10 Dates

10 Dates

Bridget Van der Eyk

For Joshua - my Wentworth Turner,
and always my biggest supporter.

I love you *10 Dates* and forever.

ISBN 978 0 6459368 03

Cover design by Bridget Van der Eyk | @authorbridgetvde
Front cover image by Maggie | @maggies_artt
Back cover image by Keeks | @keekstudi0 | www.keekstudio.com

Prologue

I have no idea what I was thinking. Absolutely no idea. When I force myself to recall it all now, I can't even begin to imagine what must have been going through my head last night, or rather the lack thereof. Reason was one, and my dignity was another.

It wasn't like it was slim pickings there last night either. The male portion of the invite list was quite impressive. It was a Niven party after all, and as much as Charlie Niven pushes my buttons sometimes, she does know a lot of very impressive guys. We're not even just talking about regularly impressive guys. No, we're talking devilishly handsome men. The kind of devilishly handsome that you see in the movies. I'm talking Jamie Dornan as Christian Grey 'take-me-home-and-ravish-me' kind of devilishly handsome.

Maybe I could blame the alcohol? I did down two glasses of champagne immediately on arrival after spotting Spencer Stevenson and his posse walk through the front double doors. Of course, the Stevenson posse was way too cool for the *Alice and Wonderland* theme, so their bad-boy musician attire stuck out like a pair of lip fillers. Thankfully, however, it did make avoiding them a whole lot easier... for most of the night that is.

I also had an unclear but excessive amount of Cosmo Jell-O shots after those two glasses of Dom. I would put any money on the fact that the inventor of Cosmopolitan Jell-O shots was a woman. Orange vodka, lime, cranberries, and Grand Marnier liqueur? Only a woman would know everything that a woman wanted in her drink. The whole Jell-O part may not be the classiest way to get the alcohol into your system, but it beats getting a Cosmo poured all down your back from the wannabe strippers trying to walk around in heels holding a martini glass.

Maybe it was the pot? I wasn't smoking it, but most people there last night were. Is second-hand pot smoke a thing? I remember I was severely craving nicotine after having gone a whole week without touching a single Marlboro. It was why Willa Nelson almost got that clichéd red lipstick smacked clean off her face when she came up and blew a cloud of smoke in my face. She was champagne-giggling something I couldn't quite make out, probably because I don't care about most things that come out of her mouth when she's intoxicated. Still, no matter how much I was craving that sweet nicotine, marijuana was never a suitable substitute in my mind, so I've never touched the stuff. He must have been smoking it though because I could smell it everywhere. It was on his breath, on his shirt, and in my hair when I woke up this morning. If he was high, he probably had the best night of his damn life. He probably felt like he was walking on water.

According to Anita Yates, who is a little too well-versed in recreational drug use, sex when you're high is the best experience of your life. Two euphorias combined into one. Maybe that's why he's still here. Maybe that's why he's still sound asleep while I try to figure out how to melt out of this bed without disturbing him so I can escape one regret to deal with another. Dealing with this mother of a hangover without the shame of a one-night stand was definitely my preference right about now.

OK, so maybe I'm exaggerating. Maybe I'm cutting to the chase and just assuming things happened last night when they didn't. I mean there's not much proof that I slept with Wentworth Turner. I only woke up this morning in the most expensive suite in the Niven

Hotel with his hair in my face and his naked body pressed up against mine under the beautifully embroidered 1200-thread-count sheets.

Oh fuck.

1

#TheBratPack

Libby Evans intently inspected the ends of her raven black hair as she twirled a few strands around her fingertips. She adjusted the dark-tinted sunglasses on her nose as the sun started glaring from behind another set of clouds. Silverlake was always busy this time of the morning, and this time of the week, so her Ray-Bans were a necessity to give the illusion that she wanted to sip her green tea in peace without being papped. Even though Hollywood paparazzi were the scum of the Earth they weren't stupid. Libby and her friends were here every Sunday for brunch without fail. Even the Scum of the Earth would have picked up on their social patterns by now, and the photographs of them splashed online tomorrow would be proof of that.

It was a brisk fifty degrees on this December morning in Beverly Hills and this was Libby's only item on the agenda for today, so she wanted to enjoy herself and relax. She had only just returned a couple of days ago from taping the *Victoria's Secret Fashion Show* in Sydney, Australia, and the mixture of nerves, long hours, and jet lag meant that she was severely lacking in the beauty sleep department. Despite all that, however, she had made it through. It was the second time she was invited to walk for the show and she had her fingers, toes, and any other body part capable crossed that this was them prepping and lining her up for the metaphorical modeling golden ticket - a Victoria's Secret Angel contract.

"Have the others messaged you?" Anita's voice pulled Libby out of her thoughts. "Cause it's 11:05 am now so they're almost an hour late, and I NEED coffee!"

Libby dropped the piece of hair she was still absent-mindedly twirling and looked up at the only other occupant at the table. Anita Yates currently had her head buried in her folded arms on the round table in front of them. Her hair was haphazardly strewn across the table, tangled in amongst the black and white printed Hérmes scarf wrapped around her neck. As per usual for a Sunday morning, Anita was a little bit hungover, and seeing as it was just Libby for now, she was saving the small amount of sparkle she had left for when their other brunch companions finally arrived. Libby couldn't help but let a small laugh escape her lips as she looked at the state of her best friend. She was, of course, met with a middle finger thrown intentionally her way.

Apart from drinking more and indulging more frequently in recreational drugs, Anita was the same as she had been when she and Libby met six years ago. This included the same natural dark strawberry blonde hair resulting from her strong desire to rebel against mainstream fashion and beauty trends. The lack of hair product and bleach was probably the reason why Anita's hair was effortlessly and enviably currently flowing down around waist length. It wasn't just the hair though, Anita's style of everything, from fashion and music to movies, was circa 1950. At Anita's fantasy dinner party, there would have been polka dot tablecloths, music playing on vinyl setting the mood, and Marilyn Monroe front and center. It was her style, and she was sticking to it.

"Sorry, I'm late!" A voice chirped to Libby's right, causing Anita to subtly roll her head to rest in the palm of one of her hands.

She tried to play out a relaxed and casual vibe, free of a hangover.

Libby stood as Willa Nelson sashayed her way over to an empty seat, greeting Libby with a double kiss on the cheeks and then giving Anita a gentle, yet condescending, pat on the head. Anita half smiled and half smirked as Willa sat in the spare seat next to Libby.

"Willow's car wouldn't start this morning, which is why I'm late," Willa announced, even though no one had cared to ask where she was, especially because the last member of their party was still yet to arrive.

"I keep telling her that she should just tell Daddy hers is broken and she desperately needs a new one so that she can stop making me late everywhere," Willa continued.

"What happened to your car?" Anita asked, suddenly interested in the conversation at the smallest spark that there could be a little gossip to be heard.

"Nothing," Willa declared innocently as she adjusted the structured black and white blazer around her shoulders, "but after that DUI a couple of months back I'm still not allowed to drive for another five months."

"So why not let Twinnie drive your car if it's just sitting there at your place doing nothing for nearly a whole year?" Anita asked.

Willa rolled her eyes as she ran her fingers through her short white-blonde bob.

"Like I would let Willow drive my baby!" Willa exclaimed. "I'm the better driver of the two of us, even when I am drunk!"

This time it was Anita who rolled her eyes and Libby knew it was time for a conversation change before more questions came flying out of her best friend's mouth in response to Willa's awful reasoning.

"So, how were your castings for Paris?" Libby asked.

"Urg," Willa sighed, "they were so long and some of them were totally pointless! Some of those designers have no idea what they're even talking about!"

Libby just nodded. Lucky for her, she had already been booked for *Paris Fashion Week* this year due to her appearance in the *Victoria's Secret Fashion Show*, so she could bypass the entire process of casting calls. Even though Willa always had something to complain about, Libby had to agree that casting calls were undoubtedly the work of the Devil for aspiring models.

"How was Australia?!" Willa exclaimed. "I heard it was so hot down there! Yuck to being sweaty for a fashion show!"

"It was super hot!" Libby nodded. "But it was so much fun! I just didn't want it to end!"

"Oh my God! Can you imagine if next year we both do the show?!" Willa exclaimed, the excitement in her voice rising with every word as she reached out and took hold of Libby's arm. "You have to put in a good word for me with them! It would be so much more fun for us to do it together!"

Libby simply smiled and tried to look as enthusiastic as Willa was, nodding her head and trying to bounce along to match Willa's excitement.

Willa Nelson craved the spotlight more than anyone else Libby had ever met. She craved it like it was something she needed and prayed for every second of every day. A little was never enough when it came to jobs, roles, or shows. Willa always wanted more. She wanted to make friends with more Hollywood royalty. She wanted to date more high-profile guys with the right connections and the right bank accounts. She wanted to be on the cover of more magazines, and if that couldn't happen, she attended all the right parties in the hope of getting papped. She wanted more people to know exactly who she was, and she was willing to do anything she could to make that happen, especially something that was currently much easier; cashing in on Libby's currently rising star.

Libby felt terrible for Willa because since the two met at a *Marie Clare* photo shoot a couple of years back, Willa was still struggling to find high-end work. It was easy for Anita because she had been on the Hollywood circuit since her early days as a child star, and despite things being easier for Libby because of her father's high profile, Libby had worked her ass off to get to where she was. Willa just wasn't quite there yet, and she wasn't at the point where she was willing to go the extra mile. Her climbing strategy was much more focused on expanding her contacts rather than doing the hard yards. Lucky for Willa Nelson though, she was exceptionally and effortlessly attractive.

For starters, she had that Elsa from *Frozen*, Scandinavian princess with milk-white skin thing going on, which was trending hard in Hollywood these days, but her attractive factor wasn't just concerning her appearance. She also had one of the most charming personalities that Libby had come across in this town, which meant that making new contacts was her specialty. It was how Willa got herself an invitation to this table after all.

"Oo, Charlie's finally here!" Willa exclaimed.

Willa practically leaped from her seat in the direction of Charlie Niven who they had all, inadvertently, been waiting for.

Libby turned in the direction of Willa's hysteria in time to catch Charlie strutting her way across the Silverlake courtyard. No doubt those gorgeous emerald-colored things were new Jimmy Choos and, of course, they matched her shiny new emerald Birken. That was Charlie Niven to a tee. The girl that had all the money in the world, or rather whose father had all the money in the world. Like Libby, Charlie and her younger sister, Camille, were also heiresses.

However, whilst Libby's great-grandfather was the founder of film production company Privileged Pictures, the Nivens were all about hotels and resorts. As of last year, there were more than six hundred Niven Hotels & Resorts properties in eighty countries and territories across six continents, so Charlie knew that she was set for the rest of her life as she walked the streets of Hollywood. No doubt it would always be in a different pair of Choos though.

"Morning ladies!" Charlie chirped.

She almost wholly ignored Willa's exaggerated greeting as she slipped into the chair between Willa and Anita, her Ray-Bans still propped perfectly on her face as she sent a small smile around the table.

"Charlie that bag is to die for!" Willa exclaimed as she reached out a hand to gently stroke the leather bag that Charlie had purposely placed in the center of the table.

"Urg," Charlie replied as she flicked her classic Charlie Niven blonde hair, straightened and then re-curled to perfection, out of her face. "I'm so sick of the color! I can't believe that they would make a special edition in only one stupid color. You can have it when I'm done with it."

"Oo!" Willa cooed, as her eyes lit up.

Libby could virtually see the reflection of the emerald Birken swirling around in Willa's irises as she continued to stroke it like it was a small puppy she couldn't take her eyes off.

"We missed you so much while you were in Australia!" Charlie exclaimed as she reached across the table to place her hand over Libby's. "Don't ever leave us again for such a gross place!"

Libby smiled. Charlie was one of those people who was hard, if not impossible, to read when it came to her true intentions. Her statement could have easily meant that she genuinely missed Libby while she was in Australia and didn't ever want Libby to leave

Hollywood again, even for a second. It could have also meant that she thought Australia and the *Victoria's Secret Fashion Show* were gross and a total waste of time so Libby should agree to never participate again, especially if it meant leaving Hollywood to do so.

"I missed you guys too!" Libby smiled. "And I've really missed eating too so can we order already?"

"Oh my gosh finally, I am starving!" Anita exclaimed, making her presence in the conversation known again.

Anita threw her right hand up in the air and started looking around for the nearest member of the Silverlake waitstaff.

A young girl with short curly red hair approached the table in a brisk walk. Freckles were scattered across her face and an unknown orange substance, resembling old ketchup, was splattered all over the front of her white apron almost entirely covering up the black Silverlake logo sitting in the apron's bottom left-hand corner.

"What can I get you, ladies?' the girl squeaked, as soon as she found a spot to stand in between Anita's and Libby's spare seat, where their own two Birkin bags were sitting.

Libby eyed the girl as she brought a pen to the docket book in her hands. Her hands were shaking, and her green eyes were squinting in the glare of the late morning sun. She was clearly nervous because she recognized them. If she hadn't already realized from the sea of designer sunglasses and what appeared to be a Birkin photo shoot, then the fact that they were always here at this same table every Sunday morning was probably a dead giveaway. They were The Brat Pack these days and everyone in Hollywood knew who they were.

"We'll have two el diablos, one ice latte on oat milk, and one Jade orchid green tea," Anita quickly answered, not even needing to consult a menu or the other girls to order their usuals.

"And to eat," Anita continued, "we'll have a selection of our usual pastries."

"And make sure the pastries are fresh," Charlie chimed in. "As in, they were made this morning, not yesterday."

Charlie didn't even bother to look at the waitress as her attention was now focused on the phone she had just retrieved from her Birken.

"Oh, and don't forget some side plates with the pastries," Willa added, "cause you guys always seem to forget no matter how many times we remind you."

"Yeah, because I love having to eat my pastry off the table," Charlie muttered under her breath.

"And bring it all out together," Willa said.

The redhead nodded and scribbled furiously on her docket book for a couple of seconds before she gave the table one final nod at no one in particular because everyone's heads were now buried in their phones, á la Charlie.

"Oh, and make sure my tea is double strength because I hate how weak it always is here too!" Libby quickly added.

The waitress had already turned around and walked a couple of steps in the direction of the kitchen when Libby called out. In response, she tried to quickly turn back around in the direction of their table and in her haste lost her footing and tripped over the leg of a chair from an adjacent table. The loud, clear sound of metal against metal, and metal against the pavement, ensued and the next thing the girls saw was the waitress on her butt on the pavement with her docket book and pen scattered in front of her. Without a second's hesitation, the four girls started to laugh as they all stared at the waitress and her mess on the floor.

"How embarrassing," Willa laughed. "Like her job is so hard she can't even remember how to walk properly."

"I guess, that's what happens when you don't have any real prospects in life," Charlie laughed. "Poor little Annie from the Hollywood slums."

"Guys, c'mon," Anita said.

Willa, Charlie, and Libby immediately stopped laughing and stared at Anita in confusion.

"I mean she probably just watched the one prospect she had fall to pieces as her ass fell to the ground," Anita laughed.

The others resumed their laughter, not caring who heard or how much attention they were drawing to their table.

"Oh my God," Libby added, "I wouldn't be surprised if they totally fired her for that."

"God, can you imagine how much shit she must break here if she's always being so uncoordinated," Charlie laughed.

"Totally," Willa said. "Zero prospects are what you get when you're not part of The Pack. Everyone wants to be us after all."

"You said it, Wills," Libby added.

Suddenly the familiar *ding* of Libby's phone, which was sitting face down next to her on the table, sounded out, interrupting their conversation.

"Let me guess," Anita said, resting her chin in her hand on the table as she looked in Libby's direction, "Mr. Thatcher calls?"

Libby rolled her eyes and smiled as she flipped her phone over to what she also expected to be a text message from her boyfriend, Ace Thatcher.

"You're so lucky," Willa sighed. "I am so over dating tech geeks and backup dancers. I want an oil heir billionaire!"

"Yeah Willa, your dating history makes me sad," Anita commented.

"Shut up, Anita!" Willa exclaimed. "I'm a sucker for a nice guy."

"Ew, I would take rich guy over nice guy any day of the week," Charlie commented, pouting into her phone for yet another selfie for her social media of choice this morning.

"You should teach Willa then Charls," Anita smirked, "so she can stop taking any and every man in sight back to her bed."

"You are such a bitch, Anita," Willa huffed, "but at least I'm not going through the biggest man drought on the west coast!"

"I see plenty of guys thank you very much!" Anita exclaimed.

She was clearly surprised that Willa was taking the bait and fighting back for a change.

"Yeah, you girls are both sluts," Charlie sighed sarcastically, still engrossed in her phone. "Congratulations!"

Libby laughed to herself as she settled back into her chair with the sound of the rest of The Pack in the background bantering away about one of their favorite topics, the many men currently on their radars. Libby removed herself from the conversation and entered the text conversation she had just been invited to by her boyfriend.

She and Ace had been officially together for only a few months, but they had been in that almost-in-a-relationship stage for nearly six. They'd randomly hooked up at Brica Dallas' Oscar's after-party earlier in the year. He was someone else's date but, in the end, had found his way to Libby Evans. Like a moth to a flame. It was a testament to the boy's good taste in women.

Over the next couple of months, however, Libby infuriatingly watched Ace um and ah over the decision to be official with her, despite the fact they were already acting like it and the tabloids were already reporting it. He claimed it was because of his crazy overseas schedule learning the ropes of his family's exceedingly profitable oil exploration business across the Mediterranean. But in the end, Libby was patient and had waited for Ace and his ridiculously sexy French accent, and now they were here. He spoiled her like no one had spoiled her before. The continuous stream of gifts was definitely a relationship plus and according to the media, dating the oil heir had put her in a new light in terms of her public image. It made her more lovable and printable to have someone as successful and good-looking as a Thatcher on her arm. Plus, it kept her name front and center in the tabloids and scandal-free for the meantime, which was precisely what she needed while she was trying to lock down her Angel contract. It was something her publicist, Felicity Reynolds, reminded her of daily.

Libby looked up from her phone as the beverages and pastries arrived at their table, carried by a couple of more coordinated, and not unfortunate-looking, male waiters. Libby rolled her eyes as she watched Willa bare her impressive set of pearly whites and full red lips in a big smile at the pair of them. The Nelson charm was just never put to rest, no matter the time or place. No wonder she'd bedded so many duds.

Libby poured herself some tea from the white teapot that was placed in front of her and smiled. She had it good. Well, she had it much better than just good. All of it was so much better than just good. She had loyal friends, a well-to-do gorgeous boyfriend, and a reputation that meant that soon she would finally have a pair of her very own jewel-encrusted Victoria's Secret wings. Life was perfect, and she intended to keep it that way.

2

Wonderland

"Urg, I should have got Marco to give me highlights too!" Charlie exclaimed in frustration. "Yours look amazing and my hair just looks shit!"

"Don't be silly!" Libby cried. "Your hair always looks awesome, Charls!"

Libby was sitting across the room from Charlie in her new and very fancy private suite at the Beverly Hills Niven Hotel, which was expected when your last name matches all the monogrammed bathrobes in the building.

Libby would never get over how over the top and gorgeous all the Niven suites were, but Charlie's was the definition of extra. She and Charlie were currently getting ready in what used to be the suite's living room but had been remodeled into a walk-in wardrobe as per Charlie's request. The closets lining two of the walls were arranged into pairs with glass-paneled double doors so that Charlie's exceptional array of designer clothing and couture could always be on show. A mahogany dressing table sat on one of the other walls matching the rest of the mahogany the room was drowning in, including the wardrobes. Charlie was sitting at her dressing table in front of a large circular mirror decked out in gold trim. What Charlie wants, Charlie gets, and Charlie always wants everything.

They were currently getting ready for the hotel's launch. The Beverly Hills hotel was the Niven's newest addition to their empire, and it didn't look like they were slowing down anytime soon. Niven hotels were exploding up all over the west coast and Charlie, being the party planner she apparently was now, always encouraged every opening to be that little bit more over the top than the last one. Over-the-top parties with over-the-top drinks, over-the-top guests, over-the-top decor, and of course, an over-the-top theme to tie it all together. Tonight, it was *Wonderland* and while it was a decent theme, Libby was pretty sure it was selected only so Charlie could go dressed as Alice. That quote from *Mean Girls* sprung to mind about Halloween being the only time of the year that a girl can dress like a total skank and no other girl can say anything about it. Libby shouldn't have been thinking like that as Charlie was one of her best friends, but she really couldn't help herself when she looked at the very short puffy, powder blue dress Charlie had laid out on the back of the black suede chaise that Libby was currently sitting on.

"You're such a lying bitch," Charlie rolled her eyes.

Her voice brought Libby back to the here and now as she watched Charlie continue to fuss over her newly bleached blonde curls in the mirror.

"Trust me," Libby said as she stood up and walked over toward Charlie, coming to stand behind her so she could look at her friend in the mirror in front of them, "you look gorgeous! Those curls are just amazing. I wish my hair would do anything other than just sitting so damn straight."

Charlie smiled and Libby smiled back as she let out a breath of relief on the inside that she'd said the right thing.

"Yeah, but the straight look works for you," Charlie replied. "It looks way too weird when you do curls. It just doesn't suit the shape of your face at all!"

Charlie then gracefully shuffled around in her seat to come face to face with Libby.

"Your wings are off," Charlie commented with narrowed eyes as she studied Libby's face. "Come here!"

Charlie gestured with her index finger and Libby crouched down and closed her eyes so that Charlie could work her magic.

"Willa better have sorted out her costume situation," Charlie said, as she swiped black liquid liner across Libby's right eyelid.

"What do you mean?" Libby asked, trying to keep her eyelids as still as possible as she talked. "What was wrong with her costume situation?"

"Urg," Charlie scoffed, "she was going to go as Alice."

"Oh," Libby replied, immediately realizing the magnitude of the situation, "but didn't she know that you were going as Alice?"

"She should have!" Charlie exclaimed. "Like I should have to spell it out for her. It's my fucking party after all!"

"True," Libby agreed.

"I'm just adding a bit of sparkle," Charlie spoke, noticing the twitch in Libby's eyelid as the eyeshadow brush touched her skin. "But I mean like how dumb is she?!"

"Ridiculously apparently," Libby agreed, knowing full well that it was exactly what Charlie wanted to hear. "So, no idea what her new costume will be?"

"Nope," Charlie replied. "As if it would matter anyway. No matter how good, or expensive, her costume is she's just going to hook up with some ugly anyway."

"Charlie!" Libby exclaimed in surprise, but not being able to stop a laugh from escaping her lips at the same time.

"What?!" Charlie exclaimed with a grin. "Don't try and be so nice, you know I'm right! She does it at every party we've ever been to! It's so embarrassing!"

"Maybe she just needs to get her eyes tested," Libby laughed.

"Yeah, like that would help her vomit worthy taste in men," Charlie laughed. "Open!"

Libby realized that Charlie was speaking to her, and she opened her eyes to allow her friend to inspect her handiwork.

"I'm a genius!" Charlie smiled as she popped her makeup tools back down on the dressing table. "You look heaps better now!"

Libby turned to face the mirror and noticed the massive overload of black liner slathered on her eyelids. It was way more than she usually wore, but she'd sort that out later in the restroom downstairs when she was sure that Charlie had had at least four tequila shots.

"You can thank me later," Charlie said as she strutted her way toward the bathroom door, grabbing her dress along the way. "Going to get changed, bitch, and then we're having at least two flutes before we head downstairs. Party starts in five."

Libby let out a sigh as the bathroom door closed. She looked at herself again in the mirror, scrunching up her nose at the over-the-top black liner. It wasn't her style, and she knew that Charlie knew that. She considered quickly grabbing a Q tip and sorting it out, but then thought twice because no doubt Charlie would notice that she didn't look like Edward Scissorhands anymore and Libby did not want to deal with that kind of drama tonight. She'd leave the antagonism of Charlie's mood to Willa, who had already started it. Instead, Libby grabbed a couple of Q tips and tossed them into her clutch for later. She closed the gold clasp and ran her fingers over the hand-embroidered beaded design. He wouldn't be here tonight, but somehow Ace Thatcher had managed to special deliver the perfect clutch to match her outfit. A red beaded heart-shaped clutch, embellished with gold and black beads. Perfect for the Queen of Hearts.

Libby looked in the mirror again and smiled. She knew that the costume wasn't exactly what Lewis Carroll had in mind when he wrote the novel, but she was sure that he, whether he was high on opium or not, would have approved. She felt like maybe across the back there was a little too much sheer red lace, and the black bodysuit cut a little high along her bikini line, but those two flutes would sort out those worries before she and Charlie headed downstairs. They might, however, make walking down that extravagant bifurcated staircase from the ballroom to the lobby a little bit tricky in her new patent leather Louboutin pumps.

Suddenly Libby felt her clutch vibrate. She felt her heart flutter as she quickly undid the clasp again to retrieve her phone, only to feel her stomach sink when she saw it was just a text from Willa asking where she and Charlie were. Typical extra keen Willa Nelson; having no concept of being fashionably late and always showing up to parties at least five minutes early. I guess she didn't want to miss a single moment of 'networking'. Or a single moment of hooking up with 'some ugly' as Charlie had put it.

"Well, I look fucking gorgeous!" Charlie exclaimed as she re-entered the room.

Libby looked at her phone again and sighed before she turned her attention to her friend with a smile.

"Yeah, you do!" Libby agreed semi-enthusiastically.

Charlie put her hands on her hips and raised an eyebrow at Libby. She looked like an unimpressed, overgrown elementary school kid with those puffy sleeves, which nearly made Libby laugh out loud.

"Now I know that you could have put more enthusiasm into that," Charlie commented as she pointed to Libby's phone, "but

I'm guessing that a text message, or lack thereof, might have just crapped all over your mood?"

Libby sighed.

"He's just being a douchebag you know, Libs," Charlie said as she popped a black headband in amongst her curls. "It's been what, three days since you last heard from him?"

"Try five days," Libby said as she rolled her eyes. "I'm getting the Dom!"

She stood up and headed for where she was sure the fridge was in amongst all the closet space and mahogany.

"Fridge is right in front of you and flutes are on top of the dresser," Charlie commented as she continued to admire herself in the mirror. "And he's an ass, but Libs you have to remember that he is a man. This is what they do."

"Yeah, I know," Libby agreed as she popped the champagne and started pouring.

"And you know he'll apologize with a ridiculously expensive gesture when he realizes what an ass he's been," Charlie added, "and you know how much you'll love that. You always do."

"Yeah, I know that too," Libby nodded as she handed one of the flutes to Charlie. "Or he'll go for the record and make it ten days this time before I hear from him."

Charlie rolled her eyes as she took a generous gulp of her champagne before she placed the flute on a nearby table and went to retrieve the whole bottle. Libby chuckled a little as Charlie topped up her flute as close to the rim as she possibly could before she smiled with the bottle outstretched in Libby's direction. Libby offered her flute, and the blonde took that as all the confirmation she needed before she poured Libby's flute in the same fashion; filled right to the rim, bubbles splashing out of the glass as they rose to the surface of the sparkly liquid.

"I honestly think you could do better than Ace Thatcher," Charlie shrugged. "I mean God knows you've done worse."

"Hey!" Libby exclaimed as she almost choked on a mouthful of champagne.

"Hamish? Basil? Woody?" Charlie started counting with her fingers. "Spencer?"

"Hamish was a sweetheart back then," Libby exclaimed.

"And the rest?" Charlie laughed with a cocked eyebrow.

"Point taken," Libby laughed. "But hey, you've been on the Spencer train as well!"

"Yes, unfortunately, we've both had the same Spencer Stevenson mental breakdown," Charlie shrugged with another mouthful of champagne. "But at least I realized how dumb I was being. You, on the other hand, keep waiting for the next stop but you never got off the fucking train!"

"I am well and truly off that train now!" Libby stated firmly. "I'm not the cheating kind. I haven't been with anyone else while I've been with Ace."

"Well don't let yourself slip up because I know you have a weakness for bad-boys," Charlie said, "and Spencer Stevenson has a weakness for you."

"And that doesn't matter in the slightest!" Libby stated, matter-of-factly. "Even if Ace and I don't work out, I don't need another trip on the Spencer train."

"Well, try and remember that tonight when you're wasted," Charlie laughed, "cause you seem to get yourself into terrible love triangles with Mr. Stevenson and vodka every time we party and him and his posse show up."

"Well, you should stop inviting them!" Libby retaliated cheekily.

"Half the girls in this town wouldn't show up if I didn't invite Spencer, Hamish, and all the other bad-boy musicians that make every girl lick her lip fillers over," Charlie stated. "And then if those girls didn't show up, the boys in this town would follow suit. It's a no-brainer. Spencer and Hamish stay on the list."

Libby went to retaliate with another smart comment, but Charlie stopped her in her tracks, with one of her fingers pointed in her friend's direction.

"But none of that matters because you promised me a fun night!" Charlie said before she quickly, and in a very unladylike manner, consumed the rest of her champagne. "So, none of this moping around. You just need to let the alcohol take all your worries away!"

"Amen to that!" Libby exclaimed with a smile as she toasted her flute into the air before following suit and letting all that sparkly liquid disappear right down her throat.

* * *

Charlie took a deep pull of her third, and last, Marlboro for the night. She truly despised the stupid California building codes and not being able to smoke inside nowadays. If only this was sixteenth-century France where smoking was essentially a fashion statement, and you were low on the social hierarchy if you were 'looking after your lungs' or 'trying to be healthier'. Charlie rolled her eyes at the mere thought of it, and because those exact words had come out of Libby Evans' mouth only half an hour earlier when Charlie had tried to convince her to join outside on the back terrace before they headed down to the party. Of course, Little Miss Victoria's Secret had to give her whole health kick spiel instead of just giving a simple 'no', and it had pissed Charlie right off.

Charlie had just spent the better part of the last hour listening to Libby complain about her relationship with Ace Thatcher. She had tried to be supportive of her friend's relationship 'dilemma' but all she could think about were all the sarcastic comments she wanted to reply with because according to Libby it was so hard to have a gorgeous boyfriend from an exotic overseas country that has status, money and always buys you expensive presents. It was all Charlie could do to hold her tongue and just let her friend vent about her 'nightmare'.

She could always just call one of the girls to vent about it, probably Willa because she was always up for bitching about anyone if it meant getting a little attention herself, but she had a party to host. She could just get blind drunk like she knew most would be tonight, especially with the free-flowing champagne and her last-minute Jell-O shot addition to the drinks menu. She wasn't really in the mood to drink herself stupid though. So, instead, she was here smoking her frustrations away into the cool Beverly Hills air out the back of her dad's fancy new hotel where she'd probably live until a new Niven popped up somewhere along the west coast.

Charlie sighed as she leaned over the railing in front of her. She wished she had brought a jacket, as it had crossed her mind seconds before she escaped her suite. The breeze was just that little bit nippy tonight, which wasn't exactly a surprise considering it was December, but a cool breeze was just about all the 'winter' you could expect in sunny California and Charlie hated that. She just couldn't wait until her annual Switzerland 'ski-cation', courtesy of the bank of Daddy Niven. She was aching to sit in front of a massive wood fire and watch the embers dance as the snow fell like little white feathers outside. She'd sit there with an extra-large mug of hot chocolate, with a dash of marshmallow vodka, and after the shocker of a year she'd had with her love life, she knew she damn well deserved it! Her heart was dying for a little chocolate, and she knew she'd have to get out of Hollywood to be able to enjoy such an indulgence and also get away from the root of the problem - Hamish Dawson.

She had it bad for him, but she'd never admit it. She'd even go as far as to drag his name through the mud anytime she had the opportunity, just like she had with Libby earlier. It was the best way, in her mind, to distract from just how bad she had it for the boy. How could she resist his gorgeous liquid brown eyes and that head of long disheveled golden brown hair that was currently long enough to be tied back into a sexy man bun? She'd known about him long before they'd ever met, but she'd never forget the night they finally did.

She'd been at a party at Bar Nineteen 12 in Beverly Hills that night. She'd managed to bum a Marlboro off Marissa Michaels, as usual, before Marissa disappeared from the porch back to the bar. Something that was not so usual though, was Marissa's spot being replaced by a tipsy Hamish Dawson. He'd smiled at her straight away, but it was obvious he didn't know who she was, even though she'd very briefly dated his best friend, Spencer. He'd thrown a casual 'hey' her way though, and she'd smiled back at him, trying to focus on the cigarette in her hand and not how irresistible he looked in that black button-up shirt and tight-fitting dark blue jeans.

"I can't believe we're the only ones out here," Hamish spoke, causing Charlie to turn to look at him again. "I remember a few years back when there'd barely be any room out the back to have a smoke because there were girls everywhere."

"Ah," Charlie sighed. "Everyone got fucking healthy it seems."

"Except me and you," Hamish replied as he pulled a pack out from the back pocket of his jeans and fiddled in one of his front pockets before retrieving a lighter.

"Guess we can share a funeral then," Charlie replied, taking a long draw of her cigarette as she tried to calm herself.

She couldn't remember the last time a guy had given her the time of day and had a conversation with her that consisted of more than a dozen words. It was making the butterflies in her stomach fly around like little psychos.

"I mean after we both die of lung cancer that is," Charlie quickly added, making sure that Hamish didn't misconstrue her words.

He laughed, and she internally jumped for joy. She could feel the heat rising in her cheeks, so she focused her attention back on her dwindling cigarette, the heat of the burnt end edging closer toward her fingertips.

"I'm Hamish," he said, as he took a step closer to her and leaned over the railing, matching her current posture.

She turned to face him and tried not to get lost in his beautiful eyes as they smiled in sync with his lips.

"Charlie," Charlie smiled, trying not to blush. "Charlie Niven."

She had replayed that conversation a million times since that night. It hadn't lasted much longer than five minutes, but it was enough to get Charlie hooked, and hooked she was still. She'd casually added him on a couple of her social media platforms after she'd felt that enough time had passed that she wouldn't seem desperate. He'd then asked for her number, and they'd been constantly texting for almost a month now, with a few phone calls thrown in there as well. It still wasn't enough for her though. She wanted more Hamish Dawson. Since her relationship with Spencer had fallen apart a couple of years ago, she'd been through the longest dry spell in the history of everything. Hamish was just moving too slow, and it was frustrating the hell out of her.

All she wanted to do was vent, and yet she couldn't, and that was the biggest problem. Unluckily for Charlie, Hamish Dawson and Libby Evans had history. An industrial-sized load of romantic history. They'd been teenage sweethearts long before Libby knew the wonders of Cosmo Jell-O shots, and before Hamish realized that a good Marlboro was the key ingredient in a night out on the town. They were first kiss kind of teenage sweethearts, and because of that Charlie never really felt like they'd ever forgotten each other. Even though Charlie and Hamish were 'on' right now, she couldn't help thinking that he was wishing her hair was black instead of blonde; imagining her eyes were dark brown instead of blue; envisioning the gold chain she always wore around her neck was of the letter 'L' instead of the letter 'C'. Maybe it wasn't the case and Charlie's insecurities were just playing up, but it wasn't that farfetched an idea considering who that brown-eyed, black-haired girl was.

Libby insisted there was nothing between them, there hadn't been for years now, but Charlie saw the way Hamish looked at Libby whenever they bumped into him at a party or a club. She honestly couldn't even blame him because Libby was gorgeous. An effortless kind of gorgeous that Charlie truly envied. Libby would play along and wear just as much make-up as Charlie and put just as much time into making sure her outfit and her hair were perfect before a party, but she didn't need to. Every Sunday when they met for brunch, 'effortless Libby' was there with her naturally, silky straight hair, her naturally modelesque figure, and her flawless complexion. Even if the biggest zit in the world appeared on her face, in the middle of her nose, Libby would still manage to pull it off with the self-confidence that just oozed out of her every pore. Confidence that Charlie knew, though she'd never admit it out loud, she would never have.

"Hey!" a voice called from behind Charlie, jolting her out of her thoughts and making her jump so high she dropped her cigarette.

Charlie sighed as she watched her little glowing cigarette fall until it landed on the concrete of the alley below. She took a deep breath and turned around to face Willa Nelson.

"My bad!" Willa exclaimed, scrunching up her nose. "But I have another if you want?"

Charlie's eyes quickly lit up as she watched Willa rummage around in her purse, before pulling out a pack of Marlboros and an awful bright orange lighter. She didn't even care that she'd promised herself just three cigarettes before joining the party and trying to find Hamish. All she wanted was to puff her cares away for at least another fifteen minutes. She'd then head down to the party fashionably late after downing at least one more flute of Dom, so she'd have the patience to deal with running into Libby again and having to listen to more of her supermodel problems.

"One more," Charlie smiled before extending her hand to accept the first Marlboro Willa pulled from the pack.

"Me too!" Willa replied excitedly before she lit them both up.

"You're going to need it if you plan on seeing Libby tonight," Charlie sighed as she turned her attention back to the dark alley, primarily so she didn't have to look at Willa's costume.

She didn't think she had the discipline to not verbally rip it to shreds in the mood she was in. It was obvious that Willa was trying to pull off the dodo sailor from *Alice in Wonderland* tonight but was only pulling off 'slutty sailor'. It was made even sluttier by the fact that, in true Willa Nelson style, she was wearing the most ridiculous push-up bra that pressed her enormous fake boobs higher and closer together.

"Oh my God," Willa groaned as she leaned on the railing with her elbows. "She's still having a big cry about Ace?"

"Like she'd be done," Charlie rolled her eyes sarcastically. "It's only been three weeks since he left, remember?"

"Maybe she's just frustrated cause she needs to get laid," Willa laughed.

Charlie laughed in response.

"You're probably right," Charlie said. "Hopefully she can sort that out tonight."

"You really think she'd cheat on Ace?" Willa asked, her eyes lighting up at the prospect of some fresh gossip. "He's pretty into her, but I doubt he'd forgive her if she cheated."

"If she gets as wasted as we all know she will, we might find out just how forgiving Mr. Thatcher is," Charlie smirked.

"Oh my God, that would be such a scandal!" Willa exclaimed.

"Such a fucking good one too." Charlie continued to smile.

"Her Victoria's Secret contract would be in the trash after that," Willa said, the volume of her voice dropping slightly as she leaned a little closer into Charlie. "I heard her publicist telling her that she won't get the Angel contract if even the smallest scandal gets out about her over the next six months."

"Interesting," Charlie nodded.

"Think she can do it?" Willa asked, her eyes fixated on Charlie's reaction. "Avoid a scandal that is?"

Charlie looked at her friend with a coy smile. If there was anything that Willa was good at, because there wasn't a lot of it, it was willing to trade any 'friendship' for gossip and a scandal.

"Let's hope she doesn't," Charlie replied, letting a small laugh escape her lips along with another trail of smoke.

3

Coyote Ugly

Libby took a deep breath as she closed her eyes tighter. She wasn't sure what time it was, but she knew from the minimal sunlight streaming in the window that it was probably just a little after dawn. She could feel the sun's warmth on her forehead, the only part of her body out from underneath the covers and, considering how much her head was throbbing, it was still too much. She could feel the alcohol wreaking its havoc on her brain cells and she couldn't help but let out a low groan as she brought her hands up to clutch the sides of her head to try and dull the pain.

As she moved her hands she realized she was naked. Her eyes flew open almost immediately. She didn't usually sleep naked because she hated it. Usually, she was dressed in at least underwear because she hated the feel of her silk sheets directly on her body when she was in a state of complete undress. So, the fact that she was naked right now was concerning. Very concerning because it meant that last night she had probably...

"Oh my God Libby," Anita exclaimed with a girlish giggle. "Slow down on the Jell-O!"

Libby giggled in reply as she tried to stop the Jell-O from falling out of her mouth before she could let its vodka goodness work its way through her system to start sedating her worries.

"I can't even remember how many of these I've had!" Libby exclaimed with another giggle as she slapped her hand across her mouth to clean herself up, the sticky feeling of Jell-O now under her fingertips.

"At least one hundred!" Anita exclaimed as she chucked back another shot herself.

Libby watched as the Jell-O spilled out the sides of Anita's mouth, causing them both to erupt into more fits of laughter.

"Hey there, gorgeous," Libby heard a voice from behind her accompanied by warm smoky breath in her ear.

Slightly startled, Libby jumped a little as she spun around in the direction of the voice. The combination of the alcohol in her system and her quick movement caused her to stumble a little, but a set of manly hands was quick to steady her. Libby's eyes rose to meet those dark blue eyes that she was all too familiar with.

"Whoa there," Spencer Stevenson chuckled. "Steady on there, little one."

"Ew, Spencer, get off me," Libby whined as she attempted to create some distance between herself and the musician.

Her attempt at displaying some strength to push his body away from hers was pitiful, and she had her Jell-O shot friends to thank for that.

"Hey, no need to be like that, Libs," Spencer cooed, his hands effortlessly pulling Libby even closer to him.

She could feel one of his large hands on her right hip and the other on the small of her back.

"You know if you want to get rough again all you have to do is invite me upstairs," Spencer whispered in her ear. "Like last time."

Libby hated how physically weak she was when she was drunk and she could feel that last Jell-O shot rushing quickly to her head, making the floor a lot less stable than she remembered a couple of moments earlier. She looked into Spencer's eyes and they were smirking, just like his lips. His eyes looked exactly like deep pools of dark blue water and Libby could feel herself desperately drowning in them.

"Spencer, we are never doing that again," Libby mumbled as she tried again to prise his grip from her body.

Her mind was screaming the words, but her conviction was sorely lacking. She was barely convincing her own ears that this is what she wanted, let alone a determined Spencer who knew exactly what he wanted because he'd had it countless times before. She could feel his breath on her skin as he dipped his face closer into the crook of her neck.

"C'mon, baby," he cooed again. "You know how much you want it."

Libby wasn't sure if it was the intoxicating smell of cigarettes on his breath or the fact that his hands felt so good wrapped around her, but he was right. It was oh-so-tempting to just give in to him, and she could feel her body sinking into his offer. An offer that was right there. Clear as day. Just as he knew what he wanted because he'd had it before, she'd also had it before, and it was tempting to experience it all again because it had been good. She could have easily closed the inch gap between her lips and Spencer's, all she needed was to lean that little bit forward and tilt her head ever so slightly toward his cigarette-laden breath...

Libby's eyes closed tightly as the memories started coming back to her and she started mentally beating herself up. She moved her leg slightly under the covers and even though she was expecting to find flesh, her breath still caught in her throat when her toes brushed against what she assumed was his warm calf.

She couldn't believe she'd slept with Spencer again. She had told herself last time was the very last time, but then again that's exactly what she had told herself the time before that, and the time before that. Why there were so many times she couldn't explain. She had tried everything to stop herself from adding to the tally; whether it was verbally beating herself up time and time again or sharing the details with Anita or Willa to shame herself out of repeating her actions. It wasn't even like their trysts left her satisfied for days on end, which would have made them worth it. It was such a fleeting feeling of satisfaction. The very next morning she always felt so dirty that she'd actually throw away her sheets and jump into a nice, long shower to physically scrub the Spencer off her. She usually followed that up with a deep tissue massage, a facial, and a mani-pedi, which wasn't entirely necessary, but she figured that all those treatments combined would completely rid her of every skin cell and bodily fluid that Spencer had transferred to her the night before. It sounded stupid but she had to find ways to help herself sleep at night after those momentary lapses of judgment and sanity.

Libby sighed deeply, yet quietly to keep Spencer in dreamland so that she wouldn't have to see that disgusting smirk on his face when he woke up and realized that she was naked in bed with him, again. The smirk usually only deepened as he wriggled his way over to get closer to her. It had only happened once that she hadn't managed to escape before he woke up and that was more than enough for Libby. Every other time she had quietly left the scene of the crime without waking him up to save herself the morning after torture. She was hopeful that it also increased her chances that Spencer wouldn't remember who he'd slept with the night before, and she'd save herself some shame by not receiving that dreaded **So I heard about you and Spencer, again...** text message that she'd probably receive multiple copies of before the end of the weekend. There was always the option that if he couldn't gossip about it then it wouldn't spread, but that was crazy talk. Even if she did have a handgun, it would probably be too big to fit in any of her party clutches anyway.

Libby slowly pushed the blanket further down her body while keeping her chest covered to protect her modesty. She could hear him breathing heavily next to her and it almost made her throw up in her mouth a little bit, or maybe that was one of the Jell-O shots resurfacing. She did take the heavy breathing as an indication, however, that he was still sound asleep, so she risked a look in his direction.

She involuntarily scrunched up her nose as she saw a head of short dark brown hair as opposed to the blonde mess she expected to see. He was facing away from her, but it was clear as day that she was not in bed with Spencer Stevenson. At the same time, however, her bed companion was naked, at least from the waist up, so it was probably safe to assume that Libby had slept with the unidentified male. She felt unnerved by the fact that she was so plastered last night that she had engaged in her very first one-night stand, even if she could sigh relief at the fact that she hadn't let Spencer back into her bed for the umpteenth time.

This was exactly why she had tried to convince Charlie not to put Jell-O shots on the drinks menu for the party last night, or on the drinks menu of any of her future parties. It was one of those things that made Libby, and Anita as her primary bad influence, revert to their teenage days of house parties in the Hollywood Hills. Back when the aim of the game was to get as drunk as you possibly could on Jell-O shots without vomiting in your Louis Vuitton handbag. Now they were legal, they could drink proper alcohol in proper glasses with the aim of the game being to not sleep with disgusting guys repeatedly, and Libby always seemed to lose that game because Jell-O shots came in and gave the disgusting guys an unfair advantage.

Libby looked around the room and realized that she wasn't in her bed, which was good because the 1200-thread-count sheets currently on her bed were new and she didn't want to have to burn them so soon. The mahogany furniture and the red down quilt covering the bed were a good indication that she hadn't made it out of the Beverly Hills Niven Hotel. The gold embroidered 'N' on the fluffy white bathrobe slung across the red suede armchair was an even more specific indication. It looked like, at least, she'd made it up to one of the master suites, but the details of how she got here were still fuzzy. She closed her eyes tightly to try to bring back her alcohol suppressed memories.

"Let's head up to one of the master suites that I know you have access to and let's just get this over with," Spencer whispered in her ear as he continued to pull her toward him tighter, one hand slipping lower down her back until it came to rest on the curve of her butt.

Libby couldn't tell if it was the alcohol coming back up or whether it was the thought of being naked with him again, but she had to fight the vodka vomit from projecting up from her stomach, out of her mouth, and all over the front of Spencer. She knew she was trashed but she also knew that she wasn't trashed enough to do this dance again.

"Tell me that you don't want to," Spencer mumbled, obviously unsatisfied by Libby's lack of an answer, as his lips connected with her jawline and then again with the hollow of her neck. "You know you want to, baby."

"No, Spencer, I don't," Libby finally blurted out as she tried to move her neck out of his lip's reach. "Let go of me."

Spencer's reaction to Libby's protests were those of a man insistent on conquering what his brain was processing that he couldn't have, at least not tonight. Libby felt Spencer's hand on her butt tighten and his lips incessantly tugging on the delicate flesh of her neck.

"Don't be like that, baby," Spencer insisted. "You feel so uptight. Let me take you upstairs and loosen you up a little."

Libby was already having the hardest time keeping down the vodka vomit, but Spencer's awful pickup lines were making it even more challenging.

"I don't need to loosen up," Libby stated, a little louder than before as she pushed against Spencer's chest that little bit harder. "I need you to get off me."

Spencer distanced himself a little from her and it took everything in her not to spit in his eye at that look of excitement on his stupid face. Before they had hooked up, back when Libby had a stronger will than she did now, he used to always say how much her innocence turned him on. He loved to talk about how much he wanted to conquer that same innocence as he looked at her with that same stupid, excited smirking face he was showing her right now.

"Spencer, leave me alone!" Libby exclaimed.

"I believe the lady would like you to back the fuck up," a voice announced from somewhere to Libby's right.

Both Spencer and Libby stopped what they were doing and turned in the direction of the new participant in their conversation. Libby could tell it was a 'he' from his voice, but his costume made it extremely hard for her to confirm that. He had definitely committed to the theme and was decked out, head to toe, in the most ridiculous, yet impressive, caterpillar costume Libby had ever laid eyes on.

"You know what, buddy," Spencer replied without letting go of Libby, "this doesn't concern you, so you can fuck off."

"You know," the Caterpillar said, "I would just love to fuck off, but it seems your ears need checking cause it doesn't sound like she wants any part of whatever the fuck it is you're offering."

Libby tilted her head, and a smile worked its way across her lips. She had never heard anyone speak to Spencer like that. He was a big deal in Hollywood at the moment, with his new album that dropped last month and his army of other broody musicians, so it wasn't an everyday occurrence that someone told him where to shove it. Spencer was just as stunned by the comment. The Caterpillar spoke again before Spencer could come up with a verbal response.

"So, if you don't mind," the Caterpillar said, "I'm going to take Miss Evans to get another drink."

Again, before Spencer could respond, the Caterpillar snuck his arm around Libby's waist and drew her away. It all happened in one quick motion, so before Libby knew it, she was headed in a direction far away from Spencer with this strangely dressed man.

"Are you OK?" the Caterpillar whispered in her ear.

Libby turned her head, so they were face to face. He was taller than her, probably around Spencer's height, and his eyes were the most beautiful green she had ever seen. Green mixed in with shards of brown and what appeared to be specks of gold. His bright blue costume covered most of his other identifying features, except for some tufts of brown wavy hair that were peeking out from where the costume finished around his hairline.

Libby sighed as she opened her eyes. It wasn't an everyday occurrence that she was rescued from the clutches of a horny musician by a knight in 'caterpillar' armor. Unfortunately, even with her hazy memory of what her knight's hair looked like, she thought it was safe to assume that she had thanked his chivalry last night in more ways than one. Libby groaned quietly, wanting more than anything to scream in frustration. She wished that she had simply thanked her knight verbally rather than physically, especially because there were at least two hundred different ways to say thank you with your clothes on, no matter how thankful you were.

Instead of screaming, though, Libby decided that it was time to bail on this bad situation. Thankfully, both her hands were free so she wouldn't have to 'coyote ugly' her way out of the bed, but she did have to locate her clothes before she could make a quick exit before her caterpillar knight woke up.

Libby looked around and shuddered at the thought of what happened last night once they got up here, considering the fact the room was littered with various items of clothing. Some of them were her Queen of Hearts costume and the rest, she assumed, were the Caterpillar's. She tentatively shuffled out of the bed, freezing when she felt him stir ever so slightly. She held her breath as he stretched out under the covers, rolling toward Libby as he did so. His eyes were still closed, but now he was lying on his side facing her. She continued to hold her breath as he sighed before settling back into sleep in his new position. His face was almost entirely buried in the soft white pillow underneath his head with the comforter lazily covering his body from the waist down. Libby resumed her regular breathing as soon as she was completely sure he was back asleep. She looked at him intently for any signs that he was about to wake up and couldn't help herself from studying the parts of him that she could see as she did so.

"I'm fine," Libby replied with a smile before she once again stumbled in her ridiculous choice of footwear.

"Whoa there," the Caterpillar laughed as he steadied her with the arm he already had around her. "I don't think your shoes are helping you make a clean getaway."

Libby smiled as she leaned into him.

"Hey, asshole!" a voice suddenly shouted from behind them, causing Libby and the Caterpillar to turn and look over their shoulders.

Libby watched as Spencer Stevenson started charging his way toward them. Libby was surprised that it had been so easy for the Caterpillar to rescue her from Spencer's clutches, so she wasn't at all surprised now that he was returning to reclaim his honor that was stolen only moments earlier. The look in Spencer's eyes screamed that he was going to do something stupid. No doubt, he was going to try and reclaim his honor with his fists, and both Libby and the Caterpillar could see it. The Caterpillar released his arm from around Libby as Spencer closed the distance between them. Libby instinctively took a step back.

"You need to mind your own fucking business," Spencer exclaimed as he finally caught up to them and shoved the Caterpillar with two hands firmly on his chest.

Libby watched on, as did several other party guests around them who had noticed the start of the commotion. The Caterpillar stood his ground, barely even moving as Spencer's hands connected with him.

"And you need to keep your fucking dick in your pants, dude," the Caterpillar replied, not a single note of hesitation in his voice.

Libby watched, as did more and more people, as Spencer's rage continued to build. She was surprised that she couldn't see steam coming out of his ears because the look on his face seemed incomplete without it. The pair of men were standing so close that had the circumstances been different, she would have thought something a little more romantic was going on here.

"I'm only going to tell you once," Spencer continued, further closing the gap between him and the Caterpillar as he used his index finger to poke at the other man's chest to make his point clearer. "Keep the fuck out of my business otherwise you and I are going to have a much bigger problem on our hands."

"And I'm only going to tell you once, pretty boy," the Caterpillar replied, completely unphased. "I couldn't give two shits about you, but what I do care about is you forcing yourself onto drunk girls, so you can either back up or I can make you."

Spencer laughed before he wound himself up and threw his first, and last, punch. Unluckily for him, his physical intentions were anticipated, and the Caterpillar sidestepped his punch easily. In another twist of bad luck, Spencer did not anticipate the right hook that the Caterpillar was going to retaliate with that knocked the musician flat on his ass in the middle of the dancefloor.

Libby's jaw dropped as she heard a thousand different gasps from the crowd that had formed around the altercation on the dancefloor. The quick-thinking Caterpillar didn't savor his victory, but instead turned straight to Libby, grabbing her hand as he did so.

"C'mon," he smiled, "before you and I both get kicked out of here."

Libby didn't know what she was doing, and she barely knew this guy, but she held his hand and ran from the dancefloor with him.

Libby smiled as the image of Spencer lying flat on his back in the middle of the dancefloor lingered in her mind. Unfortunately for her, she didn't have the luxury of time and therefore set her mind back to the task of retrieving her clothes, or at least enough clothes to assemble a makeshift outfit suitable for her to leave the room in. She was desperate to get out of here as fast as humanly possible.

Libby slowly climbed out of the bed, being careful to not move the mattress enough that it would cause the Caterpillar to wake. Although it was quite the task, she finally managed to escape the mattress, forgetting all about her modesty as she stood in the middle of the Niven suite in nothing but her birthday suit. Albeit her birthday suit was better than most, she couldn't be naked when she left the suite, so she needed to find herself an outfit.

It was both a curse and a blessing that her Queen of Hearts costume from the night before was in so many different pieces. A million pieces meant that surely something would be easy to find. A million pieces, however, also meant that the pieces she did find were not that suitable on their own. She quickly scooped up her black bodysuit and slipped that on. It covered only half of her boobs, but she also managed to find a blue T-shirt that she was sure belonged to the Caterpillar. The T-shirt wasn't her size, but it did mean that she didn't have to worry about her nipple making a surprise appearance when she fled this room and this hotel.

Libby kept looking around because now she needed some pants. She couldn't, for the life of her, find the skirt that she wore as part of her costume last night, so she was going to have to improvise. She found the Caterpillar's black pants, but they were way too big for her. Panic started to settle in as she realized that the sun was creeping further and further into the room. It meant that time was ticking, and that meant that the Caterpillar would be waking up from his beauty sleep any moment now.

Finally, she found what appeared to be a pink scarf. The Caterpillar must have been wearing it as part of his costume because pink did not go with Libby's. She figured that she could fashion it into a skirt. A very short and slutty skirt, but a skirt all the same. All she needed to do was create an outfit that was acceptable enough to get into one of the cars of her father's car service, which she had already texted to meet her by the back door of the hotel in ten minutes. Thankfully her phone was together with her clutch from last night and they were easy to find. She quickly picked up the pink scarf from the back of one of the suite chairs in the room and something fell to the floor. Libby hesitated. She was already short on time. Curiosity got the better of her. She bent down to see what had dropped.

It was a black leather wallet. Surely it was the Caterpillar's, if he wasn't a thief who had swiped it from the party last night. Libby thought against that idea though. All the guests at the party last night were wealthy and this wallet was pretty basic. No label. Arguably, even real leather. Libby placed it back on the chair and quickly secured her makeshift skirt before she decided to give in to her curiosity once more.

Libby opened the wallet and its contents looked standard at first glance. The Californian driver's license let her come face to face with the Caterpillar himself. His smile, she noted, was pretty damn cute and those brown curls were pretty damn sexy. Libby looked at his details. Six foot three inches. She had thought as much. Eyes: Green. Yep. Hair: Brown. Yep. His name was Wentworth Turner. His real name. Libby was impressed. That was a star power name if she'd ever heard one. It made her second-guess ditching him before he woke up. She assumed he was probably an up-and-coming actor or musician. He was way too attractive to be working behind the scenes as a producer or director. At the same time, however, Spencer hadn't recognized him last night and he probably would have had the Caterpillar been in the music business. Spencer knew everybody in the music business, especially those with enough contacts to make it into an exclusive Niven Hotel launch. Libby's eyes then caught the corner of a white piece of card sticking out of the notes section of the wallet. She immediately thought business card and therefore decided to look because it was probably going to tell her whether her assumption about his profession was right.

Libby's heart sank as soon as she read the business card and she had to stop herself from dropping the card and wallet altogether. He did work in the business, but it wasn't doing what she thought. The card had his full name across the top, *Wentworth Turner,* confirming that it was, in fact, his business card. Underneath his name read the words *Freelance Photographer*. It was then and there that Libby realized she probably would have been better off sleeping with Spencer.

She had slept with a paparazzo. Paparazzi were the scum of the Earth. The scum of the Hollywood circuit. Sleeping with a paparazzo was even lower than sleeping with a backup dancer, something Libby had never done because she still had a career worth hanging onto. Once you started mingling that low on the social hierarchy it was either because your career was dying or it was already dead. There were no other exceptions. Everybody knew it. It was the way the hierarchy worked in Hollywood. Everybody knew that too. If this got out, Libby would be done. Her Victoria's Secret contract would disappear. Her modeling gigs would join it. She would be back to dead-end casting calls with Willa Nelson because the only thing she would be able to land, and that would require effort as well, would be catalog modeling shoots. She would be right back, if not even lower than, where she had been when she had started on the circuit when she was a teenager. Her career would be over.

Libby was abruptly drawn out of her thoughts by a loud yawn. Her eyes darted immediately to Wentworth Turner still asleep in bed, although facing the window and therefore not facing her right now. She didn't have any more time to process this disaster because she had to get out of there as fast and as quietly as she could. She didn't have time to get the business card back in the wallet, so she just tossed it all to the floor as she very quietly and slowly moved to the chair she had placed her clutch and phone on moments earlier. Her eyes remained fixed on the man in the bed as he continued to stir. It was then that she realized she hadn't even thought about footwear for her great escape. Her right shoe was sitting neatly on the floor at the foot of the bed, but there was no time to try and find her left one. Instead, she started for the closed door. Wentworth was stirring but she didn't look back as she reached the door. She quickly, not even bothering with how much noise she was making at this point, opened it, and slipped out into the corridor, letting the airlock on the door do the rest.

She immediately started running down the corridor, thanking her lucky stars that the carpets were brand new and therefore would be cleaner than the average carpeted hotel corridor. She finally reached the lift and once it arrived at her floor she ran inside and immediately hit the button for the ground floor. She started pressing the 'close door' button like a maniac. She knew it wouldn't make the doors shut any faster, but her heart was racing, and she was desperate enough to convince herself that it would make a difference. It wasn't until the doors slid closed that Libby let out a deep breath she didn't even know she was holding. She looked down at her attire as the lift started its descent. She adjusted her scarf skirt once more as she prayed that the lift would go all the way to the ground without having to stop at another one of the thirteen floors. All she wanted to do was contemplate the monumental disaster that was her current predicament in peace.

4

Run

It wasn't until Libby found herself back in her condo that she felt her body fully relax as she closed her eyes and leaned back against her closed front door. She couldn't believe how much traffic there was from Beverly Hills back to her place, and had it been a moment more she would have lost it at the driver of the car service that had picked her up. Not only was he late, meaning that she had to spend fifteen minutes hiding in the back alley behind the Niven Hotel shoeless and in her makeshift skirt, but he spent the entire ride eyeing her in the rear-view mirror. More unwanted dirty attention is not exactly what a girl wants when she's doing a literal walk of shame. Especially because the guy was at least three times her age, and not in a sexy George Clooney kind of way.

"Where have you been slut?"

Libby's eyes widened in surprise, not expecting to hear anyone's voice in the condo she lived in alone. Thankfully it was only Anita. She breathed another sigh of relief. The blonde was currently curled up on one of Libby's grey armchairs in the middle of the living room. Her head was buried in the latest copy of *Cosmopolitan* magazine, which had only just arrived at Libby's door on Friday morning. Libby hadn't even had a chance to read it yet.

"Hope you don't mind, I was craving almonds and I thought you might have some," Anita continued, her eyes not leaving the magazine pages as she continued to peruse.

"I'm allergic to almonds," Libby stated as she dropped her clutch down on the small table next to the front door and dragged her feet to join Anita in the living room.

"Which is precisely why I didn't find any," Anita smiled as she finally looked up at Libby.

Libby collapsed onto the three-seater lounge directly opposite Anita. The soft grey cotton felt exactly like the comfort she needed right now. She closed her eyes and snuggled into the cushions underneath her. Her legs curled close into her body as she did so.

"Why the fuck are you wearing a cheap-ass scarf as a skirt?" Anita asked.

"Oh my God, Nita," Libby sighed, not bothering to open her eyes as she threw her arms over her head to cover her face in shame as the memories of last night started flooding her mind again. "You don't even want to know!"

"Hell yeah, I want to know!" Anita replied enthusiastically as she snapped the magazine shut and tossed it onto the coffee table. "Especially because that fuck ugly scarf was not part of your costume last night."

Libby sighed as she moved her arms slightly and opened her eyes to look at her best friend. She hated that Anita's blue eyes were so wide at the prospect of fresh gossip, but she knew that if the roles were reversed that she would have reacted in the exact same way. They all thrived on the gossip, no matter who it was about.

"I can't even say it. It's...," Libby sighed before she started mumbling incoherently into her arms again.

"Well, seeing as the last time I saw you last night, or at least I'm pretty sure that was you because I was pretty trashed after the Jell-O shots came out, you were with Spencer," Anita grinned. "Let me guess, you gave into his bad-boy charms again?"

All Libby could do was sigh. Sure, it would have been awful to have fallen for Spencer and all his bad-boy charm again, but her situation was much worse than that. So bad that she didn't even know how to verbalize the shame.

"I promised myself I would never get into bed with Spencer again," Libby said.

"And that's exactly what you said last time, lovely," Anita commented.

Anita was right. Libby had a hell of a lot of history with Spencer Stevenson and everyone close to her knew all about it. Sure, he was successful and his ranking on the Hollywood hierarchy was decent enough. He was cute, too. Those ridiculous blue eyes probably bumped that up to 'really cute' on a good day. Those blue eyes had also cast a spell on many a girl in Hollywood, so it wasn't like Libby was the only one to have fallen prey either. If she had to wrap it up in so few words, though, Spencer Stevenson was... icky.

She couldn't quite describe it properly, but he had this disgusting and skin-crawling quality attached to him and all his bad-boy charm. It mostly had to do with the fact that the girls he usually 'spent time with' didn't have a lot going on upstairs. They were also the kind of girls that usually spent time with A LOT of other guys. He was notorious for having a bit of a type, and that type was usually blonde, dumb, and very easy. At the end of the day, Libby Evans didn't want to be categorized as another one of Spencer's 'bed ladies'. Even if he did come back for more every time they spent the night together. Even if he did shower her with compliments and praise, which was very un-Spencer-like. She just couldn't get past the damage that being associated with Spencer would do to her reputation, especially with so much on the line right now with her Victoria's Secret contract in the works. She had to avoid a scandal at all costs, which gave her a very good reason to avoid Spencer Stevenson. If only he was the only scandal she had to worry about right now.

"So, fess up," Anita asked again. "Did you?"

"No!" Libby stated firmly. "I really meant it the last time, no more Spencer Stevenson! I was done then, and I am still done now!"

"Good girl," Anita smiled as she crossed her legs, which looked exceptionally long in the short white denim skirt she was currently sporting. "Cause I don't think Ace would appreciate hearing about something like that while he's so far away."

Libby felt the panic rising in her throat, her chest, and her cheeks. She had completely forgotten all about Ace Thatcher and the role that he played in all this mess until Anita had mentioned his name. Suddenly last night wasn't something that could just affect her reputation. It was also something that could spell the end of Libby's relationship. It wasn't like Ace meant a lot to her because they had been seeing each other for the better part of a year or anything. Except that it was exactly like that.

Libby was internally freaking out, but the look of confusion on Anita's face meant that Libby probably needed to say exactly what was going on that was causing her extended silence. Or at least verbalize some untruthful version of what was going on without having to tell the truth about last night to Anita. Libby wanted to be able to tell her best friend everything, but at the same time when she did tell Anita anything, she had to be prepared for it to get back to Charlie or Willa. She also had to accept that whatever Charlie or Willa heard would be told to more people after that, and so on, no matter how much of a 'secret' it was. Realistically in Hollywood, a secret was better defined as something kept between friends, and their friends, and their friends.

"I completely forgot that I was supposed to call Ace last night!" Libby quickly lied with the first thing she could think of. "He's going to be super pissed!"

Anita smiled making Libby sigh with relief on the inside. It was obviously a lie that was easy to believe. Easier to believe, that is, than the truth.

"You're so lucky you bagged him," Anita sighed. "I'd kill for a man with an accent. Though, I'd probably rather British over French."

"Yeah, French accents are a bit weird," Libby nodded as she got up and started heading for her phone. "Do you mind if I give him a call now?"

"The room is yours!" Anita exclaimed as she hopped to her feet. "I've got to get back to learning my lines for filming on Monday anyway."

"Oh, you've got an audition, have you?" Libby asked as she fished for her cell phone in last night's clutch.

"Oh my God no, thank God it's not an audition!" Anita exclaimed as she grabbed Libby's *Cosmo* from the coffee table again. "I've got a guest role in a new movie and my scenes shoot on Monday at Universal."

"Wow, that's awesome, Nita!" Libby exclaimed, genuinely excited for her friend. "What's the movie about?"

"I wanna say a war, maybe?" Anita shrugged as she started heading for Libby's front door. "But then again maybe it's about the end of the world? It's about something sad!"

"Cool," Libby nodded as she unlocked her phone, found Ace's number in her contacts, and then pressed the phone to her ear. "Break a leg!"

"Love you," Anita cooed as she waved goodbye and exited stage left to her condo that was just down the corridor.

"You've reached Ace Thatcher, leave me a message."

Libby rolled her eyes and hung up. Ace never answered when she called him. It was like he was allergic to surprise conversations, so he only ever talked on the phone when he was the one making the call. Usually, when she wanted to talk to him, she'd try to call, it would go to voicemail, she'd hang up, and then he'd call her right back. Caller ID was invented so people didn't have to go through this kind of time-wasting nonsense, but apparently Ace was a little behind on that concept.

Libby sighed and looked around her condo. There was way too much going on in her head to spend the evening by herself. She could always duck next door and take up more of Anita's time, but her friend did say that she was going to be busy learning lines. Judging by how little she seemed to know about the movie, however, Libby thought it was safe to assume that Anita didn't exactly have a very large or complicated role in it. Then again, maybe spending time with Anita wasn't the best idea just in case she remembered that Libby hadn't given her a straight answer on what she had been up to last night after the party, including the origins of her pink scarf skirt. Libby pondered it for a moment longer and then decided that the only thing that was going to be worse than getting grilled by Anita about last night's events, was sitting in her condo alone and dwelling on last night's events. There was only one thing that sounded better right now.

Libby unlocked her phone again and started texting.

**Where are we partying
tonight? x**

As soon as she sent the message, Libby stared at the phone screen in her hand. She knew full well that Willa Nelson was never without her phone so she wouldn't have to wait too long before she received a reply. As expected, those three little dots appeared almost instantly and then the familiar *ding* of her text message tone sounded.

Skybar at 9pm.
See you there, bitch! x

* * *

Skybar at the Mondrian Hotel was one of Willa Nelson's favorite places to go on a Saturday night. She had always wanted to travel to Hawaii, and even though she hadn't made it there yet, she was certain that bars in Hawaii all looked like this. The pool centerpiece was really what gave it the look, especially as the whole scene was open air and the stars, or what she assumed were stars through the hazy LA pollution hanging in the air, just glittered as their light reflected off the pool's surface. No one was swimming tonight either, it being December and all, so the pool's surface was still and almost looked mirror-like as it reflected the image of every one of the little seated window areas, complete with their matching tables decked out in a massive array of candles. The whole bar oozed seductive energy and Willa absolutely adored it. This was her location of choice every Saturday night, even if it wasn't The Pack's usual one anymore.

Willa was surprised when Libby texted her earlier today about meeting up tonight. Saturday nights out weren't really Libby's thing anymore unless there was some swanky Hollywood event going on downtown. She'd insisted that she was still the same 'down-to-Earth' Libby that she was when they had all started hanging out together, back when Willa and Libby were attending the same photo shoots and casting calls. However, since Libby had started on her Victoria's Secret career path, Willa knew she thought she was above them all, no matter how much she'd deny it. There were no more pre casting call girls' nights featuring rosé and mani-pedis, and there were no more post casting call celebratory shopping sprees because Libby didn't need casting calls anymore to get fashion week work. There were also no more Saturday nights at Skybar checking out cute guys as Libby didn't need that either because she had Ace Thatcher. Charlie was right, if it wasn't all about Libby then Libby wasn't really interested. Ironic as it was because Libby would say the same thing about Charlie when she was using Willa's ears for a good vent.

"Hey, have you heard from Charlie yet?" Christie Ecles asked, a new gin and tonic in her hand.

Willa shook her head and then checked her phone again and realized that it was 10:30 pm, which was well past when Charlie said she was going to meet them.

"I'm sure she'll be here soon!" Christie smiled.

Willa had met Christie just the other day and was instantly drawn to her. Sadly, her teeth were 'Britney Spears' style massive and everywhere, and her credentials were almost exclusively backup dancing gigs, but Willa saw potential in the blonde. It also helped that Christie had a ton of money that always came in regularly from her dad, the dean of some Ivy League school on the east coast. Willa hadn't entirely been paying attention when Christie was telling that story. It was partly because she'd still been adjusting to just how much of Christie's mouth she could see when the girl talked, but it was mostly because Willa had zeroed her attention in on Christie's mom, Camryn Ecles, who just happened to be the founder and CEO of Illuse Cosmetics.

Over the last couple of years, vegan cosmetic brands had started to become more in demand in Hollywood, and Illuse Cosmetics was pretty much leading the charge. This is where Willa's networking talents were going to come in handy because cozying up to Camryn's daughter was going to be the first step toward Willa's new career goal of becoming the face of Illuse Cosmetics. Commercial modeling wasn't quite where she hoped she would end up. Everyone on the Hollywood circuit knew that runway modeling would always be the more elite of the two, but being a brand ambassador changed the game entirely. Being the face of a brand as big as Illuse would trump any runway show, even the Victoria's Secret kind. A spokesmodel role for a cosmetic company meant all kinds of exposure, including magazine adverts and your face being plastered all over those billboards high above Hollywood Boulevard. It would also mean that she would have some steady work, a definite plus considering all the feedback from her recent casting calls had left much to be desired.

"Hey," Libby spoke as she returned to Willa's right hand, the three girls now completely occupying Willa's usual section of Skybar.

The window seats in each section of Skybar had a large glass window behind the lounge seats. The glass was always pristine, which gave a perfect view of the city of lights in all its glory.

"Can you believe the bar is already out of fucking limes?" Libby scoffed, rolling her eyes as she handed Willa one of the two mojitos she was carrying.

Willa noticed that Libby had returned with mojitos that were double the size of the ones that she'd brought over two rounds ago. Considering it was the night after a huge night at the Niven Hotel opening, it seemed awfully strange that Libby was hitting the juice so hard. The girl was the biggest lightweight on the west coast, and useless when she was wasted, so Willa thought it was weird that she kept heading back to the bar and bringing bigger and stronger drinks back with her.

"Are you fucking serious?!" Willa exclaimed as she scrunched up her nose at her lime-less mojito.

"The loser at the bar tried to mansplain to me that there was still lime juice in it," Libby said.

"Like a Cuban is even a real mojito without an actual lime wedge in it," Willa said rolling her eyes. "What a loser."

"Tell me about it," Libby said, taking a long sip of her drink through the bamboo straw.

"So, you girls seen any cute guys tonight?" Christie asked, leaning all the way into Willa to physically, and verbally, inject herself into the conversation.

Willa immediately saw the look of disdain plastered all over Libby's face at Christie's sudden intrusion. Libby's facial expressions always needed reminding to use their inside voices. It was obvious from the moment they were introduced earlier, that Libby wasn't interested in getting to know Christie, and no doubt she'd already forgotten what her name was. Libby never bothered remembering names, let alone the names of people who she knew were backup dancers. Models were notorious for being snobs, and Libby fit right in in that regard. Status was everything to her and she wouldn't stray from her 'kind', even if it was just for a couple of drinks on a Saturday night.

"Don't even ask her," Willa said, turning to Christie and pointing a thumb in Libby's direction. "Her boyfriend's an oil heir."

"Oh my God, you're dating Ace Thatcher, aren't you? I totally read about that!" Christie exclaimed excitedly as she smiled and flashed both rows of her teeth in Libby's direction. "He is such a babe! You are SO lucky!"

"Well duh," Libby replied as she took another long sip of her mojito and let her eyes wander to things in the club other than Christie Ecles.

All Willa wanted to do was roll her eyes. Libby was about as subtle as a punch in the face and it was making Willa uncomfortable. Tonight was all about sucking up to Christie in the hopes of getting to meet her mother so Willa's spokesmodel career could get started. Unfortunately, it was becoming increasingly harder as all her sucking up was being countered by Libby being as rude and moody as possible, in addition to her leaving every five seconds for the bar. Willa knew Libby was probably just acting over the top moody so that someone would ask her what was wrong, and Libby would have the chance to offload her 'problem' of the moment. Typical Libby Evans. It was why Willa was doing the absolute opposite and ignoring Libby's behavior while restraining herself from letting her eyes roll straight out of the top of her head at the supermodel's antics. Willa turned to face Christie, hoping to quickly change the subject but it became apparent that she didn't need to. Either Christie wasn't well versed in sarcasm, or she was a fantastic actress because that Britney smile was still plastered all over her face as she met Willa's gaze.

"I saw Chase Neron arrive not that long ago," Christie said. "He is so much more gorgeous in real life!"

"So much," Willa agreed. "I heard he's only in town for a few days because he's so busy at the moment training for the next Olympics."

"Wow," Christie swooned, as she continued to stare at Chase as he sashayed across Skybar with a few of his other athlete friends in tow.

Willa sighed as her eyes, in sync with Christie's, followed the line of athletes. They were all dressed in matching tight white T-shirts that made their well-defined arms so ridiculously obvious, which was probably intentional to draw as much female attention to themselves as possible. Willa wanted to go up and shake their hands because it was working. It was working so very well. Willa snapped out of her thoughts, though, as her eyes caught Libby watching the string of athletes pass them by as well. A smirk worked its way across her face as she turned back to Christie.

"I mean, if you want to know more about him, though, you should just ask Libby," Willa said in between sips of her mojito. "Libby could tell you ALL about Chase Neron."

Libby choked on her drink.

"Oh my God, why?" Christie asked, her eyes lighting up as they darted between Willa and Libby in anticipation of who was going to explain Willa's statement first.

Willa stifled her laughter as Libby tried to cough up all the mojito that had obviously gone down the wrong way. Luckily for her, there wasn't a lime wedge in there.

"She was OBSESSED with him a few years ago!" Willa said, as she playfully nudged Libby. "Weren't you, Libs?"

Libby coughed one last time, nudging Willa back less playfully, as she sorted her breathing out so she could finally defend herself.

"I was not obsessed with him!" Libby exclaimed.

"You were totally obsessed with him!" Willa laughed, enjoying every minute of watching Libby squirm. "That was during your 'Professional Athlete' phase I believe."

Willa continued to laugh as she turned from Libby back to Christie. Libby was really annoying her tonight so she was going to try and inflict as much pain and shame on Libby's reputation as she could right now. Even if Christie Ecles was her only audience.

"She got ridiculously drunk at a party at Nate Sherman's place a few years ago and totally called Chase up and confessed her undying love for him," Willa said, in the most condescending tone she could muster.

"Willa!" Libby exclaimed, clearly not expecting Willa to start telling the entire Chase Neron story right now.

"Poor little thing poured out her heart and soul, and Chase shut her down," Willa turned back to Libby with a condescending smile. "It took her ages to get over it, especially because it was only a few days after that embarrassing phone call that he was sleeping up a storm with backup dancer Bridget Hamilton."

"Oh no, Libby!" Christie sighed, clearly trying to sound genuinely sad for Libby but instead sounding like she pitied the hell out of her. "That's so sad. I'm sure it was just the wrong timing. You are so much prettier than Bridget Hamilton!"

Libby stared daggers in Christie's direction for only a moment before she turned her daggers back to Willa.

"Do you really want to play this game tonight, Willa?" Libby asked, taking another sip of her mojito before she placed it down on the table in front of her.

"You really shouldn't be embarrassed, Libby," Christie quickly interjected. "You're a supermodel now! I'm sure Chase regrets it big time, especially because you're practically a Victoria's Secret Angel!"

Willa had to suppress a smile, and her laughter, at Christie's continuous string of comments that were genuinely trying to make the situation better but were instead just making things worse. It was obvious that Libby was trying to control herself from absolutely losing it at Christie. Instead, Willa watched as Libby's eyes remained solely fixed on her. A devious smirk worked its way across her supermodel face as she opened her mouth to speak again.

"Well, Willa, seeing as you want to take a little trip down memory lane," Libby smirked. "I'm sure your new friend here would love to hear about how many times you've slept with 'funny man' Coen Dean."

Willa's eyes popped out of her head as she practically dropped her mojito onto the table in front of them. The hand gestured air quotations that Libby used to emphasize 'funny man' just adding insult to injury.

"Oh my God, Coen Dean is hilarious!" Christie exclaimed. "I LOVE the late show!"

Willa couldn't stop the look of sheer horror from spreading across her face, not even caring how unattractive it made her look in the middle of Skybar right now. She was caught completely off guard by Libby's comment, and she couldn't hide that.

"I cannot believe you said that, Libby!" Willa exclaimed.

The banter had quickly turned serious and all the humor, at least for Willa, had vanished from the conversation. She glared at Libby as she felt the anger boiling inside her as it replaced the embarrassment of the Coen Dean bomb that had just been dropped. Libby always pushed everyone's buttons. Whether it was hers, Charlie's, or even Anita's occasionally, which was a big achievement seeing as virtually nothing got to Anita. Tonight, it was Willa's turn to fall victim to Libby's particular button-pushing talents, and Willa wasn't impressed by it in the slightest.

When Willa was drinking, she had an especially hard time making smart decisions, including that terrible drunken phase of hers when she thought chubby, blonde comedian Coen Dean was a good idea. Sure, he was funny on TV and *The Late Show with Coen Dean* got amazing ratings, but he was not the type of guy one dates when they are trying to make it big in Hollywood. Even as an aspiring model, Willa was very much out of his league, and the idea that she'd stooped so low embarrassed her enough to try and keep their sexual tryst a few years back on the extreme down low. Tryst number one hadn't been the only tryst, though. After tryst number two, she thought coming clean about it to Libby and Anita would stop her from making another huge mistake. Unfortunately, it took trysts three, four, and five for her to finally come to her senses.

'Drinking Willa' also had a hard time letting Libby's button pushing go, which meant that she thought that tonight at Skybar, in front of Christie Ecles, was a good time to challenge Libby Evans to a verbal war. Libby was a huge deal right now in the modeling world. She didn't have her Victoria's Secret wings yet, but as far as the media was concerned, she was already there. She was effortlessly climbing her way to becoming one of the highest-ranked, highest paid, and most powerful supermodels in Hollywood. As far as Willa was concerned, one phone call from Libby could make or break Willa's modeling prospects. However, Willa wasn't seeing things clearly right now. She wasn't looking at the future and her career prospects, she was just looking at the red that was right in front of her. She was going to regret it, but she was going to give Libby the tongue lashing that only 'drinking Willa' was game enough to dish out.

"The one thing I ask you to keep your huge mouth shut about and you can't even do that!" Willa exclaimed in a hushed whisper as she leaned away from Christie and further in toward Libby. "Like seriously Libby! The one thing I trust you to keep to yourself and you have to be a complete bitch about it!"

Willa stopped in her tracks as she realized Libby wasn't retaliating, or even listening for that matter. Instead, she was gripping the side of the couch they were sitting on and her dark brown eyes, which seemed even bigger than usual, were darting from the drink in her hand to the bar. Back and forth.

"Are you even listening to me right now?!" Willa exclaimed, trying to keep her volume down but finding it extremely hard as her anger continued to rise at the fact that Libby wasn't even paying attention to her right now.

Willa's eyes darted in the direction of the bar too, trying to figure out what was going on and what on Earth Libby was looking at so shadily. Nothing seemed out of the ordinary. There were several couples either currently making out or on their way there, sitting in the love seats closest to the bar. A few single guys were packed into the right of them, seated on the stools directly in front of the bar, and were creepily spending way too much of their time ogling the couples. Then there were the other Saturday usuals; the cliched and over-the-top bachelorette party with male genitalia party favors everywhere, and the scantily dressed girls whose outfits basically screamed 'I will do anything to get famous', including sleeping with just about anyone. Unusually, though, there was also a group of what appeared to be college guys in their teenage boy T-shirts and skinny jeans with the characteristic dorm room key lanyard hanging out of their back pockets. Some were cute, but Willa wasn't really interested in a man without any status attached to him.

"I have to go," Libby announced to no one in particular.

Willa watched as Libby quickly grabbed her Chanel purse and readjusted the white bra she had on underneath her powder blue Gucci sheer midriff top. Willa went to say something to her, but before she could get another word out, Libby had jumped to her feet and literally skimmed right across the surface of the wooden floor and out of sight in amongst the crowd. Willa hadn't even realized that Libby had downed the rest of her mojito. The empty glass, complete with mint leaves still stuck to the sides, was sitting there on the table next to Willa's only half-empty glass. The ice hadn't even had a chance to melt inside it.

"What was that about?" Christie asked.

"Who the fuck knows?" Willa replied, trying to shake the confusion off her face and out of her mind.

"Oh my God, that fucking bouncer downstairs spent at least ten minutes checking my ID," Charlie Niven huffed as she strutted up to their table and took a seat next to Willa. "I don't know why you insist on coming here, Wills, it's definitely gone downhill!"

"You must be Charlie!" Christie exclaimed excitedly as she leaned across the table in Charlie's direction. "I'm Christie. Christie Ecles, and I absolutely LOVE that black dress. Is it Chanel? Oh my God, it's definitely Chanel, and it looks amazing on you!"

Charlie was obviously confused as hell as to why there was a stranger at their table who was talking to her, so instead of replying she turned her attention back to Willa, completely ignoring Christie in the process.

"Where's Libby?" Charlie asked, looking around the bar and the space around their table. "Didn't you say she was coming out?"

"Yeah," Willa said. "It was her idea."

"Weird," Charlie said. "She is never down to party on a Saturday anymore, unless it's a Victoria's Secret event."

"Right?" Willa sighed. "But she's gone now anyway, which is probably for the best because she was in a foul mood."

"Oh my God, she was totally in the worst mood as soon as she got here!" Christie chimed in as she downed the rest of her gin and tonic directly from the glass, tossing her straw on the table in front of her.

"Who the fuck is this?!" Charlie asked Willa as she looked in disgust at the straw on the table in front of her.

Willa didn't respond because she hadn't heard the question. She wasn't listening to Charlie at all. She wasn't listening to anything. Not the music in the club, which had caused the bachelorette party to burst out into high-pitched high school girl screams and giggles, or the hundreds of different conversations happening all around them. All she was thinking about was Libby, and what the hell was going on with her. It was obvious that she was bailing because of something she'd seen. Probably someone rather than something. Looking over in the general direction of the bar one more time, Willa couldn't put her finger on it right now. All she knew was that there was something going on with Libby, and judging from her behavior tonight, it was something GOOD!

5

Ten

Libby closed her eyes again and willed sleep to take her. She had checked her phone only moments earlier and it had read 1:33 am. She should have been deep into a REM cycle by now, instead of standing in the middle of her kitchen waiting for her lactose-free milk, cinnamon, and turmeric mixture to boil on the stovetop.

She had been in bed since 11:30 pm, since arriving home after bolting from Skybar and getting into the nearest taxi she could find on Sunset Boulevard. She had spent the first hour in bed just staring out at the magical Hollywood skyline through the floor-length windows that led from the master bedroom in her Sierra Towers condo onto the outdoor terrace. The next hour was spent trying to force herself to sleep by forcing her eyelids shut but to no avail. How was she supposed to sleep when her mind was racing a mile a minute with a million and one things?

She knew Willa was going to ask just as many questions about her unexpectedly bailing at Skybar last night and she was going to have to come up with an elaborate lie. She'd already lied to Anita within the last twenty-four hours, so a lie to Willa was just going to be more practice. Lying was a skill she would, no doubt, need because she was sure that more lies to her friends were in her near future. Despite how important her friends were to her, though, her impending lies to them were not at the forefront of her mind right now.

Buzz. Buzz.

Libby's eyes narrowed in confusion as to why the intercom to her condo was ringing. She stood completely still as she waited for the characteristic second *buzz* that would confirm that it was, in fact, her intercom and not her imagination that was making noises at odd hours of early Sunday morning.

Buzz. Buzz.

Libby moved to the stove and quickly turned off the burner before setting the cast iron teapot onto one of her ceramic Pottery Barn trivets on the marble benchtop. She then readjusted the pink silk Victoria's Secret robe around her body as she moved out of the kitchen toward the intercom on the right-hand side of her front door, pressing the large grey button on the small machine mounted on the wall.

"Miss Evans, I realize—" Paul the concierge spoke from the lobby downstairs.

"That it's 1:30 in the morning?" Libby said. "Seriously Paul?"

"My sincere apologies, Miss Evans," Paul replied. "However, there is a gentleman from Caterpillar Deliveries here to see you. He says it's an emergency."

"At 1:30 in the morning? What kind of delivery shows up at...?" Libby asked before she finally registered what Paul had just said to her. "Wait, did you say 'Caterpillar' Deliveries?'"

"Yes, that's correct, Miss Evans," Paul replied. "He said his name is Mr. Turner?"

"Let him up!" Libby squeaked, as her eyes widened in panic. "Let him up, Paul!"

"Yes, Miss Evans," Paul replied.

Libby instantly let go of the intercom button as she tried to slow down her breathing. Wentworth Turner was here. It was 1:30 am and Wentworth Turner was here. He had just showed up, without an invitation, at Sierra Towers where he could have been seen by anyone. The security and the concierge, and probably the valet too, had seen him here. Any one of the celebrity residents, and their respective guests, could have also seen him. It was early Sunday morning, after all, and some would just be returning to their condos after a night out on the town or after attending another swanky Hollywood party. This was not good. This was very much the opposite of good.

Libby knew she had two minutes, at least, until Wentworth Turner was at her front door. After all, her condo was on the twentieth floor. Anita's condo was also on the twentieth floor, though, which meant that she had less time than that to make sure that Anita did not hear the knock at Libby's front door that would announce Wentworth's arrival off the elevator. It took Libby thirty seconds of mental umming and ahhing before she decided that the best thing to do would be to simply wait in the corridor outside her front door until she heard the elevator arrive at the twentieth floor, and then whisk Wentworth straight into her condo before he could knock or speak. Her decision was made, and now she just had to wait the excruciating seconds until she put her plan into action. It was then that she realized that she was bouncing up and down on the balls of her feet in anticipation.

Libby heard the elevator doors open, ridiculous in their loudness. She stood across the threshold facing in the direction of the elevator. As expected, Wentworth stepped straight out of the elevator dressed in exactly what he was wearing when Libby had caught a glimpse of him at Skybar just hours earlier. Dark blue button-up shirt, black jeans, and some ugly brown lace-up shoes. Regrettably, she had a momentary memory lapse as soon as she noticed how sexy he looked with his hair pushed back. When she realized he wasn't Aaron Samuels and this wasn't *Mean Girls*, she straightened herself up and started hand gesturing in silence like a crazy woman for him to hurry across the corridor and straight into her condo. Judging by his freaked-out expression, but his quick shuffle the twenty feet to her front door, she had made her intentions clear enough. The next thing she knew she was quietly shutting her front door and ensuring that all the locks were done up before she breathed a sigh of relief. A wave of déjà-vu washed over her from yesterday morning when she'd arrived back at the condo after this whole nightmare began.

"What the hell are you doing here?!" Libby exclaimed in a hushed whisper as she spun around to face Wentworth, who was now standing in the middle of her living room.

"Nice to see you too," he smiled as he started casually wandering around the room.

Libby followed, eyeing him closely.

"OK," she said. "Let me repeat myself so I can be sure that you're listening this time – what the hell are you doing here at my condo at this ridiculous time of the morning?"

"I wanted to talk," Wentworth casually replied, as he turned back around to face her after inspecting the feature painting on the wall in front of him.

Libby's eyes were drawn to the painting as his gaze left it. It was an Australian sulfur crested cockatoo on a bright pink background, and it hung proudly between the grey armchairs on the east-facing wall of the living room. It was something she had picked up in Australia after the *Victoria's Secret Fashion Show* last year. It had been more than a hassle to get home, but it was worth it. That cockatoo was always going to remind her of Australia and the best time she'd had walking the Victoria's Secret runway again.

"You wanted to talk?!" Libby asked, cocking an eyebrow in disbelief as Wentworth helped himself to a seat in one of her armchairs. "You wanted to talk at 1:30 am?!"

"Well, I actually wanted to talk to you earlier at Skybar," Wentworth replied, "but you seemed like you were in a bit of a rush to leave."

Libby closed her eyes to avoid having to see the grin that she knew was spreading across the smug photographer's face again. It didn't help that his green eyes, the ones that she remembered well from the first night they'd met, sparkled like hell every time he smiled.

"Fine," Libby replied, crossing her arms across her chest. "What do you want to talk about?"

"I thought that was pretty damn obvious," Wentworth replied.

"What do you want to talk about?" Libby replied, not bothering to try and hide the frustration in her voice.

"OK," Wentworth replied with a chuckle as he leaned forward, resting his forearms on his knees as he clasped his hands together in front of him. "Maybe we should talk about what happened at the Niven a couple of nights ago?"

"There's nothing to talk about," Libby said.

She was getting more and more infuriated at how much enjoyment he was clearly getting out of this whole interaction, but she tried her hardest to maintain a straight face.

"Nothing to talk about?" Wentworth laughed.

"Nothing happened a couple of nights ago," Libby replied, trying to pass off the comment as nonchalantly as possible. "So, we have nothing to talk about."

"OK," Wentworth replied as he leaned further forward, reaching behind him for the back pocket of his jeans as he did so. "So, I'm assuming that these are not, in fact, yours that I found in bed with me at the Niven the other morning?"

Wentworth held out Libby's missing pair of red and pink Victoria's Secret French knickers. She'd pulled them out of the gift bag that she'd received after the show in Sydney, and they'd quickly become one of her favorites. She'd been quite disappointed when she had realized the other morning that she was missing them. She was, however, even more disappointed now that they were literally being dangled in front of her by the paparazzo she had let take them off in the first place. Taking a deep breath, Libby closed her eyes for a moment to compose herself and control the red rising in her cheeks. She then stormed over to Wentworth and snatched the pair of knickers right out of his hand.

"So, what's it going to take?" Libby asked as she balled the knickers in the palm of her hand.

"What do you mean?" Wentworth asked, the tone in his voice and his facial expression giving Libby the impression that he was genuinely confused by her statement.

"What's it gonna take to keep your mouth shut about whatever happened at the Niven that night?" Libby asked, slowly and clearly so she wouldn't have to repeat herself. "Money? Is that what you want?"

Shaking his head in amusement, Wentworth let out a small laugh.

"That is so typical of you Hollywood girls," he said. "You think you can buy anything and everything you want."

"Everyone has their price," Libby shrugged.

"Oh really?" Wentworth asked, still slightly chucking.

"Yes, really," Libby replied. "So, the question is, what's yours?"

"Maybe I just came to chat with you about a deep and meaningful connection we had the other night?" Wentworth suggested as he leaned back to get more comfortable in Libby's armchair.

"A deep and meaningful connection?!" Libby exclaimed. "Do you even remember anything about the other night?!"

"I do remember saving you from that douchebag Spencer Stevenson," Wentworth replied, "and while I was also fairly drunk, I do remember a few other things that happened after that."

"That's a lot more than I remember," Libby mumbled under her breath.

"Oh, and you bailing on me the other morning in the penthouse suite at the Niven of course," Wentworth replied.

Libby paused as she thought carefully about what she wanted to say next. It was obvious that he was trying to get her to talk about the details of what she remembered of their night together at the Niven. He did remember more than she did, but it didn't sound like it was by much. He seemed to also blame his patchy memories on alcohol. It was one of those situations where she wanted to know more, if only to confirm that they had in fact slept together, despite how obvious it already was. At the same time though, she knew that the longer she spent in this conversation, the more she would feel like she was stuck in a nightmare that she just wanted to wake up from.

"I have a boyfriend," Libby decided to reply with, her eyes locking with Wentworth's.

She wanted him to know how deadly serious she was being. She wasn't a cheater. She had never cheated before, and even though it wasn't the first thing that came to her mind the morning after, it made her uneasy when she thought about the fact that she was a cheater now.

"Oh yes, the glorious Ace Thatcher," Wentworth replied.

His eyes nearly rolled out of his head and his words dripped with sarcasm.

"I wouldn't have done it if I hadn't been so drunk!" Libby exclaimed defensively.

She was, after all, defending both her reputation and her relationship.

"Yes, you would have," Wentworth nodded, his eyes fixed on Libby.

It was his turn to let her know how serious he was being with what he was saying.

"Excuse me?!" Libby exclaimed.

"The only reason you regret what happened between us was you found out what my job is," Wentworth replied.

"I don't know what you mean," Libby lied.

"You do realize you left my business card and wallet strewn all over the floor just before you bolted the other morning, don't you?" Wentworth replied. "After you finished snooping through my stuff, that is."

Libby was busted. He was right. She had been snooping.

"This conversation is ridiculous," Libby replied, shaking her head. "I have a relationship and a reputation to protect so I'll ask you once more, what do you want?"

"How do you know that I want anything?" Wentworth asked.

"You definitely wouldn't have come here if you didn't want something," Libby answered.

Wentworth shrugged in reply.

"Despite the usual assumptions," Libby continued. "I'm not as dumb as you think I am."

"I don't think you're dumb," Wentworth replied, causing Libby to narrow her eyes in suspicion. "I know you're not."

If Libby could have narrowed her eyes further, she would have. She wanted to believe he was just trying to butter her up before he dropped the metaphorical bomb. The expression on his face, though, looked too genuine for buttering up, which meant that he'd just given her a genuine compliment. She was not expecting that, which made her feel uneasy.

"But you are right," Wentworth continued, a smile forming at the corners of his mouth. "There is something that has crossed my mind."

"Which is?" Libby asked.

She wasn't sure whether she was going to like the next words to come out of his mouth. In fact, she was sure she wouldn't.

"Ten dates," Wentworth said.

"What?" Libby asked, her nose scrunching up at how cryptic his answer was.

"I don't want any money from you," Wentworth explained. "If you want me to keep my mouth shut, all you have to do is give me ten dates."

"As in you want me to go on ten dates with you?" Libby clarified. Wentworth nodded.

"In exchange for your silence, all I have to do is go on ten dates with you?" Libby asked again.

Wentworth nodded once more.

"I can't," Libby replied. "I have a boyfriend and the tabloids would have a field day with it. The reputation and relationship that I'm trying to save would both be in the trash."

"I can guarantee that we'd go places you won't be recognized," Wentworth explained. "I mean, it'll be hard because after all, you are the great Libby Evans."

Libby rolled her eyes at his blatant use of sarcasm yet again.

"But I can guarantee it," Wentworth quickly added. "Easy done."

Libby considered his condition. As big of a star as she always considered herself to be, as a member of The Brat Pack and a Victoria's Secret supermodel, there were still places that she could go in LA and Hollywood where people didn't give her a second look. She knew a lot of those places well. Those were the places she would go to escape the paparazzi. Unfortunately, the Niven hadn't been one of those places, nor apparently was her own condo at 1:30 on a Sunday morning.

"You give me ten dates," Wentworth continued, "and I give you my silence about the mind-blowing, heart racing, out of breath, passionate sex that we had the other night."

Libby closed her eyes and cringed at his description of that night's events. She had gotten her wish. That was all the confirmation she needed that they had done the deed. The French knickers were first base, and that last comment Wentworth had just made was the entire home run. When she opened her eyes, she wanted nothing more than to slap the grin off that silly photographer's face. Taking a deep breath, she finally realized that the deal wasn't going to get any better. This was pretty much the easy way out. Had he been any other jerk who had gotten a piece of Libby Evans, he would have suggested ten bedroom tumbles to keep his mouth shut as opposed to ten dates. Or perhaps ten lap dances in a public place with lots of paparazzi. It seemed that Wentworth was giving her a pretty easy way out. This was a case of relatively easy blackmail, if such a thing even existed.

"How can I be sure that you're not using this as a way to set me up with another one of your photographer buddies so you can sell the photos to the tabloids?" Libby asked, her suspicion getting the better of her.

"I give you my word," Wentworth replied.

"Your word?!" Libby laughed. "Your word means nothing to me. I don't know anything about you or how good your word is."

"My word is good," Wentworth insisted. "I give you my word that there will be no cameras, no photos, no hidden photographers. Well, at least no hidden photographers that I have organized or set up. Anything else?"

"Nothing physical," Libby said.

"So, no holding hands?" Wentworth replied cheekily.

"You know exactly what I mean," Libby replied, pointing a stern finger in his direction. "Just because you're taking me on more than one date, doesn't mean that you're entitled to anything physical. No kissing. No hugging. No doing whatever else we did the other night at the Niven."

"I'm not a bad guy," Wentworth replied. "I don't force myself on women."

"You're not a bad guy?!" Libby laughed. "Have you forgotten where you are right now? Showing up at my place unannounced at 1:30 am with a deal that sounds a lot like blackmail?"

"Not blackmail," Wentworth winked. "Just a bit of fun really."

Libby rolled her eyes. He was actually blackmailing her with a side of cute and funny right now.

"So, Miss Evans," Wentworth said, "do we have a deal?"

6

Doubtful

Anita was almost at the point of using her hands to cover her ears to drown out the incessant bitching that was going on around her. She was usually all up for a bit of banter about her friends, but Charlie and Willa took it to a new level, especially when the current topic of conversation was Libby Evans. Instead, Anita continued to mask her real feelings as she tried to discretely check her new Tag Heuer watch in the hope that looking at the time would make Libby arrive faster.

Anita and Libby had been best friends since before Libby realized how pretty she was, and before Hollywood realized her potential for supermodel greatness. Back then, Libby was a massive dork. She knew nothing about fashion. Neither of them did. She knew nothing about boys, no matter how much time she spent daydreaming about Hamish Dawson. Anita and Libby were a part of Hollywood without really being a part of it. Anita was a stable working child actor and Libby was the sole Privileged Pictures heiress before the company started making blockbusters. They were young and carefree, living on the outskirts of the glamorous life that they now had as part of The Brat Pack. Those were the days when she and Libby would make wish lists of all the things they dreamed about doing one day. Anita wanted to star in a movie directed by Peter Jackson, preferably with Orlando Bloom, and win an Academy Award. Libby wanted to be a supermodel and walk the runway for every major fashion brand, preferably Victoria's Secret.

The difference between their dreams now was that Libby had crossed hers off her wish list, whilst Anita was nowhere near achieving hers. The transition from child star to serious adult actress had seemed straightforward in theory, but for Anita things had been rougher than she had imagined. Once Libby had gotten everything she dreamed of, she still wasn't satisfied. She wanted more and more. Once she had walked the runway for *New York Fashion Week,* she decided that she wanted to do *London* and *Paris*. Once she had walked in the annual *Victoria's Secret Fashion Show*, she wanted to do it every year. She continued to chase bigger and better goals, and now a Victoria's Secret Angel contract was her latest quest. She was now interested in making connections with more like-minded Hollywood girls in the hopes of boosting her career. It was ironic that it was one thing Libby loved to complain that Willa did all the time when she was essentially becoming the exact same way, whether she was aware of it or not.

Libby's 'connecting' meant that while she and Anita were still best friends by default, things weren't really that way in real life anymore. They lived next door to each other and yet Anita barely saw Libby outside of Sunday Brat Pack brunch. They texted a lot during the week and yet Anita had no idea how Libby spent her days, and Libby never asked Anita how she spent hers. Anita had told Libby last weekend, after the Niven party, that she started filming a new movie the following Monday, and yet not one of Libby's texts through the week asked about how filming was going. Not one of Libby's texts through the week had asked Anita how she was at all.

In usual Libby fashion, all her conversation starters were about her and her texts were either filled with stuff she wanted to talk about or were spent prompting Anita to ask her about things she wanted to talk about. Anita figured that it was just hard for Libby to care about something that wasn't about her.

Anita wasn't disappointed Libby hadn't asked about the movie though. In fact, she was relieved that every member of The Pack had forgotten entirely about it because it turned out the movie wasn't anything to brag about. Anita had shown up on Monday morning at Universal only to be left waiting for three hours, without so much as a latte offered her way. When someone finally came and told her what was going on she was told that most of her scenes were cut from the movie and therefore the studio had made the executive decision to use an extra for her role. Just an uncredited actress who Anita wouldn't have remembered even if they told her who it was.

An extra meant that they'd slash their budget because Anita was an expensive commodity, even for mediocre roles like this one. It was largely due to Anita's agent, Tiffany Yaleman. Tiffany was a darling and she always made sure that Anita was paid more than the average actress, which wasn't necessarily a bad thing except in this situation. She was also really bad at picking movies for Anita. Every movie she suggested was 'a sure-fire blockbuster hit' and most of those films, if Anita's role didn't get cut or reassigned to a cheaper/younger/sluttier actress, ended up being straight to DVD nonsense. That was, in every sense of it, the opposite of a blockbuster. All in all, Anita felt like Tiffany definitely shouldn't career change into clairvoyancy because not one of her movie predictions had been right in the three years that she'd been representing Anita.

"Oh my God, you guys, I am so sorry I'm so late!" Libby entered stage right in a flurry.

Anita sighed in relief as she knew the bitching would finally stop now Libby was here, and she would have the distraction she needed from thoughts about her dwindling acting career.

"Libs, you're like thirty minutes late," Charlie scoffed, not taking her eyes off the phone in her hands. "We ordered without you."

"Oh?" Libby replied, sounding a little disappointed. "That's fine, there was a totally inconvenient car accident on the way here that's blocked nearly the entire Sunset Strip! So annoying!"

Anita sent Libby a smile as she pulled up a seat in between her and Willa.

"It was probably Brica Dallas again," Willa said, her eyes also glued to her phone as she continued to adjust the filters on Instagram before posting a brunch selfie. "God, someone should do us all a favor and cut up that license of hers."

"Oh my God, Brica Dallas," Libby added, almost beaming at the opportunity to do some fresh morning bitching. "That girl is such a weirdo. Did you see her the other week at Valerie Nice's movie premiere after-party?"

"Urg, that party was almost as bad as that movie," Willa scoffed.

"That's only cause Valerie couldn't act her way out of a cardboard box," Libby laughed.

"I mean she is doing a great job of acting like that role is the ONLY reason she gained twenty pounds last year," Willa commented.

"Twenty pounds is a bit generous, Wills," Libby smirked. "Thirty is definitely more believable!"

Anita had to stop herself from rolling her eyes as soon as Willa and Libby launched into a new round of gossip – the first one since the calendars had ticked over into the new year. For one, Willa was still currently disqualified for DUI so shouldn't be commenting on anyone's driving skills, and two, she didn't know why Libby insisted on acting like this. It was only when they were in front of Charlie and Willa that Libby became the quintessential Hollywood brat. She'd take every opportunity to listen and contribute to a bitching session about anyone that Willa or Charlie mentioned in conversation. She'd act like best friends with a girl at a party and then the next day be throwing her under the bus if Willa or Charlie initiated a good bitching session about her. Sometimes, it made Anita wonder what Libby said about her behind her back.

"Finally," Charlie said as the waitress arrived with the table's drinks. "I thought I was going to have to go back there and make my latte myself."

The waitress simply pursed her lips together as she started putting the drinks down, something that didn't go unnoticed by Anita.

Charlie wasn't always a bitch, but she did have an awfully hard time considering others' feelings when she opened her mouth. They were all a bit guilty of it, but Charlie was by far the worst, especially when she was in a bad mood. Based on last night, Anita had anticipated that today was going to be one of Charlie's low mood days that even an oat milk latte wasn't going to fix. Her loose lips this morning was just confirmation of that.

Last night, Anita and Charlie had gone out to dinner at Château Marmont whilst Willa and Libby were at a models-only *Great Gatsby* inspired fashion show event in Westwood. They'd had way too many vodka martinis and 'drunk Charlie' was vulnerable as all hell about her current situation involving Hamish Dawson. It was at times like last night when Anita felt particularly bad for Charlie because it was one of the very raw times when Charlie showed just how low her self-esteem was. Anita didn't think she would ever do it in front of the other girls, but she frequently showed her softer side to Anita when it was just the two of them. Charlie's softer side could easily be described as kind, generous, and fiercely loyal. It was a side that Anita knew she was one of few to have seen, and it was one of the main reasons why her friendship with Charlie had lasted as long as it had. They'd grown much closer in the past six months, in line with the drifting apart that Libby and Anita's friendship had done due to Victoria's Secret and Ace Thatcher.

"I'll have my usual," Libby butted in as soon as the waitress finished placing Willa's el diablo down in front of the blonde.

Anita watched the panic in the waitress' eyes as she slowly pulled out her notepad to take Libby's order. It was a new waitress that Anita hadn't seen working at Silverlake before, so she assumed the panic was related to the fact that she had zero idea what Libby's 'usual' order was. Anita watched as Libby raised an eyebrow as the girl tentatively looked at her, her pen ready to write down whatever it was that Libby wanted to order.

"And you wanted to order....?" the young waitress started, trying to prompt Libby to finish her sentence.

"Are you serious?!" Libby exclaimed, more dramatically and much louder than any of them expected. "We are here every single Sunday, and we order the exact same thing! I order the exact same thing every single Sunday!"

"I'm sorry miss," the waitress tried to explain, her voice shaking as she spoke. "I'm new here and—"

"Don't give me that bullshit about being new!" Libby retaliated as she pointed a finger aggressively in the waitress' direction. "Go back to that kitchen and find out what my usual order is so I don't have to waste another word on you!"

The Pack sat in stunned silence as they watched the waitress meekly nod a few times before turning heel and heading straight back to the kitchen. Charlie let out a laugh and locked her phone before placing it on the table in front of her.

"Fuck, Libs, that was savage!" Charlie laughed.

"Yeah well," Libby replied, a satisfied smile on her face as she turned to face Charlie. "That waitress needs to learn her place."

Anita suppressed the urge, yet again, to roll her eyes right out of her head. It was obvious that Libby and Charlie were always trying to impress each other, even though they were both in a silent war about who was the rightful Queen Bee of The Brat Pack. Anita didn't care about things like that. She barely cared about the status that came along with being a member of The Pack let alone being the actual leader. Willa, on the other hand, was like the Gretchen Wieners of The Pack who just wanted a leader to serve, whether it was Charlie or Libby. She played the role of the dutiful servant well, too. She would tell each what they wanted to hear and would gladly join in bitching about Charlie if it earned her brownie points with Libby, and vice versa. In Willa's mind it was the same thing.

"The waitresses here are going from bad to worse," Willa added. "Like have a little respect for your elite customers, right?"

"Tell me about it," Anita chimed in, just to feel like she was part of the conversation and to stop her mind drifting to unkind things about her friends.

No one was forcing Anita to be here, and no one was forcing her to be a part of The Pack. She was a big girl, and it was her decision, so the fact that she was still here meant that there were things worth staying for. She enjoyed the company of the other girls, on most days, and she wanted to see the best in them. It was that kind of a feeling when you've been friends with someone for so long that it's hard to imagine your life without them. Like they're family – you don't always get along and sometimes they drive you crazy but at the end of the day, you love them for who they are. That was who Libby, Charlie, and Willa were to Anita. They were her family, no matter how much they bitched about each other. They were her family and she loved them.

Anita was drawn out of her thoughts by the sudden ringing of Libby's cell phone, which was now vibrating like crazy on a patch of table between them. The phone was face down so Anita couldn't see the caller ID on the screen, but that wouldn't have mattered anyway considering how quickly Libby snatched her phone off the table. Anita's eyes narrowed at the strange look on Libby's face as she quickly checked the screen herself and almost immediately jumped to her feet.

"Sorry, girls, I have to take this," Libby squeaked before she darted in the direction of the parking lot.

"Oh my God, let's hope that's fucking Ace so she can stop her whole victim charade," Charlie mumbled into her latte.

"Lay off, guys," Anita said, as her fingers fiddled with the rim of her cup.

"Don't be such a martyr, Anita," Charlie said rolling her eyes. "You're too nice to that girl when you know, just as well as we do, that she bitches about all of us behind our backs."

"She just misses him," Anita added, ignoring Charlie's comment.

"I guess that's true," Willa sighed as she finally put her phone away and folded her arms. "He's been gone for months now! I'd miss my boyfriend too if he was away for that long."

"You'd actually need a boyfriend before you could miss him, Wills," Anita smirked.

Anita loved to wind up Willa Nelson because it was so easy. Willa was the most easily offended person Anita had ever met, even when it was just casual banter. Her reaction to being offended, though, was definitely the best part. Shame the girl wasn't interested in acting because she was as melodramatic as privileged white girls in Hollywood get.

"You're such a bitch Anita," Willa said as she picked her phone up again and started scrolling through her Instagram feed. "I'm ignoring you for the rest of brunch."

* * *

Libby ensured that she had made it to the parking lot before she accepted the phone call. As soon as she had seen the caller ID she knew this was a conversation she didn't want to have in front of her friends at the brunch table. Unfortunately, in her Jimmy Choos, it wasn't the easiest thing in the world to 'run' as quickly as she just had. Once again, reputation over anything and everything else.

"I didn't think I'd hear from you," Wentworth Turner said as soon as she answered the phone.

Libby had been trying to reach him all morning. It was the reason she was late leaving Sierra Towers for brunch, and the car accident on Sunset had just amplified the situation. She'd been pacing around her condo staring at the minimal text conversation between her and Wentworth, which consisted of her one text message and zero replies from him. It had been about a month since Wentworth had shown up at her condo unannounced with a proposition for her. A proposition that would allow her to keep her reputation, her dignity, and her relationship with Ace. She had told Wentworth she would think about it, and she had done nothing but for the last twenty-eight days. Christmas in Canada with her extended family had been shit because of it. The *Victoria's Secret New Year's Party* in New York City had also been shit because of it. That, and bringing Willa Nelson to the party was a massive mistake because instead of trying to make herself seem more desirable for modeling gigs, she insisted on getting trashed on fairy floss tequila shots and hooking up with yet another backup dancer.

"Don't lie," Libby said.

She wasn't in the mood for his sarcasm this morning. It had taken him too many hours already to get back to her after that simple text message, which she sent in the early hours of the morning after yet another sleepless night.

"Alright then," Wentworth replied. "Have you made a decision about our deal?"

Libby took a deep breath. She knew what her answer was going to be as soon as she sent that first text to 'Turner Evans', even though it had taken her at least two hours to figure out how to initiate the conversation without sounding sarcastic, aggressive, or stuck up enough that he would take back his offer. He had added his number to her phone the last time she saw him and the first thing she did when he left was promptly change his name to Turner Evans to cover her ass. She figured that a mysterious relative from out of town would be a safe option to go with had one of the girls found his number in her phone for whatever reason, whether it was now or later. She needed a safeguard, even if it was just a silly code name. She usually placed her phone face down at brunch, but Turner Evans was for the times she forgot. Forgetfulness, after all, was one of her usual hangover side effects on a Sunday morning.

"Libby?" Wentworth asked, in response to her extended silence.

Libby held her tongue again. She knew what she needed to say, but at the same time it was harder than she anticipated to speak the words. She'd had no one to talk to about this whole debacle so she hadn't really said any of these words out loud. The debate that she'd been having was an internal one. Despite that, she had made up her mind and had made her choice. Although, it was barely a choice if she wanted to keep her relationship with Ace alive. She had decided that because it was just one night, and it meant nothing, she wasn't going to tell Ace about Wentworth and the Niven, so she didn't want anyone else telling him about it either. She also needed to keep her Victoria's Secret Angel prospects alive and a scandal like this would kill that too. She really didn't have a choice at all.

"Libby?" Wentworth asked once more. "Are you still there?"

"Fine," Libby spoke, her eyes closing as she composed herself to calmly speak the words. "We have a deal."

Libby anticipated a laugh or a comment that would be said in a way, or a tone, that would make it easy for her to know it was being accompanied by one of Wentworth's signature smirks.

"OK," Wentworth replied.

"That's it?" Libby asked.

"What do you mean?" Wentworth replied, the confusion evident in his tone.

"I was just expecting—" Libby started.

"Me to be more of an ass about it?" Wentworth finished.

Libby paused for a moment before she nodded.

"Well, yeah," she replied.

Wentworth stifled a laugh on the other end of the line and Libby found herself smiling a little at the sound of his laugh before she realized what she was doing and who she was speaking to. Her smile quickly disappeared.

"Well, I'm not going to be an ass today," Wentworth said. "I realize how hard this probably is for you."

"Then why are you doing it at all?" Libby asked.

"I'll tell you about it one day," Wentworth replied.

A silence enveloped the conversation as Libby realized he wasn't going to give her an answer to that question today. She took a deep breath and then spoke again.

"Answer me this then," she said.

"And what's that?" Wentworth asked.

"Why ten dates?" Libby asked. "Why ten?"

"Anything lower than ten would be too little considering the amount of leverage I have on you at the moment," Wentworth explained. "Anything higher than twelve would be pushing my luck."

"Why not eleven then?" Libby posed.

"I like even numbers," Wentworth replied. "I'll let you know about date number one soon."

Libby scrunched up her nose as she pulled the phone away from her ear and looked at the screen. Wentworth had spontaneously ended the call before she even had a chance to respond to how weird a statement it was that he randomly liked even numbers. This guy was weird, and it made Libby unnerved to think about what she had now gotten herself into.

7

Date #1

Of course, her phone was glitching right now. Libby started slamming the red end call symbol on her phone screen as she watched the call time tick over and the call not end like she had wanted it to seconds before. She could feel the rage inside her burning as she continued to aggressively slam her phone screen with her index finger before the tenth slam finally ended the call. She proceeded to lock her phone and toss it into her Birkin before she realized she wanted to check the time because Wentworth Turner was still not here.

She let out a melodramatic sigh, adjusting the oversized Ray-Bans on her face as another person passed her in the New Beverly Cinema lobby. She knew as soon as she reached into her bag that it was going to take way too long to find her phone, as her purse was always a mysterious abyss when she needed to locate something in a hurry, and that was just going to compound her anger. Libby Evans was on the downward rage spiral, and she knew exactly how that was going to end.

Libby heard her phone *ding* in her bag and after what seemed like an eternity, she finally managed to locate it and noticed that she had one new message from Willa Nelson. This made her less angry, seeing as it wasn't Ace, but at the same time also angrier that it wasn't Ace texting to apologize for the monumentally shitty phone conversation they'd had moments earlier.

You bitch! Why haven't you text me all about the Weeknd video shoot from Sat? ;)

Wills, you would not believe the shitty day I've had!

Oh no – what's up?

Libby could almost hear the sarcasm in Willa's text message. She knew that her consistent whining was exhausting, and she knew that it rubbed people, especially her friends, the wrong way. She knew it because she experienced it firsthand when any of her friends tried to whine about their own first-world Hollywood problems. They were all the same. She also knew it because Willa had told her that Charlie was bitching about her whining just the other day at brunch when she'd been late.

She shouldn't be having a shitty day. Felicity had just sent through some stills from her appearance in The Weeknd's newest music video and she looked totally hot in them if she did say so herself. The Weeknd did love his models, particularly those of the Victoria's Secret kind. After all, what man didn't love a whole bunch of models dressed scantily in white fur and lingerie. Libby, along with four other models from the Sydney show, were invited through Victoria's Secret to appear in the music video. Most of the other girls were already Victoria's Secret Angels so it was nothing short of an honor to be invited to join in all the music video fun. Libby was also hoping it was a taste of more good things to come.

Fucking Ace and his fucking lies!

Typical! What the fuck did he do this time? Doesn't he know he's fucking lucky to have you?!

Libby always loved talking to Willa when she was in a bad mood. She knew that Willa was everybody's best friend, but when she was acting like hers, Libby loved it! Willa knew all the right ways to stroke Libby's ego and make her feel better about the decisions she'd made, no matter how terrible they were.

Did he finally call you?

He sure did. 4 weeks later and all he's got to say is that he's not going to be back for another month. Another fucking 30 days!

Libby was furious and the aggressive way she was tapping her phone screen to text made that glaringly obvious. She couldn't type fast enough. Yesterday it had been exactly four weeks since she had so much as heard from her boyfriend. Four weeks. Twenty-eight days. No texts. No reply texts. No phone calls. No emails. Nothing after the five-minute phone call on Christmas Eve when he basically just called to see whether his ridiculously expensive Cartier earrings had reached her in Canada. He usually 'ghosted' her for days at a time when he was out of the country, with his busy schedule always to blame, but this was the longest period they'd gone with zero communication since they'd been doing the long-distance dance. It was infuriating that a man could spend that much time on his phone, and Ace was always on his phone, and yet couldn't push a few buttons to send the 'love of his life' a simple text message.

So, wait what? He's not
coming home for your
mother fucking
birthday?!!!!!!!!

Lucky fucking me!

Reason number two that Libby was furious was that it was her birthday in two weeks. The first birthday she was going to have with Ace, and he wasn't going to be here with her. What was the point of having an oil heir billionaire boyfriend on her birthday if he wasn't even going to be here to shower her with lavish gifts and treat her like a princess? Libby was wondering what the point of having an oil heir billionaire boyfriend was at all when she never heard from him or saw him.

That's bullshit Libs!
Absolutely bullshit! As if he
can't fly on his dad's private

jet for the weekend to come
and see you?! It's been
FOREVER!

It is bullshit! And it has
been forever! It's ALL
FUCKING BULLSHIT!

Did you ask him about that
slut we saw him with
online??

Libby had forgotten all about the photo that Willa had found online. The dimly lit paparazzi photo of Ace and some mystery girl at a bar in Paris. The same Paris where he was supposed to be 'working all day and all night' with his dad sorting out new locations around the Mediterranean for further oil exploration. Willa should quit modeling and start working for the FBI because she'd be miles better at that. She was a genius when it came to digging up dirt on people and finding things that people wanted to remain hidden. Libby wasn't sure how she did it, but she always managed to find something, including that photo of Ace and his Parisian slut.

The girl in the photo with him hadn't been that pretty. Whether that was better or worse Libby didn't know. She was blonde-haired, blue-eyed, and lacking the long legs and supermodel figure that Libby had, but that didn't stop the jealousy from raging inside Libby as she remembered what Ace was doing behind her back. What else was he doing in Paris that Libby didn't know about? How many average-looking mystery blondes were there in Paris that were taking up so much of his attention that he couldn't even send Libby one stupid text message?!

> I should have, but I was too
> preoccupied yelling at his
> lying ass. He's probably
> screwing her and God knows
> how many others in Paris.
> Probably the reason he can't
> pick up the fucking phone
> and—

"Libby?" a voice spoke, causing Libby to nearly jump out of her skin mid-text.

Libby was so engrossed in her text conversation with Willa that she hadn't noticed that Wentworth had arrived at the cinema and was now standing directly in front of her. He wore a small smile on his face and was dressed decently, considering he was a paparazzo and the scum of the Earth. Libby ignored him for a little longer as she finished writing her text to Willa. She then locked her phone in her hand before she locked eyes with Wentworth again, still refusing to remove her sunglasses despite the fact they were inside. She folded her arms across her body, which wasn't an easy task in the oversized H&M coat she was currently sporting. She'd found it at the back of her spare wardrobe, and it seemed like the perfect item of clothing to hide who she was by way of hiding all the supermodel that was obvious in most of the designer clothes she usually wore.

"Let's just get this over with," Libby said, the anger being kept at bay in her tone but not in the unimpressed facial expression she knew she was throwing in Wentworth's direction.

"Are you OK?" Wentworth asked, his brow furrowing as he looked intently at her like he was searching for clues as to why she was in such a bad mood.

"I'm not here for a therapy session, Turner," Libby snapped. "Now let's just get this thing over with already, OK?"

"Wow," Wentworth sighed as he rolled his eyes.

"What did you say?" Libby asked, her eyebrow cocked.

She could feel the anger inside her from earlier slowly finding its way back to the surface.

"Nothing," Wentworth replied with an extremely forced smile. "Absolutely nothing."

"Good," Libby replied as she turned her attention back to her phone.

"I'm just going to get the tickets," Wentworth mumbled as he turned around and started walking in the direction of the ticket booth.

Seriously Libs, what the fuck are you wasting your time with him for?

> **Felicity says I need to stay scandal free for VS, and staying with Ace is good for my image.**

Yeah, she's probably right, which sucks balls. But it does stop you from finding your way back into Spencer's bed... haha.

> **You're such a bitch!**

Libby smiled as she sent the text. Talking about Ace was only going to make her angrier, so she needed the distraction. She was hoping that Willa was going to provide her with that, even if that included conversations about Spencer Stevenson and Libby's torrid past.

You just need to get laid girl! It's been way too fucking long and that's probably why you're so wound up!

Libby leaned against the wall next to her as she watched Wentworth from across the cinema lobby. If only Willa knew it hadn't been that long since Libby had expressed her sexual frustrations. Willa's text could have been the opening that Libby needed to confess her secret and ask for advice on the situation because she desperately needed to talk about it, and currently had no one to do that with. Unfortunately, it was too risky to talk to anyone about a scandal this big and because of that, it was certainly too big a scandal to expect Willa to keep it to herself. She trusted Willa, but she didn't trust her that much.

Fuck, it has been foreverrrrr!

She sighed as she scrunched up her nose as images started flooding her memory about the last time she'd had sex. She felt the anger rising in her chest again as she started mentally kicking herself for being in this situation. She was at a dingy downtown cinema waiting to see a black and white movie she didn't even care about with a paparazzo that she had accidentally slept with and was currently being blackmailed by. On top of that, she was so uncomfortable underneath the stupid coat and multiple layers she was currently wearing. It's common knowledge that Californians cannot deal with a little chill, so the heaters in the cinema lobby were blasting. It was chilly enough outside that the coat was bearable then, but now it was just playing a starring role in her shitty day. The more she thought about her current situation, and the more she saw Wentworth smiling at the skanky redheaded cashier like he was having the best day of his life, the angrier she became. As Wentworth started back toward her, she realized that the only way she was going to keep her anger about this entire day under control was to busy herself texting the crap out of Willa.

I feel ya sister! Maybe you should just dump Ace and you and I can hook up with some hot male models at that event next week?

"I didn't know what you wanted so I got popcorn, Mike and Ikes, and m&ms?" Wentworth smiled. "Ready to go?"

Libby didn't even look up from her text message as she continued to text Willa back. She simply shrugged her shoulders. Wentworth didn't say anything else as he started walking in the direction of the individual cinemas. Libby followed behind him.

OHHHH SOOOO TEMPTING!

Seriously though, it wouldn't

be the worst thing in the
world if you had a little fun
whilst Ace is out of town...
what he doesn't know won't
hurt him...

You know I'm not like
that....

You mean you're not like
that anymore...? ;)

You are such a fucking
bitch Willa, haha.

"Libby?" Wentworth whispered. "Did you hear what I said?"

"Huh?" Libby asked as she finally looked up from her phone and came face to face with the frustration etched all over Wentworth's face.

They were standing in the middle of the cinema entrance, previews rolling on the large screen in front of them. Libby looked up from her phone and noticed how full Wentworth's arms were as he juggled a couple of different packets of candy, a bucket of popcorn, and what appeared to be an extra-large cup of Pepsi. Wentworth rolled his eyes at her.

"Where do you want to sit?" he whispered.

His words were much slower than normal, suggesting it wasn't the first time he'd asked her this question.

"Wherever," Libby shrugged as she turned back to her phone. "Like it even matters."

Without another word, Wentworth proceeded into the closest row of seats and Libby followed behind him, taking the seat immediately next to him when he finally sat down.

Bzzt! Bzzt! Bzzt!

Libby looked down at her phone. Ace Thatcher's photo appeared on the screen as it started to vibrate like mad in her hand. She shook her head as she declined the call.

Bzzt! Bzzt! Bzzt!

Libby sighed in frustration as she declined the call again. Ace Thatcher was nothing if not persistent. He hated not getting exactly what he wanted and apparently right now he wanted to talk to her.

Bzzt! Bzzt! Bzzt!

Libby groaned as she stood up from her seat.

"I have to take this," Libby casually remarked in Wentworth's general direction as she rushed out of their row and into the corridor outside of the cinema.

She looked down at her phone one last time before she pressed the phone to her ear.

"What do you want, Ace?" Libby asked coldly.

"Look I'm sorry I'm not coming home," Ace said, his tone sounding more annoyed than anything else, including sorry.

"Yeah, you sound it," Libby said, rolling her eyes.

Ace had a way of making all his apologies sound absolutely nothing like actual apologies and it infuriated her. More so because he had spent a very large chunk of their relationship having something to be apologetic for.

"Babes, I miss you, ok?" Ace said. "I really wish I could come home sooner but I just can't. Work here is crazy busy and my dad—"

"Don't call me 'babes', Ace," Libby groaned. "You know I hate it when you call me that, and if you missed me so much then you'd do a much better job of actually talking to me while you're away. Or hey, maybe you would have put more effort into actually coming home when you said you were going to. Just more and more empty words, Ace. You seem to be an expert on that."

"Libs—" Ace started before he was cut off by Libby ending the call.

Libby tossed her phone into her Birkin with a groan of frustration as her hands rushed to her head and she tugged at the hair underneath her palms. Despite how clueless and annoying he was, Libby knew that at the end of the day the reason she was so angry was that it was going to be another thirty days until she saw Ace again. She loved him so she hated that it would be so long until they could spend time together. When Ace was in California, the time they spent together was always amazing. They would wine and dine at fancy restaurants in LA, like Urasawa. They would spend whole days lying in bed in his ridiculously oversized mansion in Beverly Hills. They would take his dad's helicopter out to Napa Valley and take a private tour around one of the wineries there. The last time they did, they got exceptionally drunk during a wine tasting and then had risked indecent exposure in one of the cellars after they'd ditched their tour guide. She missed all that, and she missed Ace.

Libby composed herself as she decided it was time to go back into the cinema. It sounded like the previews were over now. She continued to think about Ace as she slowly walked her way back to her seat. As she mulled it over, she realized that whilst she was angry, part of her was also sad. Missing someone tended to do that to a person, especially when it was someone you love. Unfortunately, she had a bad habit of masking her sadness with anger when it came to Ace. It was the way she coped with the lows of their relationship. It was the way she coped with the lows of everything in her life. Whether it was something as trivial as breaking a nail, or something that meant a lot more like when her mom died.

Libby stopped in her tracks and looked right, left, forward, and backward. She was distracted when she'd originally entered the cinema with Wentworth, but she was sure that the empty seats directly in front of her were their seats. She was sure that she should have found Wentworth sitting in the seat directly in front of her all settled in to watch *Model Shop*, but he wasn't there. There was almost no trace that he had been in the now empty row at all until she noticed the almost full popcorn box at her feet.

Libby started to panic. It was wishful thinking that he'd left due to an unrelated emergency, which was why the popcorn was tragically strewn across the floor in a giant mess. Realistically, though, he'd probably left because she'd been the worst date in the history of the world. Not that she really cared how bad a date she was because this wasn't a real date. What she did care about, though, was whether she had been a bad enough date that he was going to call off their whole deal.

Maybe she was just going to have to wait for Detective Willa to call her tomorrow and let her know about the new dirt that she'd found online. That new dirt being about a certain supermodel/socialite called Libby Evans who had gotten so trashed at another swanky Hollywood party and royally fucked up her whole life.

8

Christie Ecles

"Wooo!" Willa and Libby exclaimed in unison as they slammed their shot glasses down on the table in front of them, their faces scrunching up as the tequila hit the back of their throats.

Charlie laughed from her spot opposite the two girls as she, too, threw down a tequila shot of her own. She was feeling the vibe tonight at 1 OAK, and it made her wonder why she had only been here once before tonight. It reminded her of the nightlife of New York, which she adored! From the chic chandeliers to the leather booths all lined up in perfect symmetry. It helped that the guest list was a little more exclusive than some of the other places in town, like Skybar. She was getting over that place the more college kids she had to see in there on a Saturday night. Every one of them looked like they had either rolled straight out of bed or come straight from a football game.

She watched Willa and Libby clink their shot glasses together as they braced themselves for another round before she started looking around at who was present tonight. There were a lot of faces that she recognized, from The Sports Stars to her right to The Back-stage Geeks that were tucked away in one of the booths near the restrooms. It was hard not to stare at all the muscle that was bursting from The Sports Stars' booth, but she knew she had to unless she wanted to lock eyes with her ex, Matt York, who was inconveniently sitting directly facing her. It was also hard to avoid looking in the direction of The Backstage Geeks because they were obviously, and truly sadly, staring at her and her friends. It made Charlie feel like flipping them off whenever she felt their stares burning holes into her flesh.

There was Sylvan Wachs, one of Libby's exes, and two of Willa's exes, Basil Shatz and Brian Davidson. Libby and Willa had gone through a phase when they'd been desperate enough to venture to the back booths at 1 OAK, and for the sake of all their reputations, Charlie was hoping that neither ventured there again. Yeah, they were smart, and they weren't terribly unfortunate looking, but they were just really weird. Charlie was still having nightmares about the time Willa and Libby brought Brian and Sylvan to her Oscar's after-party a couple of years ago. They spent the night talking to all her guests about the chemical composition of different alcoholic drinks, and Charlie nearly strangled Sylvan when he then tried to tell her what the exact volume was of a bottle of tequila she was downing at the time. She was never inviting another Backstage Geek to one of her parties again.

Despite so many familiar faces in here, Charlie was still having trouble spotting the one face that she wanted to see, and it was making her feel unsettled as well as a little pissed off. He had, after all, told her he was going to be here tonight and that he was looking forward to seeing her. It was already 11:20 pm though, and Charlie was starting to wonder if those had just been words and that Hamish Dawson wouldn't grace her with his presence tonight. Maybe it was just his default farewell to text **I'll definitely see you there!** and it didn't mean that he was actually going to see her at 1 OAK tonight.

Maybe he was just being polite and trying to let her down gently without her knowing that he was letting her down. Or maybe he crashed his car on the way here and was now sitting in the hospital with a broken leg. On top of that, his phone had run out of battery so he couldn't text her back and let her know that he wasn't going to make it even though he really wanted to. She knew she was just grasping at straws at this point, and it was pathetic.

"Look I'm sure he'll be here soon," Christie whispered in Charlie's ear.

Charlie shrugged, trying to play it cool and pretend that she wasn't doing what Christie Ecles had just caught her doing, which was daydreaming about Hamish Dawson being in a car accident. Christie just smiled in Charlie's direction before she took another sip of her espresso martini. Christie had had some rough nights on tequila, so she stayed away from it altogether now. The martini also made her look super sophisticated, and it made Charlie a little bit jealous. Even if Christie was a backup dancer who was wearing a pink sequin mini dress that was clearly from Forever 21. It made her feel like maybe she needed an espresso martini too, even if it was just to hold rather than to drink. After an out-of-control girl's night in San Francisco three years ago, the taste of Kahlua still made Charlie instantly throw up.

"So, where's Nita tonight?" Libby asked the table as she pulled a compact out of her purse to ensure that her bright red Taylor Swift lip wasn't smeared all over her face from all the shots.

Charlie resisted the urge to roll her eyes as she noticed the black compact was a Victoria's Secret one. Libby Evans was like a walking, talking Victoria's Secret billboard that was both ridiculously large and ridiculously obnoxious.

"Is she still bummed about that role?" Christie asked.

"Oh yeah," Willa chimed in. "I heard it ended up going to Valerie Nice."

"Oh, God!" Charlie exclaimed as she wrinkled up her nose in distaste. "Nita would have been so pissed about that!"

"Tell me about it!" Willa nodded.

"What are you guys talking about?" Libby asked as she looked around the table with a confused look on her face.

"She lost out on that role she auditioned for last week," Willa explained as she recounted the gossip in her typical Willa Nelson way.

She was all perked up, her massive boobs nearly spilling out of her Versace Baroque printed bralette top, and bright-eyed as she told a bit of gossip that she knew and someone else didn't.

"She mentioned it in the group chat on like Wednesday," Charlie added, raising an eyebrow in Libby's direction.

"Oh yeah," Libby shook her head as if just remembering it. "That role."

"Poor Nita," Christie sighed as she took another sip of her martini.

"Yeah, I know," Willa said. "She was so excited about that role too!"

Charlie barely heard Christie and Willa's exchange as she was busy looking at Libby. Libby may have successfully convinced Willa and Christie that she knew what was going on with Anita, but she hadn't convinced Charlie. It was, after all, in true Libby Evans style that she had no idea what was going on outside of her little bubble. Unless the information or the conversation had to do with her, Libby only paid enough attention to make it seem like she was interested. She was too busy, after all, being interested in her own life to care about those of her friends. Even though Anita was supposed to be her best friend, Libby still had too many things in her busy supermodel life to care about what was going on with her.

"So Charlie, when are you going to tell us about Marc Jacobs?!" Christie squealed.

The shrill of excitement in Christie's voice could have easily been interpreted as the sound someone made when they'd had a glass of ice water poured down the back of their cheap, tacky dress. Despite that, though, Charlie couldn't help but smile. For a backup dancer, Christie was quickly learning what it was going to take to establish herself on the Hollywood circuit. Listening to all of Charlie's problems was a good start, but giving Charlie the opening she needed to brag about herself and her recent accomplishments was much better.

"Oh my God, what about Marc Jacobs?!" Libby exclaimed.

Whether it was genuine excitement for Charlie or whether it was excitement at hearing some new gossip, Charlie didn't care right now. All she cared about was all eyes being on her.

"C'mon, Charlie!" Willa exclaimed. "Spill!"

"Well," Charlie started, purposely drawing out her words as she savored the attention, "I got a call from a secretary at Marc Jacobs the other morning because it turns out that Marc saw a picture of me at Silverlake a couple of weeks back with that Marc Jacobs bag that I customized."

"You mean the camera bag one that you took the strap off and replaced with a silk scarf?" Christie asked excitedly.

"Yep!" Charlie nodded. "I mean the strap was totally ugly and I had a totally cute Marc Jacobs skinny silk scarf that matched way better anyway!"

"So, what happened when the secretary called?!" Willa asked.

"So, she said that Marc wanted to set up a meeting with me to organize a potential collaboration based on my little customization of his bag that he LOVED!" Charlie exclaimed.

Christie, Willa, and Libby let out a squeal of excitement in unison, almost like they'd rehearsed it prior.

"Charlie that is AMAZING!" Libby exclaimed.

"You would make such a kick-ass handbag designer!" Willa exclaimed. "I can't believe you've been keeping this news all to yourself!"

"Well, it's not like it's a done deal just yet," Charlie added, trying to play up her modesty and downplay her success just so her friends could build it up.

"It sounds like it pretty much is!" Libby exclaimed, reaching out a hand to touch Charlie's forearm. "You're going to be amazing!"

"Oh my God, Char, you totally are!" Christie jumped in, practically bouncing on her side of the booth. "I cannot wait to hear how your meeting goes! When is it?"

"Monday, February third," Charlie answered. "It's at his house in Westchester too."

"That is so ridiculously exciting!" Christie beamed. "Don't forget us when you're a famous designer, Char!"

Charlie resisted the urge to scrunch up her nose at Christie's incessant need to call her Char – a nickname that she had never been called. She also had to resist the urge to look over in Libby's direction because she knew that Libby was displaying that scrunched-up nose that Charlie was holding back. Libby had been particularly moody tonight, even though it was now subsiding due to all that tequila she was watering it down with. All that tequila, however, was bringing out 'loose lips Libby' who let anything on her mind fly out of her mouth without so much as a second thought. Charlie loved a bitch as much as the next girl, but she knew that the bitching in Hollywood needed to be sneaky because you never knew who was going to hear what, or who had connections with whom. Christie may have been a former backup dancer, but her parents had connections and Charlie didn't think that she was ready to discard those connections just yet, particularly the connections that came along with Christie's mom. Fortunately for Libby, a lot of her success was drawing a lucky hand, so her abilities at playing the Hollywood game were still taking baby steps.

"I'm going to the restroom," Libby exclaimed, as she started sliding out of their booth. "Charlie, wanna come with?"

Charlie immediately saw the look of disappointment on Willa's face at not being asked to go somewhere private like the restroom to, no doubt, have a little girl chat. Charlie didn't really want to leave with Libby but the temptation of more gossip and the thought of how much it would annoy Willa were too much to resist.

"Sure," Charlie replied, as she picked up her Marc Jacobs clutch and got to her feet.

Libby immediately linked arms with Charlie as they started walking in the direction of the restrooms. It didn't go unnoticed to Charlie just how many men stopped to stare at them as they passed. She wanted to think that it was her new black Elie Saab strapless mini because it was gorgeous and had cost her father a fortune when she asked for it after seeing it in last month's *Vogue*. Or that maybe it was the string of Tiffany pearls that she'd received for Christmas that she was debuting in LA tonight. Unfortunately, she knew that neither of those things was what every set of manly eyes was staring at as Libby and Charlie passed them.

It wasn't even like Libby was trying, which was the most infuriating part. Sure, the Givenchy top she was wearing was low plunging, but it was plain and wasn't like Libby was well endowed enough for it to be that eye-catching. Unluckily for Charlie though, she couldn't compete with the supermodel when she insisted on wearing six-inch Manolos and skin-tight Saint Laurent black leather pants. She knew that Libby did it on purpose and Charlie couldn't even really fault her for it. After all, if Charlie had Libby's legs, she probably wouldn't wear anything lower than six inches either.

"So," Libby whispered in Charlie's ear as they approached the restrooms, "what the fuck is Christie Ecles doing here?"

"What?" Charlie asked, missing the first part of Libby's question as she was still lost in her thoughts.

"Christie?" Libby asked. "Why the hell is she here?"

Charlie simply shrugged as Libby went into one of the stalls. Charlie, instead, started fixing her hair in the mirror. She smiled as she noticed that her beachy waves were still looking on point. It had been well worth the four hours she'd spent in front of the mirror at home perfecting them.

"It's really sad how desperate she is to be friends with us," Libby called out from the stall.

"Oh my God," Charlie laughed, "so sad. Could she be any more of a backup dancer?"

Charlie continued to stare at herself in the mirror, working her way down to her eyebrows and then her eye makeup.

"So, who the fuck invited her anyway?" Libby asked as she exited the stall and joined Charlie at the mirror, just as Charlie pulled her Kohl liner from her clutch and started to fix her eyeliner wings.

Truth be told, Christie was starting to grow on Charlie. It was totally unfortunate that she was a former backup dancer, but Christie had been playing the role of dutiful best friend to Charlie awfully well lately, and Charlie was loving it. Christie would listen when Charlie talked and then she'd text to follow up on things that Charlie had mentioned. Whether it was lunch with her dad or her conversation with the secretary at Marc Jacobs. It was refreshing to not have to repeat herself every brunch about what was going on in her life because people were too self-involved to pay attention the first time she mentioned it.

"I did," Charlie replied, a smirk working its way across her face as she finished her liner touch up and continued to stare at herself in the mirror.

"Why the fuck did you do that?" Libby asked as she, too, started to dissect her appearance in the mirror next to Charlie.

"Well," Charlie answered, knowing exactly how to play it, "I figured that I'd fuck with her a little for a laugh."

It was true that she had invited Christie tonight, but it wasn't for that reason. She knew she couldn't be honest with Libby about that though, especially considering the way Libby was making her feelings about Christie crystal clear. Libby stopped fixing her eyebrows as she turned to face Charlie.

"Let her get comfortable and think she's a part of The Pack," Charlie continued, "and then rip it all out from underneath her."

"Savage, Charls," Libby laughed. "I love it!"

"Thanks!" Charlie replied as she turned to the mirror one last time and smiled.

Libby's phone *dinged* from inside her clutch, also a piece of Victoria's Secret merchandise Charlie noted with an internal groan. Libby immediately stopped cleaning rogue lipstick from around her lips and tried to open her clutch as quickly as possible. Charlie narrowed her eyes at the speed of Libby's movements and the frustration evident on her face as she, for a couple of moments, battled with the clasp on the little black clutch in her hands.

"You're a fucking mess, Libs," Charlie laughed as Libby finally got into her clutch and retrieved her phone.

"Shut up!" Libby laughed.

Libby unlocked her phone and then stared at the screen for longer than Charlie deemed necessary to read one simple text. The pair of them stood in silence as Libby continued to zone out.

"Are you OK?" Charlie asked.

"Um, yeah," Libby replied, barely taking her eyes off her phone to look at Charlie. "Can I meet you back in there?"

"Ace troubles?" Charlie asked, hoping for a bit of a gossip update on Libby's relationship to relay back to Willa and Christie at their table.

"Um," Libby replied, still distracted by the phone in her hands. "Something like that. I'll meet you back in there, K?"

Charlie narrowed her eyes at Libby. Libby was clearly trying to get rid of her and Charlie was unsure why if all she had to do was text, or not text, Ace back. From experience, if it was a good text, Libby would have been smiling and giddy like a schoolgirl, but if it was a bad text then she'd start on one of her Ace Thatcher bitching tirades. Neither of those reactions was what Libby had just given Charlie, though. It made her curious as to what was really going on in that text message and whether it was from her boyfriend at all.

Charlie waited another moment, in the hopes that Libby would elaborate on what was going on, but she didn't. So, Charlie exited the restroom without another word and mentally pinned this moment and this conversation for another time. Probably the next time Libby was drunk and much more pliable when it came to spilling all the details.

* * *

Libby sighed in relief when Charlie left the restroom. She quickly looked down at the text message in her hands again.

Meet me at Alleys Alleys Alleys next Tuesday at 12:45 am.

Libby started quickly typing a response to Turner Evans. She was relieved beyond belief that he was still talking to her. After all, she hadn't heard from him since their disastrous first date. The disaster had been pretty much, if not all, her fault, but it was only because she was having such a shitty day.

**I thought you might
have been still mad at
me for the other night?**

Libby felt her heart racing as she fiddled with her phone in her hands waiting for a reply. She looked in the mirror again to distract herself and noticed that her eyebrows needed a wax and a tidy. She made a mental note to book Damone for a house call tomorrow morning so she could sort that out.

Libby nearly jumped out of her skin as she heard her phone message tone again and felt the phone vibrate violently in her hands. She quickly turned the screen over and was pleased to see another message from Turner Evans. Upon opening the message, however, she was unsure how she felt about its length and quality.

See you Saturday.

She wasn't sure what that text meant in terms of whether Wentworth was still mad at her if he was even mad at all. If he was mad though, she wasn't sure whether she could consider their arrangement still on and whether her reputation was still safe. She wasn't sure about anything right now, except for the fact that she still really didn't like Christie Ecles.

9

Date #2

Wentworth had barely turned off the engine before he had his seatbelt off and his door opened. He knew he was running late as he checked his watch for the nineteenth time. He was sure that Libby was going to be waiting by the back door being propositioned by some weird character that was either homeless or looking for a hooker.

South LA wasn't exactly the best place to be at 12:45 am, even with its proximity to the USC campus and the Staples Centre. It was definitely a place best visited during daylight hours even if one was driving a beat-up old Civic like he was. It also probably wasn't the best location for his and Libby's second date, but here he was, hoping that date two was going to be more successful than the last date he and Libby had been on.

Wentworth quickly retrieved the keys from the back pocket of his jeans as he slipped into the lane that would lead him to the backdoor of Alleys Alleys Alleys, which was currently closed for business. He fumbled with the small brass keys on the keychain as his mind drifted back to Libby Evans and two weeks ago; to the disaster that was date one.

He wasn't sure what he was expecting considering he had technically blackmailed her to go on not one, not two, but ten dates with him. He wasn't sure if he had expected her to greet him with open arms and a massive smile, or whether he had expected her to throw the Pepsi in his face as soon as they sat down to watch a movie he thought she might actually like. He wasn't sure what he had honestly expected, but it hadn't been her being unable to tear herself away from her phone and what he assumed was the endless drama that made up her fabulous Hollywood life. He'd been looking forward to a date with Libby Evans for a long time, which was part of the reason why their arrangement was what it was, so he was disappointed that it had started so badly.

"Oh my gosh, thank God you're already here!" a woman's voice exclaimed from behind him, causing him to drop the keychain at his feet in startle.

Wentworth's head whipped around in the direction of the voice and his eyes settled on Libby rushing toward him.

"I was praying that you were already here when I realized we were meeting in South LA," Libby said, her eyes scanning her surroundings. "I almost told my driver to turn around and take me back to the Hills at least eight times on the way over here."

Wentworth heard her let out a sigh of relief as she locked eyes with him. He was trying his hardest to hide the fact that he was staring at her. In his defense, though, she made it incredibly hard not to stare when she was so God damn beautiful with all her gorgeous dark hair flowing loosely down around her shoulders. Her attire was a lot more casual and relaxed than the last time he had seen her. Simple blue jeans cut off at the ankles, ridiculously clean white Sketchers, and what appeared to be a black tank top underneath a grey zip-up hoodie. Wentworth almost laughed at the fact that Victoria's Secret was spelled out in rhinestones across the front of the hoodie but decided to keep his opinion of the over-the-top clothing item to himself in the hopes of preserving the civility of this date.

Wentworth quickly snapped himself out of his thoughts as he bent down to pick up the keychain and resumed his search for the right key.

"Aha!" he exclaimed in victory as he turned around to face Libby again, surprised that she was standing even closer to him than she had been moments earlier.

"That's great, genius, you found the key," Libby replied sarcastically as she started jumping up and down on the spot. "Now can we please get the hell out of this rapist back alley and inside?!"

Wentworth laughed as he quickly opened the door. He let Libby inside in front of him before he closed and locked the door behind them. As expected, Libby didn't need a push as she rushed inside and didn't stop until she reached the bar, which overlooked the entire bowling alley.

Wentworth, knowing his way around, quickly headed for the main light switches, turning on virtually all the lights in the main bowling alley as well as those in the bar section right above Libby's head as she remained where she was. He followed in her footsteps until he was standing next to her, taking in the surroundings as she was.

Once the lights were all on, Alleys Alleys Alleys was quite an impressive space considering its location. Open from 10 am-10 pm, it was more popular during the day, particularly for tourists looking for something to do in this part of the city. The array of flashy neon lights and jukeboxes scattered around the place gave it that old 80s diner vibe. The bar took up most of the eastern wall where Wentworth and Libby were standing, and between the bar and the lanes was casual dining seating. Each table was decked out in cheap vinyl tablecloths, all red and white plaid. Wentworth could feel Libby's eyes on him as she finished looking around and he answered her, assuming what her question would be.

"Mal, a buddy of mine, works here most nights," Wentworth explained. "His uncle owns the place."

Wentworth turned to face Libby and she simply nodded, suggesting that her question had been answered.

"So 1:00 am?" Libby asked.

Wentworth took a deep breath as his gaze lifted to the space in front of him.

"To be honest," Wentworth said, "I figured that something private like this was going to be more relaxing for you. Don't have to worry about anyone recognizing you or taking photos."

"Hmmm," Libby replied with another nod, "and bowling?"

"Oh God," Wentworth sighed as he ran his fingers through his brown curls, "please don't tell me you don't like bowling."

"I don't like bowling," Libby replied.

She was clearly trying to remain stony-faced but failed as a smile crept its way across her features as she started venturing forward into the dining area.

"Said every un-fun person ever!" she continued with a wide smile. "I LOVE bowling! I can't even remember the last time I bowled!"

"They don't do bowling at your fancy Victoria's Secret lingerie parties?" Wentworth asked sarcastically as he leaned forward on the bar in Libby's direction.

"No, but they definitely should!" Libby smiled as she took a seat on the other side of the bar and started swiveling around on the stool underneath her.

Wentworth was taken back by her lack of sarcastic retaliation to his Victoria's Secret comment, which his facial expression clearly gave away as Libby stopped swiveling. Her face softened as she took a deep breath.

"I'm trying, OK?" she spoke, her eyes darting away from his for a moment. "And don't act so surprised, I'm actually a very nice person."

Wentworth laughed as she smiled again before jumping off her stool and heading in the direction of the closest lane. She was effortlessly graceful as she swished between chairs and tables to get there. Wentworth, again, had to remind himself that the date would continue to go well if he remembered to stop staring at her butt, no matter how well the jeans she was wearing fit and hugged her in all the right places.

"So, are we bowling, or did you just bring me here to show me that you like to spend your spare time in dingy places in South LA?" Libby asked cheekily over her shoulder.

"We're bowling," Wentworth spoke, as he cleared his throat and bent down to get into one of the fridges underneath the bar counter. "But first drinks."

Wentworth found the beer and grabbed one out of the fridge for himself before he stood back up to see Libby currently inspecting the range of bowling balls that were at the lane she had chosen.

"Looks like they only have wine coolers," Wentworth called out, in amongst walking the length of the bar to double-check that statement. "I can make you a mojito, but it'll take me a while because I have no idea what the hell even goes in a mojito."

Libby laughed as she picked up a small pink bowling ball and turned in his direction.

"What are you drinking?" Libby asked.

"Beer," Wentworth replied.

"Yes!" Libby exclaimed. "Give me a beer."

"Since when do you drink beer?" Wentworth asked an eyebrow cocked at her.

"I drink beer," Libby replied as she placed the small pink ball back down and started inspecting another small one, this one blue, "I just haven't had one since I was like sixteen."

She turned to face Wentworth again.

"Beer is not exactly what is socially acceptable for us models to drink at our fancy lingerie parties after all," Libby replied sarcastically.

Wentworth knew she was mocking him, and he was enjoying it. This was a side of Libby Evans he had never seen before. She was quick and witty, and he found that unbelievably sexy.

"So, give me whatever you are drinking unless it's Bud," Libby said.

Wentworth laughed as he reached down and grabbed another Bud from the fridge and started heading to the lane where Libby was.

"Well, we have Bud, Bud, and Bud Light," he said as he exited the bar area.

"Ew," Libby sighed in exaggerated disgust at the mention of Bud Light. "Just bring me a Bud then."

Wentworth smiled as he looked down at the two Buds in his hands.

By the time he reached Libby, she was sitting at one of the small seats directly behind the machine that allows you to enter names for each of the players bowling in that lane. The blue bowling ball she had been holding earlier was sitting in the ball retriever machine for lane three, right next to where she was sitting. Wentworth didn't say anything as he placed her Bud down on the table in front of her and looked up at the names she had entered.

"*Libby* and *Loser*?" Wentworth asked as he turned to face her.

Libby looked extremely pleased with herself as she pressed the confirm button and her name lit up on the screen indicating that it was her turn to go.

"I thought it was pretty accurate," Libby smiled as she grabbed her Bud and took a generous swig.

Wentworth followed suit as he took a swig of his beer and took a seat next to her.

"So, I assume you're starting?" he asked.

"That is correct!" Libby exclaimed as she popped her beer back on the table and stood up to retrieve her small blue bowling ball.

"So now I just have to sit here and watch you be completely terrible at this then?" Wentworth asked, a cheeky smile playing on his lips.

"Honey, in your dreams," Libby replied.

Wentworth watched in silence as Libby focused on the task at hand. She looked well and truly in the zone as she lined up her bowl down the lane and finished her first round with a strike. Libby turned back to Wentworth with a satisfied smile on her face and simply bowed in his direction.

"Wow," Wentworth nodded. "It appears I underestimated you."

"I'm used to it," Libby commented as she resumed her seat next to him and turned her attention back to her beer.

"Better not take it easy on you then," Wentworth winked at her as he got up from his seat and found the closest black ball that looked about the right size.

* * *

It was about one hour later when Wentworth counted eight beers on the table and realized that Libby was well and truly drunk. Five cans were his but the other three were hers, and they had obviously all gone straight to her head, especially considering how quickly she'd downed each one. It wasn't surprising though, considering he had guessed three to four beers to be the alcohol tolerance of a 110-pound female supermodel.

"Alright, your favorite movie?" Wentworth asked as he leaned on the top of the table in front of him.

Libby was sitting in front of that table but on the floor. She was leaning up against the bowling ball retriever machine for their lane, a nearly empty beer number four sitting at her side.

They had somehow found themselves locked in a game of 'What's Your Favorite?' and were working their way through the basics – color, song, animal, band, and were now at movies. Libby was finally relaxed, and she appeared to be enjoying herself a lot more than she had on their first date. At some point, she'd pulled her hair back into a messy bun on top of her head and her hoodie had been discarded and was currently sitting in a pile on the floor next to Wentworth's feet. The bowling had taken a bit of a hiatus as the screen read that they were only up to round five. Libby was absolutely destroying him, with a three-strike streak, so Wentworth was happy to have a little break. His competitive nature was banking on her losing all her bowling skills after a couple more beers.

"I can't tell you," Libby laughed, furiously shaking her head.

"Why not?" Wentworth smiled, noting how cute she looked sitting on the floor the way she was.

"Cause you won't believe me," Libby answered, laughter spilling out of her mouth.

"Try me," Wentworth replied.

"Well," Libby said as she took another swig of her beer before slowly getting to her feet.

Wentworth watched her intently in case a chivalrous catch was needed so she didn't slam face-first into the floor as she stumbled over to him.

"When I get interviewed for a magazine or an online interview thingy, I tell people my favorite movie is *10 Things I Hate About You*," Libby continued.

She had now reached Wentworth and the small bowling table in front of him. She leaned forward on the table in his direction.

"But your actual favorite movie is…?" Wentworth prompted, waiting for her answer.

"*Sharknado*," Libby whispered before erupting into a fit of giggles and falling into a heap on the floor.

"No!" Wentworth exclaimed in a surprised fashion that was seventy-five percent the truth and twenty-five percent exaggerated.

"Yes!" Libby exclaimed, her long legs splayed out in front of her as she sat up and rested her arms behind her for balance.

"That cannot be your favorite movie!" Wentworth laughed.

"But it is! I love *Sharknado!*" Libby enthusiastically nodded.

"And you should never ever admit that again," Wentworth said.

"Why not?!" Libby exclaimed in her defense.

"Because it is truly, truly horrifying that anyone would admit to liking that terrible excuse for a movie!" Wentworth replied.

He was trying his best not to stare at the fact that at some point during her fit of giggles, one of the straps of Libby's top had fallen off her shoulder causing the top to fall just a little. It was enough, however, for Wentworth to now know that her bra was strapless, pink, and lacy.

Beep! Beep Beep! Beep! Beep Beep!

Libby and Wentworth both nearly jumped out of their skin, not aware of how quiet it was in the alley as the sound of Libby's phone started to ring loudly from its place on the hardwood floor next to them. Libby's eyes immediately darted to the phone, the camera now flashing like a strobe light as it was screen down on the floor. She took the very last swig of her beer before she picked up the small device and turned it over.

"Oh," Libby gasped as she looked at the phone screen in her hand before she looked at Wentworth, turning the screen in his direction as she did so. "It's Ace."

Wentworth laughed at her shock as he downed the rest of his beer. Libby didn't say anything as the phone continued to ring and she continued to just stare at him as if she had asked him a question and was waiting for an answer.

"Well answer it, silly!" Wentworth exclaimed.

"Oh yeah," Libby gasped again as she fumbled with the phone, nearly dropping it in the process before she answered on speaker.

"Hello," Libby slurred as she started giggling directly into the microphone.

"Libby?" Ace Thatcher's voice sounded through the phone speaker.

"Hello," Libby giggled.

"Where are you?" Ace asked.

"Um," Libby mulled, as she scrunched up her face, "out some-where."

Wentworth tried his hardest to remain quiet and not laugh, but that was proving to be harder by the second at the look of confusion that was still etched all over Libby's face. This look included a scrunched-up nose, one of her eyebrows sitting impossibly high on her face, and another one of her eyes doing a terrible job of what looked like an attempted wink.

"Are you drunk?" Ace asked, confusion evident in his tone as he tried to decipher what was going on.

Libby burst into a fit of laughter, making it harder for Wentworth not to say anything. He didn't think it was a good idea for Libby's boyfriend to know that she was out somewhere with another guy at 2:00 am on a Tuesday. Nothing had happened, well at least nothing had happened tonight, but Wentworth knew exactly what Ace would assume was going down, especially now he knew that Libby was drunk.

"No," Libby laughed into the phone as she looked at Wentworth and jokingly gestured with a finger to her lips for him to be quiet.

"It's a Tuesday, Elizabeth," Ace stated. "Why are you out drunk on a Tuesday?"

"That," Libby said, "is a good question. A very good question."

"Why aren't you at home?" Ace asked, seemingly ignoring Libby's drunken stupor as he continued to probe her for answers.

"Um, I am at home," Libby spoke, trying to be serious before bursting into a fit of silent giggles.

"Well, no you're not," Ace stated, "because I'm at Sierra Towers and you're not here."

"You're what?!" Libby exclaimed.

Her eyes widened in panic as she looked up at Wentworth from her phone. Ace's name had come up once in their conversations, but it hadn't been anything special. Wentworth knew nothing about the guy, except that he was one of those rich, spoilt oil shipping heirs. He didn't know what the guy looked like, what the relationship between Ace and Libby was, or where Ace had been tonight whilst Libby was here with him. Judging by Libby's facial expression though, Wentworth assumed that Ace was not supposed to be at her condo waiting for her.

"I wanted to surprise you by coming home early," Ace continued. "As soon as my jet landed, I came straight over to Sierra Towers to see you but you're not here, obviously."

"Um," Libby answered, closing her eyes, and shaking her head as if she were trying to sober herself up and de-clutter her thoughts. "I'm out right now."

"Well yeah, you already said that," Ace replied.

Wentworth scrunched up his nose as he listened to the annoyance and sarcasm in Ace's tone. It wasn't Libby's fault that she wasn't home. Ace had wanted to surprise her so, of course, she didn't know that he was going to come over, so she'd gone out. It seemed like Ace was the type of guy that wanted his way all the time, and when he didn't get his way, or things didn't go his way, then he was not going to be happy about it. Libby seemed to be one of those 'things' that Ace wanted his way, whenever he wanted.

"Yeah, I know," Libby replied, her eyes still closed as she reached up and started fiddling with the scrunchie in her hair.

"Well?" Ace asked, still clearly annoyed at the answers Libby was giving him.

"Um," Libby answered, "I'll be there in like half an hour."

Libby didn't bother to wait for Ace's response, nor did she bother saying goodbye before ending the call. She spent a few moments just staring at the phone in her hands before she looked up at Wentworth from her spot, still sitting on the floor.

"I'm sorry, but—" Libby started, as she struggled to find the right words.

"Go," Wentworth said before Libby had a chance to say anything else. "He's your boyfriend. You should go."

Libby opened her mouth, as if she was going to say something else but then quickly closed it. He'd tried to sound casual in the way he spoke but judging by the look on Libby's face, he hadn't achieved that. She simply nodded and took her hoodie from his outstretched hand before she headed for the back door they had come in through. Wentworth didn't bother to watch her leave but did hear her talking to, what he assumed was, her car service on the phone as she asked for someone to come and pick her up. It was only a few seconds later that Wentworth heard the back door close shut behind her and he was left alone with an unfinished bowling game and his jumbled-up thoughts.

Libby had sounded almost guilty, maybe disappointed, that she had to leave so suddenly. He, on the other hand, had sounded jealous when he'd told her to go, maybe even upset about it. Wentworth sighed as he looked at the scoreboard once more. This wasn't the way that he had wanted this date to end, especially when it was going so well. It was probably the first time in his life that he enjoyed getting his ass beat at bowling.

10

Play Your Ace

Libby downed her second bottle of water as she sat impatiently in the back seat of the car service as it took her back to Sierra Towers. Thankfully, it being 3:00 am and all, there was barely any traffic on the back roads as the driver took her across Los Angeles and Hollywood. According to Google Maps, the drive shouldn't take more than thirty minutes. That was good because she wanted to get home as soon as possible, but also bad because it meant her time to sober up was limited.

Libby tossed the empty water bottle onto the seat next to her, to join the first bottle she had already finished. She hoped that the water would start to put her in a better state of mind to have a face-to-face conversation with her boyfriend. The same boyfriend who had apparently, and completely unexpectedly, flown back early from Paris to surprise her at her condo. She noted that they were only a few streets away from Sierra Towers and figured that she needed to come up with a story for Ace that would explain her drunken state and being 'out somewhere' in the middle of the week in the early hours of the morning. Even though it was LA, it wasn't a common occurrence for there to be heavy drinking on a Tuesday at 3:00 am, and less likely that if there was that Libby would be involved in it. Ace knew Libby well enough to know that random heavy drinking wasn't really her thing anymore unless there was an event on, so Libby knew that she had approximately three streets to figure out what event was on tonight that explained this whole scenario. Three streets to down one more bottle of water as well.

It was a matter of minutes before the car service pulled up outside Sierra Towers and Libby exited the vehicle as soon as Antoine, one of the security personnel, opened the door and greeted her with a warm smile. She simply nodded in response, unable to force much of a smile when she was so nervous about what awaited her up on the twentieth floor. As the elevator climbed floor by floor, she could feel her heart pounding in her chest as she nervously fingered the side seams of her jeans. She rehearsed the story in her head, making predictions as to how Ace would respond to her answers to all the questions he had already posed over the phone and no doubt more after that. She knew Ace, so she knew there would be a thousand and one questions. The doors pulled open as soon as the elevator *dinged* at the twentieth floor. That was when Libby laid eyes on Ace Thatcher for the first time in what felt like an eternity.

He was leaned casually up against a patch of wall next to Libby's front door, fiddling with his phone in his right hand whilst his left hand remained half-buried in his jacket pocket. He was wearing the monochrome Ace Thatcher special that Libby knew she would see him in as soon as she stepped off the elevator. That same jacket that he wore everywhere, even though he had enough money to buy every jacket that existed in the world, teamed with black jeans, some new ugly black shoes, and a white button-up shirt. He was predictable if nothing else.

"You cut your hair," Libby commented as she pulled her keys from the front pocket of her hoodie and finally pulled Ace's attention away from his phone.

"Miranda, my new publicist, says it's better for my image," Ace smiled.

Libby simply shrugged as she opened the door, without so much as looking Ace in the eye, and entered her condo.

"It's nice to see you too," Ace mumbled under his breath as he followed behind her.

She was too tired to argue so she let it slide. Instead, she placed her keys where they belonged and took off her hoodie as she relaxed into the comfortable room temperature courtesy of her thermostat. It felt like a cool spring day rather than the crisp winter night it was outside. It made Libby long for her bed and a good night's sleep, but she knew that she was probably far away from that right now.

"So, a big Tuesday night?" Ace spoke as he brushed past her.

Libby took a deep breath, suppressing the urge that her eyes had to roll out of her head as the interrogation began. She watched as Ace made himself at home and helped himself to a seat in her living room. She locked eyes with him as she remained where she was standing.

"Yes," Libby forced a smile. "Me and some of the Victoria's Secret girls were having a few drinks to celebrate the music video release."

"What music video?" Ace asked.

"For the Weeknd's new single," Libby replied, trying to limit her sarcasm even though she'd mentioned the music video multiple times over the last couple of months.

She watched as Ace mulled over the information and she braced herself for more questions because she knew they were coming.

"So where was this 'celebration'?" Ace asked.

"One of the girl's places," Libby replied.

"Whose place?" Ace asked.

"Claire," Libby answered. "Claire Hemmings."

"Where does she live?" he asked.

"Hollywood Hills," she answered.

"And it took you thirty minutes to get back here from the Hills?" Ace asked, his brow furrowing as he leaned forward to rest his forearms on his knees.

"Yeah," Libby answered, just as she rehearsed because she knew that he would nit-pick her answers like this. "Her place is all the way up on Mulholland Drive."

Ace nodded as he processed the information. Libby folded her arms as she watched him sit there. This was Libby's least favorite part about Ace getting back into town. He would interrogate her like he didn't trust her and was always looking for the holes in whatever story she gave him. Her stories were always ninety-nine percent the truth, with the remaining one percent being harmless details that she would omit to prevent an argument. From some sleazy guy hitting on her at a photo shoot or a bar, to how many drinks she had at one of her model parties. Tonight was different though because the percentages were reversed and ninety-nine percent of her story was false, if not more. Ace's interrogations usually made her a little nervous, but mostly angry that after all this time he still didn't trust her. Tonight was also different because she didn't have time to be angry. She was too busy trying to keep to her script of carefully constructed lies.

"Look, I'm sorry," Ace said, causing Libby to narrow her eyes at him. "It's just that I've been away so long, and I've missed you so much."

Libby's eyes narrowed further as Ace finally looked up from his hands and locked eyes with her.

"Being away from you makes me a little crazy," Ace smiled.

Libby pushed aside her anger as she remained where she was. Ace was never too proud to apologize, but usually, his apologies were nothing more than a way to end an argument. They never sounded like anything more than words, except for tonight. Libby could complain about him all she wanted to Willa or Charlie, but at the end of the day, if there wasn't something about him that she loved, she wouldn't still be here. If she didn't see something good in him, she wouldn't still be with him, no matter how good their relationship was for her career.

She looked at him sitting there staring at her hopefully, like an expectant puppy or a kid on Christmas morning. His brown eyes watched her intently as he remained perfectly still. Her thoughts started drifting back to when they first got together and how in love she had been with him right away. In love with the low tone of his voice, his Parisian accent, and the way that on that first night he had made the first move. He'd just taken her into his arms without asking permission. She had loved the confidence he showed when he'd surprised her by kissing her like they were old lovers rather than two people who had just met and who each had different dates at the start of the night. She'd fallen in love with how he swept her off her feet and within a matter of days she was head over heels. Those days, only months ago, felt like years ago. Unfortunately, it had felt like the honeymoon period, all bells and whistles, romance and sex, hadn't lasted as long as she expected it to.

"I'm sorry, Libs," Ace spoke again, his voice soft, yet strong enough to break Libby out of her thoughts. "I trust you and I love you, and I'm sorry that we've been apart for so long. I realize that that is entirely my fault and I'm sorry for that."

Libby could feel a lump rising in her throat as she listened to his apology. She could feel herself caving. She could feel the anger and the defiance she felt toward him earlier disappearing as the seconds passed. While it felt like their honeymoon days were an eternity ago, she still felt the same way about him that she had when they had first fallen in love. She still loved him, and it was moments like this, and him saying things like this, that made her realize that he still loved her too. Despite the crazy interrogations, the long distance, and the fights, he still loved her.

Libby sighed as she smiled at Ace before making her way over to him slowly. She watched as a smile crept its way across his face as she took a seat, without a word, in his lap. She wrapped her arms around his neck as she felt his arms tighten around her small frame, his head burying into the crook of her neck.

"I love you, Libby," he whispered as he kissed the side of her neck.

"I love you too," she whispered back.

She felt her eyes flutter shut at the feeling of his lips as they trailed sweet kisses from her neck along the underside of her jaw.

"I love you," he whispered as his arms tightened again around her, his hot breath leaving little drops of condensation in her ear.

He kissed around her ear lobe before trailing his kisses in search of her lips.

Libby surrendered to his kiss as he roughly and passionately captured her lips with his. She could kiss Ace Thatcher for days. His lips were utterly intoxicating, and Libby often found it hard not to give in to the touch that followed when he started kissing her like that, but she wasn't really in the mood tonight. He was her boyfriend and she hadn't seen him in months, but he had also been interrogating her like a fugitive just moments earlier. No matter how smooth he talked and no matter how good she knew the sex would be, because it always was, she just wasn't feeling it tonight. Even if she had wanted to, the little voice in her head was making her very aware of every finger he laid on her skin and tonight it just didn't feel right. If she was being honest, for some reason his touch on her skin somehow felt uncomfortable, almost like an itch that she couldn't scratch.

Libby gave Ace one final kiss before she gently pushed against his chest with her small hands. Ace sighed as he took her cue and allowed her to create some distance between them. His arms remained around her, but his hands only loosely held her waist. His fingers entwined as they stopped trying to coax the skin of her lower back where her tank top had ridden up. Libby closed her eyes and took a deep breath herself.

Now that they were no longer kissing and she was almost completely sober, she couldn't stop thinking about how angry she still felt at Ace considering everything that had gone on between them over the last few months. There was so much unfinished business they had yet to discuss so Libby started to feel uncomfortable sitting where she was. She attempted to create some distance between them as she slowly slid off Ace's lap in the direction of the kitchen, under the guise of getting a drink of water.

"I brought you some gifts back from Paris," Ace said.

Libby's back was currently turned as she opened her fridge to retrieve a bottle of Evian. She rolled her eyes as her head remained in the fridge for a moment. She took a deep breath and turned back around to face Ace with a forced smile.

"You know you didn't have to bring me back anything," Libby said, trying not to sound as sarcastic as she felt.

It wasn't exactly a surprise that Ace had brought her back presents to try and mend the rocky ground that had fallen between them while he'd been away. This was a typical Ace Thatcher move, and while Libby had loved being spoilt with expensive gifts at the beginning of their relationship, the novelty had worn off quickly. Now she associated the expensive gifts with apologies, fights, and the low points of their relationship. She knew that Hollywood girls lapped up this kind of thing, and she had for many months, but the same old song and dance was just getting stale now. Rather than filling her up, the gifts just made her feel empty.

"But I knew that I couldn't come back from Paris without diamonds for my favorite girl," Ace replied.

The charm just oozed from his every word as he stood up and walked toward her. Libby watched as he removed a sizeable gold box from his jacket pocket. With a wide smile, he stopped directly in front of her as he offered her the box and she readily accepted it. She knew it was jewelry. Apart from the fact that Chaumet Paris was stamped across the center of the box, she knew it was jewelry because Ace had always been the jewelry-type boyfriend. One could say that it was because he loved to deck his woman out in the most expensive jewelry that money could buy. Others, including Libby, knew it was more likely his go-to because he could walk into any jewelry store anywhere in the world and get one of the shop assistants to pick him out something that a Hollywood girl would love. Spoilt rich girls, after all, love nothing more than diamonds.

Libby carefully opened the lid of the box, and sure enough, there was a piece of very expensive-looking diamond jewelry staring back at her from the brown cushion that lined the inside. Like other Hollywood girls, Libby knew her jewelry, so she knew that the brilliant-cut diamonds in the pendant cost more than the average man's salary. They were, of course, flawless, but nothing of lesser quality could be expected from jewelry that came from Chaumet. Libby continued to inspect the pendant and chain and had to stop herself from rolling her eyes and laughing when she realized the chain and setting were white gold. No matter how much rose gold jewelry she wore when they were together, and no matter how many times she'd told him she loved the look of rose gold, he would forever believe that because white gold was more expensive that it was clearly what she wanted. Another typical Ace Thatcher move. It was like he didn't know a single thing about her. Whether it was because he genuinely didn't know or because he didn't care, Libby wasn't even sure anymore.

"So?" Ace spoke to fill the silence that had wrapped around them in Libby's kitchen.

Libby's eyes immediately rose to meet his for a moment before she looked back down at the necklace and smiled.

"It's beautiful," she said as she took a hold of the chain and removed it from the box. "Will you help me put it on?"

"Sure," Ace replied as Libby unfastened the chain and handed it to him before turning around so her back was facing him.

Ace carefully took the ends of the necklace and threaded his arms around Libby so that he could fasten the chain around her neck. She felt herself staring into space as Ace's fingers struggled with the clasp. She slowly fingered the diamonds in the pendant that were now sitting around her neck.

"There," Ace said as he finished.

He released the chain, and it hung daintily around Libby's small neck. She smiled as she felt his arms wrap around her.

"It looks perfect on you," Ace whispered in her ear as he pulled her close to him, his head resting on her shoulder.

His lips gently pressed against the soft flesh of her neck.

"I love it," Libby replied, almost as if the words were automatic because she had said them so many times before. "Thank you."

"You're welcome," Ace replied as he continued to nuzzle her neck.

Libby could feel his five o'clock shadow roughly tickling her jawline.

"Can I stay here tonight?" Ace whispered in her ear again, joined by another kiss on her neck.

Libby wanted to say yes. There shouldn't have been an issue with him staying over. He usually stayed over when he was back in town so they could spend as much time as possible together before he had to jet back off again. The kisses on her neck, and the fact that he had just given her expensive jewelry, however, meant that Ace was expecting his stay here to include more than just a little cuddling. Again, there shouldn't have been an issue with that either. He was her boyfriend and she had slept with him many times before, but there was that little voice in her head again. That little voice that was telling her that even though there shouldn't have been an issue with any of those things, there suddenly was. It was nearly 4:00 am, though, and she simply didn't have the energy to start a fight, which was exactly where this was going if she asked him to go home to his perfectly good mansion.

* * *

Fifteen minutes after she had finished her sleep routine and crawled into her bed, Libby felt Ace beside her as he finished in the bathroom and turned off the last of the lights in the bedroom. She didn't even know why she bothered with lights in the bedroom sometimes because of how bright the LA skyline was out of her bedroom windows. It was like falling asleep to a view of millions of fairy lights, which was doable some nights, and other nights impossible. She didn't need the lights in the bedroom, but she needed the blockout curtains.

Libby could feel Ace's body, dressed in just his boxers, pressed up against her and she knew that she needed to remain as still as possible if she wanted him to believe that she was already asleep. She didn't want to deceive him, but she knew that there was no other way to get out of having sex with him tonight. She had purposely worn a full set of pajamas to bed, as uncomfortable as it made her to sleep in clothes, and had also rushed her skincare routine just so she'd beat him to the bed. It still, however, wouldn't have been enough to get her message across loud and clear. Thankfully, though, it was only a matter of minutes before she heard Ace's rhythmic breathing. She felt his movements still with his head buried in the pillow behind hers as he fell asleep.

Libby sighed as she dared to move slightly to get more comfortable. She was confused. She was still mad at Ace for everything that had happened while he was away. The pap pics of him with another girl, the lack of calls and text messages, and then the third-degree interrogation when he'd finally gotten himself back to her. Usually, the gifts he brought were enough to at least put her in a better mood so she could enjoy the welcome home sex with him, but tonight was different. She should have wanted to sleep with the gorgeous boyfriend who had come home early to surprise her considering they'd been apart for so many months. Tonight, though, she just didn't want to, and that was not normal. It was out of the ordinary for her.

Libby sighed again as she closed her eyes and then opened them to look at the skyline out her window. She knew that tonight was going to be restless and mostly sleepless as she dissected everything that had happened in the last twenty-four hours, including the fact that she didn't want to have sex with her boyfriend tonight and why unexpectedly, she couldn't stop thinking about Alleys Alleys Alleys and Bud Light.

11

Fashion Week

Libby looked at herself once more in the mirror and knew that she looked ridiculous, but that was the point of high fashion, wasn't it? Tonight was one of the few night shows she had to do for *LA Fashion Week* this year and it was at the Majestic Downtown for an up-and-coming American designer, Laurena Carter. The whole theme of the show was 'military', as one of the big trends of the summer, and pulled inspiration from every predictable military trend you could imagine. Think 90s military caps, which every model was wearing tonight, khaki, and double-breasted everything. Libby was fortunate enough to be closing the show for Laurena tonight. Closing a show was always a massive honor during the craziness of fashion week, so tonight was extra special, no matter how much Willa and Charlie had tried to convince her otherwise.

It wasn't that her friends were unsupportive of her modeling career, except that they were. Charlie claimed that being a model was beneath her, but with her 5'3" stature, there weren't a whole lot of things that were actually beneath her. Willa, on the other hand, had struggled to land any gigs during *LA Fashion Week* this year so the whole event, particularly casting call rejection, had left a big sour taste in her mouth. It was a big enough sour taste that Libby had tried to avoid talking about *LA Fashion Week* altogether, as she wanted to avoid another Willa Nelson gasbag special. However, when Willa and Charlie had invited Libby out to dinner and drinks at Catch LA tonight, she had to decline and give a reason. Willa had proceeded, as expected, to verbally bash all the designers that were lined up this year, particularly Laurena Carter. Libby smiled and nodded as usual and tried to play it off that she'd tried to get out of it with her agency, which she hadn't, but had failed, and therefore had to walk the show as a matter of courtesy. Thankfully this had gone down well with the blondes, and they had simply changed the subject in the group chat after that.

"Libby Evans!" a voice exclaimed from behind Libby. "You look fucking gorgeous as always!"

Libby didn't even need to turn around from the backstage dressing table she was currently seated at to know who that voice belonged to. She also bet that when she turned around, she would find not only the owner of the voice but another two of her fellow models as well – one blonde and one brunette.

"Brooke!" Libby exclaimed as she turned around and jumped to her feet in time to be enveloped in an over-the-top hug.

"Fuck, girl, you look amazing!" Brooke said as she broke Libby's hug and looked her friend up and down. "That Bora Bora tan is perfection!"

Libby couldn't help but laugh as she looked at Brooke and her model friends, who were always in tow, Cameron and Melissa. LA had a growing alternative model scene and Brooke was leading it. She booked just as many shows as she did before the gratuitous facial piercings and the pink streaks in her hair, if not more. Hollywood was absolutely lapping up the change in mood that Brooke and her alt girls were bringing *LA Fashion Week* this year.

"Oh my gosh, we saw all the photos online!" Cameron exclaimed.

"Yeah, talk about hot and steamy," Melissa added. "You and Ace Thatcher were blowing up the tabloids this weekend!"

"What a way to spend Valentine's Day!" Cameron swooned as she clutched her chest melodramatically, causing her low-cut khaki top to nearly expose more than her terrible acting skills.

Libby laughed as she shook her head. They were referring to the trip she and Ace had just taken to Bora Bora. She hadn't told them personally about the trip, but with the way the media works in Hollywood she didn't have to. Ace had insisted after Willa had told him that everyone knew about his Parisian tryst with the mystery blonde, that Libby deserved a relaxing getaway in celebration of Valentine's Day and her twenty-third birthday. Libby had wanted to continue to be mad at Ace after he basically admitted to cheating on her when he finally apologized, but she knew that she hadn't exactly been true to their relationship while they were apart either. So, without admitting that she had one-upped him and slept with someone else, she graciously accepted his apology and happily agreed to join him on an all-expenses-paid vacation to work on her tan and her relaxation. It was exactly what she needed, and it turned out that it was exactly what her relationship with Ace had needed as well. In Bora Bora, he was the Ace she fell in love with. There were no business calls the entire time they were away, and no arguments. Everything was perfect, and it reminded Libby of all the reasons she wanted to stay with him and all the reasons she would continue to.

"So, enough about Bora Bora," Brooke said, completely ignoring Cameron and Melissa as they chattered away, diverging into a conversation about Brazilian waxes for summer. "Excited about closing tonight?"

Libby smiled. She loved that when it came to modeling, she and Brooke were friends. There wasn't an ounce of competitiveness between the two, which meant that she could genuinely be excited about being the model to close the Laurena Carter show tonight. The opening and closing spots of a show were always the most coveted in the line-up, even if Laurena was a smaller designer compared to the powerhouses that are Marc Jacobs, Prada, and Calvin Klein.

"So excited!" Libby admitted. "Pretty excited that I actually get to wear a jacket over this super skanky thing too!"

Brooke laughed as she looked at Libby's attire and then at her own. Apart from the double-breasted black jacket, Libby was wearing, she and Brooke were dressed in the same khaki-colored bodysuit that rose dangerous high on the bikini line. Brooke's had long sleeves with matching shoulder pads, whilst Libby's top half finished in cap sleeves. It wasn't obvious though as Libby was already wearing her jacket to take the cool edge off in the breezy backstage area.

"Girl, these are definitely going to be riding straight up the ass on the walk back!" Brooke laughed as she exaggeratedly hiked the sides of her bodysuit up, causing Libby to laugh. "Ace coming to watch you tonight?"

"Yep!" Libby beamed. "He managed to score front row on the right at the last minute so he's here with a couple of business associates."

"I heard the whole military theme is bringing in a lot of musicians tonight," Brooke said, in a hushed whisper. "I'm hoping Spencer Stevenson is one of them!"

Libby held her tongue and her desire to vomit in her mouth at the thought of Spencer Stevenson being here to creepily check out the models in the show, including herself. She didn't want to explain the whole saga to Brooke, who was clearly completely oblivious, so she decided to keep her mouth shut.

"Five minutes ladies!" a stagehand yelled across the backstage area, causing Libby and Brooke to jump a little.

"See you out there!" Brooke exclaimed excitedly.

She hugged Libby one more time before she followed Melissa and Cameron, who were already heading out of the dressing area to get in the walk line-up.

Libby took a deep breath and did a once-over in the mirror in front of her. Her hair and make-up had all been sorted earlier by one of the hair and make-up girls backstage, so she was essentially ready to go. She resisted the urge to tone down the over-the-top gold glittery eyeshadow all over her eyelids and instead just quickly topped up her black mascara and lip balm. It all looked ridiculous in the dim backstage lighting, but she knew that as soon as she hit the runway the blinding lights were going to make it look like she had barely any make-up on at all. She wasn't even sure how much eye make-up was going to be visible on the models when they all had to wear matching black military newsboy caps, that looked less high fashion and more like she should have been driving a cab in downtown London. The jacket was cute though, she had to admit. She would probably try and take this one with her when the show was finished or get Felicity to follow up on it later.

"Thirty seconds!" the stagehand cried again as the music that was playing throughout the Majestic increased tenfold before Taylor Swift's 'ME!' started blaring from the speakers.

Libby wasn't surprised this song was playing right now. The marching band drums in the bridge just screamed cliché when teamed with the military theme. Libby adjusted a few stray strands of her artificially straightened hair and added the black cap to the mix. She quickly ran, as fast as she could in her thigh-high black stiletto boots, to where she needed to be, ready to close the show.

* * *

Libby kissed Laurena Carter on each cheek once more when they arrived at the backstage area as the music started to die down and the house lights came back on so people could find their way out of the Majestic. Libby had only met Laurena right before the final walk at the very end of the show but she was well versed in how these things worked. She was to be quiet, polite, and, of course, gracious when meeting the designer in the hopes that they would be pleased enough to re-hire her for their next show or ad campaign. Libby had only had the privilege of closing a couple of shows up until this point, but Felicity had given her a specific run down yesterday about what was required from both the opening and closing models, and it was non-negotiable from a designer's point of view.

Once Laurena had thanked Libby for the umpteenth time, and Libby had stopped to hug a few of her model friends that had also walked the runway, she quickly worked her way back to her dressing area. The first thing she did was rid herself of the ridiculously un-comfortable boots. Next, she pulled her phone out of her bag and decided to sit and relax for a couple of minutes and let the adrenalin running through her system settle. No matter how many shows she did, the runway was always a thrilling place for her. She loved the atmosphere of the blasting music and the lights as soon as she stepped onto the runway. Then there was a rush at the end of the runway when the camera flashes would go nuts as photographers tried to get as many photos of each model from as many angles as they could in the few seconds they had. It was exciting and Libby loved every second of it. It always took her a few minutes to come down from that high at the end of a show, which was why she always took her time when it came to getting dressed and leaving the venue. However, as soon as Libby looked down at her phone screen, she realized that it wasn't going to be that hard to come down from her high tonight.

**I hope your show went
well my love! I'm so
sorry I missed it. Got a
call that Dad is unwell so
had to take the jet back
to Paris tonight. Will call
you soon x**

Libby knew she couldn't be mad at Ace for missing the show because his dad was sick. Unfortunately, it didn't stop her from being incredibly disappointed, and yet she still wasn't entirely surprised; not entirely surprised that Ace had let her down again, that is. She was, however, very surprised at how stupid she had been to believe that this time was going to be different. Sure, his dad was sick and he couldn't control that, but if it wasn't that it would have been something else. There was always something, no matter how genuine. Always a reason why Ace had to let her down and break a promise or go back on his word.

Libby sighed and decided to not even text back just yet. Maybe she'd slowly work her way through removing the make-up off her face, get dressed, and then head home for a long magnesium bath first. She'd done a killer Pilates session the other day with her trainer and her muscles were still a bit sore. It was only when Libby exited Ace's text that she realized there was another unread message on her phone. This one was from Turner Evans, and it made her heart start pounding in her chest.

She hadn't heard or seen Wentworth Turner in over a month now, so she had pushed him to the back of her mind, but it had left a very dull worry in the pit of her stomach. She was nervous about why she hadn't heard from him as well as what date three was going to be and when. She was also confused as to why she had thought so much about Wentworth when she was with Ace these last forty days, including in Bora Bora, and why that made her feel guilty. It didn't feel like guilt because she was thinking about another guy when she was with her boyfriend. It felt like the opposite almost. Like she was almost feeling guilty that she was spending time with Ace while Wentworth was still playing in her thoughts. She had tried to not think too hard about it because she could feel a cold sweat coming on every time she tried to make sense of it all. The good part, though, was that this new worry was taking her mind off her original worry about Wentworth spilling the beans and ruining her Hollywood reputation. Libby snapped out of her thoughts, realizing she was working herself up again and closed her eyes tightly before opening them and Wentworth's text at the same time.

The confusion hit her as soon as she realized that he had sent her a photo. That confusion lifted a little when she realized that it was a photo of her, and then a little more when she realized that it was a photo from tonight. She had no idea that Wentworth was going to be here, but it wasn't surprising considering being a photographer was his job and what better place to photograph models than at a fashion show during *LA Fashion Week*. This photo, however, hadn't been taken from the end of the runway where the other photographers were. It looked like the photo was taken from the opposite entry onto the runway, where the models exited.

In the photo, she was wearing the outfit that she was still currently dressed in, and it was taken seconds before she took to the runway. Libby saw that she was smiling and laughing in the photo because Brooke had just exited the runway and had pulled a weird face at her as she did so. Libby shook her head as she remembered how the stagehand behind her had yelled at her when she laughed, which reminded her that this wasn't Victoria's Secret, and they did not want you to smile when you walked the runway. The photo was so candid, so she didn't look her best in it. She had Christie Ecles' style teeth everywhere and she was slouched over in laughter so the fabric at her waist had cinched, which made it almost seem like she had anything less than a washboard stomach. Even though she didn't look perfect, though, she looked so happy and she looked like herself. Had Wentworth sent her the photo because he thought that she'd love it because it was fundamentally 'natural Libby', or had he sent it because he knew it didn't look perfect and was angry at her for not contacting him for forty days? She had had her fair share of boy troubles in the past and, as a result, she figured she was pretty good at figuring out guys. Wentworth Turner, though, was like no guy that she had ever known, or had ever tried to figure out before.

Libby snapped out of her thoughts and realized she was dumbly smiling down at her phone as she looked closely at the photo. She then realized that the photo was accompanied by a second text message. Another from Wentworth.

**Date 3. Your place, next
Sunday morning at 9.**

She didn't know why but reading that text and realizing they had another date on the cards so soon made her stomach flutter a little and made that dumb smile appear on her face again.

12

Date #3

Libby couldn't help but wish that she was drinking a very strong mimosa right now as she sat across from Wentworth Turner in the middle of her dining room. Sure, the coffee was great this early on a Sunday morning, but watching him fiddle with the Scrabble tiles on the rack in front of him in silence made her want a little liquid courage to settle her raging nerves. She nearly lost it when he started licking his lips in concentration.

She didn't really know what the nerves were about. She was relieved when Wentworth had texted her after the Laurena Carter show scheduling their next date because it meant that their arrangement was still on. However, she hadn't just been relieved to receive that text. She'd also been almost excited about date three, which had her extremely confused as to what on Earth was going on in her head. She had, surprisingly, really enjoyed their bowling date, and it hadn't just been because she was all tipsy on Bud. She had genuinely enjoyed it, but she was scared to admit that she may have enjoyed the date so much that she'd been looking forward to the next one. She was scared to admit it because the reality was that she was in a relationship with someone else. A relationship she was desperately trying to save, which was why she was partaking in these dates in the first place. There was just too much to think about right now.

"Your turn," Wentworth smiled, bringing Libby's focus back to what had become a very competitive game of Scrabble.

Libby smiled to herself as she noticed that Wentworth had left the board open exactly where she had planned to place her tiles while he was contemplating his move. She didn't think in a million years that date three was going to involve Wentworth turning up at her doorstep at 9:00 am on a Sunday with coffees, blueberry croissants, and a game of Scrabble. When she had truthfully admitted to him that she hadn't played Scrabble since she was about eleven years old, it appeared that Wentworth had gotten a little overconfident about his chances of beating her. What he'd forgotten from date two, however, was that Libby Evans should never be underestimated.

Libby slowly but surely arranged the four Scrabble tiles she had selected from her rack on the board between them. She could feel Wentworth watching her intently, so she purposely took her time as she made sure each tile was in its exact place before she sat back and smiled at him.

"'GAZED'," Libby announced, reading out her word. "Thirty-six."

"What?!" Wentworth exclaimed. "That is not worth thirty-six!"

"You left the triple word score wide open!" Libby exclaimed, half laughing, as she watched Wentworth eyeball her tile placement. "Z is worth ten, so triple ten is thirty."

"No way!" Wentworth exclaimed, obviously still in shock that she had managed to score so big on such an easy move.

"I can get you a dictionary if you don't believe me," Libby smiled as she folded her arms across her chest, her white Prada cashmere sweater bunching at the elbows.

Wentworth rolled his eyes as he picked up the pencil and started adding thirty-six to Libby's score. Libby watched as he added up the scores once, and then twice more for good measure.

"So how much am I beating you by now?" Libby replied cheekily as she looked over at the score sheet.

"Oh, not by much," Wentworth brushed off as he leaned back into his chair and took another swig of his coffee. "Just eighty-three, but who's counting?"

Libby shook her head, a small laugh escaping her lips, as she grabbed the small green pouch and reached in to replace her four used tiles.

"So, I guess the lesson to be learned here is to really never underestimate you, is that right?" Wentworth asked.

Libby shrugged, still smiling. She kept her eyes on the tiles she had just drawn as she started to arrange them on her rack.

"How'd you get so good at Scrabble anyway?" Wentworth asked, this time drawing Libby's eyes up to him.

Libby had to remind herself where she was and who she was with as soon as she locked onto those green eyes.

"My mom used to play it with me," Libby replied as she reached for her coffee, taking a swig, and trying to distract herself from all the things running through her head with the smooth caramel taste.

She didn't usually have coffee so she was impressed that Wentworth had known to order her an almond milk caramel latte. The almond milk and caramel combination were sweet enough to counteract the bitter coffee taste that she really didn't care for.

"Judging by how much you're kicking my ass at this," Wentworth laughed, "I find it hard to believe that your mom hasn't been sneaky Scrabble coaching you all this week!"

"She died five years ago," Libby blurted out.

The words tumbled straight out of her mouth before she could even think about them. She didn't want another second of this conversation to involve Wentworth thinking her mom was still around. It was bad enough thinking about it without having to talk about it with someone she barely even knew.

"Oh shit," Wentworth sighed under his breath.

"Don't worry about it," Libby replied, her hands reaching out to fiddle with the arrangement of her Scrabble tiles to keep her mind distracted. "It was a long time ago."

The conversation paused for a second. Wentworth opened his mouth to speak again, and Libby expected him to reply as everyone else did. Some kind of half-assed sorry to break the tension, or just a sorry to try and change the direction of the conversation to something a lot less awkward.

"Five years is a long time," Wentworth nodded, "but I bet it still feels raw as hell."

Libby's eyes narrowed at the tiles in her fingers as she stopped fiddling. They remained narrowed as her gaze raised to lock with Wentworth's. There was something in his eyes that looked sympathetic without looking like he pitied her just because her mom was dead.

"Every day," Libby nodded.

She didn't know what else to say. It was like he was reading her mind. How else did he know exactly what to say and exactly how to react to everything she said or did? Was this all part of some elaborate act – was he acting the part of a guy he knew would be completely and utterly perfect for her? Or maybe this was just him? Maybe he was just that smooth and she would have to give him that? Maybe there was a lot about him that she had also underestimated? She didn't want to think about it like that because it made her that much more confused, but what else was she supposed to think when he said things like that?

"So, how was fashion week?" Wentworth spoke, reaching for another blueberry croissant.

Libby realized they were having another break from the game like they had a couple of times earlier on. Maybe his ego needed time to recover.

"You don't really want to know about that, do you?" Libby scoffed as she shook her head.

"Why not?" Wentworth asked. "It's obviously a big deal to you."

"But it's not to you!" Libby snapped. "I get enough crap about being a brainless model from the tabloids without having to hear it from you this early on a Sunday."

Wentworth raised an eyebrow at her. She knew it was a cheap shot, but it was starting to get on her nerves the more she thought about the possibility that this was all an act. It might not have been, but she couldn't be sure right now and that was worrying, and annoying, her.

"No one said anything about you being a brainless model," Wentworth said. "Those were your words, not mine."

"Oh really?" Libby asked, feeling herself becoming angrier.

It was almost like she was baiting him, and she knew she was doing it. She did this a lot, particularly with Ace. It was almost as if a guy being an asshole to her was more genuine and believable than a guy being a decent human being. It was like it made her feel more comfortable dealing with males that were assholes because that's what most were in Hollywood.

"So, you actually think models are smart, is that it?" Libby laughed.

"I didn't say that either cause I don't know every model in LA or the world," Wentworth replied, not breaking her eye contact, "but I know that you're incredibly smart and you're a model so it's not a completely outrageous combination."

"Are you kidding me right now?!" Libby exclaimed.

"What?!" Wentworth exclaimed in his defense, his hands gesturing in confusion.

"What is your deal?" Libby asked.

She took a deep breath to try and calm herself down as she realized they were talking too loudly for this early on a Sunday morning in a building full of residential units.

"What deal?" Wentworth asked, lowering his volume to match Libby's.

"I have no idea how to take you," Libby said, shaking her head.

"Take me where?" Wentworth asked, the confusion written all over his face. "Are you having a stroke right now? You're not making any sense."

"Why are you here?" Libby asked. "What do you want from me?"

Wentworth sighed as the room fell silent. The only sound that could be heard was that of the clock in Libby's kitchen.

"It's just ten dates," Wentworth finally answered. "You know, seven if you don't count this one and the two we've already been on."

Libby sighed before she nodded.

"Just let me get to know you," Wentworth answered, the honesty clear as day in his voice. "Just pretend it's like we're two strangers who are dating to get to know each other a little better. I know the circumstances between us aren't exactly like that, and I know that any kind of physical contact is strictly off-limits but other than that it's just like ten regular dates, right?"

Libby nodded again, though she kept her mouth shut as she processed his words. She tended to speak before thinking and it usually got her in trouble. Either igniting an argument or saying something she instantly regretted.

"I think you're worth getting to know better, and I wish that I could get to know you under different circumstances, but here we are," Wentworth continued. "You're one of the most interesting girls I've ever met, so I just want to get to know you better because I know there's a lot more to you than you let most people see."

Libby could feel that lump rising in her throat. She didn't know what was happening right now. Real guys didn't say things like this. Real guys didn't tell girls that they were worth getting to know better. Real guys didn't tell girls that they were more than what they appeared to be on the surface. She didn't think she would ever hear any guy say those words to her, so it made her feel like that lump in her throat, that was bursting with emotion, was either going to explode out of her in tears or yelling. It also made her feel something in the pit of her stomach that felt like butterflies and tornadoes at the same time.

"Is that OK?" Wentworth asked and Libby realized it had been a really long time since she had said anything.

It had been so long that her mouth felt dry, and she had to swallow before she could even form words to speak.

"OK," Libby nodded.

There was too much going through her mind for her to say anything other than that. She was relieved to know that despite the blackmail and the circumstances that had led to these dates, Wentworth was probably actually a genuine person. They'd had an interesting string of dates so far, from her being a bitch, to him being jealous about her leaving early to see her boyfriend. Then there was today where she pushed him in the hopes that he would crack. That he would realize that it was all too hard to keep going with this façade so he would leave her alone to live her life, but things were quite the opposite. So much so that when Libby thought about everything now, she decided that she would probably have to give him the benefit of the doubt from now on. She hadn't met many, so she was convinced they were a bit of an urban legend in Hollywood these days, but it seemed like Wentworth Turner was a decent guy. Plus, it wasn't like they were going to end up married with three kids or anything so maybe she could let herself just enjoy his company. The company of someone that actually thought she was a smart model for a change.

"So, can you pass me that dictionary over there so I can make sure this is actually a word before I embarrass myself by putting it on the board?" Wentworth said, changing the direction of the conversation.

Libby rolled her eyes and smiled as she passed him the Scrabble dictionary sitting next to her.

"Don't hurt yourself there," Libby laughed as she watched his brow furrow intensely as he flipped through the dictionary pages. "You're going to lose anyway."

"Savage!" Wentworth exclaimed in mock horror as he continued to flip pages. "I could have been taking it easy on you up until this point."

"I think the time for chivalry has come and gone, Went," Libby replied as she downed the rest of her latte before eyeing off the remainder of the blueberry croissants that, up until this point, Wentworth had been solo wiping out.

She hadn't meant to call him Went, especially because it was the first time she'd used his first name out loud. It had just slipped out, and she was hoping that he hadn't noticed, but considering she could feel him staring at her, she realized that wasn't true. She tried to focus on the croissant in her hands as she took a couple of deep breaths to try and calm her nerves. She wanted to act like it wasn't a big deal that she'd just called him by what was probably a nickname that was reserved for close friends and family. It was a big deal, though. She barely knew him and yet she'd said it.

"Found the word you're looking for yet?" Libby finally said, trying to avoid a conversation about what had just happened.

"Turns out 'EXOWINP' is not, in fact, a word," Wentworth replied as he sat the dictionary back down next to him.

"You're an idiot," Libby laughed.

"Evidently, yes, it appears I am!" Wentworth laughed as he sighed and glanced over his tiles again. "Twister would have been a much better idea."

"It would have been," Libby smiled as she popped another bit of croissant in her mouth, "but we are more than halfway through this game so I feel like I should make you finish it so you'll learn your lesson."

"And what lesson is that?" Wentworth said as he collected the 'W', 'I', and 'N' tiles from his rack and placed them on the board to make 'WINE'.

"That you should never ever underestimate me again," Libby smiled.

Wentworth smiled back and shook his head as he added his score to the scoresheet.

* * *

"Happy birthday, Charlie!" Anita exclaimed in excitement as she grabbed her mimosa, which was really just ninety-nine percent champagne, and raised it in a toast.

Charlie was absolutely beaming as she watched Christie Ecles and Willa Nelson grab their mimosas too and all toast in the center of their table.

"How the hell are we this old already?" Charlie sighed as she swallowed a mouthful from her flute of mimosa.

Eat This Café did the best mimosas and the best French toast. The Pack didn't usually frequent here, Silverlake was always going to be their brunch spot, but today was a special occasion and on special occasions, the rules didn't apply. Charlie scrunched up her nose as she eyed off the bottomless Grand Marnier French toast platter sitting in the middle of the table and thought about how many pieces she'd already had and how many calories that equaled. From all the powdered sugar and butter to the maple syrup and fresh fruit, she was going to have to consider throwing it all up later, or not eating for the next couple of days. Especially because she was going to have at least one more piece before brunch was over. It was her birthday after all.

"Hun, you don't look a day over twenty-one," Christie smiled, touching Charlie's arm reassuringly.

"Christie's right," Willa added as she downed the rest of her mimosa.

She then threw her hand up in the air to indicate to the waiter that they were ready for another round.

"Yeah, you look fucking amazing, Charls," Anita chimed in as she picked a blueberry off the French toast that was sitting on her plate in front of her. "Especially in those jeans!"

Charlie couldn't help but widely grin at that comment. Six months ago, she had bought these Levi's that were two sizes smaller than she usually wore as a bit of extra motivation to get herself down to a size two. It wasn't quite the size zero that Libby and Willa were sitting at, but she was getting there. No matter how close they were as friends, Charlie would always be competing with the rest of The Pack to be the skinniest, most successful, or best looking, and she was sure that the feeling was mutual.

"So, have you heard from Hamish this morning?" Willa asked, never being one to shy away from fueling her gossip needs.

Charlie smiled again. There were a lot of things to be happy about this morning, apart from the mimosas and her Levi jeans. Hamish Dawson had finally realized he was desperately in love with her. Well, maybe a little less on the desperate and a lot less on the love part, but he had called her all the same. They'd had drinks last night at The Bungalow and although she wasn't a girl to kiss and tell, she'd done both by the time the French toast was served at brunch this morning.

"He may have sent me a birthday message this morning," Charlie said, trying her hardest to sound as nonchalant as possible, even though she was squealing like a twelve-year-old girl on the inside.

"OMG so cute!" Christie cooed.

"You guys are going to be the hottest new couple!" Willa exclaimed. "I can just see it now. The tabloids are going to go crazy for this!"

"Yeah, they better," Charlie added. "It's been way too long since the tabloids have given me any kind of publicity."

"You're telling me, honey," Anita sighed, "and at least you have work coming your way. I have no work and no publicity."

"Don't worry about it, Nita," Christie said, turning her attention momentarily to Anita across the table. "That was totally unfair that you lost out on that role, but another will come up surely! You're way too talented to be out of work for long!"

"But I mean on the plus side, Charlie is totally working the dream with Marc Jacobs!" Willa said, knowing that there would be hell to pay if anyone stole Charlie's thunder today and talked about themselves for more than five seconds. "And now you've got a sexy new boyfriend too! You are just living the dream!"

Charlie smiled.

"As if the tabloids wouldn't want to write about you!" Willa added.

"At least if they write about Charlie, they can have a break from sucking up to Libby," Christie said, rolling her eyes.

"Fuck me, right?!" Charlie exclaimed, excited that someone had finally brought up the should-be occupant of the empty chair at their table. "Did anyone see that fucking spread on TMZ about her last week?"

"About her Victoria's Secret contract in the works?" Anita said, rolling her eyes. "I couldn't be on any of my socials without it fucking popping up everywhere!"

Charlie was a bit taken back by Anita's sudden contribution to this morning's Libby bitch session. Usually, the actress kept the dramatics to herself and stayed out of verbally bashing her so-called best friend. Lately, though, Charlie had noticed a change in Anita's attitude since Libby had been anything but a comforting best friend when Anita missed out on her dream role a few months back. It didn't help that Libby also kept missing brunches, like today.

"Speaking of the 'Hollywood Princess'," Willa said sarcastically, "where the hell is she this morning? This is like the third brunch in a row that she's missed."

"And it's Charlie's birthday!" Anita added before she turned her attention back to conquering her recently topped-up mimosa for the third time that morning.

"Said she had a breakfast meeting with her dad," Charlie said.

"Yeah right," Christie exclaimed. "Char, give me your phone."

"Why the hell do you need my phone?" Charlie asked.

"Trust me," Christie replied, with another wide smile.

Charlie hesitated for a moment but then saw that twinkle in Christie's eyes and what appeared to be a little deviousness in her smile. Charlie reached forward on the table, grabbed her phone, and unlocked it before passing it to Christie.

Christie tapped away on the phone screen silently before Charlie leaned over her shoulder to see what she was up to. Christie had found the number for Privileged Pictures, the film production company that Libby's great-grandfather founded and that was now being run by Libby's father as CEO. Christie tapped the number on the screen and then put the call on speakerphone. It rang three times before someone answered.

"You've reached Privileged Pictures Santa Monica; you're speaking with Avery. How may I direct your call?" the receptionist said.

"Hi Avery, this is Camryn Ecles, CEO of Illuse Cosmetics," Christie said.

"Good morning, Ms. Ecles," Avery replied. "How may I direct your call?"

"I'd like to speak with Lance Evans, please," Christie replied. "Is he available this morning?"

"I'm terribly sorry, Ms. Ecles, but Mr. Evans is currently out of town on business," Avery replied. "Can I direct your call to someone else at Privileged or would you like to leave a message for Mr. Evans for when he returns in two weeks?"

Christie broke out in a wide smile as she turned to Charlie.

"You know what, Avery, you've been very helpful this morning," Christie replied. "I'll call Lance back in a couple of weeks to chat, no rush. Thank you."

"You're welcome, Ms. Ecles," Avery replied. "Have a wonderful Sunday."

"You too," Christie replied as she tapped the screen and ended the call.

"Breakfast meeting with Daddy my ass," Charlie commented as she took another big swig of her mimosa. "Nicely done, Christie."

"There is nothing I wouldn't do for my friends," Christie replied as she handed Charlie back her phone.

"So, if she isn't at breakfast with her dad," Willa said, "where the hell is she?"

13

Date #4

"Hey there!" a voice called from somewhere behind her, causing Libby to quickly turn around.

She hadn't even had time to second guess her outfit choice and whether this was going to be a classic *Legally Blonde* prank at 45 Dunstan Street. Libby supposed, though, that even if it was, it was too late now to bail. She was going to have to own it, Elle Woods style. Libby shook herself out of her thoughts as she focused on the situation at hand and the young man walking her way.

There he was. Wentworth Turner was walking toward her, illuminated enough under the campus streetlights that she could recognize him. Even though he was dressed in the most ridiculous cow costume she had ever seen, Libby decided at that moment that she liked his walk. It made her want to smile as he walked. It was pretty much a manly version of a supermodel strut, and he pulled it off well. For a man that wasn't in the business, he carried himself with enough confidence and posture that he could have fooled anyone. Especially with that ridiculous glam-worthy name.

She and Wentworth had been 'dating' for about three months now, and the more she thought about it the more ridiculous it was.

She did, after all, have a boyfriend, and these 'dates' were technically blackmail, but she tried not to think too much about the logistics of it all these days. Partly because she had made her bed and therefore now had to lie in it in the form of seven more dates, including this one.

It was also partly because it was kind of exciting to date someone new. Someone who knew nothing about you and, therefore, wanted to get to know you. Someone who didn't care about how famous you were or how dating you would help their image. Libby would also be lying if she said that she didn't also like the excitement that came from all the sneaking around and keeping secrets, which was confusing. Excitement and blackmail tended to not go together after all, but Libby didn't want to think about that either right now. Tonight, she was giving herself permission to just enjoy the night and whatever Wentworth had in store for her on date four.

When Libby snapped herself out of her deep mess of thoughts and confusion, she realized that Wentworth had nearly walked across the entire courtyard toward her. She also realized, now that he was so much closer, that he was pretty much gawking at her, and he was doing little to hide the fact that he was.

She knew that the black leather catsuit was a little much, but her instructions were to dress for an 'animal-themed' costume party. She also knew that if there was already gawking then the outfit was serving its intended purpose. That made the whole thing worth its money, and the twenty minutes it had taken her to get herself into it. Luckily it was still cooler, even for April, because she wasn't ever going to attempt getting into the catsuit in summer. The whole costume thing, especially the black leather cap mask that came with it, also gave her a little more peace of mind that no one was going to recognize her tonight.

"I take costume parties very seriously," Libby said as she placed her hands on her hips, a matching white pawprint purse dangling from her wrist.

It was like Wentworth hadn't even heard her. He was still blatantly staring, and his eyes were now starting to roam from the top half of the catsuit all the way down to the black leather boots she had teamed with the outfit.

"Hey!" Libby exclaimed with a small laugh as she reached out to hit Wentworth in the side with her clutch. "Quit staring like that!"

"Sorry!" Wentworth laughed, as he finally broke his stare. "It's just a little hard considering how..."

Libby laughed as he let his words trail off, his stare lingering on her and all that black leather again for a moment, before he physically shook his head.

"I'm done," Wentworth smiled. "But seriously, that looks amazing on you. You look. Wow."

Libby ducked her head as she felt a rush of red fill her cheeks. She got compliments on her appearance every day because her appearance was her job, but the genuine ones were rare even while she had a boyfriend.

"Now that's not fair," Libby replied, changing the subject. "It's probably only so wow because of your... costume?"

"C'mon now," Wentworth replied gesturing to his head-to-toe white cow costume, complete with bright pink udders in the crotch region. "What girl isn't going to want a piece of this tonight?"

"You mean apart from the girls with eyes?" Libby replied with a laugh.

"Savage, Miss Evans," Wentworth said, shaking his head. "Savage."

"So, which way then?" Libby said, changing the subject and looking around the courtyard for any signs of this party they were supposed to be attending. "And who do you know that goes to Caltech anyway?"

"Apart from me?" Wentworth asked with a smile as he motioned for Libby to follow him across the courtyard.

"You go to Caltech?" Libby asked in disbelief. "As in you go to Caltech as a student?"

"Sure do," Wentworth replied. "Is that so hard to believe?"

"I mean, no," Libby said. "I just thought—"

"That I take photos of the rich and famous for a living?" Wentworth asked, raising an eyebrow at her.

Libby shrugged.

"To be honest," Libby replied, "yeah. I thought it was your full-time gig."

"I get that a lot," Wentworth replied as they continued to walk. "Which is amusing because I'm a God-awful photographer really."

"Then why do you do it?" Libby asked.

"Easy money," Wentworth replied honestly as he led Libby down a narrow path between two large, brick buildings. "Plus, I get free invites to fancy parties where I get to meet hot girls."

Libby rolled her eyes as Wentworth's eyebrows danced suggestively at her.

"So," she spoke, changing the subject, "can I expect a lot of people to be at this party tonight?"

Wentworth nodded, seemingly unshaken by the new direction of the conversation.

"Yeah," he replied. "It's the last party before everyone will be buckling down for midterms so I'm pretty sure the whole dorm should be there."

"And do you usually bring dates you've been blackmailing to these parties?" Libby asked, not sure if she was trying to be serious or funny.

"Now now," Wentworth replied, a smile on his face as he assumed the latter. "I prefer to call this a business arrangement, remember?"

"Ah, that's right," Libby replied, suppressing a smile as she rolled her eyes.

"But I mean you don't have to come if you don't want to have a fun night," Wentworth commented as he shrugged his shoulders.

"It took me a really long time to get into this costume so you can be damn sure I won't be wasting it," Libby replied as she motioned again to her catsuit, drawing back Wentworth's gaze.

"Well, I mean it would also be a shame," Wentworth replied.

"How so?" Libby asked.

"It would be a shame to miss seeing that look on all my friends' faces when I walk into this party with you looking like that," Wentworth answered.

"Oh, so that's what this is about?" Libby replied. "You're using me tonight, is that it?"

"I mean," Wentworth shrugged again, "aren't you using me?"

"I don't think so," Libby answered, her brow furrowing in confusion as she watched Wentworth intently for his answer.

"I mean, aren't you also just using me to keep your secret?" Wentworth replied.

Libby continued to watch him intently as he remained looking in the direction they were heading. His face appeared expressionless and difficult to read. It made Libby feel uncomfortable but also annoyed that he was already trying to put her in a bad mood when the night, and their date, had just begun. It was already hard and confusing enough 'dating' this guy when he was in a good mood, but when he made snide remarks like that it really annoyed her. He was, after all, the reason they were here and doing this in the first place.

"Let's just go to this party, OK?" Libby said, breaking the silence as she refused to head down this train of thought because it was surely just going to continue to kill her partying mood.

It was then that Libby heard what sounded like music to her left and she automatically turned in that direction. Surely that was the party, and surely there would be alcohol there. She thought about just heading toward all that good stuff by herself but hesitated for a moment, which was enough to make Wentworth reach out and grab her arm.

"Look, I'm sorry," Wentworth said as Libby turned back to face him. "That was a shitty thing to say."

"Well, it certainly wasn't great," Libby sighed.

"I'm sorry," Wentworth repeated. "That was out of line. I appreciate you being here. I really do."

"Well, you promised me a party," Libby said.

"And a party I will deliver!" Wentworth smiled.

It was at that moment Libby realized that Wentworth's hand had slid down from where he had been holding her arm. His hand and fingers were now entwined with hers.

"C'mon," Wentworth spoke again, taking the lead whilst still holding her hand. "I know Libby Evans is always up for a good time!"

Libby rolled her eyes at his suggestive dancing eyebrows as she allowed him to lead her.

"Why is there always some kind of sexual innuendo in literally everything you have to say?" Libby asked. "Are you that sexually frustrated?"

"I think you're only interpreting it that way because you're the one that's a little frustrated," Wentworth replied. "How long has it been now?"

"And there you go again," Libby replied.

"What?!" Wentworth said with a small laugh.

"Maybe you'd get laid more if your words were a little less sexual and a little more genuine," Libby replied.

She noticed the music had gotten louder and they were approaching what looked like a mass of college students up ahead.

"Valid," Wentworth replied. "I'll take it under advisement."

"I hope when we get to this party that someone beats you up for talking like that," Libby said.

Wentworth laughed as he and Libby caught up with the group of college students Libby had spotted before. She and Wentworth were definitely in the right place as everyone around them was dressed in some sort of animal-themed attire, which meant that they didn't look out of place anymore. Libby remained silent as she took it all in and followed Wentworth, his hand still entwined with hers as he led her through the crowd and into the closest building, one of the Caltech residential dorms. She looked from one person to another as she tried to make out what animal inspired each outfit. She made out five cats, most of them scantily dressed girls wearing cat ears, and at least fifteen dogs because dog onesies were super easy to find in LA. She also noted several guys that were already so drunk that they either hadn't bothered with costumes, or their costumes had been lost on their journey to the party.

Once Libby and Wentworth had made it inside the building, it was so jam-packed with students that they had to literally squeeze themselves through the red-carpeted corridors. She felt herself involuntarily grip Wentworth's hand tighter, in fear of getting lost in the animal-themed haze, and felt him squeeze it back as he continued to lead her. As they ventured further into the dorms, Libby noticed the music was getting louder. She resisted the urge to roll her eyes and groan at the choice of music playing over the speakers. 'Animals' by Maroon 5 was an obvious and very cheesy animal-themed party choice.

"Turner!" a voice yelled as Wentworth and Libby finally reached the lounge area they were apparently heading for. "We've been waiting for you!"

Libby's eyes were drawn to the owner of the voice: a tall blonde surfer-looking guy dressed up as Toothless from *How to Train Your Dragon*. By the time Libby had spotted him, he was halfway across the room and bowling Wentworth over in a manly embrace, causing Libby and Wentworth's hands to separate.

"Toby," Wentworth said, "you guys started without me!"

"Oh yeah, cause this is your party is it, Turner?!" a short girl with piercings and violet-colored hair chimed in from her spot on one of the many red couches around the common area.

She easily downed the rest of her beer as she cuddled up to a guy wearing the same tiger onesie as her.

"And who is this?" Toby spoke again, drawing Libby's attention back to him as she realized he was talking about her.

"A friend," Wentworth replied as he turned to face Libby.

"Right," Libby nodded.

"From New York," Wentworth added, turning back to face Toby.

"We know each other from high school," Libby added.

"She's in town for a few days visiting family," Wentworth said.

"Right," Libby said with a smile and an outstretched hand. "It's Beth."

"Nice to meet you, Beth," Toby said, shaking her hand before he turned back to Wentworth. "I dare say, Turner, you're going to have your hands full tonight keeping everything with a dick away from your 'friend' here."

"Ah, no worries," Libby said, "I can look after myself."

"Yeah, Toby," a tall blonde that had just entered the room spoke as she nudged Toby, causing him to nearly spill the contents of his red solo cup all over himself. "The girl can look after herself."

Libby smiled and locked eyes with the girl.

"Beth," Libby said.

"Gigi," she replied with a wide smile that revealed her braces. "I'm this idiot's better half."

"It's true," Toby shrugged as he wrapped his arm around Gigi's shoulders, causing her to roll her eyes in response.

"Beer?" Wentworth leaned into Libby's ear and whispered, causing goosebumps to race down her back at the sudden feeling of his breath on her skin.

She turned to face him and only managed a small nod while she calmed herself down before Wentworth disappeared into an adjacent room. Libby took a deep breath and shook herself out of her thoughts as Gigi motioned her over.

"Take a seat over here with us!" Gigi exclaimed as she linked arms with Libby and led them to a couch opposite the pair of tigers. "Your costume is sexy af, Beth!"

Libby laughed out loud as she took a seat next to Gigi, leaving a spot on the end of the couch for Wentworth when he returned.

"Yours looks much more comfortable though," Libby commented as she eyed Gigi's black and white panda costume, one of the few in here that wasn't just a onesie.

"I told her she should have gone as a giraffe with those gangly legs of hers," Toby said as he perched himself on the arm of the couch where Libby and Gigi were seated at.

Gigi rolled her eyes and nudged Toby so hard he nearly lost his balance and the rest of his drink, again.

"So, what is the deal with you and Turner?" Gigi whispered quickly, as they both noticed Wentworth return to the room juggling three solo cups full to the brim with what Libby assumed to be keg beer.

"Nothing," Libby laughed as Wentworth reached them and handed one of the cups to her and the other to Gigi.

"Thanks, Turner!" Gigi exclaimed loudly, before returning her volume to a whisper as she leaned into Libby's ear. "Yeah right! I can see the way he's been looking at you since you guys got here."

Libby stifled another laugh.

"We're just friends," Libby replied, matching Gigi's whisper.

"Friends with benefits?" Gigi asked, wiggling her eyebrows as she took a generous sip of her beer.

"No!" Libby exclaimed, nearly choking on the mouthful of beer she'd just taken. "Just friends. Just friends."

* * *

Libby laughed again, feeling the back of her jaw starting to ache with the amount of laughing she had been doing over the last couple of hours. Wentworth's friends were funny. She was, as unexpected as it was, having a really good time. She took another swig of what was probably her fifth solo cup of beer before she realized that her other hand was resting precariously high up on Wentworth's thigh. She didn't know how it got there or how long it had been there. She also wasn't sure if he had drunk enough to be oblivious to it, but she didn't want to move it and draw attention. Instead, her eyes raised to look at his face as he, and Jeremy the lion, recounted the time they were Caltech freshmen and tried to sneak into the Vanity Fair Oscar After-Party so that Jeremy could profess his love to Taylor Swift.

As he spoke, Libby watched Wentworth closely. She noticed the numerous wrinkles around his mouth as he laughed and how his eyes lit up as he told the classic story, although Libby was sure that most of them had already heard it many times over the last four years. Every time she looked at his eyes, she found herself mesmerized by the specks of gold and brown swimming around in the bright green. She always found herself staring at them when they were talking, though she was usually much more subtle than 'five beers Libby' was being about it now.

As Jeremy finished off the last part of the story, she felt Wentworth's fingers on her waist as he readjusted them, a small smile on his lips as he did so. It wasn't his usual smirk, which made her want to withdraw. It was a small genuine smile, and it made the corners of her mouth start to curl as well. She didn't know if that was the alcohol talking, but it felt nice.

"I'm telling you guys, I saw her heading to the restroom with Lorde!" Jeremy exclaimed as he adjusted the thick orange mane around his neck. "If I had had another five seconds, I would have met her!"

"Dear Lord, you are a sad sad man, Jeremy," Anna, the purple-haired girl, laughed as she snuggled in closer to her matching tiger man.

"So, are you at college in New York, Beth?" Gigi asked, changing the subject.

Throughout the evening, Gigi had worked herself into Toby's lap, so along with the increasing proximity between Libby and Wentworth, there was now a giant gap between the girls.

"Yeah, at Columbia," Libby replied.

Her reply was so quick that Wentworth narrowed his eyes at her, trying to mask his surprise at her response.

"Damn," Toby replied. "You've got yourself an Ivy League girl, Turner."

Libby laughed.

"My mom went to Columbia so I'm a legacy," Libby explained.

"What exactly is it you study again, Beth?" Wentworth asked, causing Libby to smile.

He seemed to be intrigued by the story she was telling his friends.

"Communications," Libby replied, facing Wentworth directly.

"Nice," Wentworth nodded.

"What is yours again?" Libby asked playfully. "I almost totally forgot that you go to college at all."

Wentworth laughed.

"Nerd brain over here and I," Jeremy answered, pointing to Wentworth, "are pre-vet."

"Pre-vet?" Libby asked in surprise, her voice so quiet that only Wentworth could hear her.

Wentworth nodded.

"Jeremy majors in Zoology," Wentworth added, loud enough for the whole group to hear. "I'm a Bio major myself."

"So, Nerd brain," Libby added, "where are all these girls you said were going to be all over you tonight?"

Toby and Jeremy laughed out loud.

"All the girls after his massive brain, you mean?" Jeremy laughed.

"Oh no, he said the costume was going to bring all the ladies in tonight," Libby added, elbowing Wentworth in the side.

Wentworth laughed as he used the arm around her waist to draw her even closer.

"I guess they're all just a bit intimidated by you, my dear," Wentworth replied to Libby.

"Well, I mean, yeah man," Toby added. "I wouldn't have brought Catwoman over there to this party if you were planning on picking up."

"So, I mean, that sounds like a you prob, Turner," Gigi laughed before she turned to Toby and quickly jumped to her feet. "Oh my God, Tobes, I love this song! Come dance with me!"

Toby downed the rest of his drink and then saluted the group.

"Boyfriend duty calls, friends," Toby added before he disappeared with Gigi into another part of the building in the direction of where 'Hungry Like the Wolf' was coming from.

"C'mon then, Catwoman," Wentworth said jumping to his feet. "Enough of this making fun of me in front of my friends."

"Where are we going?" Libby said as she finished off her beer and placed the empty solo cup on the table in front of her.

"To dance of course," Wentworth said, taking Libby's hand in his own.

Libby let him lead her in the direction of Toby and Gigi, which happened to be the part of the house where a DJ was set up and a dance floor had formed. Before Libby knew what was happening, she and Wentworth were in the middle of a college kid mosh pit with every American college stereotype in play; from the jock wearing his high school varsity jacket because he was too cool to adhere to the theme, to red solo cups in every set of hands she could see. Libby couldn't wipe the smile off her face as she watched Gigi, Toby, and everyone around her absolutely scream the lyrics to 'Hungry Like the Wolf'. Libby felt Wentworth's hand in hers as he smiled at her. It felt nice to be here.

Everything about tonight felt nice. Being at this college. Being in this college party mosh pit. Being around people who were more worried about having fun than what they looked like if they were worried about anything at all. This wasn't the type of party you'd find Libby Evans at. This was, however, Beth's type of party, so tonight she wasn't going to be Libby. Tonight, she was just going to be Beth.

* * *

Beep! Beep Beep! Beep! Beep Beep!

Charlie closed her eyes tighter. She felt Penelope's fabulous hands continue to work into her shoulders as she buried her face deeper into the head cushion beneath her. This was the first time in months that she'd managed to find the time to get a masseuse around to her place for one of her Saturday night pamper treats. The last time around it was a facial but this time she decided a massage was just what she needed.

She had also been dying to try a trendy lymphatic drainage massage. All the Victoria's Secret models last year in Sydney were treated to one. Charlie knew because Libby would never shut up about it anytime anybody mentioned anything remotely related to massage. Charlie wanted to roll her eyes at just the thought of it, even if Libby was right about how amazing these massages were. Charlie had also done her own research and read about how drainage massages diminish water retention and eliminate fat deposits. She could already feel her skin softening and her puffiness from last night's cocktails disappearing.

Beep! Beep Beep! Beep! Beep Beep!

"Oh my God, who on Earth is bothering you now?!" Anita sighed in frustration, causing Charlie to raise her head out of her head cushion so she could look at her friend.

Christie and Willa were all pouts when Charlie announced that this month it would be Anita joining her for Saturday night pamper. Usually, it was Willa, and Christie had been sucking up big time this month, so naturally, they had both expected it to be them. However, Charlie knew that Anita had had a rough couple of months, with her only film prospect getting canned, so she needed it more than the two blondes. Charlie, as per usual though, also had ulterior motives for inviting Anita and they involved Anita's dwindling patience and love for Libby Evans. Anita and Libby had been best friends since their teens, but lately, Anita was starting to get sick of Libby's egocentric attitude and therefore was much more willing to participate in a little verbal Libby bashing. Something that Charlie thought went well with a night of massage.

Beep! Beep Beep! Beep! Beep Beep!

"Oh my God!" Charlie exclaimed, reaching Anita's frustration level as she angrily motioned for her phone. "Penelope! My phone!"

The young masseuse was startled by Charlie's outburst but quickly collected herself and retrieved Charlie's phone from the coffee table and quickly handed it to her. Charlie looked at the caller ID and scrunched up her face.

"Who is it?" Anita asked as she lifted herself onto her elbows, adjusting the silk sheet around her chest.

"Ace Thatcher," Charlie answered, her face still scrunched up in confusion as she turned the phone screen in Anita's direction.

"Why the hell is Ace calling you?" Anita asked, obviously just as confused as to what was going on.

"Who the hell knows?" Charlie shrugged as she watched the call disappear. "But he's called four times in the last ten minutes."

"Must be important," Anita shrugged as she laid back down to allow her masseuse to continue.

Charlie hesitated for a moment before she motioned for Penelope to stop so she could sit up on the table. She unlocked her phone and tapped into her phone's recent calls.

"Hey Charlie," Ace said as he answered. "How are you?"

"What do you want, Ace?" Charlie said, cutting straight to the chase as she clutched the silk sheet closer to her body. "Why are you calling me instead of your supermodel girlfriend?"

"I've already tried calling her eight times," Ace replied. "She's not answering her phone. Is she with you?"

"She's not here, Ace," Charlie said. "I don't know where she is."

"She was supposed to meet me for dinner at Citrin two hours ago," Ace added.

"I don't know what you want me to tell you," Charlie replied, sighing in annoyance that this conversation was currently cutting into her massage time. "She's not here and I don't know where she is."

"Fine," Ace replied, obviously annoyed that Charlie couldn't give him the answers he wanted. "Will you tell her to call me back if you talk to her tonight?"

"Sure, whatever," Charlie replied before she simply ended the call.

"What was that all about?" Anita asked through her head cushion, not even bothering to lift her head this time.

"More Ace and Libby drama," Charlie replied as she re-locked her phone.

Her eyes glanced around the room as she started thinking. It wasn't like Libby to miss dinner plans with Ace, especially when he was out of town for long periods at a time. It wasn't like Libby to miss plans at all, but it seemed like all she'd been doing lately was missing plans.

Charlie looked around the living room and noted that some of Libby's birthday gifts were starting to look a little worn out. In apology for missing birthday brunch the other day, Libby had a Marc Jacobs extravaganza delivered to Charlie's hotel suite in twenty-threes, in honor of Charlie turning twenty-three. Twenty-three bottles of Marc Jacob's new Daisy perfume, Daisy Love, were sitting on her coffee table and twenty-three bouquets of half-wilted week-old daisies were scattered around the room too. It wasn't like Libby to miss things, but it really wasn't like Libby to try so hard. Charlie knew something was off and she was sick and tired of waiting to find out what it was. She was going to find out herself.

14

Date #5

No one goes putt putt golfing on a Monday.

That was Wentworth's reason for scheduling date five today, or at least that's what he told Libby, so she didn't have a chance to query why this one and date four were so close together. The truth was, he hadn't been able to stop thinking about her after the college party they went to on Saturday night. It was another date fueled by beer, but it had also been another date where he was glad that he'd blackmailed her in the first place.

After spending what felt like hours in the Fleming House make-shift mosh pit, Wentworth had walked her to the other side of campus so her driver could pick her up. What should have been a nice walk from the party to her pickup spot, ended up with her spending most of her time not being able to answer his questions properly because she was so distracted by numerous missed calls and messages. Missed calls and messages of reality, no doubt. A reality called her boyfriend.

Wentworth had thought a lot about Ace Thatcher this morning and what kind of guy he was. He'd thought about him all day

Sunday when he should have been studying for mid-terms, and during the nearly two-hour drive to get here. He'd even been thinking about him every spare minute that he got when Libby was busy being truly awful at putt putt on the previous five holes. He wasn't sure whether it was because she was actually bad at putt putt, or whether it was because, like him, she had a lot on her mind.

She'd barely spoken the whole morning, but it hadn't been in a supermodel attitude way like their first date was. It seemed like she was genuinely distracted by what he could only assume were a million things running through her mind. It made him wonder if he and Libby were thinking the same thing – that Ace Thatcher would have kicked his ass if he knew that Wentworth was on his fifth date with his girlfriend.

"Hey?" Wentworth said, causing Libby to stop lining up her putt.

He was momentarily distracted as he looked at her. He wasn't sure if he'd ever met a girl that was quite as beautiful as Libby Evans. Obviously, she was beautiful, being a supermodel and all, and Wentworth had seen photographs of her in lingerie more times than he'd honestly admit to Libby herself. However, she was beautiful today because she wasn't being a supermodel. She was, for the first time on one of their dates, not wearing any more make-up than a little mascara and a pink Chapstick he had watched her reapply multiple times this morning. Today, in her jeans, classic white Rolling Stones T-shirt, and truly sucking at putt putt golf, she was just being an exceptionally beautiful regular girl.

"Yeah?" Libby eventually asked, breaking the silence, as Wentworth didn't follow up his 'hey' with anything else.

"You OK?" Wentworth asked. "You wanna take a break?"

"What do you mean?" Libby asked a bit puzzled as she finally broke her putting stance and turned to fully face him.

Wentworth found himself distracted again as he watched her flick her long, straight hair over her shoulder in one graceful movement. The hand she casually placed on her hip drew his eyes to her very sexy, womanly hips.

"You just seem distracted today," Wentworth continued, the voice in his head screaming at him to get a hold of himself as he focused hard on keeping her eye contact rather than letting his eyes roam her body. "Like you've got a lot on your mind."

Libby paused for a moment before she returned to her putt, lined it up, and miraculously got it into the hole in just one more shot.

"Don't even tell me how many that was for that hole," Libby said, with a small laugh. "I am well aware of how much I suck today."

"Wasn't going to say a thing," Wentworth smiled.

He headed for a wooden picnic table just up ahead, just past their next scheduled hole.

Libby looked behind her, double-checking that no one had joined the course and was waiting for them to play the next hole before she joined him. She placed her putter on the table as she sat down. Her fingers played with the metal club as she sighed.

"I'm sorry I'm not being much fun today," Libby said as she looked up at Wentworth and managed a small smile.

"Don't worry about it," Wentworth replied. "You wanna talk about it?"

"I don't know," Libby replied honestly.

"What do you mean?" Wentworth asked.

"Well, I mean, it's a bit weird if we talk about my boyfriend, right?" Libby asked.

"Well, I mean, maybe," Wentworth said with a small laugh, "but if you want to talk about it and it'll make you feel better, then we can talk about it. Sure."

Libby sighed.

"And hey, maybe it'll make your putt putt game better?" Wentworth offered.

"Like you want that to happen," Libby said rolling her eyes. "You are absolutely loving kicking my ass at this after bowling and Scrabble."

"You know me so well," Wentworth replied with a wink, causing Libby to break out in a small laugh of her own.

Libby silently rolled her putter in between her fingers as they sat in silence for what felt like longer than the several seconds it was. It wasn't an awkward silence, so Wentworth didn't feel the need to say anything. He let Libby sit on it and talk when she was ready. She sighed again and finally looked up at him.

"I slept with Ace last night," Libby said.

Wentworth simply nodded. He didn't feel great about hearing Libby's statement, but at the same time, there wasn't much he could do about it. Ace was her boyfriend after all. She was more than entitled to sleep with him as often as she wanted to. All he could do was sit there and try and control his facial expressions, especially if she was going to elaborate on what last night specifically entailed.

"I felt bad, guilty almost, for missing our dinner the other night to go to that Caltech party with you," Libby continued, "and he just kept asking and pressing about where I was and why I wasn't there, no matter what explanation I gave him. I just. I dunno."

Libby trailed off as her gaze returned to the putter in front of her. Her fingers fiddling like crazy as she clearly continued to shuffle through the thoughts in her head. Wentworth could almost see them flying around in there like crazy as he watched her eyes glaze over.

"And then part of me felt bad about sleeping with him because...," Libby continued, not quite able to find the words she wanted to say as she and Wentworth locked eyes again. "I dunno. I just did it and I had to, but I just. I just don't feel great about it today."

Wentworth nodded again, waiting a couple of moments to see if Libby would continue before he decided to speak.

"How long have you guys been together?" he asked.

"Do you really want to know about me and Ace?" Libby asked, raising an eyebrow at him.

Wentworth paused.

"Look at it like this, I guess," he explained. "This is our fifth date now, yeah?"

Libby nodded.

"Surely this is fifth date conversation material then, right?" Wentworth continued. "I mean, ignoring the fact that you actually have a boyfriend, who is not me, and we're not in a relationship and all that technical garbage."

"Right," Libby laughed. "All that technical garbage."

"Ignoring all that," Wentworth continued, "this sorta heavy conversation stuff is what I'd consider fifth date material, right?"

Libby took a moment to process what he'd said before she shrugged and then nodded.

"OK then," Libby answered. "We haven't really been together that long, officially that is. All in all, nearly a year."

"A year's a long time," Wentworth commented.

"Yeah," Libby said. "It feels like so much longer than that though."

"Is that a good thing or a bad thing?" Wentworth asked.

"I don't know to be honest," Libby replied.

"The last thing I remember seeing in the tabloids about your dating life was about you and Woody Kirk?" Wentworth said.

"Oh God, let's please not play this game," Libby said as she buried her face in her hands melodramatically. "Most of my dating history has been a string of my not so finest moments."

Wentworth laughed.

"Ace is my first serious relationship," Libby said, directing the conversation away from Woody Kirk and all the others that Wentworth could name drop right now.

"Really?" Wentworth asked.

"Yeah," Libby answered. "I mean, like we've just mentioned, I've had other boyfriends, but Ace is my first serious one."

"What makes it serious?" Wentworth asked as he folded his arms in front of him and rested them on the table.

"We talk a lot about the future," Libby said. "Getting married one day down the track. Having kids, which is even further down the track."

"You're a bit young to be talking about things like that, aren't you?" Wentworth said.

"True," Libby said, "I guess."

"But that's why it's serious to you?" Wentworth asked. "Because you see yourself being with Ace for the long haul?"

Libby mulled over Wentworth's words for a moment, one of her hands reaching up and absentmindedly toying with the ends of her hair.

"I guess," she nodded.

"You guess?" Wentworth pressed.

"I guess I don't even really know these days," Libby shrugged. "I mean, I still want all that stuff. Marriage, kids, one day. I just..."

Libby trailed off and Wentworth narrowed his eyes at her and hesitated for a moment before speaking again. It was the first insight he was getting into Libby's relationship with Ace, which was not only intriguing as the other guy 'dating' her but also because her answers were giving him more insight into what she was really like. What she wanted. Who she really was.

"I realize we're already talking about pretty personal stuff here, so stop me if I'm pushing it," Wentworth said, trailing off as he waited for Libby to indicate that he should continue.

She nodded.

"You mean, you're sure you still want all those things," Wentworth continued, "but you're not sure if you see all those things happening with Ace anymore?'

Libby paused. Wentworth watched as she sighed and then started speaking without looking at him. She remained focused on the putter in her hands that she had started fiddling with again.

"When we first started dating," Libby said, "Ace was amazing. He was charming and funny. We had so many good times. I remember this one time; we were just hanging out in his bedroom in his mansion in Beverly Hills. I think I was between meetings with Victoria's Secret about the runway show in Sydney, and he was in town for a week or so doing business stuff for his grandfather's company. He had this random acoustic guitar there in his room that he'd just brought over from France with him. We were just hanging out and talking, and then he just picked the guitar up, made me lie down on the bed and he just played and sang to me. It was probably one of the most romantic moments of my life so far."

Wentworth smiled as he watched Libby smile, and also in response to her 'life so far' comment. She was clearly a romantic. He hadn't known that about her until just now.

"When it all first started, I knew he loved me, and I knew I loved him," Libby continued. "I also knew he was dating me for me. Just for me."

"You don't think he is anymore?" Wentworth asked, clarifying her words.

Libby sighed.

"I worry that the romance in our relationship is gone because it's more of a job for him now," Libby continued. "For us both now, I guess. Having me on his arm for events to do with his dad's company is good for his image, and my publicist says the same thing for mine especially when it comes to my Victoria's Secret contract."

"Which I hear is a super big deal in your world," Wentworth said, immediately regretting his choice of words when he went with 'your world'.

"It is a super big deal," Libby nodded. "It's everything every model wants. It's prestigious, it's money, it's everything. I don't know a single model that doesn't want an Angel contract."

Wentworth nodded.

"So, it's more of a business arrangement?" he asked. "Your relationship with Ace, that is."

"No," Libby smiled, "this is a business arrangement."

"What's the difference?" Wentworth said.

"Well, despite my better judgment for what I'm about to say," Libby said, "this arrangement is actually fun."

"Your relationship isn't fun?" Wentworth asked, raising an eyebrow at her.

"Let's just say that you know something in your relationship is wrong if you're having more fun with a guy that isn't your boyfriend," Libby added. "But don't let that go to your head or anything. After all, this is still business."

"Of course," Wentworth replied.

He decided to go with his better judgment and leave it at that, even though a million witty remarks were floating around in his head. She had genuinely opened up to him about something important in her life, and with very little pressing on his part too. It was what he had wanted, so he decided that whatever he was doing correctly he was going to continue to do it, which probably meant laying off the smart-ass comments for now.

"OK, so your turn before we pick up where we left off," Libby said as she looked in the direction of the next five holes of putt putt they still had left. "Which is probably just going to be me dragging my dignity through the mud with this putter."

Wentworth laughed.

"My turn for what then?" he asked.

"Tell me about your last relationship," Libby answered. "This being me presuming that you don't currently have one as well."

"I do not currently have one," Wentworth replied with a laugh. "Haven't since I left high school."

"Go on," Libby asked, resting her face in the palm of her hand as she watched him intently.

Wentworth smiled at her attempt to show her enthusiasm and willingness to hear all he was about to share about Ellie Love.

"So, Ellie and I were high school sweethearts," Wentworth said. "She and I were a couple of nerds who had lived in San Fran our whole lives but didn't meet until sophomore year in high school when we both joined the school decathlon team. I even think our first kiss was on one of the school decathlon field trips to Sacramento on the bus trip home."

"Aw," Libby cooed, causing Wentworth to roll his eyes unsure of how genuine her sentiment was.

"We dated for the rest of sophomore year and then into our junior and senior years as well," Wentworth continued. "We broke up the night of senior prom, which wasn't great. Breaking up is a shitty thing to do at your prom apparently."

"What happened?" Libby asked.

"She wanted me to go to New York with her after graduation," Wentworth replied. "She had gotten into film school at NYU and I'd gotten into NYU as well, so she wanted us to go together."

"So why didn't you go?" Libby asked, her words tumbling so quickly out of her mouth that Wentworth wanted to laugh.

Her romantic side was showing again. She was obviously already very invested in his story.

"I wanted to," Wentworth answered, "but I couldn't. It was a bad time for my family."

"How so?" Libby asked.

"In May of my senior year my dad was diagnosed with Non-Hodgkin's Lymphoma," Wentworth explained. "By the time graduation rolled around he was receiving regular chemo treatment from UCSF and my mom was a mess while it was all going on. She and my dad had been together since they were thirteen and fourteen, so the thought of life without him just sent her into this downward spiral. She wasn't eating anything, and she wasn't sleeping unless it was in a chair in the corner of my dad's treatment room in the hospital. Even though he was scheduled to finish his treatments before I would have started at NYU, I didn't feel like it would have been right to just get up and leave to the other side of the country. So, I did—"

"What you had to do for your family," Libby finished.

"Something like that," Wentworth replied. "And Ellie got it. She understood why I couldn't go with her, as much as I wanted to, but it didn't make it any less painful when we broke up. We just knew that it would never be the same long distance and we didn't want to put each other through that."

"Wow," Libby exhaled.

"Yeah," Wentworth nodded.

"So, I guess you're actually a nice guy then?" Libby asked, causing Wentworth to laugh.

"Well, I mean apart from being a scum of the Earth paparazzo, right?" Wentworth added.

"Unless you're going to tell me that the reason you do the whole paparazzi thing is to help with your dad's medical bills...?" Libby said, trailing off as she raised an eyebrow in Wentworth's direction.

"Well...," Wentworth started with a shrug.

Libby rolled her eyes.

"Of course, you are," Libby replied. "Is your dad OK now?"

"He's been in remission for the last couple of years," Wentworth said.

Libby smiled and nodded at him, and he smiled back. He noted, for at least the fifteenth time this morning how gorgeous her smile was, especially when it was one of those small ones where she didn't show any teeth. It was a little lopsided, a little more to the right, and covered in that pink Chapstick that brought out the natural flush in her cheeks. He had to stop himself from literally shaking his head as he realized that he had it bad. He had it bad for this girl and the more time he spent with her, the harder it was becoming to keep that realization to himself.

"Thank you," Libby said, breaking Wentworth out of his thoughts.

"For what?" Wentworth asked.

"For being a real person today," Libby shrugged as she leaned forward, her arms coming to rest over the top of her putter on the table between them. "I mean, for listening to me talk about my relationship, as awkward and weird as that must have been."

"I mean it wasn't that weird," Wentworth replied. "Maybe a little."

"I don't get the chance to have many real conversations with the people in my life so thanks," Libby added.

Wentworth swallowed hard as he felt his earlier realization rising to the surface again. He hadn't known what to expect today when he had planned this putt putt golfing date with Libby. He had thought that they'd probably have some fun, and he thought she was going to be naturally talented at it too, and kick his ass every single hole they played. He had also hoped they'd have more of a chance to have some proper conversations, but he wasn't prepared for today's conversation and how vulnerable Libby would be in the things they spoke about. He didn't even know if she realized how vulnerable she was being and how much more it made him want her.

"I mean, that's what fifth dates are for, right?" Wentworth smiled.

"Right," Libby smiled back.

Wentworth looked at her, straight into those dark brown eyes, and he knew that this was his moment if he wanted it to be. She was looking at him like maybe she was waiting for him to say something. She was also looking at him like maybe she was waiting for him to do something, but that could have easily just been his ego talking.

He wanted to kiss her so badly. He'd wanted to kiss her on every date they'd had so far. It was so hard not to do it at the Caltech party, especially when all that beer had meant that one of her hands always found itself resting on his thigh while they were sitting with his friends. Right now, though, after that conversation, he was barely holding himself back from just closing the small gap between them. She was maintaining his eye contact, and it felt like they had been staring into each other's eyes for days. Wentworth was trying to control the look in his, to make sure his lust wasn't showing, but he wasn't sure how well he was doing that. He could almost feel the lust exploding out of him with each second that passed.

"You're welcome," Wentworth said, breaking the silence and the moment as he suddenly stood up and grabbed his putter.

He motioned for Libby to follow him to the next putt putt hole, and she did without so much as a reaction to the moment they'd just shared in Wentworth's mind.

He knew that he'd blown it, and he liked to think that maybe she had also been disappointed by him not making a move. In reality, though, he had to remind himself that this wasn't his fairy tale. He got the dates, but she went home to Ace Thatcher's bed like she had last night. He got to have the relationship conversations, but not the actual relationship. While he was starting to feel things for her that he hadn't felt since Ellie Love in senior year, he had to assume that she had those feelings too, but they weren't for him. He wasn't sure, but he figured it would be safer to assume it anyway. Even though she had told him today that she used to love Ace, and that he used to love her too, Wentworth couldn't help but wonder if Libby still did love her boyfriend.

15

Mutiny

"Wills, you OK?" Libby asked.

Willa looked up from her oat milk latte and realized that she had spent the last five minutes stirring it while completely lost in thought. The Pack, minus Anita, were in New York City for the weekend having coffee at the Café Charlotte on the first floor of the Niven Hotel in midtown Manhattan. She and Libby were here for casting for the *Sports Illustrated Swimsuit Edition* at Sports Illustrated Headquarters a couple of blocks away, and Christie and Charlie were along for a glamorous weekend in NYC.

This was Willa's first time being invited to the casting for the swimwear edition after many years of struggling to even be considered. No matter how many modeling jobs, particularly swimwear, she had managed to book over the years, she'd still missed out. Her agency, Aurora Models, was an up-and-coming agency that had been representing her for two years now. They were great at landing her jobs, but most of them were catalog shoots, which paid the bills but weren't going to launch her career. It was, just by luck, that she had tagged along with Libby to a Victoria's Secret photo shoot a couple of months ago and had made some contacts that worked for Sports

Illustrated. Those contacts had then gone through Aurora to send her an invitation to come to casting calls this weekend. Only twenty-five models would make it into the magazine this year and, despite how competitive it always is, Willa was hoping that she would be one of the models that landed one of those coveted spots.

"Yeah, all good," Willa nodded.

"Right well, Christie and I are off to do some shopping on 5th Avenue before high tea," Charlie announced as she got up from her seat, swinging her limited-edition Marc Jacobs x Charlie Niven handbag over her shoulder.

"Oo, where are you girls off to for high tea?" Libby asked.

Charlie locked eyes with Libby for a split second before she disappeared behind her phone, typing away on the screen as if she were replying to an important message. Christie watched Charlie for a second before sending a small smile Libby's way.

"The Russian Tea House," Christie replied as she flicked one of her blonde curls over her shoulder. "We have reservations at 11:00 am."

Willa looked from Charlie to Libby and could feel the tension building between the two. Before anyone could say anything else, though, Charlie turned heel and started walking toward the elevators. Christie quickly waved at Libby and Willa before she ran off after Charlie. Her feet nearly falling out of her clearly ill-fitting Jimmy Choos.

"Since when does Ecles wear Choos?" Libby said, rolling her eyes as she returned to her bottle of Evian.

"Who knows," Willa replied, as she looked down at her latte and then at Libby's bottle of water.

Libby had refused to order her usual green tea this morning with her fruit bowl, claiming that the last thing she wanted before casting was to be all caffeine bloated in her bikini. Willa pushed her half-drunk latte aside. She then stared at her half-eaten açai bowl and knew that that was pretty much all of it she was going to feel like eating right now. Especially because the oat milk made her latte taste like sewer water.

"And what the hell is up Charlie's ass this morning?" Libby asked. "As a matter of fact, she was all moody and grumpy last night at dinner too."

Willa looked up from her food and had to stop herself from smiling. What better way to distract herself from those pre-casting jitters than with a little bitch session? They had the time. SI headquarters was only two blocks away after all.

"She's been in such a mood lately," Willa said, resting her arms on the table in front of her as she gave Libby her full attention. "She and Christie have been non-stop bitching too."

"About who?" Libby asked.

"Well," Willa replied, "you."

"Me?!" Libby exclaimed, in surprise.

It took everything Willa had not to roll her eyes at Libby's reaction. She was Libby Evans, after all, and she thought everyone loved her. Willa simply answered with a nod.

"Why?" Libby asked. "I haven't done anything to Charlie!"

Again, Willa bit her tongue and controlled her eyes.

"She and Christie are totally pissed because you keep canceling on us," Willa explained. "You've missed the last four brunches."

"Seriously?!" Libby exclaimed, clearly shocked by Willa's words.

Willa nodded again.

"I couldn't help any of that," Libby explained. "I had meetings and a breakfast with my dad and all that. I can't believe they're being so unreasonable! You get it right?"

"Of course, I get it!" Willa lied so well that it might as well have been the truth. "To be honest, I think Charlie's just in a foul mood because Hamish didn't call her back last night."

"Hamish?" Libby asked. "As in Hamish Dawson?"

"Yep," Willa nodded. "They've been dating. Well, I don't know if I'd call it dating more so as casually sleeping together. It's been going on for like a month now."

"Really?!" Libby asked again, the surprise in her voice still clear as day. "Hamish Dawson? As in my Hamish?"

Of course, Libby thought she owned Hamish Dawson. They had dated, but that was so long ago Willa could barely remember it. In typical Libby Evans fashion, though, she had to make even the smallest amount of Charlie gossip all about her.

"Yep," Willa replied. "She's been into him for ages, but you didn't hear that from me, OK?"

"Oh yeah, of course," Libby said.

"Yeah, so he didn't call her back and this isn't the first time it's happened," Willa continued, pleased with how not well this news was sitting with Libby.

"Hmmm," Libby replied.

"I mean, after all," Willa continued, "I don't think she's the only girl he's seeing right now."

"Well, I mean, that's what you get for dating a musician," Libby added.

"Totally," Willa said.

Willa could tell that Libby was distracted by the news about Charlie and Hamish as they sorted the check at Café Charlotte and then started the walk to SI headquarters. Libby had clearly been taken back by the news that Charlie was seeing her ex behind her back, which meant that she was very quiet as she mulled everything over as they walked. Willa was beyond thankful for a little peace and quiet as she tried to compose herself for what was finally about to happen.

Willa looked down at her attire. She and Libby were dressed in pretty much identical outfits. Strutting down the streets of Manhattan in their white T-shirts, jeans, and nude pumps screamed that they were heading for SI headquarters. After all, every model in the industry knew that the casting call for the swimsuit edition was being held this weekend. Willa looked at Libby as she walked next to her. Even though she was engrossed in thought, Libby walked with a self-confident strut that told the world she was a supermodel. Her usual straight black hair was blown out and in loose curls. It even looked like she'd gone the extra mile to have her natural black dyed over so it looked even glossier and shinier than usual. Usually, for casting calls, she and Libby both opted for a low ponytail to show off their bone structure, but the swimsuit edition casting was completely different. They want you to look like a model, but at the same time, they want that combination of sparkle and personality to shine right out of you. It was why Willa's hair was also blown out and deeply conditioned, and why she and Libby had spent yesterday getting facials, mani-pedis, and skin massages. It seemed like a lot of work, but it was a small price to pay if it meant that Willa could finally get herself in that magazine and pull herself out of the non-working slump she was currently in.

"Libby! Libby! Over here, Libby!"

Willa was caught off guard as she and Libby rounded the corner that would take them right up to the SI headquarters building. The outside of the building was swarming with paparazzi waiting to get a glimpse of the aspiring models showing up for casting calls today. So, of course, they were looking straight through Willa to get a photo of Libby. Willa and Libby pushed their way through the sea of paparazzi and made their way inside the building. They were followed closely behind by a couple of other tall, white-shirt and jean-clad women who were obviously headed in the same direction.

"Oh my God," Libby exclaimed as she adjusted her hair. "Paparazzi are so annoying!"

"Yeah!" Willa exclaimed. "Like they have nothing better to do than follow the pretty people around."

"They really don't," Libby laughed. "It's pathetic really."

"Such scum," Willa said as she and Libby continued to walk through the lobby, following another trio of aspiring SI models just ahead of them.

They took the elevator up and when the doors opened it was obvious where they were. Apart from the mass of models all dressed identically, the tropical-looking signage providing everything from directions to motivational phrases made it clear as day. '*Welcome to the Sports Illustrated Swimsuit Edition Casting Calls!*' was the biggest sign in the room and it was plastered all over one of the feature walls right next to the elevators. The display also included blow-up palm trees, beach balls, and deck chairs. Clearly a photo op for the models to post all over their Instagram pages, which is exactly what Willa would be doing once her interview was over and she could relax a little. She was not above selling her image on social media if it gave her a better chance of making it a successful casting call this morning.

Libby and Willa strutted in the direction of one of the unoccupied white couches in the middle of the room.

"You know, I'm convinced that Charlie is only acting like this because of that Christie Ecles," Libby said. "Who invited her to be part of The Pack anyway?"

Willa rolled her eyes on the inside. She didn't know whether SI had spies hanging around in the room watching the models and their behavior before their interviews, so she was going to be on her best behavior for the rest of their time here.

"Who knows?" Willa replied, carefully placing one of her loose blonde curls behind her ear as she sat down on the couch as elegantly as possible. "I don't even like her. She's so annoyingly chirpy all the time and those teeth of hers are so fugly."

"Urg, tell me about it!" Libby said as she sat down next to Willa. "Don't we get a vote or something? Can't we just kick her out?"

"You should definitely say something to Charlie," Willa said, as she placed her Birkin down at her feet before retrieving her phone to check her messages. "I mean, Christie's only a backup dancer after all. The Pack should be way more exclusive than that!"

As much as Willa wanted to continue this bitch session, she didn't want to waste any time before her interview. She had interview prep and make-up touch-ups to do after all. Another unwritten rule of casting calls was to wear as minimal make-up as possible, without looking like you just rolled out of bed. SI was no different, except their minimal make-up requirement was a fresh, outdoors, beachy look. Minimal mascara, shaped brows, foundation sans contouring, and fresh pink lip-gloss were on the agenda this morning.

Beep! Beep Beep! Beep! Beep Beep!

Libby's phone started ringing at the exact same time a black woman, with the most beautiful looking afro, called Libby Evans to one of the interview rooms. Libby grabbed her phone, turned it on silent, and then chucked it back in her own Birkin before greeting the woman with all her charm and a million-dollar smile. It was ironic that Libby was obviously made for casting calls, with all that self-confidence and charisma, and yet she didn't need them the way Willa did. Libby probably didn't even need to attend these SI casting calls because she'd been in the swimsuit edition for the past two years in a row.

Willa placed her phone back in her bag and placed her hands on her lap as she looked around the room. Checking out her competition was only going to hype up the butterflies in her stomach, so she needed something to distract herself with. She looked at the door to the interview room that Libby had just gone in and figured that she was going to be at least ten minutes, if not longer. She hesitated a moment before she reached into Libby's Birkin and retrieved her friend's phone to check who the missed call was from. Whilst the phone was obviously locked, you could still see the missed call sitting there, followed by a text message. Both were from Camryn Ecles. As hard as she tried not to, Willa could feel her eyes bulging out of her head as her jaw dropped in shock. She was shocked that Camryn was calling Libby on a Saturday morning, let alone why she was calling Libby at all.

Willa looked at the locked symbol once more, hesitating for a second before she figured that she might as well give it a go. She knew that she had five attempts before the phone would disable, so she had four tries to crack Libby's passcode. She thought for a moment and then entered '*0216*' into the keypad. Willa rolled her eyes as the phone immediately unlocked. It was so predictable of Libby for her phone passcode to be her own birthday. Anyone could access her private text messages with that level of predictability.

Willa opened Libby's messages and found the message from Camryn Ecles sitting there just ready to be read. She opened it, looking around once more to make sure that Libby was still in her interview in another room before she started to read.

**Darling Libby, it was such a
treat to meet you last**

**Sunday for brunch! Felicity
was right, you are an
absolute dream! I can't wait
to have you represent our
new perfume line! I will send
through the paperwork
Monday morning! Good luck
in NYC this weekend!
Camryn x**

Willa barely made it through the entire text message before she started feeling the heat rising in her cheeks and a scream of pure frustration bubbling in her throat. Libby knew how much it meant to Willa to work with Illuse Cosmetics. Willa had gotten drunk on rosé a couple of weeks back at Anita's condo and divulged her new career aspiration to the rest of The Pack, including Libby. In Willa's mind, it was the only reason why Christie Ecles was still allowed to exist in The Brat Pack. She couldn't believe that Libby had sneaky gone behind her back to land a contract with Illuse and their soon-to-be-released fragrance line. Willa knew all about the new line, even the fact that it was going to be called Nine Seven because it was made of ninety-seven percent certified organic ingredients. Camryn had told Willa and Christie all about the new Illuse venture when they had dropped by the Ecles' Hollywood Hills mansion for lunch for Christie's birthday about a month ago. Willa had been sucking up big time to Christie, and Camryn as well when given the opportunity. She just knew that she would have been a shoo-in for the fragrance spokesmodel role if it wasn't for Libby. It was so typical of Libby too. She had to have everything. She had her Angel contract in the works so she didn't even need this Illuse one.

It was then that Willa noticed there was still one unread message on Libby's phone. She contemplated marking the Camryn Ecles message as 'unread', a little hacker trick that Basil Schatz had taught her back when she had dated him for like five seconds, and locking the phone. However, another glance at the closed interview door convinced her that she had the time to do a little more snooping. The message was from Turner Evans. Willa had never heard Libby mention anything about a Turner Evans, and Libby should have considering how many messages on her phone were from this mystery guy. Willa opened the messages and started to read.

> I'm out of town this weekend for casting calls. Next weekend?

Can't. Mid-term exams for the next couple of weeks. I'll text you when they're over.

> Good luck with your exams!

Thanks :) I'll see you soon.

Willa only got the chance to read the last couple of messages when the sound of one of the interview doors opening scared her out of her skin. Thankfully it wasn't Libby's, but Willa decided to play it safe, marked the messages as unread, and re-locked Libby's phone. Willa returned the phone to exactly where she had found it, inside one of the inner pockets of Libby's Birkin.

Willa straightened herself up and grabbed her compact out of her own Birkin to touch up her lip-gloss. Surely her interview wouldn't be too far away. She should have been rehearsing her candid answers for her interview – how long she'd been professionally modeling, why she loved modeling, what she liked to do in her spare time, and why she thought she'd be perfect for the magazine. Instead, she was trying to rack her brain and figure out who Turner Evans was. The last name Evans suggested he was a relative of Libby's. Maybe a cousin or half-brother, but what was Libby doing texting him so often when she had never mentioned him at all to Willa or the girls? The texting sounded friendly too, so they'd obviously been hanging out and chatting a lot. Maybe it was who she was hanging out with lately when she kept canceling on the rest of The Pack? It sounded reasonable enough, especially if he was family, so why was Libby keeping it a secret?

"Willa Nelson?" a voice called, breaking Willa out of her thoughts.

A short blond guy, probably not much older than her, was standing next to one of the open interview doors clutching a clipboard and looking around the room.

"Willa Nelson from Aurora models?" he called again.

"That's me!" Willa answered with a wave and a smile in the guy's direction.

As usual, he couldn't help himself from matching her broad smile. Willa smoothed out her white T-shirt and strutted her way across to the blond. She felt ready and confident, probably because she hadn't spent the last few minutes stressing out and overthinking everything. At least she had one thing to thank Libby Evans for this morning, even though she was going to take her down for stealing her Illuse deal. Right after she figured out who Turner Evans really was. It was game on.

16

Date #6

Libby could feel the heat in her hands rising. Her palms felt like they were on fire and her fingers felt like they were going to fall off, but she wasn't going to let go. Libby Evans was nothing if not competitive. No matter how stupid and pointless this contest was, she was going to win, and she would have all those Victoria's Secret boxing classes to thank for it. Her arms were barely hurting right now at all because of those grueling classes, it was just her silly skinny hands that were struggling. It didn't help that she had forgotten to take off her Tiffany T ring that was currently digging into the middle finger on her right hand as it pressed against the gymnastic bar she was gripping so tightly onto.

Libby took a deep breath as she adjusted her right hand, then her left, turning to look at Wentworth to her right. She couldn't help but let out a laugh as she watched the strained look on his face. He was clearly struggling more than she was right now. It made sense though. He didn't really look like the type that worked out and chose morning protein powder over a cooked breakfast. To be honest, though, she would have chosen bacon any day over protein powder too. No matter how good some of the protein powder was that she had tried, nothing beat bacon.

"Evans, I am so ridiculously impressed at your upper body strength right now," Wentworth groaned as Libby watched him adjust his grip on the bar.

"How many times have you underestimated the hell out of me?" she laughed. "It's like you never learn!"

"Never," Wentworth groaned again. "I never do."

Libby winced as she felt her ring digging further and further into her finger. Her hands were burning so bad right now, but she knew that she probably didn't have to hold on much longer. Wentworth would cave soon, and then she'd win this pointless contest to see who could hang the longest from the gymnastics bar above the foam pit in the Caltech gymnastics center.

"God, this hurts so badly!" Wentworth groaned again. "Aren't your arms killing you?"

"Yeah, of course, they are!" Libby exclaimed. "But I refuse to lose!"

Wentworth let out a frustrated sigh, obviously realizing that she wasn't going to give up.

"I'm done!" he exclaimed as he started readjusting each of his hands on the bar.

"Let go then!" Libby laughed. "You have to let go first!"

"Maybe," he replied.

"What?!" she asked.

Libby watched as Wentworth picked each of his hands off the bar one by one as he started moving closer to her.

"What are you doing?!" she suspiciously asked.

"Ending this nonsense!" Wentworth said before he completely let go and launched himself in her direction.

Before Libby realized what was going on, Wentworth had taken her out at her mid-section and they both went crashing into the foam pit below them. Libby landed hard on the mass of soft foam blocks underneath them. She felt his arms around her waist and his body pressed against hers for longer than necessary after they landed, even though it was only for a couple of seconds. It made her very aware of the fact that the fall had caused her red varsity shorts to ride up a little. Her left butt cheek was now pretty much only covered by the foam surrounding her.

Once Wentworth finally released her, Libby found herself having to wriggle to the surface of the pit as their combined weight had dropped them a fair way in. When she broke the surface, she was barely an arm's length away from Wentworth who had already adjusted himself so he looked like he was comfortably reclined in a La-Z-Boy.

"You really hate to lose, don't you?" Libby laughed as she adjusted herself so she was lying parallel to him in the very same reclined position.

"Oh yeah," Wentworth admitted freely. "It's one of my worst qualities."

"What's your best then?" Libby asked, trying to discretely sort out her shorts situation.

Wentworth pursed his lips together as he contemplated her question.

"Listening, I reckon," he replied.

Libby shrugged.

"I'll give you that," she replied. "You're a pretty good listener."

Wentworth raised an eyebrow at her.

"What?!" Libby laughed.

"No smart-ass comment today to accompany that compliment?" Wentworth asked.

Libby smiled and shook her head.

"Guess it's just a genuine compliment, Turner," Libby replied.

"Wow," Wentworth nodded. "Must be my lucky day."

As she laughed again, Libby looked down. She caught sight of her white T-shirt and realized just how see-through it was. She would have normally picked a white T-shirt bra to wear underneath the white cotton fabric, but unfortunately, all of hers were sitting in her overflowing laundry basket ready to be hand washed. So she wouldn't be running any later than she already was this morning, she picked the first bra that she thought could potentially pass for white. The ivory-colored lace bra was, however, not the best option as it would have only maybe passed for white if they were in a completely dark room and she was underneath a thick weighted blanket. She sighed as she realized the color wasn't the only issue. The lace was obvious through the cotton and sticking out like the sore thumb that was Christie Ecles' fashion sense.

"So, humor me this," Wentworth said, "because I feel like putting my fantastic listening skills to the test."

Libby turned her head to face him and realized that he was now lying on his side, completely facing her. She could have also sworn in her moment of distraction that he had moved three or four inches closer to her. The grey fabric of his T-shirt was now close enough that it was brushing against a couple of stray leg hairs that indicated she was overdue for a wax. She raised her eyebrows at him as an invitation for him to continue.

"The other night," Wentworth said, "at that party I took you to."

"Yeah?" Libby asked.

"The name Beth seemed to roll off your tongue pretty quickly," Wentworth continued. "So, I mean—"

"Where did it come from?" Libby asked, figuring out what Wentworth was trying to ask her before he found the words he was looking for.

He nodded. Libby broke their eye contact as she looked straight ahead at the rock-climbing walls in front of the foam pit.

"Beth was what my mom used to call me," Libby replied. "I haven't gone by Beth since she died. Actually, no one's called me Beth since she died, not even my dad."

Wentworth nodded as Libby turned back to face him.

"You don't talk about your mom a lot, do you?" he asked.

Libby shook her head.

"Honestly?" she asked.

Wentworth nodded.

"Apart from you," she continued, "I don't know a lot of good listeners, so I don't really bother."

Wentworth nodded again.

"So, you said it'd been five years?" Wentworth asked.

Libby could hear the hesitation in his tone. Like each of his words was tiptoeing on eggshells. Asking someone about their dead parent, no matter how well you knew them or what the circumstances were, wasn't ever an easy conversation to start.

"It was five years in February," Libby answered.

"What happened?" Wentworth asked.

Libby sighed and turned on her side so that her position was the mirror image of his. She propped her arm up underneath her head and let her head rest in her open palm. She placed her other hand in front of her chest to balance herself, and to also cover up her horrible bra choice.

"Do you really want me to tell you about it?" Libby asked.

Wentworth adjusted himself as if he were trying to convey with his body language that he was ready to listen to her story.

"That's your call," Wentworth replied. "Your story. Your call."

Libby nodded. She hesitated for a moment as she tried to shuffle through her thoughts to figure out where to begin. She hadn't told someone about Yolanda Evans since she'd briefly mentioned her to Ace when they first got together. At the mention of her mom in passing, Ace's response was, *"I'm sure it's hard to talk about your mom so I don't want you to have to tell that story. I can just Google it."* Whilst her mom was definitely Googleable, being the first wife of the Privileged Pictures CEO, unfortunately, the first ten search results were no longer about her many philanthropic ventures and all the good she did for the homeless communities in downtown LA. Now when you Googled her, it was all about how she died and photos of what her funeral looked like.

"My mom," Libby said, "was the most beautiful woman."

Wentworth smiled at her, and Libby found herself smiling back.

"I mean, I don't just think that because I'm her daughter," she continued, "she genuinely was the most beautiful woman ever. I remember when I was younger, just absolutely idolizing her. Her skin was flawless, this beautiful olive color. Her hair was perfect. She had these beautiful dark brown curls that just sat perfectly all the time. They weren't natural. Her hair was like mine, dead straight, but gosh she pulled off curls like they were made for her."

"I remember at the party you said something about her going to Columbia," Wentworth said. "Was that true?"

Libby nodded.

"She majored in English at Columbia in the 90s," Libby continued. "She wanted to be an editor, so after college, she moved to LA and started working as a publishing assistant at Paperdoll Books. I think she said that she met my dad at a book launch for the company."

"Did she want you to be a legacy?" Wentworth asked.

"How did you know?" Libby asked, her eyes narrowing at him.

"My dad went to UCLA back in the late 80s," Wentworth explained. "Unfortunately for him, what I wanted to do I couldn't do there, and whilst he was supportive about me forging my own path, I knew he was disappointed I didn't go to his legacy school."

Libby nodded.

"Mom wanted me to go to college," she continued. "Columbia would have been her first preference, had it been up to her, but really she just wanted me to go to college period."

"And you didn't want to?" Wentworth asked.

Libby sighed.

"I mean, I thought about it a lot but then I kind of fell into modeling," she said, "and I..."

Libby's voice trailed off as she focused on her fingers as they stroked one of the foam blocks sitting directly in front of her.

"And what?" Wentworth asked.

"And I love it," Libby replied, still looking at her foam block as she smiled. "I love modeling. Every time I walk down a runway it's the best time I've ever had. It's just such a rush. It's a bit hard to explain, but there's nothing like it."

Libby lifted her gaze and noticed that Wentworth was watching her intently. A smile formed at the corners of his lips as he continued to listen to her story.

"Mom got it," Libby smiled. "She let me model all I wanted in my teens. She let me finish high school through homeschooling so that I could focus on building my portfolio. She supported what I wanted, but at the same time, she wanted me to have options. So, she made me a deal when I got my high school diploma. I could keep modeling if I sat my SATs and got at least a 1400."

"Wow," Wentworth said, "that's quite the expectation."

"Yeah, it was," Libby nodded, "but, like you, I'm competitive by nature and wanted to prove to her that I could do it. I was only seventeen, but I knew I didn't want to go to college back then. I wanted to make it as a model, and I was willing to do whatever it took. I was willing to work my ass off for it. Whether that meant attending a million casting calls every season. Whether that meant getting every inch of my body waxed religiously every four weeks. Whether that meant working out six days a week, or whether that meant sitting the SATs and getting a 1400. I was going to do whatever it took."

"Wow!" Wentworth exclaimed again.

"Modeling is a lot of work," Libby added. "Most people don't realize how much work it actually is because it appears to be so glamorous."

"I can't believe that you get waxed every four weeks!" Wentworth exclaimed. "That is a lot of torture to put yourself through! That's like twelve waxes a year! At least!"

Libby laughed. Of course, the only part of what she said that registered with him was about her body waxing regime.

"You get pretty used to it," she explained, "and it hurts less the more you do it."

"So, you sat the SATs?" Wentworth asked.

Libby was glad for the change off the topic of something with as many sexual connotations as body waxing. She was very much aware of several reasons why discussing things of a sexual nature with Wentworth was inappropriate right now; one was her boyfriend, two was how long it had been since she'd had sex, and three was how aware she was that Wentworth's hand was now just inches from hers, balancing on the same foam brick.

"I did," Libby replied, snapping herself out of her thoughts. "I sat them a month before I turned eighteen."

"How did you go?" Wentworth asked.

"I got my score back a couple of weeks after the test like you usually do," Libby started. "I remember calling my mom to tell her my score and I was so pissed off at her because she didn't pick up her phone. I can't remember a time when she ever answered my call on the first try, so of course, that time wasn't any different. I remember I left her an annoyed voicemail telling her how pissed I was that she was, as usual, not answering her phone when I called. I told her what my score was and then I hung up. I didn't hear back from her like I usually did whenever she missed my first call. I texted her after an hour and still didn't hear anything. I texted my dad an hour after that and I didn't hear back from him either. It wasn't until it had been four hours after I made that first call that my dad called me."

Libby paused. She could feel how labored her breathing was becoming and she could feel the heaviness in her eyelids as her vision started to blur. The only thing that was keeping her together was the feeling of Wentworth's hand on hers. She didn't know when his hand had finally closed the gap and found hers, but the feeling of his warm flesh on hers was what she was currently trying to focus on. Her eyes were locked on one of the foam bricks underneath one of her feet. Her mind was focused on the rose gold Tiffany toe ring she was currently wearing as she traced the engraved leaf pattern backward and forward with her eyes.

"I can still hear my dad's voice when he told me that she had died," Libby continued. "He could barely breathe let alone talk when he called me from the hospital. He told me that she'd been in a car accident on the I-10. A driver that was fucked up on MDMA had crossed into her lane and caused a head-on collision. The paramedics that arrived on the scene first did all they could do to stabilize her, but she died in the ambulance on the way to the hospital."

Libby took a deep breath as she had finally composed herself enough to look Wentworth in the eye. His face was expressionless but now that she was looking at him, he squeezed her hand. Libby looked down at their now entwined fingers for a second before she looked back at him.

"I can't remember the last thing she said to me," Libby sighed. "I can't remember the last thing I said to her. I don't know whether she got my voicemail before she died and knew that I'd gotten a 1500 in the SATs like I knew she believed I could. Every day that goes by, I remember less and less about her and it fucking hurts. I can't remember what her voice sounds like anymore. I can't remember what she smells like. It's only been five years and it feels as raw as if it happened yesterday, but at the same time it feels like it's been a lifetime since she was here."

Libby suddenly stopped talking. She stopped when she realized where she was in her recount of her mom's death. She realized how heavy the conversation had gotten and just how unexpected it was that she was getting so in-depth and personal with this guy that she still didn't even know that well. She'd never gotten this in-depth and personal about her mom with Ace. In fact, she'd never gotten this in-depth and personal with Ace about anything.

"Wow, that was a hectic trip down memory lane," Libby laughed, trying to shake herself out of her thoughts as she sat up from her reclined position.

As she sat up, she retracted her hand from Wentworth's and tried to make it look like she had something that she needed to do with her hands. She saw the scrunchie around her wrist and used it to throw her hair up into a messy bun on the top of her head.

"You OK?" Wentworth asked, watching her intently as she continued to slowly tend to her hair.

Libby couldn't look him in the eye, but she could feel him staring at her.

"Yeah," she replied as she threaded her hair through the scrunchie.

"You sure?" Wentworth asked again.

Libby took a deep breath as she realized that she was doing a poor job of hiding her bullshit right now. She secured the scrunchie in her hair, drew her legs into her chest, and then finally looked Wentworth in the eye.

"I'm OK," Libby said, forcing a small smile.

Wentworth nodded as he adjusted his position so that he was now sitting cross-legged and facing her. Mirroring her new position.

"You know," Libby said, as she rested her hands on her knees, "I haven't told that story to a guy before."

"Why not?" Wentworth said.

"No one's ever asked," Libby replied.

"Ace?" Wentworth asked.

"Nah," Libby said, shaking her head. "It's hard for him to ask about things he doesn't care about, and he doesn't care about a lot of things that aren't about him."

"I care about you," Wentworth said.

Libby could tell by the look on his face that he hadn't meant to blurt out those words just then. Regardless, the words were now out. He'd said them and she'd heard them, clear as day.

"I know you do," Libby smiled. "I wouldn't have told you all that if I didn't, on some level, know that."

"Libby," Wentworth said.

Libby could feel his breath on her face as she tried to avoid looking him in the eyes. She was painfully aware of how close they were. They had been this close before, but this was the first time she knew for sure that she wanted him to kiss her. They'd come close a few times on their last few dates, but she knew for certain right now that she wanted him to kiss her. She wanted to feel his lips on hers. She wanted to close her eyes and surrender to this moment, and it made her so nervous. She could feel her heart pounding in her chest, and she could hear it in her ears. It was taking every bit of concentration to remind herself to breathe.

It was then that she felt Wentworth shuffle even closer to her. They were both still sitting cross-legged in the middle of the foam pit. His movement caused her eyes to dart and suddenly they were locked on his. Those bright green eyes were completely unreadable as they stared back at her almost blankly. She took a deep breath as she forced herself to keep his eye contact like it would pull him toward her and close the small gap between them. She wanted to do it herself, but she was too chicken. She wanted him to make the first move. She wanted him to kiss her, not the other way around. In this moment right here, time almost standing still as green eyes mixed with brown, she just wanted Wentworth to kiss her. No thought of the consequences. No thought of Victoria's Secret, Ace, or The Brat Pack. No thought of anything except the two of them. Libby was so sure it was going to happen, but just as quickly as the moment appeared, it was gone.

Wentworth rolled onto his back, sinking slightly into the foam bricks as he did so. Libby drew her knees into her chest and started fiddling with her T ring so that her eyes would have something to focus on. Wentworth just stared blankly up at the gymnasium ceiling.

"I'm sorry," Wentworth finally mumbled.

"For what?" Libby asked, looking at him carefully as she tried to read him.

He just continued to stare at the ceiling.

"I'm just sorry," Wentworth said.

Libby didn't say anything. Again, silence surrounded them for what felt like an eternity. Libby was very aware, for the first time today, that Wentworth was wearing a watch. Only because the ticking of the watch's second-hand now sounded like it was booming in the quiet empty gym without the sound of their voices. She went back to fiddling with her ring. Noting how dull the rose gold was, she made a mental note to polish it up when she got home.

"It sounds like you and your mom were really close," Wentworth finally said.

Libby watched him return to a sitting position as he spoke, and she smiled at him. She wasn't expecting such a thoughtful comment. She was, honestly, just praying for any change in conversation topic that would break the deafening silence, especially based on what had almost happened just moments before. Even though she hadn't said it out loud, she felt almost embarrassed that she had wanted the kiss so badly. Even though she hadn't said it, she still felt like Wentworth knew it too.

"She was the person I went to for advice about everything," Libby said. "Fashion advice. Love advice. Life advice. I'd been going to her for everything since I was a little girl. When she died, I lost all that. When she died, I had to rely on my friends for more than I think they were willing to be relied on for."

"Sounds like you might need some new friends," Wentworth added.

"Don't say that," Libby snapped. "They're good people."

Wentworth threw his hands up in defeat.

"Hey, they're not my friends," Wentworth said. "You obviously know them better than I do."

Libby rolled her eyes. Maybe it was time to cut her losses and avoid another embarrassing moment of thinking that Wentworth kissing her was anything other than a horrendously terrible idea. Maybe it was time to call it a day before this conversation continued its direction south.

"Look I think should just go," Libby said.

"You don't have to be like that," Wentworth sighed.

"Like what?" Libby snapped back.

"Like that!" Wentworth gestured toward her.

"Well, I don't feel like sitting here and listening to you verbally bash my friends!" Libby exclaimed.

"Well then forget I said it!" Wentworth exclaimed back.

Libby eyed him and he sighed.

"Forget I said anything," Wentworth repeated, his voice returning to its normal tone and volume.

Libby watched him intently and she could see that he meant well. She knew that he hadn't meant to raise his voice and say what he had about her friends, but she could already feel the heat rising in her cheeks. Her emotions were already heightened to the point of no return.

"No," Libby said shaking her head. "I need to go."

"Why do you need to go?" Wentworth pushed.

Libby ignored his question and uncrossed her legs as she looked around for the best way to exit the foam pit.

"Why do you need to go?" Wentworth repeated, reaching out to catch her arm.

"I need to go!" Libby exclaimed again as she brushed away his outstretched hand.

"You don't," Wentworth said.

"Why should I stay?" Libby asked. "This is stupid anyway."

"What's stupid?" Wentworth asked.

"This," Libby said gesturing between them. "All of this. This date. All these dates. All of this."

"Why is it stupid?" Wentworth continued to probe.

"Because you're not my boyfriend," Libby bit back. "I already have a boyfriend and I'm doing this for him. I'm not doing this because I have a choice. You didn't give me a choice."

"You had a choice," Wentworth said.

"Like hell, I had a choice!" Libby exclaimed.

Wentworth's probing and pushing were really starting to make her blood boil. Whether he was trying to do it intentionally or not she wasn't sure, but it didn't even matter at this point.

"Either I do this with you, or you ruin my relationship and my reputation," Libby continued. "Yeah. It was a great choice you gave me."

"I know it's not ideal but we're here now," Wentworth said.

"What does that even mean?" Libby asked, looking Wentworth dead in the eyes as if she were trying to get an answer from them while she waited for one from his lips.

"Tell me that you don't feel something here," Wentworth said. "That you don't feel something between us. Tell me that you don't feel something for me."

Libby didn't say anything. She had gotten the straight answer she wanted. He had answered her, plain and simple, but now she was the one who couldn't find the words. She knew that it was just a matter of time before he threw those words in her face. The ones about how he felt about her. The ones about what was going on between them. She knew it because it was the same thing that popped up in her mind every single time he looked at her. She felt it every time he touched her, and every time she was with him.

"There's something here, Libby," Wentworth continued. "I can feel it, and I know you can feel it too. Tell me I'm wrong."

Before Libby knew it, she could feel his hand on hers again, and it was then that she realized that she'd stopped trying to leave. She was still sitting cross-legged in the middle of the foam pit having this conversation with him.

"I love Ace," Libby said.

She knew full well it was a cop-out and that it probably wasn't going to go down well, but it was the truth. It probably wasn't as true as it had once been, but somewhere in her heart, she knew she still loved Ace.

"Yeah, well I seriously doubt that," Wentworth mumbled.

He'd mumbled it under his breath, yet it was loud enough that Libby had heard it because they were sitting so close.

"This is ridiculous!" Libby exclaimed, realizing that this was the wrong place to be right now as she quickly retracted her hand from Wentworth's again. "I don't have to listen to this."

"OK, that was out of line," Wentworth said calmly. "I shouldn't have said that. I'm sorry."

"Damn straight it was out of line!" Libby exclaimed. "I am done with this right now."

"Beth, please," Wentworth said.

"Don't you ever call me that!" Libby exclaimed.

Wentworth stopped where he was. Libby could see in his eyes that he knew he had stepped over a line, but it was too late. It was done, and if she hadn't been angry before, she was definitely angry now. If he had any chance of getting her to stay before, he had shattered that chance with just one word. She felt the heat rising in her cheeks and she felt the tears building behind her eyes.

"You don't ever get to call me that," Libby repeated. "Ever."

She knew that he wasn't going to try and stop her from leaving, and she was thankful for that because it turned out to be a lot harder to get out of the foam pit than she initially thought. She made sure that part of her exit strategy required her back to be turned away from him because she knew that she wasn't going to be able to stop the tears this time.

She hadn't brought a bag with her today, so she left straight out the double glass doors to the gym as soon as she had escaped the foam pit. No words were spoken by either of them as she left. It wasn't until she felt the brisk May air on her cheeks that she realized they were covered in tears. She hurriedly brushed them off her face and just kept walking. She needed to compose herself a little before she could even think about calling her car service and retreating to Sierra Towers.

She was frustrated with her tears. Not just because she was shedding them, but because of what they represented. Her tears were a combination of sadness from all the dredging up of stories about her mother, memories that she hadn't faced properly in five years, and heartache. That feeling in the pit of her stomach that felt like she'd just had her heart broken or had the wind knocked right out of her. She wasn't sure why she felt it, but it was unmistakable because she was no stranger to heartache.

It was strange to feel it today though because she wasn't sure if that heartache was to do with the boyfriend that she was sure she still loved and had betrayed, or whether it was heartache for the other boy in her life. The one that wasn't even supposed to be in her life at all. The one that made her feel things that she wasn't sure she'd ever felt before. The one she knew she could never be with. Whether it was because of Victoria's Secret or Ace Thatcher, she knew that she could never let herself love Wentworth Turner.

17

Date #7

"Hey," Wentworth said. "How've you been?"

He ran his fingers through his hair in frustration before he quickly looked around to check that no one had just heard him having a conversation with himself out loud in the middle of downtown Hollywood. Truth be told, however, with the number of homeless people downtown he probably wouldn't have stood out that much anyway.

He had been waiting for Libby to show up for date seven for the past twenty-five minutes. She was running late, which wasn't like her, so he was starting to panic about what it might mean. It was 7:00 am on a Saturday, though, so maybe she had overslept after the *MTV Movie and TV Awards* last night. Even though she hadn't told him she was going, he knew she was there because he saw her on the red carpet. He was working the awards show and had nearly dropped his camera in the paparazzi mosh pit when he saw what she was wearing.

He didn't know designers or anything about couture, but he did know that she looked absolutely stunning in the white bodysuit pants thing she was wearing. It was almost like watching her in slow motion as she walked the red carpet, the curls in her hair almost floating in the breeze. Thankfully his job last night was to take photos of all the beautiful people on the red carpet, so he had plenty of reasons to just stare at her. Just how much staring he had done was pretty evident by the hundreds of photos of Libby he had racked up on his camera.

Last night was the first time he'd seen her in weeks. The last time was at the Caltech gym when things had gone from good, to bad, to good again, and then to really bad. It meant that Wentworth was particularly nervous about seeing her again this morning. So much so that he was making an idiot of himself rehearsing what he was going to say when he finally did see her. That was if he saw her at all.

She had been pretty upset at him the last time they'd met, evident by her storming off out of the Caltech gym, and he had been kicking himself for the last sixteen days for not keeping his stupid, big mouth shut. He wasn't sure how he had expected her to react when he had said the things he had. Maybe he had expected her to profess her love for him and break up with her oil heir billionaire boyfriend. It sounded even stupider now that he was thinking about it for the eight hundredth time.

Ding! Ding!

Wentworth nearly jumped out of his skin as his phone went off in his hand. He looked down at the screen and saw that a text message from Libby had just come through. Part of him was relieved that she wasn't ignoring him, but another part of him was freaking out just thinking about what she had to say. He took a deep breath and opened the message.

So sorry – I am running

> **really late! Text me the
> address and I'll meet you
> there!**

Wentworth sighed in relief. He started walking in the direction of where date seven was going to be and started texting Libby back as he did so.

> **3740 Sunset Blvd. See
> you soon!**

He ummed and ahhed for longer than he would admit about whether to finish the message off with an exclamation point or a period. He shook his head at himself as he shoved his phone back in his pocket and continued walking, wondering how he was keeping himself upright considering how hard he was mentally kicking himself for being such an idiot. He headed a little further down the block to his destination and entered without a second thought.

He'd been volunteering at least once a week at FETC(h): For the Ethical Treatment of Canines since his sophomore year. FETC(h) was a canine specialty animal shelter in downtown Hollywood. It was just the one shelter for now, but they did have plans to expand the brand to other parts of California over the next couple of years. The facility had developed in leaps and bounds since Wentworth had started volunteering here and now consisted of shelter facilities for stray dogs, as well as a dog washing parlor and a small retail store that sold everything from dog toys to clothing and accessories.

Wentworth waved to Karen as he entered through the front door. He headed straight through the clear PVC strip doors that led from the front of the store, which could be seen from the road through the glass windows, into the shelter. Karen was the usual shop assistant that worked on a Saturday morning and Wentworth was the usual shelter assistant until Parker and Immy showed up at 11:00 am, when Wentworth's shift ended. When his shift started at 7:00 am there generally weren't that many people who came through to the shelter portion. Business only picked up around midday, so it seemed like the perfect place for him and Libby to have their seventh date.

Wentworth had just retrieved the working smocks from the storage cupboard when he heard the front doorbell. He rushed to the strip doors and poked his head through them just as Libby was entering the front shop.

"She's with me, Karen," Wentworth called out as he motioned, with a nod, for Libby to head over in his direction.

"Sorry, I'm late!" Libby exclaimed as she rushed over to him.

"Don't worry about it," Wentworth smiled as he pushed some of the PVC strips aside so that Libby could follow him through to the animal shelter.

Just like when he had entered, Libby's entry caused most of the dogs to start barking like crazy as their collar tags started hitting the bars of the metal cages, making an absolute racket.

"Yeah, we know guys," Wentworth called to the dogs as he looked around. "We know. We know."

Wentworth turned to Libby, who was smiling from ear to ear as she looked around the room.

"You like dogs, right?" Wentworth asked as he handed her one of the smocks he was holding.

Libby nodded enthusiastically. Wentworth threw his smock over his head and watched as Libby did the same. He had picked a blue smock for himself whilst Libby's was red, but they were both covered in the same bold yellow and orange paw prints. Libby laughed as she looked down at how baggy her smock was, even though it was ridiculously short.

"None of the sizes are good, unfortunately," Wentworth also laughed as he noticed what was going on.

He looked down at his smock. Whilst it was always his go-to because it fit him reasonably well height and width wise, there were at least three holes on the front of it and what appeared to be a tear that was fraying along the front hem

"Eh," Libby shrugged. "It's not important."

"If it helps," Wentworth offered, "I'm pretty sure everything looks good on you."

Libby didn't say anything, she just looked down at her smock once more and adjusted the hem, so it sat flatter than it had moments earlier. Once she was satisfied with it, she placed her hands on her hips and her eyes lifted to meet his.

"Is it weird when I say things like that?" Wentworth asked when Libby didn't respond to his comment.

He started walking toward the back of the shop to start putting things together for the first job of the morning.

"Like what?" Libby asked.

"About how hot you are," he said.

Libby laughed. She had obviously noticed that he had started moving around and had decided to follow him.

"No," she said shaking her head as she smiled back at him.

"Are you sure?" Wentworth asked.

"Yeah, I'm sure," Libby said. "Don't stress it."

Wentworth paused and stopped walking, causing Libby to nearly run into him. He turned around to face her and had she not quickly shuffled backward, he was sure that they would have been touching.

"Look, I'm really sorry about what happened on our last date," Wentworth blurted out.

It had been playing on his mind all morning but, unfortunately, he had a lot less chill than he thought he had. Even after that pep talk he had given himself about half an hour earlier.

"It's fine, Went," Libby said.

He felt his heart flutter in his chest as she called him 'Went'. There was something ridiculously sexy about the way she spoke his name that just made his insides do all kinds of ridiculous gymnastic stunts. It made him thankful that she called him 'Turner' most of the time.

"Are you sure?" Wentworth asked. "I really am sorry. It wasn't my place, and it was way out of line for me to make that kind of comment about your boyfriend and—"

"Don't stress it," Libby said, cutting him off. "It's fine. Really."

"You're sure?" Wentworth asked one more time.

"Yes!" Libby exclaimed with another laugh as she reached out to playfully punch him in the arm. "Now, are you going to tell me exactly what we're doing here?"

Wentworth thought about apologizing just one more time but decided to leave it and take Libby's word for it that it really was OK. Whether it was OK because she was over it or whether it was because he had apologized, he wasn't sure, but he decided to leave it anyway. He gave Libby the grand tour of the small animal shelter, including the dog cages that lined two and a half of the walls in the large room, as well as the examination table and the storage facilities that held all the equipment they needed. He explained that his job on a Saturday was to pull all the individual dogs out of their cages, clean their water bowls and cages thoroughly with hot soapy water, and refill water and food.

"Whatever we don't get done this morning, the afternoon shift will get done when they come in at 11:00 am," Wentworth finished.

"Cool," Libby nodded. "So, I suppose I'm here to help you out today?"

"I thought it might be fun," Wentworth replied. "Plus, if anyone sees you here you can always say that you're doing charity work for your image?"

"Sure," Libby laughed.

"OK," Wentworth smiled. "Want to get the first pup out?"

"Yeah," Libby replied, her eyes lighting up as she looked from one end of the cages to the other. "Right side?"

"Yep," Wentworth replied as he moved to the sink to get the hot soapy water mixture started. "Tatum. The big golden lab. He's always first."

Wentworth watched Libby as she confidently approached Tatum's cage. The lab's tail started going crazy and he let out an excited little howl as Libby bent down in front of his cage. Wentworth got the hot water running into a bucket in the sink as he watched Libby start chatting away to Tatum. She opened the cage door and gave him a multitude of pats and cuddles before clipping one of the communal yellow shelter leashes onto his collar.

"Where do you want him?" Libby asked as she walked Tatum over to Wentworth.

Wentworth watched as Tatum sat down next to Libby as she stopped walking. Her hand absentmindedly started running through the fur on the top of his head. Tatum was a tall dog, so Libby didn't have to bend down to reach him, even with those long supermodel legs of hers.

"I didn't realize you were such a big dog lover," Wentworth commented.

Libby smiled as she looked down at Tatum and increased the intensity of his head pats.

Wentworth was a massive dog lover himself so watching Libby be with a dog in such a natural and loving way made something inside him feel warm, as cheesy as it was. He could feel that warmth radiating all through his body as he watched her hands gently stroke Tatum's head. She seemed to not mind at all when Tatum started rubbing himself against her leg to get closer to her. Wentworth could already see the thick layer of golden fur building up on Libby's jeans.

"Did you honestly bring me here not knowing whether or not I liked dogs?" Libby laughed.

"Honestly," Wentworth replied, "I had a feeling you were a dog person."

"Would have been a shitty date if I hated dogs," Libby said.

"You'd be a pretty shitty person if you hated dogs," Wentworth added.

Libby eyed him for a second and crouched down to give Tatum, who was getting restless more cuddles.

"It's one of your deal-breakers, isn't it?" Libby asked.

"For what?" Wentworth asked.

"For relationships," Libby clarified.

Wentworth thought about it for a moment. He hadn't really given it much thought before now. Obviously, when he pictured his life in the future with his wife and children, the ones he knew he wanted someday, he always saw a dog sitting there in the picture too.

"Yeah," Wentworth nodded. "I mean, I hadn't given it much thought before, but yeah it's definitely a deal-breaker."

Libby nodded.

"I mean you're pre-vet," she added as she stood up again. "It makes sense that animals would be an important part of your life."

Wentworth showed Libby where to tether Tatum's leash so they could get to work on his cage.

"What's your deal-breaker?" Wentworth asked. "Or at least one of them?"

Libby made a face that indicated she was mulling the question over. She headed back in the direction of Tatum's cage to retrieve his food bowl so it could be refilled with the dog biscuits from the large black bin sitting in the back corner of the room.

"Kids," Libby replied. "That's probably the biggest one."

"As in a guy not wanting to have kids?" Wentworth clarified.

"That would definitely be a deal-breaker," Libby nodded. "You weren't expecting that answer, were you?"

Wentworth was caught off guard by Libby's question and realized that his facial expression must have given his thoughts away.

"No, I wasn't," he replied honestly. "I didn't think supermodels thought much about things like that."

"Well, I don't plan on being a supermodel forever," Libby smiled before she turned away and got back to her job of filling up the dog feed.

Wentworth smiled back, even though her back was turned and she couldn't see him. He watched her for a moment longer before he got back to work too.

Wentworth and Libby spent the next couple of hours working from Tatum to Georgie and all the shelter dogs in between. Wentworth worked on cleaning the cages and dog bowls whilst Libby darted here and there to fill in the rest of the jobs. Once the water bowls and the feed were refilled in each dog's cage, Libby often had some downtime before Wentworth was ready for the next cage to be emptied.

Wentworth caught her biding her time by sitting on the floor and giving cuddles to the dog whose cage was currently being cleaned. The dogs were clearly in love with her as Wentworth often saw them lying on the floor, on their backs, begging for every single pat that

Libby had in her. Her face was lit up the entire time, which meant that Wentworth had a hard time focusing on what he was supposed to be doing. Occasionally he found himself just staring at her, only realizing it when the hot soapy water that was meant to be inside the cage ended up all down the front of his smock and had started soaking his T-shirt underneath. It was just so hard not to stare when he was seeing a side to Libby Evans that had started to appear more often the more dates they went on.

It was almost like she was a different person from the person she was on their first date. He still didn't know everything about her, because after all, it had only been seven dates, but he was starting to be sure that the Libby Evans he was seeing now was the real one. Not the pretentious supermodel and member of the famous Hollywood Brat Pack that he'd constantly read about in the tabloids. The one that was happier than he'd ever seen her sitting on the dirty floor of a downtown Hollywood animal shelter, wearing a ridiculous paw print smock, and cuddling as many dogs as she could get her hands on. Even if those hands were perfectly manicured, those hands were getting incredibly dirty, and she didn't seem to mind one bit. This person that was starting to shine out of her was one that Wentworth was having a hard time keeping out of his mind.

"Do we have another bag of this particular feed?" Libby said, breaking Wentworth out of his thoughts and forcing him to reverse out of the cage he was currently in on his hands and knees. "This bin is nearly empty."

"Yeah," Wentworth said, getting to his feet. "It's just in the storeroom. Come. I'll show you."

Wentworth headed in the direction of the storeroom. Libby followed close behind him, leaving Salt and Pepper, two Maltese terrier crossbreeds, tethered to the metal leash hooks on the wall.

Wentworth didn't realize how narrow the storeroom was until both he and Libby were in there. It was mostly filled with cleaning and medical supplies, such as worming and flea tablets, at least fifty different types of dog shampoo, grooming brushes, and gentle dish soap. Wentworth flicked the light switch, and it took a moment before the fluorescent light above their heads turned on and illuminated the room.

"Feed is all the way back here," Wentworth explained as he walked in between the shelves, being careful not to knock anything down.

The narrow room meant that he couldn't see Libby walking behind him, but he could hear her footsteps and her voice, indicating that she was still following him.

"It's a little jam-packed in here," she commented.

"Yeah," Wentworth said. "It's not exactly the biggest storeroom for what we need it for, and the loading bay is all the way at the end, which is why the feed is back here."

Wentworth and Libby reached the roller door, which was the exit into the alley behind the building and the loading bay where feed supplies were dropped off on a fortnightly basis. Next to the roller door were bags upon bags of dog food. Most of it was the same flavor they always ordered - chicken in the purple packets. However, they'd been branching out with different flavors recently so there were also some green tuna and red beef bags in the mix. Wentworth turned to Libby.

"Think you can carry a bag?" he asked. "They're thirty-two pounds each."

Libby leaned around him to properly inspect the bags.

"I kicked your ass last date in that gym, remember?" Libby asked cheekily.

Wentworth laughed.

"But my arms were sore from a grueling day at the gym the day before," Wentworth replied.

Libby laughed out loud.

"Since when are you ever at the gym?" Libby laughed.

"I could be at the gym!" Wentworth exclaimed in his defense.

Libby cocked an eyebrow at him, and he laughed in response.

"This is my gym," he replied, using his arms to gesture to all the bags around them. "I get to lift at least thirty-two pounds every time I'm here."

Libby laughed.

"OK, OK, Schwarzenegger," Libby said. "How many bags are we taking back in?"

"Let's just take one each for now," Wentworth replied. "We can always restock the bin once we've finished with the cages. Plus, I think if we leave Salt and Pepper alone any longer, those two are going to Houdini themselves out of their collars."

"OK," Libby laughed.

It was then that they locked eyes and Wentworth knew that this was his moment. Libby looked like a mess from all this morning's activities. She was covered in dog hair all down her work smock and jeans. Her hair, which always seemed to be up in a messy bun on top of her head with a grey scrunchie, was falling in loose little bits everywhere, and her cheeks were flushed from how high Karen had pumped the heaters, even though it was June. She looked like a mess, but it only made him want to kiss her more.

He had wanted to kiss her the other week in the Caltech gym. They'd had a moment, or so he thought. He had felt like she had wanted him to kiss her as well, but he had hesitated, and he had lost his chance. He wasn't going to lose it again.

"OK, I'll just grab a purple one then," Libby spoke as she pushed one of the stray strands of hair out of her face before she turned to her right to grab the nearest bag.

Just as she turned, Wentworth reached for her arm before his brain could even register what was happening. It was probably a good thing, though, because otherwise, he would have talked himself out of doing what he was about to do. Libby stopped dead in her tracks and turned back around to face him. A small look of confusion crossed her flawless features as their eyes locked.

Wentworth took a deep breath and pulled Libby flush against him. One hand remained on the part of her forearm that he'd managed to catch as he tried to stop her from leaving the storeroom, whilst the other had found a spot on her lower back. His lips met hers in one swift motion, firm at first and then more tender as he relaxed into the feel of her lips.

Something about it felt familiar, which was no surprise. This was, after all, not technically their first kiss. It was, however, the first kiss he could, and would, remember. He felt himself subconsciously holding his breath as he waited for a response from Libby.

He had accepted the fact that the kiss was going to catch her off-guard, which was why she felt so tense up against him. He knew he would have to wait a moment for her initial shock to wear off before he could read a reaction from her. It was either going to be what he was hoping for – that she had wanted the kiss too and would kiss him back. The other option, which was just as likely though, was that she was going to push him away and probably slap him for breaching the terms of their business arrangement. He could almost feel the slap coming, as he mentally anticipated it, but then Libby kissed him back.

He felt her relax into his arms, which instinctively made his hand from her forearm move toward her face as he cupped her cheek to deepen the kiss she returned. He felt her soft hands on his body. One coming to rest on his shoulder, and the other wrapping around his waist. It was only when the kiss was interrupted by the sudden barking coming from the shelter that Wentworth realized he could have stayed in that kiss forever.

Libby was the first to break away as the sound of Salt and Pepper's high-pitched barks shattered the silence in the storeroom. Wentworth watched her intently as she breathed heavily. Her eyes focused on a spot of floor just in front of her. Her arms, whether intentionally or not, retracted into her body slowly. Her hands clasped together as she drew them tightly into her chest. He wanted to say something, but he didn't know what. The plus side was that she still hadn't slapped him, but that didn't make it any easier for him to read her as she just continued to stand there, breathing heavily as she did so.

Wentworth waited another moment for any kind of reaction from her before Salt and Pepper started barking more vigorously. He sighed as he ran through the storeroom back to the shelter area where he was met with the sight of Salt playfully gnawing on Pepper's neck. Their leashes were completely entwined so their collars were now touching, and they had very limited range of movement away from each other.

"What the hell are you two idiots doing?" Wentworth laughed as Salt and Pepper's tails started going crazy when they realized he was talking to them and walking their way.

Wentworth removed the two leashes from the tether and untangled them whilst the two small dogs bounced up and down the entire time. They scratched his jeans with their small paws and the claws of their front feet. He put them back in their cage together, noting that Libby had already filled up their food and water.

Once Salt and Pepper were contained, Wentworth turned around and noticed that Libby wasn't behind him, or in the shelter area at all. He double-checked the room, making sure Salt and Pepper's cage was fully locked, and that no other dogs were out of their cages before he headed back into the storeroom in search of Libby. He worked his way through the narrow room to the roller door and found her exactly where he had left her.

She was still staring at that same spot of concrete floor in front of her and her feet hadn't moved an inch. Her hands, however, were now resting loosely at her sides. Wentworth waited a moment to see if she would acknowledge his presence by moving in some way, but when she didn't, he decided to take a step forward so he was standing directly in front of her. When she still didn't move, he did the first thing that felt natural to him and that was to reach out and take her hands in his.

Wentworth expected her reaction to hold a little more surprise or shock, but she easily let him take her hands and she closed her fingers around his. As her gaze finally rose to meet his, he realized how much taller than her he was when she was wearing sneakers, as opposed to those black leather heeled boots she was wearing at that costume party. As he stared into her eyes, he knew that kissing her again wasn't an option.

She didn't look upset or angry, but the vibe he was getting from her indicated that now wasn't the right time to kiss her again, no matter how much his body was urging him to do so. Her eyes were drowning in emotion, but they were emotions that Wentworth was still struggling to read.

He thought that he could see some confusion in there as to what had just happened and what she was now feeling, which was exactly how he was feeling right now. He wasn't sure if he could also see a little frustration there, or maybe a little guilt. He wasn't even sure if he was just assuming these things based on the emotions that he could feel bubbling up inside of him.

His thoughts were interrupted as he heard her sigh and her eyes drifted away from his for a moment before her body slowly fell against his. He felt her hands draw into her chest again as he wrapped his arms around her waist. His left arm stayed around her whilst his right moved, and his right hand came to rest at the base of her head. His fingers moved slowly through the hair around her neck and shoulders as she rested her head against his chest.

He felt her relax deeper into his embrace, so he held her tighter. Trying to understand what she was feeling. Trying to read her body language cues. Trying to give her what she needed right now, what she wanted. If only it was that simple. If only he knew what she needed and what she wanted. If only he knew what he wanted other than to hold her for as long as she would let him.

18

Busted

I can't believe you're late again Libby! Why don't you just get yourself a Rolex?!

We've been waiting for hours, as usual! So, we just went ahead and ordered without you!

Maybe we should just switch to lunch instead of brunch because Libby is ALWAYS so late!

Libby rolled her eyes as she mentally ticked off the phrases that she would, no doubt, hear this morning once she finally arrived at brunch at Silverlake. At least she would only be twenty minutes late this week, as opposed to last week when she hadn't woken up until well after brunch had started. She had to make up some lame excuse about being sick that she then had to maintain for the next couple of days. That meant canceling her appointment at Carasoin Day Spa & Skin Clinic with Anita the next day, which she had really been looking forward to!

It wasn't like she meant to be late, but with all the stuff living rent-free in her mind right now, there was just no time for sleep. It was why she needed that day spa appointment with Anita because the dark circles around her eyes were getting worse by the day.

Between Ace, Wentworth, Victoria's Secret, and the endless politics of being a member of the illustrious Hollywood Brat Pack, her mind was always running around in circles. She had spent nearly every night for the last two months mentally tracing the shape of every crystal on the chandelier above her bed and locating every loose thread on her block-out curtains. Her eyes were always deer-in-the-headlights wide every time she crawled into bed, no matter how late it was or how many cinnamon and turmeric mugs of warm milk she pre-emptively drank. It meant that Sunday morning brunch, as important as it was socially, was just trivial enough that she felt justified in hitting snooze on her alarm one more time this morning.

"Fucking finally!" Charlie exclaimed overdramatically as soon as she spotted Libby a couple of tables away.

Libby rolled her eyes underneath her Ray-Bans. She tried to focus on not falling over as she weaved her way in between the tables in the Silverlake courtyard. She'd grabbed the first pair of boots she could find in her wardrobe this morning, a pair of Manolos that she had bought when they were in New York for *Sports Illustrated*. They were a gorgeous black suede ankle boot that really completed the off-duty supermodel look she was going for this morning, with her favorite frayed denim shorts and a basic white cotton T-shirt. Unfortunately, she hadn't had a chance to break in her Manolos yet, so they were not luxuriously hugging her feet like Manolos usually did. Both her pinky toes were screaming at her, and she was sure that all the rubbing her pinky was doing inside her left boot was going to result in a blister. Libby ignored the pain as she took a seat next to Anita, throwing her Marc Jacobs x Charlie Niven bag over the back of her chair.

"Morning!" Libby exclaimed, forcing a chirpy attitude and a smile.

Her lack of sleep plus Charlie's comment were not helping her mood this morning, so she thought it best to try and just smile through it all until she could get some food and green tea into her.

"I ordered your green tea for you," Anita leaned over and whispered into Libby's ear.

Libby turned to her best friend and sighed.

"Thank you," she mouthed to Anita before she took her phone out of her front shorts pocket and placed it on the table in front of her.

"Morning Libby!" Christie Ecles chirped from her spot across the table.

Libby looked up and forced a smile in Christie's direction as her gaze drifted around the table and saw Charlie sitting to Christie's right and Willa to her left. She wasn't sure what Christie was still doing here but it looked like she was making herself very comfortable. She also wasn't sure why Christie thought that bright pink was appropriate for a Sunday brunch, especially when the hideous top was teamed with white denim jeans that went out of fashion at least fifteen years ago.

"Morning!" Willa chirped, following Christie's lead before she leaned forward on the table and turned toward Charlie. "So, like I was saying, it was the coolest thing ever!"

"What was?" Libby asked, leaning forward herself to try and join in the conversation.

Charlie rolled her eyes in Libby's direction, evident even through her Ray-Bans. Willa waited a moment to see whether Charlie was going to explain, but after a couple of seconds, it was evident that Charlie was instead going to bury herself in her phone again. Willa turned to Libby and smiled.

"Anna Wintour was photographed front row at a show at *Milan Fashion Week* last weekend with her own Marc Jacobs x Charlie Niven handbag!" Christie exclaimed excitedly.

Libby had to suppress a laugh at the look of disgust that crossed Willa's porcelain face, just for a second, because Christie had stolen Willa's opportunity to share the latest gossip with Libby.

"Oh my God, Charlie!" Libby exclaimed, being overdramatic and clapping her hands together to show Charlie how excited she was. "That is beyond amazing!"

"Yeah, I know," Charlie smiled, locking her phone, and placing it down on the table in front of her.

"And didn't you say you saw a couple of big names using them at the *MTV Awards* as well?" Willa said as she turned to face Anita.

"Yeah, I saw Zendaya with one," Anita replied, "and the Hadid sisters as well!"

"Oh, I know!" Charlie smiled. "Bella is my absolute favorite supermodel so when Marc and I were talking about who to send promo bags to she was at the top of my list!"

Libby knew Charlie's comment was a direct stab at her, and it became very clear that this morning Charlie was baiting Libby into losing her shit and making a scene. This was pretty Charlie Niven type behavior when she was pissed about something. The underhanded comments were just the beginning and Libby was starting to see that this morning was going to be full of them. With her current backlog of sleep playing against her, Libby knew she was going to have to try extra hard to keep her cool. Thankfully their drinks had just arrived, so the caffeine was at least going to give her a bit of a helping hand.

"That's amazing, Charls!" Libby exclaimed, forcing herself to sound super excited and supportive of her friend. "It sounds like just a matter of time before you and Marc collab on another limited edition!"

"It is," Charlie smiled in Libby's direction. "I was telling Christie the other day that I've been brainstorming with some of Marc's team about a tote next."

"That would be super cute!" Christie said.

"Maybe that would be good enough for you to wear to the next *MTV Awards* then, Libby?" Charlie said, the sarcasm dripping in her tone.

"Of course," Libby smiled.

It was typical that Charlie couldn't focus on the fact that Libby had bought dozens of bags when they were first released and sent them to everyone she knew. She couldn't focus on the fact that Libby had been religiously using her Marc Jacobs x Charlie Niven bag in navy every time she left the house so that she could get papped with it at every opportunity possible. She couldn't even focus on the fact that Libby was using it now at brunch, even though the bag was ridiculously small and couldn't fit half of what Libby usually put in her handbag. Charlie could only focus on the fact that Libby hadn't worn it to the *MTV Movie and TV Awards* the other night.

The white Balmain jumpsuit she was gifted for the occasion was an absolute dream to wear and Libby had been so excited that she had finally reached the point in her career where designers were starting to gift her clothing and accessories for events. It was a huge step in the model world. It meant, however, there were conditions. To wear the white Balmain jumpsuit, she had to team it with the blue satin embroidered clutch from Balmain as well. If she was being honest, though, it went better with the white jumpsuit than her Marc Jacobs x Charlie Niven would have anyway. Libby turned to face Willa and was about to open her mouth to change the subject when she was beaten to the punch.

"So, tell me, Libby," Charlie said, "where were you yesterday?"

Libby narrowed her eyes at Charlie, which thankfully couldn't be seen through her Ray-Bans.

"I had a late lunch with a couple of the Victoria's Secret girls at The Ivy," Libby smiled.

That was the truth. After her date with Wentworth, she went home, had a shower to get the smell of dog off her, and then she'd met a couple of her model friends from the Weeknd's music video for a 1:30 pm lunch at The Ivy in Santa Monica.

"Oh my God, how good are the chips and guac at The Ivy?!" Christie exclaimed.

"OK," Charlie said, totally disregarding Christie's statement, "but where were you before that?"

Libby narrowed her eyes at Charlie again. She wasn't sure where the conversation was going but she was starting to realize that she probably wasn't going to like it.

"Um... at home?" Libby offered.

"You weren't in downtown Hollywood by any chance?" Charlie asked as she propped her Ray-Bans on top of her head.

Libby saw the twinkle in Charlie's eye, and she knew that Charlie already knew the answer to that question. Charlie knew that Libby had been in downtown Hollywood yesterday morning. The question was, however, how much did Charlie exactly know? Libby had to play it cool and choose her next lies very carefully.

"What the hell were you doing in downtown Hollywood?" Anita asked.

"Yeah," Willa added. "Downtown Hollywood is so gross."

"Downtown Scummywood you mean," Charlie added. "So, what were you doing there, Libby?"

"Oh, yeah, I was in Hollywood yesterday," Libby said, keeping her cool as she took another big sip of her green tea.

"Doing what?" Christie asked.

Libby could feel the panic rising in her chest as the interrogation continued. She took a deep breath.

"I was doing some boring charity work," Libby brushed off casually.

"Charity work?" Charlie asked, clearly not believing a single word coming out of Libby's mouth as she cocked an eyebrow in her friend's direction.

Libby nodded as she too propped her sunglasses on top of her head so she could lock eyes directly with Charlie. She wanted to look Charlie in the eye as she masterfully delivered this next lie. She needed every member of The Pack to believe her charity story enough to drop it, Charlie included.

"Yeah," Libby nodded. "Felicity set it up for me a couple of weeks ago, but it was totally boring stuff to boost my image to lock in this Victoria's Secret contract. That's why I didn't mention it before."

The table went silent for a moment and Libby held her breath.

"That's such a good idea!" Willa exclaimed. "I should do that! Felicity is a genius. I need a new publicist."

"What charity work is it, Libs?" Anita asked.

Libby turned to look at her best friend and realized that Anita was also going to be a problem. Anita had known her longer than any of the others, so she knew when Libby was lying. Not all of Libby's story was a lie, but most of it was going to be, and it was the lie parts that Libby had to sell.

"I'm volunteering down at the FETC(h) shelter on Sunset," Libby continued as she settled into her seat, and her lie, a bit more. "It's absolute filth down there but if it's good for my image—"

"Ew," Willa said, scrunching up her nose. "You're not like cleaning up dog poo, are you?"

"Ew," Christie added.

"Oh no," Libby laughed. "The workers there do all that manual labor and dirty stuff. I just get to pat the dogs and fill up their food and stuff like that. It's so easy."

"How long do you have to do it for?" Anita asked.

"Not too much longer," Libby continued. "I've only done it the once and then maybe I'll do it another couple more times before my Angel contract comes in. Then I won't have to bother with it anymore, which is great because it's totally gross down there!"

"Make sure you tip the paps off too!" Willa said.

"Oh yeah, of course," Libby said.

"Not much point doing it if the paps don't see it, right?" Charlie added.

Libby looked Charlie in the eye and could see the blonde was less than impressed with her story. Not all of it was a lie considering Wentworth had already set her up with the perfect cover, but something about Charlie's reaction gave Libby the impression that she wasn't quite buying the whole story. Thankfully for Libby, Charlie could accuse her of lying all she wanted, but at this stage, she didn't have any proof to back it up with.

"Exactly," Libby smiled back at Charlie before she turned to Anita. "I'm going to the restroom. Anita, come with me."

"Oh yeah," Anita said, obviously caught off guard as she quickly placed her cup of el diabolo back on its saucer and got up from her seat.

As soon as Libby knew they were out of earshot, she grabbed Anita's arm and drew her closer as they walked toward the restrooms.

"Oh my God, what the hell is up with Charlie today?!" Libby whispered.

"What do you mean?" Anita whispered back.

"What's with Charlie and the third degree today?" Libby asked.

Anita shrugged her shoulders as they weaved in and out of the tables.

"She wasn't giving you the third degree," Anita brushed off.

"Um, yeah, she was!" Libby exclaimed. "She's in such a bad mood this morning!"

"Hmmm," Anita replied.

Libby looked at her friend and noticed that Anita wasn't entertaining her bitching about Charlie as much as she usually did.

"Did you know she and Hamish Dawson are hooking up?" Libby whispered in Anita's ear. "Maybe that's why she's in such a bad mood! He's obviously doing someone else on the side. I can't believe that she's being so naïve about it all."

"Who told you about Charlie and Hamish?" Anita asked, her eyes narrowing at Libby.

"Does it matter?" Libby said. "He obviously didn't call her back again or canceled on her or something. I can't imagine anything else would put her in such a bad mood."

"Sure," Anita replied. "So, was that true about your charity work in Hollywood yesterday?"

Libby's eyes widened in both shock and panic.

"What do you mean?!" Libby blurted out. "Of course, it was the truth!"

"Just asking," Anita said, throwing her hands up in defense as they reached the courtyard restrooms.

Libby stood in front of Anita as they stopped walking and she released Anita's arm.

"Yeah, well it was," Libby repeated. "Why else would I have been in Hollywood yesterday?"

Anita shrugged her shoulders and Libby rolled her eyes.

"I have to pee," Libby said as she pushed open the door to the ladies' restroom.

"I'll just wait out here," Anita replied.

Libby looked her friend in the eye and realized that something was wrong, but just shrugged it off as she went into the restroom solo. Anita was acting way moodier than she usually was, even when she was hungover. It was probably her time of the month, or at least that's what Libby was going to tell herself. She had way too much going on now to try and figure out what was up Anita's ass. She had way too much on her mind and way too much to worry about without having to worry about Anita and her problems too. If she had any real problems, she'd come and talk to Libby about them anyway. That's what best friends did. They talked to each other about their problems, no matter what, and she and Anita were best friends.

* * *

Beep! Beep Beep! Beep! Beep Beep!

Charlie looked down at her phone and immediately stood up when she read the caller ID. Without even telling Christie and Willa where she was going, she got up from the table and headed in the same direction as Libby and Anita, to the restrooms and the parking lot. She needed some privacy to answer this phone call, and she did so as soon as she knew she was out of earshot of Willa and Christie.

"About fucking time you called," Charlie said on the phone.

"I'm sorry," William Twain replied. "I meant to get back to you sooner, but I got held up with—"

"I really don't fucking care about your excuses," Charlie replied, "so don't even bother wasting my time finishing that sentence."

William went silent on the other end.

"Those photos you took on Saturday morning didn't work," Charlie said. "It was probably because you didn't get me enough of them, so I couldn't tell exactly what she was doing or who she was with!"

"She caught me off guard," William explained. "I didn't realize it was her until it was almost too late. She was alone when she arrived and when she left though."

"That's a bullshit excuse!' Charlie snapped. "What the fuck am I paying you for if you can't even do your creepy, stalker PI thing properly?!"

"I'm really sorry, Miss Niven," William said. "It won't happen again."

"It better not," Charlie warned. "Otherwise, you won't get the rest of your payment."

"Do you still want me to keep following Miss Evans?" William asked.

"Yes," Charlie said. "Willa said something about her going out of town for some supposed photo shoot in a couple of weekends. I don't know where she's going but I need you to follow her."

"I can do that," William replied.

"Let's just hope you do it right this time," Charlie said sarcastically. "I'll let you know more details when I know."

Charlie hung up the phone call before the Niven family private investigator could utter another word. She looked around again to make sure no one was within earshot. That's when she saw Anita staring off into space, soaking up the morning sun in the Silverlake parking lot. Libby was nowhere to be seen. Charlie approached her friend, the rhythmic click-clack of her Jimmy Choos echoing as she walked across the paved courtyard.

"You don't believe her either, do you?" Charlie spoke from behind Anita as she approached her.

Anita nearly jumped two feet in the air as she whipped around to face Charlie, her mane of strawberry blonde hair nearly whipping Charlie right in the eye.

"Jesus Christ, Charlie!" Anita exclaimed. "You scared the shit out of me!"

Charlie laughed as she watched Anita clutch her chest dramatically like she was genuinely having a heart attack. Charlie watched as her friend took a few deep breaths before she spoke again.

"What did you say?" Anita asked.

"I said," Charlie repeated, as she lowered her voice, "you don't believe little miss supermodel either, do you?"

Anita paused for a moment like she was really thinking about what Charlie had said. She looked over her shoulder at the doors to the restrooms before she turned back to face Charlie.

"No," Anita shook her head. "I don't understand why she would lie about it though. We're her friends."

Charlie rolled her eyes. No matter what Libby Evans did, Anita continued to be loyal to her. It used to be sweet in an 'Anita's so naïve' way, but now it was just annoying. Libby had everything; she didn't need Anita's loyalty too. Especially when Charlie knew she didn't deserve any of their loyalties at all.

"Exactly," Charlie said. "Wake up, Anita! If we were her friends, she wouldn't be lying to us."

"Maybe it's not what you think," Anita said.

"You're way too loyal to her, Nita," Charlie said, not being able to help herself from rolling her eyes. "She doesn't deserve it!"

"She's my best friend," Anita sighed.

Charlie watched her friend's gaze fall to the ground for a second. There wasn't much conviction in her words. It was obvious that Anita believed that statement about as much as Charlie believed it.

It was about as much as they all believed that Willa Nelson's boobs were actually real, which wasn't much at all.

"She used to be your best friend," Charlie said, as she placed a hand on Anita's shoulder. "She hasn't been your best friend in years. She doesn't care about you."

Anita looked at Charlie but didn't say anything. Charlie took this as her opportunity to continue to make her point in the hopes that it would bring Anita back over to where she needed her to be. At least where she needed Anita to be so that she could win.

It had always been in the back of Charlie's mind that Libby couldn't stay in The Brat Pack. Charlie didn't want Libby and her supermodel ambitions and achievements anywhere near her Pack. Libby didn't belong here anymore, and Charlie knew it. It was just a matter of time, and some convincing on Charlie's part, for the others to see it as well. Christie was already there, and Willa could easily be blown over to Charlie's side if it seemed like everyone else was doing it, so Anita was the last one left. Libby could have all the modeling contracts and all the spokesmodel roles for all the companies in the world, but Charlie wanted The Brat Pack.

"Did she even care to ask about that new Netflix series you booked?" Charlie asked. "Did she even care when you lost that movie role that you really wanted? Did she even ask about how your auditions went last week?"

"How did you even know she was in downtown Hollywood yesterday anyway?" Anita asked, changing the subject.

Charlie smirked.

"I have my sources," she shrugged.

Anita's eyes narrowed at her, and Charlie's smirk grew wider.

"What have you got planned?" Anita asked.

"What do you mean?" Charlie asked, feigning innocence.

"I mean," Anita said, "what have you got planned?"

Charlie smirked again. There was no fooling Anita. No wonder she was so good at seeing through Libby's lies.

"Nothing," Charlie said.

"Don't be a bitch, Charlie," Anita said, rolling her eyes as she looked over her shoulder at a couple of customers that walked past them. "You're better than that."

"If Libby's not going to tell us the truth," Charlie said, "we'll just have to find someone that will."

19

Date #8

It was like a pre-requisite that every girl who attended any wedding would look around the room and decide what things she liked, and what she didn't, for her own wedding. Libby Evans was no exception, even if she was as far away from marriage as she could possibly be right now, and not just because she couldn't envision who she would even be marrying. The wedding that she and Wentworth attended that night at the Julia Morgan Ballroom was for a couple of Wentworth's high school classmates. From the five hundred white roses scattered throughout the venue to the seven-tiered white chocolate mud wedding cake, Ace Thatcher could have easily afforded a wedding this extravagant, and yet Libby still couldn't envision walking down the aisle to him.

Ace could, like it was loose change in his back pocket, give Libby the wedding of her dreams along with everything else in her life that she could ever want, and yet she still couldn't see herself marrying him anymore. Six months ago she would have said yes in a heartbeat if he had asked her and she would have gladly told everyone about the Paris proposal as she flashed the ten carat Harry Winston on her perfectly polished supermodel finger. However, things weren't like that anymore. A lot of things had changed in the last six months.

Libby looked up at the giant clock on the ferry building and noted that it was only 11:00 pm, which was a lot earlier than most people would leave a wedding. However, after getting hit on by several well-to-do thirty-something males, whose dates found it highly unamusing, Wentworth and Libby had escaped out the back door and decided to walk back to the Four Seasons via Embarcadero. It was, truth be told, very out of the way when the walk back to the hotel should have only taken ten minutes, but Libby was glad for the detour if only so the night went on for a little bit longer.

"They were out of mint chocolate chip," Wentworth called as he started walking back toward her.

Libby got up from the bench where she was sitting and started walking over to meet him. She had attached the silver-tone fastenings on her Jimmy Choo Bay sandals together so that she could carry them easily in one hand without fearing that she was going to drop a single shoe, and around five hundred dollars, somewhere on the streets of San Francisco.

"Well, that's because it's 11:00 pm on a Saturday," Libby laughed.

"So, I got you the next best thing," Wentworth said as he offered her one of the ice cream cones he was carrying.

"Cookies and cream," Libby said as she looked at the cone in her hand.

Wentworth simply smiled at her as he looked down at the ground.

"You're really going to continue to walk through the city without any shoes on?" he laughed as he pointed to her bare feet on the pavement underneath them.

"I'm eating ice cream at nearly midnight in this dress and it's sixty-two degrees out," Libby said, motioning to the strapless powder blue cocktail dress she was wearing. "I'm clearly a crazy woman!"

"Well then," Wentworth replied, "at least let me carry your crazy woman shoes then."

Libby placed her sandals in Wentworth's outstretched hand as they started the walk back to the Four Seasons.

"So," Wentworth said, "you said earlier that you got good news today?"

"Yeah," Libby nodded, as she took another lick of her ice cream. "My publicist, Felicity, called this morning and said that Victoria's Secret reached out and offered me the Angel contract."

"That's great news!" Wentworth exclaimed. "Right?"

"Yeah, of course, it is," Libby smiled.

"So, it's a done deal then?" Wentworth asked.

"Well, all the paperwork needs to be sorted," Libby explained, "but according to Felicity, Victoria's Secret will announce it formally at the launch of their newest fragrance next month, as they want me to be the face of it."

"That's amazing," Wentworth commented. "You must be really pleased."

Libby didn't answer as her train of thought went to where it had been going all day when she thought about the Angel contract. Since her modeling career had started, and ever since she walked her first runway show for the brand, she knew she wanted to be a Victoria's Secret Angel. She loved everything about the Victoria's Secret brand and, as a model, there was nothing more prestigious than an Angel contract, especially when it came to really launching her career outside of the US. This was what she had always wanted, and yet, all she could think about was Ace Thatcher.

She used to think that when she got her Angel contract that she and Ace would ride off into the sunset together and live happily ever after. She'd have everything she ever wanted all wrapped up in a big pretty Victoria's Secret bow. Now that she finally had it all she should have been elated, but she wasn't.

It was probably because all she could think about was the decision she had made or had kind of made, about her relationship with Ace. It wasn't a decision that she had come too easily, and it had not come to her overnight, but once her phone call with Felicity this morning had ended, she knew exactly what she had to do. She wanted to break up with Ace. Realistically, though, she knew that as soon as she spoke to him that that might not happen, so she resigned herself to the fact that it was either going to be a breakup or at least a break so she could evaluate their relationship; whatever felt like the right decision the next time they spoke. She loved Ace, but at the same time, she wasn't sure if she was in love with him enough to stay with him anymore.

"Alright," Wentworth said, "so when was the last time you were in San Fran?"

Libby shook herself out of the deep abyss that was her thoughts and turned to Wentworth and smiled. It was like he had read her mind and knew she desperately needed a conversation change right now.

"It was like three years back," Libby said. "It was for Charlie's twentieth."

"Charlie Niven?" Wentworth clarified.

"The same one," Libby nodded.

"According to the tabloids," Wentworth said, "you two have been friends for a lot longer than the average Hollywood friendship."

Libby laughed. He had a way with words, and those words always seemed to make her laugh. She loved that about their dates. She loved to laugh.

"We have been," Libby said. "Unfortunately, our friendship isn't quite what it used to be."

"What do you mean?" Wentworth asked, as he reached out and grabbed Libby's free hand and entwined his fingers with hers.

Libby noticed that he was currently wearing her sandals as a scarf around his neck, and it made her smile. Her fingers entwined with his almost automatically, without her mind telling her to do it. Just like her mind had told her that it was OK that he had reached for her hand in the first place. Her hands and Wentworth's always seemed to find their way back to each other. They seemed to fit together so perfectly like they were always supposed to be like that. Like they always had been.

"Charlie and I used to be really close," Libby explained. "When she first moved to LA, we were inseparable. We were so alike and had so much in common that we just clicked right away. It was easy to be friends with her. We'd spend every weekend together, just talking about anything and everything, whether we were at her suite in one of the Niven hotels or having cocktails at Skybar. As time went on, though, the things we had in common and the things we had to talk about became less and less. I started modeling more and Charlie started trying to make something of herself. I had always known that I wanted to be a model, and I was good at it. Charlie never knew what she wanted to be or what she was good at, and that really caused a rift between us. The more success I had, the more Charlie resented me for it, and the more our friendship suffered."

"That's crap though," Wentworth commented. "You shouldn't have to apologize to your friends for your success."

"No, you shouldn't," Libby replied.

"But you still consider her one of your closest friends?" Wentworth asked.

"I know it's hard to understand," Libby said, "but Charlie has her bad points, like everyone, but she also has her good points. She has been there for me through a lot of shitty things that have happened. She's been a good friend to me. I think it's just a phase we're going through, maybe."

"Maybe," Wentworth nodded, "or it could just be that you guys weren't meant to be forever?"

Libby turned to face Wentworth as they continued their walk along Market Street.

"What do you mean?" Libby asked.

"Well," Wentworth said, "friendships are like relationships, right? Some of them are strong and unbreakable. Those friendships last for years and years, but others aren't meant to go the distance. It doesn't mean the short ones are any less meaningful, but they just weren't meant to last forever."

Libby went silent for a moment as she considered Wentworth's words. What he had said had made a lot of sense, she'd just never thought about it like that.

"Oh yeah," Wentworth grinned, "I can be deep."

Libby laughed out loud, nearly losing her balance as she veered them slightly left so she could toss her ice cream cone napkin in a bin they passed.

"Alright then, Aristotle," Libby said, "How many forever friendships are you still holding onto?"

* * *

It took another fifteen minutes of walking, and it would have taken longer if Libby hadn't decided to go barefoot, to reach the Four Seasons. It ended up being fifteen minutes of her and Wentworth doing what they did best, which was talking about anything they could think of. Libby couldn't remember the last time she'd become this comfortable this quickly with someone, especially a guy. They'd had their ups and downs during these last eight dates, but, and Libby wasn't quite ready to say it out loud, these were probably some of the most fun dates she had ever been on.

She knew that these dates hadn't exactly been made with the purest of intentions, they were blackmail after all, but what had started as something she had to do was quickly becoming something she wanted to. She also wasn't ready to say that out loud but considering she had kissed Wentworth back at the animal shelter two weeks ago, she was pretty sure she didn't need to. She was pretty sure he knew how she felt, and as scary as that was, the scarier part was not knowing how he felt. Even though she wasn't ready to tell him how she felt, she knew that she needed to hear how he did.

"Well believe me," Wentworth said as he held open the hotel room door to allow Libby through, "he was definitely checking you out."

"His fiancé and his ex-wife were both there!" Libby laughed. "You'd think he would have been on his best behavior."

"My cousin is a jackass," Wentworth said. "I'm surprised, at this stage, that he only has one ex-wife. I was sure by the time he hit thirty he would have had at least three."

Libby sighed as she became momentarily distracted from the conversation once she felt the lush, soft carpet underneath her feet. It felt like pure five-star luxury, especially because she'd just walked through half of San Francisco barefoot.

She watched as Wentworth took himself straight to one of the accent chairs in the corner of the room near the window that overlooked the city, and started to take his shoes off. The chair was conveniently pointed in the direction of the window so she figured that she would take the opportunity to get a bit more comfortable too. Her silk robe was draped over the bedhead above her bed, so she faced the wall as she unzipped the back of her dress and let it fall to the floor. She had her arm through one of the robe sleeves when she heard Wentworth speak again.

"Look I just couldn't believe—" he started. "Sorry! Didn't realize you were..."

Libby secured her robe by the tie around her waist and turned around to face Wentworth, only to find him staring at the wall opposite her.

"It's OK," Libby laughed. "Nothing you haven't seen before, I'm sure."

Before he could reply, she made her way over to the window to look at the city. She found something soothing in staring at all the lights of the city in the darkness of the night. She supposed it reminded her of the night view from her condo back in LA. She had been living there for nearly five years now, so the night view of a city was pretty much home to her, no matter what city it was. She curled her legs underneath her as she sat on the window couch.

"Well," Wentworth said as he took a seat next to her, his back against the window and his legs hanging over the side of the couch, "nothing I remember seeing, unfortunately."

"Alright, perv," Libby said, rolling her eyes.

"C'mon," Wentworth said, "I'm an all-American male – it's like programmed in my DNA to be sexually charged toward super-models."

"And that was definitely one of the weirdest things you've ever said," Libby laughed.

She shuffled so that she was fully facing him. Her legs still tucked up underneath her.

"I didn't realize you were keeping score otherwise—" Wentworth started before he was interrupted with a kiss.

As usual, it was Libby's lack of thinking that led to her and Wentworth sharing a kiss. She wasn't usually this forward with guys that weren't her boyfriend, especially when she was pretty much sober because all the wedding champagne had worn off on their walk back here.

She felt Wentworth kiss her back and she found herself completely lost in the kiss. She didn't know where she was or what she was doing. It felt like hours when really the kiss had only lasted seconds before Wentworth pulled away from her. She was very aware of how heavy her breathing was, and she could hear that his was just as heavy.

"I have to know what this is," he whispered.

"What do you mean?" she whispered back.

Wentworth gave her a single kiss before he sat up straighter to create some distance between them.

"You and Ace...," Wentworth started.

"Not the best foreplay I've ever heard...," Libby replied.

Wentworth laughed.

"No," he said, "you know what I mean."

Libby sighed. She did know what he meant.

"Isn't this what you want?" she asked.

She had wanted her voice to sound more normal than it came out. She hadn't wanted it to sound so soft. She hadn't wanted it to sound so vulnerable.

"Of course, this is what I want," Wentworth said, his hands seeking out hers. "I've only ever wanted you."

Libby entwined her fingers in his as her eyes focused on their hands, together in her lap.

"Then why are we talking about Ace?" she asked.

"Because I don't want this to be another night at the Niven," Wentworth replied.

Libby's eyes raised and narrowed at him.

"I don't understand what you're saying," she said.

Wentworth sighed. He looked down as he squeezed her hands in his before his eyes rose to meet hers once more. Libby could sense his hesitation. Like he knew what he had to say but he was holding back because of what his words were and what they would mean once he said them.

"I don't want this to be another night you wake up tomorrow and regret," Wentworth finally said.

Libby could feel her heart as it skipped, even if it was just for a second, and her breath hitched in her throat at the same time. It was then, at that moment, that she realized she was staring into the eyes of a guy that was in love with her.

She had felt for months the building connection between them, and she knew that he had felt it too. Maybe it was the things that he had said that made her believe that he felt that way about her, or maybe it was that voice in her head screaming it at her because it was so obvious. At the end of the day though, she knew it. She knew that Wentworth Turner was falling in love with her.

"Libby?" Wentworth asked, breaking her out of her thoughts.

"Sorry, I zoned out for a moment," Libby said, bringing her focus back to him.

"That's OK," Wentworth replied.

A silence enveloped them, the only sound being the late-night San Francisco traffic outside their window.

"What do you want from me?" Libby asked, not breaking Wentworth's eye contact as she spoke.

She wanted to see his facial expression as she asked the question. She also wanted to see his facial expression as he answered.

"I told you," Wentworth replied. "I want you. All of you. I'm here because I have only ever wanted you."

Libby took a deep breath before she leaned forward and kissed him again. This time the kiss was more tender. Softer. Slower, and when she pulled away her forehead rested against his.

"I never thought in a million years that this would turn into this," Libby whispered.

"What is this?" Wentworth whispered back.

"I don't know," she said.

"What do you know?" he asked, one of his hands detaching from hers.

Her eyes fluttered shut at the feeling of his skin on hers as he used his free hand to cup the side of her face. The pad of his thumb gently brushed her cheek. She savored the moment for only a few seconds before she opened her eyes again. Her eyes locked with his as she finally spoke the words that she had been holding back for so long. The words she knew would change everything.

"That I want you," Libby said, "all of you, and I don't care why anymore."

Just like that, Wentworth kissed her with all the reckless abandon that he had been holding back until now. Libby surrendered quickly and easily into his arms as his hands ravished every part of her skin that he could find.

She had wanted this moment for longer than she was happy to admit, and probably even longer than that. She had wanted him for so long, and she was done caring about what it would mean for her career and her relationship. She had wanted Wentworth Turner for so long, and she was done caring about anything else.

* * *

Ding! Ding!

Charlie downed the rest of her espresso martini and placed it next to her phone, which was currently face down on the table. Libby was out of town, Anita was too hungover from last night to party again tonight, and Willa was busy on a date with some guy that was too ugly and unimportant for Charlie to remember his name. So, it was just Charlie and Christie having cocktails at 1 OAK tonight.

Charlie wanted to come out and drown her sorrows after her high had become a massive low when Hamish Dawson had blown her off yet again. Even though they were not official just yet, Hamish and Charlie had spent the past week in Exuma getting to, as Hamish put it, 'indulge themselves in each other's company'. They'd stayed at the Musha Cay Niven Hotel for the whole week and Charlie spent every day in her bikini.

Whilst she usually wouldn't have fancied a week of tropical sun, lying on the beach staring at the incredibly drool-worthy body that belonged to Hamish was exactly what she had needed. She was a little bit pissed off that the rest of The Pack couldn't be here for her to brag about what a dream her week was. It was especially exciting because Charlie knew it was just a matter of time before Hamish asked her to be exclusive with him, which she knew was a big step for a big-time musician that had to swat the fangirls away left, right and center, seven days a week. Even though he had blown her off tonight, she was going to focus on the amazing week they had just had, and that was all she was going to tell The Pack about tomorrow at brunch.

Charlie turned her phone over and a wide smile appeared across her face as she saw that she had a new message from William Twain.

"I'm going to get another round," Christie said as she got up from the booth. "Another for you, Char?"

"Yep, sure," Charlie smiled.

Charlie watched as Christie headed in the direction of the bar before she returned her attention to her phone and opened William's text message. There was just a photo and when Charlie opened it, it caused her smile to widen when she saw what the photo was of, or rather who.

Charlie analyzed the photo from top to bottom, starting with Libby, who was the first person she recognized. Libby was wearing a strapless, powder blue dress that ended at her knees and, of course, looked like it was tailored just for her even though it was probably just an off-the-rack design. She was wearing her hair in a ponytail and the high quality of the photo meant that Charlie could even make out the Tiffany diamond hoop earrings hanging from her ears.

Charlie scrunched up her face in disgust at the fact that Libby was barefoot as she noticed that the photo had been taken in some city. The background of the photo was too generic for Charlie to be able to figure out which city it was though. Charlie shook her head as she realized she was focusing on the wrong part of the photo. She should have been focusing on the male in the photo that Libby was with, especially because he and Libby were holding hands.

Beep! Beep Beep! Beep! Beep Beep!

Charlie was annoyed that someone was calling her mid-photo inspection until she saw the caller ID. She smiled as she answered the call.

"Impressive work, Twain," Charlie said, as she pressed the phone to her ear.

"I'm glad you're happy with what I sent you," William replied. "I have more."

"Oh, I am more than happy with that photo you sent," Charlie said, "but just to make sure—"

"I've already emailed you all the other photos I took," William said, interrupting Charlie as if he was reading her mind.

Charlie smiled.

"Excellent," she replied.

A silence fell in the conversation before Charlie spoke again.

"Anything else?" she asked.

"Actually yes," William said. "Do you know who the guy in the photo is?"

Charlie's eyes narrowed.

"I'm listening," she said.

"Wentworth Turner," William said.

Charlie rolled her eyes.

"Is that name supposed to mean something to me?" Charlie asked, not sure that she could deal with this conversation much longer, no matter how good William's news was and how many espresso martinis she was currently running on.

"It shouldn't," William replied.

Charlie rolled her eyes so hard that they actually hurt.

"What the fuck are you trying to tell me, Twain?!" Charlie snapped. "I've got a million better things to do than stay on this phone call with—"

"He's a no one," William said.

"A no one?" Charlie asked, her patience still teetering on the edge.

"Well, worse than a no one," William continued.

"What is worse than a no one in Hollywood?" Charlie asked, not quite sure what he was trying to tell her.

"Wentworth Turner's a paparazzo," William said.

Charlie couldn't quite believe her ears. Her jaw was starting to hurt as her smile continued to grow. This was better than she could have ever expected. Not only was Libby Evans cheating on her boyfriend, Ace Thatcher, but she was cheating on him with Hollywood scum. She was cheating on a billionaire with a paparazzo.

"Here you go!" Christie exclaimed as she arrived back at their booth.

Charlie ended her call and smiled as Christie placed another espresso martini in front of her.

"Who was that on the phone?" Christie asked as she shuffled into the booth next to Charlie.

Charlie didn't say a word. She simply opened the text message from William and clicked on the photo before placing her phone in front of Christie. Christie leaned forward to have a look and her eyes widened in shock.

"That's Libby," Christie commented as she turned to look at Charlie.

Charlie resisted the urge to roll her eyes for the millionth time tonight.

"Uh-huh," Charlie smiled.

Christie turned back to the phone to inspect the photo once more.

"But that's not Ace," Christie said.

Charlie's smile grew wider.

"No, it's not," she replied. "No, it's not."

20

Date #9

"Stop it," Libby giggled. "Someone is going to see us."

Wentworth stopped kissing her neck as he looked around. It was the middle of Caltech's summer term, so the campus was virtually empty. He could count the number of students in the Caltech courtyard on one hand.

He and Libby were currently standing inside one of the many archways on campus. Her body was pressed in between his and the stone structure, shielding her entirely from view. Instinctively, his hand on the small of her back drew her closer as a couple of girls passed them, but they didn't even give Wentworth and Libby a second look. He turned back around to face her and noticed how flushed her cheeks were as he drew her in for another kiss.

"No one is on campus during summer term," he replied. "No one is going to see us."

Libby smiled at him as she stood up on her tiptoes. Her hands tightly clutched the T-shirt on his chest as she kissed him again. He had to stop himself from groaning against her lips as they resumed where they had been moments earlier.

They were well and truly into the honeymoon phase of whatever it was they were doing since getting back from San Francisco yesterday afternoon. They hadn't discussed what had happened in the hotel room after the wedding. They also hadn't discussed what it all meant to their business arrangement or Libby's relationship with Ace Thatcher, but that really didn't matter right now. It mattered less than that if it meant that Wentworth got to indulge himself completely in Libby, and indulge himself he had been for the last twelve hours.

Upon returning from San Francisco, they had driven back to Caltech and he had waited for her to call the car service to take her back to Sierra Towers, but she never made the call. He had waited for her to call it a night after they took the walk from the parking lot back to his dorm room, hand in hand, but she had never done so. He had waited for her to tell him that everything that had happened over the weekend was a mistake as he brought her bags inside his room with his, but instead, she had stayed.

They talked like they were months deep into a relationship that had zero complications. She curled up into him, in his bed, like it was what they did every night as she fell asleep on his chest, in his arms. She acted the way Wentworth assumed she would have had she been his girlfriend rather than someone else's. Like she had meant what she said at the Four Seasons – that she wanted him, all of him, and she was done caring why.

"I should really go," Libby said as she broke away from him once more.

"Back to my dorm room?" Wentworth said suggestively, as he pulled her closer. "I completely agree."

"No," Libby giggled. "I should really go home."

"Why?" Wentworth asked.

"Because I haven't been home in three days," she replied.

"So?" he asked again.

He watched her as she narrowed her eyes in thought like she was trying to figure out the answer to that question herself. He smiled as he watched her brow furrow as she drew her bottom lip into her mouth. Something she tended to do when she was deep in thought.

"What?" Libby asked.

Wentworth realized she had caught him staring at her.

"Nothing," he smiled.

Libby smiled back.

"What are you staring at?" she asked again.

"You," Wentworth replied.

Her smile widened as she wrapped her arms around his neck, a rush of pink filling her cheeks. He wrapped his arms further around her waist, almost lifting her off the ground as he drew her in for another kiss.

"You are so God damn beautiful," he muttered, as their lips met once more.

"Wow," Anita said.

Charlie rolled her eyes as Anita said that same three-lettered word for what felt like the hundredth time this brunch.

"You said that already," Charlie commented, trying to sound less sarcastic.

"I just can't believe it," Anita repeated, staring at Charlie's phone that was sitting on the table in front of her and Willa.

"I knew Libby was dumb," Willa said, "but this is, by far, the stupidest thing she's ever done."

"It's crazy right?!" Christie exclaimed. "I couldn't believe it when Charlie showed me the photo last night!"

Charlie could see Willa's eyes narrow at Christie as Christie continued to emphasize that she was the second person to hear this latest bit of prime gossip. It did, however, make Charlie delighted in the fact that she was the first.

"I don't know why you girls are so surprised," Charlie said. "This is classic Libby."

"Yeah, but selfish is one thing," Anita commented. "A cheater is another."

"I mean we all know that Ace has cheated on her too," Willa added. "At least once."

"Yeah, so it was just a matter of time, wasn't it?" Charlie said.

"Charlie's right," Christie said. "Ace is always away."

"Still though," Anita added, "there's no excuse for cheating. Distance or not."

Charlie had to try and keep her smirk under control. It appeared that it was going to be easier than she expected to get the girls on board with the idea that she and Christie had come up with.

"So, the question now is," Charlie said, reaching across the table for her phone, "what do we do with this photo?"

"So, is this whole date just going to be us making out all over campus?" Libby asked.

Wentworth smiled against her lips as he kissed her one more time, giving her butt a playful squeeze.

"I thought about it," Wentworth replied, "but then I thought that at some point you were probably going to need to eat something too."

"That is probably all this make-out session is missing," Libby replied. "Pizza."

Wentworth laughed.

"We had pizza last night!" he exclaimed.

"Your point?" Libby asked.

Wentworth laughed again as he created some distance between them, offering his hand to her in the hopes that she would take it. She did.

"C'mon then," he said. "There's a great place on the other side of campus that does amazing sushi."

Wentworth led the way, his fingers entwining with Libby's as they walked.

"So, what time do you have to be back?" Libby asked.

Wentworth looked down at his watch.

"Not for a couple of hours," he replied.

"So, remind me again what exactly you're doing here whilst everyone else is on summer break?" Libby asked.

"It's part of my conditional entry to Cornell," Wentworth explained. "One of the activities I used on my application to the Veterinary Medicine College there was volunteering for one of the Caltech Summer Exploration Camps. So, I stay here for a couple of weeks during summer break and volunteer for bits and pieces."

"And then you're heading off to New York?" Libby asked.

Wentworth felt her grip on his hand tighten as she drew herself closer to him. Her free hand crossed over her body to hold his forearm as they walked.

"Yep," he nodded. "I start Veterinary School in August, but I have a summer job for a couple of weeks in Syracuse starting next month."

Wentworth turned to face Libby in time to see her nod as she processed what he had just said.

"Are you excited about moving?" she asked.

"I've never been east," Wentworth shrugged, "so there's that, but at the same time I'm sort of happy for a fresh start. Get out of Hollywood and all that comes with it."

"I assume your pap days are over then?" Libby asked.

Wentworth laughed.

"Won't have time with Veterinary School, I don't think," he replied.

"I've always loved New York," Libby said.

"So, come with me," Wentworth replied.

"What do you mean?" Willa asked.

"Well," Christie continued, "now that Charlie has this photographic evidence of Libby's indiscretion—"

"How did you get that photo anyway, Charls?" Anita asked, her eyes narrowing at Charlie as she folded her arms.

"Why does it even matter, Nita?!" Charlie exclaimed. "It wasn't exactly like she was hiding her cheating. They were out in the open."

"Charlie's right," Christie said. "Anyone could have taken that photo."

"Who is the guy in the photo anyway?" Willa asked. "The one that Libby's with."

"Oh my God, that's the best part!" Christie exclaimed.

"What does that mean?" Anita asked.

"He's a paparazzo," Charlie replied.

"Wait," Libby said, stopping in her tracks. "What?"

"Come with me to New York," Wentworth repeated.

"No, I heard you," Libby said. "I was just checking that you meant to say it and you weren't having a stroke or something."

Wentworth laughed as he continued walking. Libby followed suit.

"I mean, go to Columbia like you said your mom always wanted you to," Wentworth said, trying to lighten the conversation. "You said last night that you always wanted to have the college experience, right?"

Libby nodded.

"So, did you mean it?" Libby asked.

Wentworth knew what she was talking about. Honestly, the words had just tumbled out of his mouth before he could think about the consequences of them, and how much they were going to weigh down their conversation this morning.

"About you coming to New York with me?" he asked.

He wanted to be careful and clarify her question before he launched into an embarrassing, and potentially unnecessary, explanation.

Libby nodded again.

"I think so," Wentworth replied. "I mean, I realize how heavy that sounds, but at the same time I'm not ready to say goodbye to you yet."

He turned to look at Libby and she was smiling as she continued to look at the ground in front of her as they walked.

"Me neither," she replied.

"Hey," Wentworth said, this time being the one to stop in his tracks.

Libby's gaze flicked immediately to meet his as she stopped in time with him. Still holding one of her hands in his, Wentworth reached for her other hand, not caring that they were in the dead center of the Caltech courtyard where anyone, no matter how few were on campus, could see them. Wentworth took a deep breath as he looked deep into her dark brown eyes. He took a step forward so that their foreheads were nearly touching.

"I have no idea what we're doing," he said. "I have no idea what this is, but whatever it is, I'm not ready for it to be over."

Wentworth watched her carefully as a small smile tugged at the corners of her mouth, starting at the left corner, as usual. Her eyes moved between his and the concrete beneath their feet, making it look like her eyes were almost completely closed as they stood in silence. Wentworth could feel his heart beating frantically in his chest as he waited for her to say something. Even though his words were honest, and he was relieved to have finally said them to her, it still made him nervous as hell as he waited for her response.

"I don't know—" Libby started.

"Shut up!" Willa exclaimed in disbelief.

"Are you serious?!" Anita exclaimed.

Charlie smiled.

"Dead serious," she replied. "Not only is she cheating on Ace behind his back, and ours too, but she's doing it with the scum of the Earth."

"Someone needs to tell Ace," Anita replied, "because this is going to be massive if it hits the press."

"WHEN it hits the press," Charlie smiled.

"You're going to leak it?!" Willa replied in disbelief.

"Why not?!" Christie said.

"Because Libby's our friend!" Anita exclaimed. "I can't believe we're even discussing this."

"Libby has made her bed," Charlie said calmly. "Now she needs to lie in it."

"A scandal like this would absolutely destroy her career," Willa said, verbalizing what they were all thinking. "Not to mention her Victoria's Secret Angel contract would be buried in the garbage."

"And?" Charlie asked. "She brought this upon herself."

"I can't believe you'd do this to her!" Anita exclaimed. "Libby may be a bitch sometimes, but she's our friend! This would destroy everything for her – her relationship with Ace, her career."

"Maybe you need to see exactly what kind of guy she's been messing around with behind our backs," Christie said, a smirk forming on her lips as she turned to Charlie.

"What do you mean?" Willa asked, her eyes lighting up at the insinuation that there was more gossip to be shared.

Charlie smirked as she unlocked her phone again and opened her photos.

"The pap's name is Wentworth Turner," Charlie explained as she placed her phone in front of Willa and Anita once more. "You may be familiar with some of his work..."

Charlie wasn't even sure that Anita and Willa had heard her last few words as they were so deeply engrossed in the new photos Charlie had presented them with. She watched as the color slowly drained from both Anita and Willa's faces as Anita swiped through the photos. She swiped slowly at first and then more frantically when she realized how many photos there were and what they were of.

The Pack was silent as Charlie reached for one of the blueberry croissants in the middle of the table. Three danishes at Sunday brunch was usually her limit, but she was going to make an exception because today was turning out to be a fabulous day. She didn't even care that the blueberry croissants were now cold considering they'd been sitting out on the table for at least half an hour.

"Leak it," Anita said as she stood up.

Charlie didn't want to upset her friend, but it was so satisfying to hear the go-ahead from Anita's lips. Charlie silently watched as Anita then gathered up her things and stormed off out of Silverlake without so much as a goodbye. Charlie smiled as she turned to face Willa.

"Any other objections?" Charlie asked.

Willa shook her head as she looked down at Charlie's phone on the table once more. Her eyes flicked back up to meet Charlie's. Her blue eyes looked extra icy as she too gathered up her things.

"Ruin that bitch," Willa said as she stood up and left brunch in the same direction as Anita.

Charlie smiled as she turned to Christie.

"Mission accomplished," Christie smiled, "and that was so much easier than we thought it was going to be with those two."

Charlie didn't reply, she was too busy opening her email drafts and hitting send. The smile on her face lingered as she popped another piece of blueberry croissant into her mouth.

"Turner!" a voice called from across the courtyard, interrupting Libby mid-sentence.

Libby and Wentworth instinctively took a step back from each other. Only one set of their hands remained connected as they turned in the direction of the voice.

Wentworth recognized one of his classmates, Phil Sullivan, instantly. He was dressed in the same red T-shirt Wentworth was with *Caltech Summer Exploration Camp* splashed across the front in bright yellow. It made sense, considering Phil was also volunteering these next couple of weeks.

"Oh," Phil said as soon as he reached them, "and you're here, too."

"What is that supposed to mean?" Wentworth said as he pulled Libby by the hand to stand slightly behind him.

Wentworth immediately noticed that Phil's comment and eyeline were directed at Libby, and she must have noticed it too as she easily moved in behind him, squeezing his hand as she did so.

"Oh, nothing man," Phil mumbled as he locked eyes with Wentworth.

"So, what's up?" Wentworth asked, trying to get Phil back on track so that this conversation could be over as quickly as possible.

"You're famous!" Phil exclaimed.

"What?" Wentworth asked in confusion.

"You obviously haven't checked your phone this morning, have you?" Phil said, narrowing his eyes at Wentworth.

"What are you talking about?" Wentworth repeated as he retrieved his phone from his pocket with his free hand.

His other hand squeezed Libby's as she remained where she was.

Wentworth realized his phone was still on silent and his screen was full of missed calls and messages. He quickly unlocked the phone and opened the first message, which was from Gigi.

Beth?

Wentworth didn't understand the message but noticed that Gigi had also sent him a link. He clicked on it and that was when everything became clear. Wentworth felt Libby lean around him, which meant that as soon as the link loaded, they both came face to face with a photo of themselves in San Francisco.

The photo had been taken of them walking back to the Four Seasons after the wedding on Saturday night. There was barefooted Libby, Wentworth carrying her shoes, and the pair of them holding hands. It was a great photo of them and the smile on Libby's face made Wentworth want to smile because she looked so happy. What didn't make him want to smile though, was the headline of the article the photo was attached to - *More than one Ace up her sleeve: supermodel Libby Evans caught in cheating scandal!*

"Oh my God," Libby whispered.

Wentworth looked up from his phone and realized that Phil had, at some point, left them, and they were now the only ones there in the middle of the courtyard. He turned to look at Libby and all the color had drained from her face. Her eyes were fixed on his phone screen and her breathing was getting more ragged the longer she stared.

"Libs," Wentworth said, but before he could say anything else Libby had snatched the phone from his hands and started scrolling.

He watched as the panic started to show on her face as her scrolling became more frantic. Her eyes were glued to the screen, almost unblinking.

"Libs," Wentworth repeated as he gently placed a hand on the small of her back. "I honestly had no idea."

She looked up at him and he could see the tears already welling in her eyes.

"I have to go," Libby said as she shoved the phone back into his hands and started running.

He wanted to stop her, but he didn't know what to say. He didn't know what he was supposed to say or do considering all of this was his fault. He'd slipped up and taken her somewhere out in public that had left her exposed for something like this to happen. Something he had promised her wouldn't happen.

Of course, there were paparazzi in San Francisco. The paparazzi were everywhere, and he knew that firsthand. It was his idea for them to have their date there, so even though she hadn't said it, he knew this was his fault. This whole date debacle was his fault because he really hadn't given her much of a choice when he proposed the arrangement six months ago. Everything was his fault, and now he could feel in the pit of his stomach that things were starting to crumble around them. Whatever it was between him and Libby was about to be over.

21

The Storm

Libby could feel her cheeks burning as her hot tears continued to fall faster and faster. She couldn't even pinpoint exactly what the tears were about either. Whether they were tears of embarrassment, tears of sadness, or tears of anger. There were so many emotions flooding her small body that maybe it was the combination of all of them that was the reason she was a crying mess on the floor of one of the elevators in Sierra Towers right now.

She knew that she had to press the STOP button on the elevator soon, otherwise the fire brigade was going to be called. They would have assumed that there was an actual emergency in the building that had caused one of the main resident elevators to suddenly stop. In Libby's mind, however, what was happening was enough of an emergency for her to press the STOP button in the first place. Nevertheless, she knew she didn't have much time. She just couldn't bring herself to press the button again just yet because she knew that when she did, she was going to have to ride the elevator to the twentieth floor and come face to face with Ace Thatcher. The boyfriend who she was sure, by now, knew that she was cheating on him with a paparazzo named Wentworth Turner.

After missing her on more than one occasion when he made his surprise trips back from Paris, Ace had somehow talked his way into getting an extra copy of the key to her condo so that he could always just let himself in. At the time it made sense for Libby to agree to such an arrangement, but right now she was mentally kicking herself for allowing him to talk her into it. Now she wouldn't even have the chance to have a few minutes to herself before she had to face him about the scandal that had just broken on every major media outlet across the country. No doubt he would be there, and he would start yelling at her as soon as she got off the elevator. If she knew Ace, which she was pretty sure she did by now, he wouldn't even wait until she closed the front door behind her to start his tirade. Considering he wasn't directly in the wrong on this occasion in their relationship, Libby was expecting him to rub in her face very loudly what a mess she had made of things. There was no arguing there though, she really had made a mess of everything, and now she had to face the consequences.

Libby noticed that the endless stream of tears had settled, so she wiped the strays from her cheeks. She closed her eyes and took five deep breaths before she pulled herself to her feet. She looked around to double-check that she hadn't missed any of her personals that had fallen out of her bag when she threw it to the ground in frustration just minutes earlier. Her phone was among the items that she had to put back in her Birkin and she knew there were going to be at least eight hundred messages on it, but she refused to look at them right now. She refused to focus on anything other than what she was about to face back in her condo.

She finally pressed the STOP button and felt the elevator spring back to life. The lights flickered a few times as it restarted its ascent the five remaining floors. She wiped at her cheeks again and her eyes too for good measure. She raked her fingers through her long hair, sorted out the knots she found, and used the grey silk scrunchie around her wrist to tie it up in a ponytail at the back of her head. Hopefully, that would at least make her look less messy than she felt right now. She couldn't even bring herself to take her compact out of her bag to check her reflection, even though that probably would have helped too.

"Is this why you sent me that stupid text yesterday?!" Ace practically yelled as soon as Libby opened the door to her condo.

She knew he was there as soon as she stepped off the elevator. Not only could she smell his terrible cliched FCUK cologne in the corridor outside, but he had conveniently left the front door ajar. Almost as if he was inviting her to come inside, join him, and cop some abuse.

Once inside, she closed the front door and turned around to find a livid Ace standing in the middle of her living room frantically waving a bunch of magazines at her. She could only make out the front covers of *US Weekly*, *Hello!* and *OK!*, but she could see there were more in the bunch. Libby sighed. She could have easily lied to him like she had so many times before. She could have used Wentworth's blackmail card as a much bigger part of the story than it was, but she couldn't see the point in that. She knew she was already the villain, so there was really no point in lying anymore.

"Honestly?" Libby said as she walked into her living room. "Yes."

"So, you fuck some paparazzo behind my back, and YOU have the audacity to break up with ME?!" Ace exclaimed as he slammed the magazines down on the floor in front of him.

Libby took a deep breath. As she usually did before she was going to meet Ace with something hanging over her head, she had already anticipated some of the things he was going to say and the hurtful things he was going to throw in her face. She had, therefore, rehearsed a few things to retaliate with. Mostly to keep herself calm because no matter what he said to her, she had betrayed him and she had, no doubt, hurt him. He was entitled to throw a little verbal abuse her way.

"I didn't break up with you," Libby replied.

"Of course, you did!" Ace exclaimed back. "What, am I too STUPID now to know when my girlfriend breaks up with me?! Like I'm clearly too STUPID to know she's cheating on me in the first place?!"

"I didn't break up with you," Libby repeated, trying to remain calm even though it was becoming harder by the second.

She had anticipated a little bit of anger on Ace's part, but this current level of rage really illustrated just how much she had hurt him and his pride. She was happy to admit that she was in the wrong about cheating on him, but she wasn't the only reason their relationship was as broken as it was. She wasn't the only reason they were standing there, amongst the wreckage of all those broken pieces.

"I just wanted a break," Libby continued. "I just needed a break from us."

"Yeah, so you could continue to fuck that pap behind my back, right?!" Ace exclaimed with his finger pointed aggressively in Libby's direction. "You just wanted me out of the way so you could continue to be a slut!"

"That's not what happened," Libby replied, her eyes closing for a moment as she tried to compose herself.

"How many were there?!" Ace continued to rage, his hand gestures getting more and more pronounced. "How many paps were there that you were fucking behind my back?! How many other guys were you opening your legs to?!"

"Don't you dare speak to me like that in my own house," Libby warned, her tone sharp even though she didn't raise the volume of her voice.

"How exactly should I be speaking to you then?!" Ace exclaimed. "How exactly should I feel about all this?"

"I don't know," Libby replied, shaking her head.

"You broke my trust!" Ace exclaimed.

"I know I did," Libby said.

"I loved you!" Ace exclaimed. "I gave you everything and you fucking cheated on me!"

"And I was the only one that did that?!" Libby exclaimed, not quite being able to keep her emotions in check any longer.

Of course, Ace was playing the role of the dutiful boyfriend and the victim. Libby had wanted to come here and at least have, what resembled, a civilized conversation. She wanted to let Ace get some of the anger off his chest, but she couldn't do that when he insisted on playing the role of the perfect boyfriend that had never done anything wrong. Unfortunately, this was classic Ace though.

"What the fuck does that even mean?!" Ace exclaimed.

"How many times have you cheated on me since we've been together?" Libby questioned, raising her eyebrow at him. "I mean I'm only aware of that one time, but I don't doubt there have been more."

"That's irrelevant," Ace retorted.

"Of course, it is!" Libby snapped sarcastically. "Because it paints you in a less than perfect light, right? Because you're the perfect boyfriend, aren't you?!"

"Don't you try and turn this around on me!" Ace yelled back. "This isn't about me, it's about you being a slut and getting caught out doing it!"

"You cheated on me too, Ace," Libby stated, "and I forgave you for that."

"And you expect me to forgive you too?!" Ace exclaimed. "Is that it?"

"No," Libby admitted. "I'm not asking you to forgive me at all."

Ace stopped where he was, obviously confused by what Libby was saying and where she was going with this. Libby was thankful for the lull in conversation to have a few seconds in silence to collect her thoughts. She sighed as she took a few steps backward and sat on the couch behind her. She grasped at her neck and her shoulders with her hands and gently massaged her skin, hoping it would help calm her down.

"I'm sorry," Libby finally spoke as she sought out Ace's eyes. "I'm sorry for cheating on you and I'm sorry for the way you had to find out about it."

Ace didn't say a word as he maintained her gaze. Libby clasped her hands together in her lap.

"I'm sorry for hurting you," Libby continued. "I never wanted to."

Ace nodded as he processed what she was saying. He was so hard to read at the best of times and now was no exception. Libby wasn't sure if his silence meant that he was digesting everything, including his anger, and he was going to speak to her more calmly the next time he opened his mouth. The silence could have also been him going over everything she'd said and done, which would make the anger boil up inside him again until it bubbled over into whatever he was going to say next.

"How long has this been going on?" Ace finally spoke.

Libby looked him in the eye. His eyes were cold as they stared at her, obviously analyzing her facial expressions and her movements carefully. Like he was studying her reaction before she had a chance to filter her words.

"I don't think that's a good idea," Libby said.

"What is that supposed to mean?!" Ace snapped back.

Libby rolled her eyes without even thinking about it.

"And what is THAT supposed to mean?!" Ace exclaimed in response.

"It means that me telling you any more about this situation isn't going to help," Libby replied. "Going into detail isn't going to make either of us feel any better."

"I don't give a fuck about what YOU think is going to make things better!" Ace snapped. "You're going to tell me everything because you owe me at least that!"

"No, I'm not," Libby said, "and I don't owe you anything other than the apology I just gave you."

"You're not sorry!" Ace exclaimed. "You're just sorry you got caught!"

"I'm sorry about a lot of things," Libby replied, "and getting caught and embarrassing you are definitely two of them. I didn't want you to find out like this."

"You didn't want me to find out AT ALL!" Ace replied.

"Of course, I didn't want you to find out!" Libby exclaimed. "I didn't want to hurt you and I knew you finding out would do just that. That's why I texted you yesterday and told you I needed a break. I needed some space from you to figure things out."

"Figure what out exactly?!" Ace exclaimed.

"Figure us out," Libby replied. "You and I haven't been on the same page with our relationship in a long time."

"So that justifies you cheating on me, does it?!" Ace retaliated sarcastically.

"Of course not!" Libby replied, "but the fact that I cheated on you says something about what kind of condition our relationship is in!"

"Oh, so it's MY fault then, is it?!" Ace exclaimed, starting to get worked up again. "I'm the problem with our relationship, am I?!"

"You're not listening to me!" Libby exclaimed. "That's the problem!"

"Fine," Ace replied, folding his arms across his chest defiantly. "I'm listening!"

"You only hear what you want to hear and when I tell you something is wrong you completely disregard it and think you can patch it up with some expensive piece of jewelry or some fancy dinner," Libby explained.

"I've given you EVERYTHING!" Ace practically shouted. "I have given you everything you've ever wanted!"

"But I don't want all of those things!" Libby answered. "I don't want any more jewelry and I don't want any more stuff. All I've wanted is for you to be here with me!"

"This is complete bullshit!" Ace exclaimed. "You're just looking for some excuse to justify you cheating on me like the WHORE you are!"

"Don't you dare speak to her like that!" a voice suddenly exclaimed.

Libby and Ace turned in the direction of the front door where Wentworth Turner was now standing.

Libby had forgotten to lock the door when she entered the condo. She had obviously been so distracted by Ace yelling at her and now Wentworth had walked in and joined the conversation without an invitation. She had no idea how he got through the lobby and to the elevator, but she knew she was going to have a strongly worded conversation with the concierge and security when this entire mess was done with. Right now, however, she had to figure out what she was going to do. What was she going to do with Wentworth and Ace in the same room that didn't involve them beating the shit out of each other and destroying her condo in the process?

"Oh my God, what the hell are you doing here?!" Libby exclaimed in a hushed whisper as she jumped up from her spot on the couch and rushed over to Wentworth.

She quickly positioned herself between the two men, knowing it was just a matter of time before Ace figured out who Wentworth was.

"Who the FUCK are you?!" Ace demanded as he started to slowly approach Wentworth and Libby.

"None of your fucking business," Wentworth replied as he completely ignored Libby, instead looking Ace straight in the eye. "But it is my business if you continue to talk to her like that."

Libby looked from Ace to Wentworth and back, catching the exact moment that Ace figured out what was going on. The look in his eyes said it all.

"You're that fucking pap, aren't you?" Ace said as the lightbulb lit up upstairs.

"You need to go!" Libby exclaimed, physically pushing on Wentworth's chest to cue him to leave.

"No, you should stay," Ace smirked. "We were just discussing what a slut Libby is, but you probably have a better idea about that than I do."

"You don't get to talk about her like that!" Wentworth warned, pointing a finger strongly in Ace's direction. "EVER!"

"I can talk however the hell I want to MY girlfriend!" Ace replied, taking a few more steps toward them.

"You're still going to stay with him?!" Wentworth exclaimed in surprise, locking eyes with Libby for the first time since he entered the room. "After all this?!"

It broke Libby's heart to see the look in Wentworth's eyes. He was clearly hoping for a different outcome, one that didn't involve Libby and Ace staying together.

Libby had called a break with Ace as of yesterday, right before she and Wentworth spent another night together. They hadn't slept together in San Francisco, nor had they last night in his dorm room, but the feelings she had for Wentworth meant that she needed a break from her and Ace. Whether it was to explore those feelings for Wentworth, or whether it was to figure out if there was anything worth salvaging in her relationship with Ace. She still didn't know the answer. She hadn't told Wentworth about the break with Ace, and it didn't seem like the right time to do that now. Especially when Ace was clearly pretending it hadn't happened at all.

"I don't—" Libby started, as she maintained Wentworth's gaze.

"You don't get a say in this, buddy!" Ace exclaimed, reminding Libby he was still in the room. "She's MY girlfriend and this doesn't fucking concern YOU!"

"Libs," Wentworth said, clearly ignoring Ace altogether. "You don't have to stay here. We can just go right now."

"Hey, DICKHEAD!" Ace shouted, his voice getting louder in response to being ignored. "Stay out of it!"

"We can just go," Wentworth repeated, looking deep into Libby's eyes as he reached for her hand. "You don't have to take this from him."

"Went, I—" Libby started.

"Get the FUCK OUT OF HERE!" Ace started yelling, his footsteps heavy as he started stomping his way over to Wentworth and Libby at the front door. "This doesn't FUCKING CONCERN YOU!"

"This does concern me!" Wentworth finally retaliated, as he took Libby's hand and pulled her behind him as if to protect her from the growingly irate Ace Thatcher.

"Oh, does it?!" Ace replied.

"Yeah, it does!" Wentworth exclaimed.

"What part of this conversation with MY girlfriend do you think concerns YOU, dickhead?!" Ace asked.

"I will not stand here and let you speak to her like that!" Wentworth exclaimed.

Libby watched Wentworth carefully study Ace like he was trying to anticipate his next move. All the while, Wentworth hadn't let go of her hand and still had her behind him in a gesture of protection.

"I will speak to my girlfriend however the fuck I want!" Ace shouted. "I'm FUCKING ACE THATCHER and you are NO-BODY!"

"You will NOT speak to her like that!" Wentworth shouted back.

Libby could feel the tension in the room rising as the voices of Ace and Wentworth started getting louder, and their retaliations started getting more repetitive. Obviously, neither were thinking straight and that was dangerous. Two hot-blooded males in proximity fighting over a girl was how every good bar brawl started, and Libby was starting to worry that her condo was going to be the bar in this scenario.

"She doesn't FUCKING care about you!" Ace yelled, breaking Libby out of her thoughts. "She's just messing around with you to get back at me for being away."

"Spoken like a billionaire that just got cheated on for a lowly nobody," Wentworth replied.

Libby liked this new scenario even less than the pair of them yelling at each other. Wentworth trying to be a smart-ass to piss off Ace and rile him up even more was definitely a worse scenario.

"GET THE FUCK OUT OF HERE!" Ace yelled, obviously taking the bait like the predictable egotist he was.

"Went, you should go," Libby whispered. "Please just go."

"I am not going anywhere without you," Wentworth said, his volume dropping as he looked at her.

"SHE'S NOT GOING ANYWHERE WITH YOU, YOU NO-BODY!" Ace yelled. "YOU don't mean anything to her!"

"I'm not leaving her here with you," Wentworth retorted strongly as he turned to look at Ace again.

"Why not?!" Ace asked. "I'm her boyfriend—"

"Because I love her," Wentworth replied.

22

Poker Face

Libby looked at the clock on the wall and realized that she had been standing at the door of her fridge for about five minutes. She was counting the pieces of bread and cheese that were left in what was otherwise an empty fridge. She wondered how long she could live on just rye bread and jalapeño cheddar. Sure, she would probably gain a whole lot of weight, but considering her modeling prospects, including her Victoria's Secret contract, were in the trash anyway, she could eat all the bread and cheese she wanted now. All that sugar, carbs, and dairy were about all that was going to make her feel better right now anyway. That, and the three blocks of rocky road chocolate and two and a half bottles of rosé Moscato.

It had been four days since the explosion that was the leak of her cheating scandal. Her name had been dragged through the mud that was every tabloid, both print and online. It had been four days since she had even looked at her phone which was probably overflowing with four days' worth of unread text messages and unheard voicemails that she couldn't bear to open right now. Her Lesjour! matching set had had four days of continuous wear and her bath had been filled with a different bath bomb every day for the last four days straight. It had also been four days since Wentworth Turner had told Ace Thatcher that he loved his girlfriend. Four days since Wentworth had said that he loved her.

She couldn't even remember what happened after Wentworth had blurted out those three little words. She couldn't recall any words that were said after that, or whether any of those words had come out of her mouth. Someone in the building must have heard the commotion on the twentieth floor and called security because before the situation could escalate any further, two security guards showed up at her front door and escorted both Wentworth and Ace off the Sierra Towers premises.

Libby pushed those thoughts to the back of her mind as she pulled a half-open bottle of rosé from the fridge. She turned it on its side to see how much was left before she decided to drink straight from the bottle in the solace of her bed. The same place she'd been seeking refuge for the last four days.

Dragging her feet back to her bedroom and into her bed, Libby pulled the comforter and organic cotton cover over herself, hoping it would swallow her whole and take her away from the disaster that was her life. She took a generous swig of the rosé and at that moment the magazines sitting on the end of her bed caught her eye. She had read the articles in them at least five hundred times in her self-isolation. All of them called her, in not so many words, a 'slut' for what she did to poor innocent oil heir billionaire Ace Thatcher.

Libby reached for the magazine closest to her and looked at the photograph of her and Wentworth on the cover, trying to ignore the headline in all caps: *LIBBY CHEATS ON ACE*. Libby was sure that the caps made that magazine stand out amongst all the others on the shelf so that people would be intrigued enough to pay the four dollars to read more. She flicked to the corresponding article inside and there were more photos, including another copy of the cover image - her and Wentworth walking together with their ice cream cones along Market Street in San Francisco.

She couldn't believe that she thought walking barefoot through a filthy city was a good idea, but it didn't look like she minded at all in the photos. She looked so happy. Part of it was probably the fact that she'd been on a bit of a post-wedding champagne buzz, but she knew that most of it had to do with the fact that she was holding hands with Wentworth. It was, in reality, a little more complicated than that though. Wentworth was, after all, the paparazzo that was blackmailing her into dating him and cheating on her now former boyfriend.

The last text message she read was one from Ace that clearly said they were over. That he was done with her, and he was ending it. It must have made him feel like he had won as he got to be the one to officially end their relationship. Libby could almost hear the smugness in his message as she read it. However, if this was what he needed to gain back the pride she had stolen from him, then she'd just let him have it. Ace wasn't a bad guy and she had hurt him. No matter what the circumstances, she was genuinely sorry for that, whether Ace would believe it or not.

After reading that text from Ace she knew that she couldn't face any more fallout from the scandal right now, so she'd just left her phone on the kitchen table and had refused to look at it. It hadn't been that easy though, especially when her phone wouldn't stop ringing, beeping, and then buzzing. Eventually, she turned the phone off altogether, after seeing that she had already racked up twenty-five missed calls from Wentworth. Another man in her life that she couldn't bring herself to talk to right now.

It wasn't because he had finally said how he felt about her. She had known for a while that he was in love with her, but it did still catch her off guard when he had eventually said it, especially because it ended up being in front of Ace.

Whilst the magazines that Ace had left all over her living room floor four days ago were full of tabloid rubbish, they were also full of more information about who Wentworth Turner really was. Libby cried the first time she read the article in *US Weekly* that detailed Wentworth's work. She was familiar with his part-time gig as a paparazzo, but what she wasn't familiar with was what his work included.

The *US Weekly* article showed all kinds of paparazzi photos that were taken by Wentworth over the years, and a lot of them were of The Brat Pack. Her tears had started when she saw that Wentworth was responsible for the 'fat' bikini photos that were taken of Willa at a terrible angle while she was on vacation in Cancun with actor Benjamin Rushmore. The tears continued as she saw the photos he had taken of Anita's cocaine scandal that had nearly landed her in jail a couple of years ago. Unfortunately, nothing quite prepared her for the photos she then saw of her at her mother's funeral five years ago. Photos that Wentworth had taken and sold to the highest bidder.

Buzz. Buzz.

Libby immediately recognized the buzzing as the sound of her intercom. She thought long and hard about ignoring it entirely as she had on day two of her self-isolation.

Buzz. Buzz.

Libby mentally calculated the day of the week and sighed as she realized it was Thursday and the guy on the other end of the intercom would mostly likely be Paul. Unlike Gerard on Tuesday, Paul was always a bit more persistent with the intercom and buzzing the condos. He wouldn't take silence for an answer. He would probably just keep buzzing until he got a response because he knew she was home.

Buzz. Buzz.

Libby rolled her eyes as she rolled out of bed and quickened her unenthusiastic shuffle to the intercom near her front door. She pressed the button as soon as she was within reach.

"Miss Evans," Paul said.

"Yes, Paul," Libby replied, trying to sound less annoyed than she was.

"I have a Miss Nelson here to see you," Paul replied.

"Tell Willa I'm not taking visitors right now," Libby said.

"No, I'm sorry, Miss Evans," Paul continued, "but it's a Miss Willow Nelson that is here to see you."

Libby's eyes narrowed in confusion. Willow Nelson had not visited her condo in at least two years.

"Shall I let her up, Miss Evans?" Paul asked again.

"Yes, Paul," Libby replied. "Let her up."

Libby let go of the intercom button but not her confusion. She wasn't sure why Willow Nelson was here right now, or if she and Willow were even friends at this point. They hadn't talked since Willow and Willa's joint twenty-first, which was almost two years ago. Libby only remembered because it was a classic Halloween party given the twin's birthday was October thirty-one.

Willa had insisted on coming as Catwoman and her leather catsuit had split right down the crotch when she had tried to twerk on the dancefloor in the middle of the Metropolitan Nightclub in LA. It was the result of one too many apple martinis, her drink of choice at the time. Willow had been forced to come as a matching superhero and nearly died laughing at Willa's catsuit fail while she remained perfectly content in her super baggy Batman costume. Willow had never been one for the politics of Hollywood, so she took pleasure in rebelling against it all. It was part of the reason why she left The Brat Pack after that Halloween party.

Libby heard the elevator stop at the twentieth floor and opened the front door before Willow could even knock.

"Hey, Libs," Willow said as she immediately reached forward to draw Libby into a tight hug.

Libby was caught off guard by the hug but relished the comfort as she closed her eyes and hugged Willow back.

"Hey, Lo," Libby said.

The twins' parents clearly thought they were only having one child when Saoirse Nelson fell pregnant. As a result, they were less than creative in naming the girls when they were born. They had their heart set on the name Willow, but when two girls arrived, they didn't know what to do. The names Willa and Willow were ridiculously similar sounding, and it caused a lot of confusion when Willow was part of The Brat Pack. As a result, Libby took to calling Willow 'Lo'.

Libby felt Lo start to pull away from her and she did the same thing. She then motioned for Lo to come inside.

"I'm sorry I haven't called," Libby said, as she closed and locked the door once Lo was inside.

"Yeah, it's been like two years since you called me back, you bitch," Lo said sarcastically.

Lo grinned, which made Libby laugh. It was the first time she'd laughed in four days, if not longer.

"Yeah, I've been a bitch to everyone apparently," Libby replied.

Lo frowned as she adjusted her hands on either side of the box she was carrying, that Libby had just noticed.

"I saw the photos online," Lo said. "The articles were way harsh."

"Yeah," Libby sighed as she motioned for Lo to follow her back to her bedroom. "Everyone knows what a slut I am now, I guess!"

"You're not a slut!" Lo exclaimed as she followed Libby through the condo.

Libby returned to her spot on her bed underneath the covers and Lo sat in the middle of the king-sized bed. She placed the box she was carrying down in front of her. It wasn't until Lo drew her bare feet in toward her and crossed her legs that Libby realized she had, at some point, ditched the Givenchy slides she had arrived in.

"Just some things I thought you'd need," Lo said, gesturing to the box on the bed. "I figured you were going to spend at least one or two more days in self-isolation so there are some essentials that will hopefully lift your spirits and keep you alive."

Libby laughed as Lo pointed to the portion of the box that contained a variety of fresh fruit, an extra-large packet of trail mix without almonds, and what appeared to be her favorite coconut cupcakes from Magnolia Bakery. Libby continued to inspect the box and saw a variety of cliched self-care items from bath bombs and face masks, to face creams and chapsticks. Willa, no doubt, had something to do with the fact that all those items were from the Illuse Cosmetics line.

Libby had read online that Willa had just signed on to be the face of Illuse's new fragrance. It was the spokesmodel role that Libby had already lined up with Camryn Ecles, but that had fallen apart after the scandal had broken. It was what Willa had always wanted so Libby knew she would have been pleased as punch.

"I'd have said to crack this open," Lo said as she grabbed one of the small bottles of Skinnygirl Spicy Lime Margarita out of the box, "but I see you already started without me."

Libby looked at the nearly finished bottle of rosé on her nightstand before she leaned over and grabbed it. The rest of the liquid in the bottle disappeared in one swig and was quickly replaced in Libby's hand with one of the Skinnygirl bottles that Lo quickly cracked open for her.

"I'd also have asked how you've been doing but I think I already know the answer," Lo said as she opened her own bottle of Skinnygirl and took a sip.

"Fan-fucking-tastic," Libby said sarcastically as she took a more generous swig.

"You know it'll all blow over, right?" Lo said.

"After my relationship and my career are dead, sure," Libby replied.

"Take me back to the very start," Lo said.

Libby took a deep breath and told Lo everything. She started at the *Wonderland* opening of the Beverly Hills Niven Hotel and finished with what happened in San Francisco and Wentworth proclaiming his love for her in the middle of her condo four days ago.

"That's a lot," Lo said as she processed everything Libby had told her. "A lot. A lot."

"Yep," Libby said, as she reached for another one of the coconut cupcakes.

She tossed the wrapper into the growing pile of food and drink wrappers that she and Lo had made on the bed.

"So, you and Ace are completely done then?" Lo asked.

"Seems that way," Libby said.

"So, what about you and Wentworth?" Lo asked.

Libby sighed.

"I have no idea," Libby replied.

"Do you love him?" Lo asked.

Libby shrugged her shoulders. It was all she could muster right now when she brought herself to think about him. She had tried to put him out of her mind these last four days, but it was hard to forget him when every time she passed her phone on the way to the fridge it reminded her of the growing number of voicemails that he was probably leaving.

"Well, and I could be totally out of line and completely off track in saying this," Lo said as she helped herself to one of the chocolate-covered strawberries she retrieved from the bottom of the box, "but maybe you're not in love with him so much as you're in love with what he made you?"

Libby scrunched up her nose.

"That doesn't make any sense," Libby said, "but that could be because I'm pretty drunk right now."

Lo laughed.

"What I mean is," Lo explained, "maybe you're in love with how he made you feel. Like he made you feel like you were just some normal girl, rather than the socialite and supermodel you actually are. He fell in love with the Libby underneath all the Hollywood crap, and it made you feel good and happy. Maybe you're just in love with that feeling he gave you?"

Libby pondered Lo's words for a moment and realized that she hadn't once thought about her relationship with Wentworth in that light. The more she thought about it now, though, the more sense it made.

When they were together, it was always without the expectation of what the media or her peers would think of her and what she was doing. When they were together, it was always out of the public eye where she could just relax; where didn't have to wear any make-up, she didn't have to make sure her hair was perfect, and she didn't have to kill her feet in a pair of heels. Maybe the part of her relationship with Wentworth that made her so happy was the fact that, for the first time in a long time, she could just be herself. Maybe what made her happy was being a normal girl. One who didn't have to worry about any of the pressures of being a Hollywood girl.

"So, have you heard from the girls?" Lo asked, drawing Libby out of her thoughts.

Libby shook her head as she finished off her second bottle of Skinnygirl, thankful for Lo's change of topic. She could feel the hangover looming in her head as a dull headache, so she eyed one of the mini bottles of Evian sitting in Lo's care box and knew that she should probably make that bottle her next.

"Willa's been busy," Lo said, almost like she was trying to make excuses for her sister, "with the whole Illuse contract thing just kind of popping up so quickly, she—"

"It's seriously fine, Lo," Libby interrupted, refusing to hear more on the topic. "I get it."

"So, nothing from Charlie?" Lo asked.

Libby shook her head.

"Nita?" Lo asked.

Libby shook her head again.

"I did try calling Nita on Tuesday night, but it went straight to voicemail," Libby continued.

"She probably just needs some time," Lo said. "I mean, the photos aren't your fault, and when you explain the whole blackmail thing to her—"

"Yeah, I know," Libby said, interrupting Lo again.

Libby reached forward and touched her hand to Lo's knee.

"Despite everything that's happened between us," Libby said, "thank you for coming and being here for me right now. I wouldn't have expected it in a million years."

"That's cause you're a dumb supermodel, remember?" Lo said.

Libby laughed at the sarcasm in Lo's voice and the grin on her face.

"I really mean it, though," Libby smiled. "Thank you."

Lo smiled back, but that smile quickly disappeared and the change didn't go unnoticed. Libby narrowed her eyes at Lo and waited for those blue eyes to meet her gaze again.

"Look," Lo said, "I came here for you today because I thought you could use a friend."

Libby quickly nodded, as if trying to urge Lo to continue.

"But there's something you should know about how this whole scandal broke," Lo said.

"What do I need to know?" Libby asked.

She wasn't even sure if her words had come out clearly because she had spoken them so quickly. She needed to know what Lo was talking about and she needed to know right this second.

"You need to know who leaked the story to the media," Lo answered.

Libby took a deep breath. Her heart was pounding in her chest as she waited for Lo to break the news to her. To tell her who was responsible for the last four days. The person who was responsible for taking her relationship with Wentworth and essentially telling the entire world about it. The same person who was responsible for Ace Thatcher dumping her and killing her Victoria's Secret Angel contract as well.

"It was Charlie," Lo finally said. "She hired a PI to have you followed. She found out about you and Wentworth. She was the one that leaked the story."

23

Face-Off

Lo had only been gone ten minutes and Libby was already doing exactly what she told her not to do because it was not a good idea. She hadn't changed, brushed her hair, or even had that bottle of Evian she knew she needed. Instead, she had popped open the last remaining Skinnygirl bottle in Lo's care box and downed the entire thing as she headed out the front door.

Thursday night was girl's night in for The Brat Pack. Thursday nights had always looked a little different over the years, but at the moment The Pack would indulge in a little Thai food, a couple of bottles of Sauv Blanc, and watch re-runs of *The Bachelor* on Hulu. Apart from the fact that they were all obviously not talking to Libby, nothing suggested that Thursday nights had changed, so that's why Libby was about to knock on Anita's front door. Anita's condo was only down the hall so what better way to really top off her pathetic look than by being barefoot when she knocked. It was how she was in San Francisco when Charlie's PI had taken those photos of her after all.

Libby hadn't thought twice before knocking, which was probably due to all the alcohol buzzing around in her system, but she was thankful for it. This was a confrontation she needed to have with the rest of The Pack, and she would never have been game enough to do it if it hadn't been for all those margaritas and rosé. She wasn't a confrontational person in the slightest after all.

Libby listened hard to what she could hear behind the door. She heard footsteps approaching her, each step louder than the next.

"Oh my God, it's Libby," Christie Ecles' high-pitched voice spoke from behind the door.

Libby forgot that Anita's condo was exactly like hers, and therefore had the same peephole installed on the front door. So, Christie had seen Libby standing on the other side of the door and was reporting back to the rest of The Pack about it.

"Of fucking course, it is," Charlie sighed.

Libby could almost hear Charlie's eyes rolling as she spoke.

"Should we let her in?" Willa asked.

It was Libby's turn to roll her eyes. Willa loved to play the innocent bystander when shit was going down. If she could play both sides of the fence she would in the hopes of maintaining all her friendships, all her networks, and so she could capitalize on gossip from all angles.

"I'm not letting her in," Charlie said.

"I'm with Charlie on this one," Christie agreed.

The volume of Christie's voice compared to the others suggested that she was still standing right next to the front door. Her words were clearer, and Libby didn't have to squint in concentration to listen to what she was saying.

"What do you think she wants?" Willa asked.

"Who the fuck even cares, Willa!" Charlie exclaimed.

"Don't speak to her like that, Charls," Anita chimed in.

It was the first time that Libby had heard Anita's voice, which meant that she was alive and was, therefore, definitely avoiding

Libby's calls. Up until this point, 'drunk Libby' had let her mind go wild with assumptions about why Anita hadn't returned her many text messages or phone calls. All those assumptions, including Anita getting kidnapped and having her phone stolen, had given Libby the slightest bit of hope that Anita wasn't mad at her. Unfortunately, the fact that she was here in her condo about twenty feet away from Libby's front door suggested otherwise. It seemed that Anita simply didn't want to talk to her.

"Whatever, Nita," Charlie sighed dramatically. "If you want that bitch in here then you can let her in."

"I don't want her in here any more than you do," Anita snapped.

"Then what the hell is this conversation we're having?" Charlie snapped back.

"Guys, don't fight," Christie said.

"Yeah, don't fight," Willa repeated.

"Will you just shut up for once, Willa?!" Charlie snapped again.

"Hey!" Willa exclaimed in her defense.

"You guys know that I can hear everything you're saying, right?" Libby finally spoke, surprising herself as the words just tumbled out of her mouth.

She had obviously surprised every person on the other side of the door too as the voices stopped and it was like time stood still in the dead silence that followed.

"Open the fucking door, Christie," Anita was the first to speak.

The silence continued on both sides of the door for a few more seconds before Libby heard the locks on the back of the door being fiddled with. The next thing she knew the door opened and she came face to face with a smirking Christie Ecles, who was trying to pull off a boho-chic look but only succeeding in looking like a homeless woman that had just stepped off the 720-bus heading straight to Skid Row.

Libby could feel every bit of liquid courage wearing off as soon as she stepped past Christie into Anita's condo and walked the few steps she needed to come face to face with the rest of The Pack. She could feel all their eyes on her as she stopped where she was. Charlie had even placed her phone on the coffee table in front of her so she could dramatically fold her arms across her chest.

Libby felt a lump rise in her throat as she looked from Charlie to Willa, and then around to Anita. All of whom were staring daggers at her. Christie was probably doing the same but drunk or not, Libby had zero time for the likes of Christie Ecles. Libby felt like an intruder who had just entered the territory of a wolf pack and was being circled to test for weakness before being attacked when the first opportunity arose.

Libby thought about just bailing on this terrible idea then and there. She could have just headed back to her condo, called Lo to tell her she was right, and then packed her bags for Guam, but then Charlie opened her mouth and Libby knew that she was stuck here now.

"What the fuck do you want?" Charlie asked.

If she hadn't been over the other side of the room Libby would have probably just reached over and used her remaining margarita high to slap Charlie Niven straight across her face. She would have, however, ended up with a hand caked in foundation because even though it was a girl's night in, Charlie was still wearing a full face of make-up, including her classic foundation matching lipstick.

"What the hell is going on?" Libby asked.

She decided to just play it cool. She didn't know for sure that the girls were mad at her, even if their facial expressions did speak volumes to that effect.

"You're seriously just going to stand there and pretend you don't know what this is about?" Charlie asked, a small laugh leaving her Maybelline Fit ME number 115 ivory lips.

"You don't have to be such a bitch about it, Charls," Anita muttered.

"If you ask me, she deserves it," Christie chimed in as she resumed her seat next to Charlie.

"Well, it's a good thing that no one did ask you, Ecles," Libby said rolling her eyes. "You've been here for like five minutes—"

"And yet she's been a better friend to all of us than you have," Anita snapped.

"What is that supposed to mean?" Libby asked.

"Classic Libby Evans," Charlie said as she turned to face the rest of The Pack and then looked Libby dead in the eyes. "Always playing the victim."

"It means that lately, you've been a shitty friend to all of us," Willa chimed in.

"I have not!" Libby exclaimed in her defense.

She immediately mentally kicked herself for retaliating with such an elementary school rebuttal.

"Seriously?!" Anita exclaimed.

"Seriously," Libby nodded, deciding that she was going to have to own that terrible statement now. "I've had a lot on my plate lately. I've been busy—"

"And that is your excuse for everything," Anita said.

"Well, I have been!" Libby exclaimed. "Work has been crazy, Ace has been MIA, and—"

"You've been fucking a paparazzo behind our backs don't forget," Christie chimed in.

"That is not what has been happening," Libby replied, holding her tongue from snapping at Christie again for butting her nose into business that didn't concern her.

"Well then, enlighten us," Charlie said as she relaxed further into her chair.

Libby turned to face the most satisfied-looking Charlie Niven that she had ever seen. The look on her face was one of pure happiness. Pure happiness at the position that she was in because of the situation that Libby had found herself in.

"Go on," Charlie continued, "tell us what has been happening then."

Libby sighed. She couldn't believe that she hadn't seen it coming that the girls would want to know everything about the whole Wentworth Turner situation. Libby had walked herself straight into that the minute she walked into Anita's condo, and now that she was here, she was going to have to tell them the truth. She didn't see another way of getting out of this argument without telling them the whole story. The story she'd avoided telling them for months now, but that they had found out about anyway. The story they thought they knew, but they didn't.

"Look, I'm sorry I didn't tell you about what was going on with me and Went," Libby started.

"Went?" Christie asked with a raised eyebrow.

"It started that night at the Beverly Hills Niven," Libby continued, ignoring Christie's comment yet again.

"It's been going on for SIX MONTHS?!" Willa gasped in shock.

"Seven months, you blonde," Anita corrected, rolling her eyes as she did so.

"You've been keeping this from us for SEVEN MONTHS?!" Willa exclaimed again.

"It wasn't like I planned for this to happen," Libby said. "I was super drunk that night, no thanks to those stupid Jell-O shots, and—"

"Honey, don't blame the alcohol for another one of your stupid men mistakes," Charlie said. "That is just so—"

"Wait," Anita interrupted. "Is that what happened to you that night?"

Libby paused for a moment and recalled the morning after that night. She had escaped the Niven without having to face Wentworth and had taken a car service back to Sierra Towers only to come face to face with an inquisitive Anita. Anita had asked where Libby was, and Libby had dodged a bullet by changing the subject. Unfortunately, that bullet was back, and this time there was no dodging it. Seven months ago, she had avoided telling Anita the truth about where she had spent that night, and who she had spent that night with, but there was no avoiding it now. Libby looked Anita dead in the eyes and nodded.

"I can't believe this," Anita said.

"So, wait," Willa said. "You hooked up with that paparazzo back in December at the Niven launch party?"

Libby nodded again.

"I thought you hooked up with Spencer that night?" Willa asked in confusion.

"No!" Libby exclaimed. "I did not hook up with Spencer! Did you guys seriously think I did?!"

Willa nodded furiously, obviously bewildered at this new revelation. Anita shrugged her shoulders, almost to say that it was what they all thought happened because it was so easy to believe.

"Wouldn't have been the first time," Charlie muttered under her breath.

"Oh my God," Libby sighed. "Spencer Stevenson and I are done, and we have been done for so long. I cannot believe that you guys didn't believe me when I told you that!"

"Can you blame us?" Anita asked. "I mean, after all, you don't exactly have the best track record for honesty these days."

"What is that supposed to mean?" Libby asked.

"This!" Anita exclaimed. "Look at where we are! You lied to us about all of this!"

"I didn't lie to you," Libby said. "I just didn't tell you guys the whole truth."

"Which is exactly the same as lying," Anita scoffed.

"So, you've been hooking up with that paparazzo since December?!" Willa asked, directing traffic back to the conversation topic at hand.

"No!" Libby exclaimed.

"Literally everyone has seen those photos of you two in San Fran," Charlie commented. "You can't lie your way out of this one, Libby."

"We only slept together that one time," Libby said, "back in December, at that party."

"So, then what on Earth has been going on between you two since December?" Anita asked.

Libby turned back to face Anita. She noted that her best friend's tone had somewhat calmed down and so had her volume.

From what Libby knew about Anita from their years of friendship was that, above all, Anita responded well to honesty. It was the reason that Libby was so afraid to finally come clean to Anita after months of deception. She knew that it wasn't going to go down well, which was why she wasn't surprised that Anita was the one in this conversation that was getting the most worked up. It was also the reason why, now that Libby was coming clean and being honest, Anita had somewhat settled.

"We've been going out on dates," Libby replied.

"You've been dating that scum?!" Willa gasped in shock.

"He's not scum," Libby sighed.

"He's a pap," Charlie commented. "They're all fucking scum. We know it and so do you."

"Paps are scum," Libby nodded, "but not him. He just graduated college. He's not a full-time pap."

"Oh, so he's part-time scum, is that it?" Charlie scoffed.

Libby turned to face Charlie, about to snap back at her when Anita steered the conversation back on track.

"Why the hell would you be dating him when you're dating Ace?" Anita asked.

Libby sighed, trying to figure out whether it was time to tell them the whole truth about the ten dates arrangement. No one knew about the arrangement except her and Wentworth. Ace didn't even know, so there wasn't any way that the rest of The Pack would find out about it if she didn't say anything right now. Libby looked Anita in the eye though and realized that if she wanted to try and salvage any part of their friendship, she was going to have to tell the whole truth. She didn't care about Christie or Charlie, or even Willa, but she did want to at least try and make things right with Anita.

"I had to," Libby finally spoke, realizing how silent the room was as the others waited for her to answer.

"You HAD to?" Charlie sneered.

"Yes," Libby said, "otherwise he was going to leak to the press that we hooked up at the party."

"So, he blackmailed you?" Christie asked.

"Yes," Libby repeated. "He told me that he would keep our hook up a secret if I dated him for a while."

Libby found it hard to speak the words as she explained the truth about her predicament to the rest of The Pack. Partly because it was true, but partly because it wasn't. The relationship between her and Wentworth back in January when they had started this arrangement was vastly different from the relationship they had a few days ago. Whilst it was the truth, he had blackmailed her into dating him in exchange for his silence, their relationship was no longer that black and white.

Somewhere along the line, she stopped feeling like she had to be there on those dates with him and instead felt like she wanted to be there. She wanted to spend more time with him and eventually found herself wanting to be closer to him, both physically and emotionally. She found herself craving their conversations and at the same time craving his touch, so it felt wrong to tell the girls about the situation without adding in the back story. Without the context of the situation, it just felt wrong.

"And you really expect us to believe that?" Christie asked.

"Well, it's the truth," Libby said.

"Like we would even be able to trust you after all this," Christie replied.

"I really don't care what you think, Christie," Libby snapped, not being able to hold her tongue any longer.

"So, he just wanted you to date him?" Charlie chimed in.

Libby turned to face the blonde and was met with a raised eyebrow in her direction.

"Yes," Libby replied.

"And you didn't sleep with him at all except for that night in December?" Willa asked.

Libby nodded.

"And Ace didn't know about any of it?" Willa asked.

Libby nodded again.

"What were the dates?" Willa asked.

"All of this sounds incredibly farfetched," Charlie said, interrupting Willa's game of 20 Questions. "I really thought a seasoned liar like you could do a little better than that, Libby."

"That's what he wanted," Libby shrugged. "I went on his dates, and he kept his word about not telling anyone about that night. Not that it mattered anyway did it, Charlie?"

"And what is that supposed to mean?" Charlie asked.

"You know exactly what that means," Libby replied.

Charlie went to say something, but instead closed her mouth and simply smiled.

"I don't know what you're talking about," Charlie replied, the smile still plastered across her face.

"Of course, you don't," Libby said. "You're Charlie Niven. You don't care what you have to do or who you have to step over if it means getting exactly what you want."

Charlie didn't reply. She simply maintained her smile in Libby's direction as she started twirling one of her blonde curls in between her fingers.

"I know that you hired a PI to follow me around," Libby said. "I can't believe that after everything we've been through that you would stoop this low just to get me out of The Pack."

"You hired a PI?" Willa asked.

"Maybe I did," Charlie replied, seemingly unfazed by Libby's revelation. "Maybe I didn't. It doesn't really matter though, does it? Because he caught you doing something that you can't deny. He didn't make anything up. What he found, those photos he took, is all you. Not me."

"I can't believe you hired a PI!" Anita exclaimed, turning to face Charlie. "That is beyond fucked up, Charls!"

"Get over it, Nita," Charlie said as she rolled her eyes, not even bothering to meet Anita's gaze. "We all wanted to know what Libby's 'Victoria's Secret' was, so I did what I had to do to find out."

"Oh, because I'm the only one here with secrets?" Libby asked as she looked around the room.

Libby watched as a temporary shade of fear washed over the eyes of every girl in the room as they all started racking their brains as to whether Libby was referring to them and the secrets they had.

"I know all about you and Hamish Dawson," Libby said as she looked Charlie dead in the eyes. "I know you've been obsessed with him for months now and that you guys have been hooking up on the DL."

"And?!" Charlie replied. "I'm not allowed to date him because you did, Libby? Because he belongs to you, does he? Or is he still in love with you? Is that it? Or is it both because everything's about you isn't it, Libby? Everything in everyone's life revolves around you."

"That's not what I said," Libby replied, immensely regretting dropping the Hamish Dawson bomb as it was just backfiring on her.

"You didn't have to," Christie chimed in. "It's just who you are."

Libby watched as Christie scooted over in her seat toward Charlie as if to demonstrate where her allegiance lay.

"That is not true," Libby shook her head.

"Except it is," Charlie continued. "Everything is always about you. You don't want to be part of a conversation unless it's about you, or Victoria's Secret. We can't talk to you about anything unless it's something to do with you, or modeling, or something else to that effect."

"Willa's a model too," Libby said with a pointed finger in Willa's direction. "She talks modeling just as much as I do!"

"Nowhere near as much as you," Willa replied.

Libby's jaw dropped as she looked in Willa's direction, not quite believing that Willa was helping Charlie drag her under the bus right now.

"Or heaven forbid we have to listen to another Libby Evans pity party about you and Ace Thatcher," Charlie added.

"So, I can't even talk to my own friends about my relationship problems is that it?" Libby asked.

"We just can't take the constant whining you do about it all," Anita added. "We get it, you're dating an oil heir, and you know what, considering the other trash guys in Hollywood, dating a billionaire is not actually that bad."

"I can't believe that I'm hearing this right now," Libby said.

She started frustratedly running her fingers through her hair, realizing for the first time how badly her greasy locks needed a wash.

"So yeah, I didn't tell you about Hamish Dawson," Charlie continued, "because I didn't want to have to listen to you go on and on about your long history with him and listen to you make the whole thing about you like you do everything else."

"I don't make everything about me!" Libby exclaimed.

"Did you know that Willa didn't get any gigs for fashion week this year?" Charlie asked.

Libby shook her head.

"That's because you didn't care to ask after I talked to you about how shitty all my casting calls were," Willa mumbled. "You didn't care to listen because it wasn't about you."

"I didn't know," Libby said.

"Did you know that Anita's Netflix series about Joan of Arc starts shooting next week in the south of France?" Charlie asked.

Libby shook her head again as she turned to face Anita. Anita, however, avoided her eyes altogether, focusing instead on the glass of wine in her hand that was almost all out of rosé.

"Truth hurts, doesn't it?" Charlie smirked.

Libby looked over in Charlie's direction and simply shook her head.

"So, that's why you felt you were entitled to destroy my reputation by leaking that scandal to the press, is it?" Libby asked rhetorically.

Charlie shrugged her shoulders.

"So, because I was a bad friend, I deserved what I got, is that it?" Libby asked again, this time looking around the room from Christie to Willa and then Anita.

Christie looked pleased as punch, as did Charlie, but Libby could see the little bits of hesitation in both Willa and Anita's eyes at what she had just said. However, they both still looked pretty upset, no doubt about the wounds that Libby had caused and that Charlie had just reopened.

"If I've been a bad friend, of course, I'm sorry for it," Libby said honestly. "I didn't set out to hurt any of you so I'm sorry, but no one deserves what I got because of it."

"That's what happens when you think you can keep secrets from The Pack and pull the wool over our eyes," Charlie muttered.

Libby looked over in Charlie's direction and shook her head again.

"I'm glad you got exactly what you wanted, Charlie," Libby said. "I'm glad you got to see my downfall. I'm glad you got to see me fail. I'm glad you got to see me lose everything."

Libby watched as the satisfied smile on Charlie's face started to slowly fade. Less satisfaction and more disdain started to appear as Libby decided to continue.

"Even if it doesn't seem it, I have been nothing but supportive of everything you all do," Libby said looking around the room. "Except

Christie because who the fuck knows what she actually does except run around Hollywood trying to fit in where she doesn't belong."

Libby knew the blow was low and uncalled for but the shocked expression on Christie's face was worth the sneaky throw-in comment. The truth was that she didn't know Christie at all, but after all of this, she really didn't even care to change that.

"It doesn't matter," Anita spoke, surprising Libby as she did so.

"What do you mean?" Libby asked.

"The damage is done," Anita continued. "You slept with someone else and dated someone else behind your boyfriend's back for seven months, so Ace was right to dump you."

"We heard your Victoria's Secret Angel contract got revoked," Christie said, "and you deserved that because you couldn't even stay scandal-free for just six months."

"And you lied to us about everything," Charlie added, "so The Pack is done with you."

"You're 'done with me'?" Libby asked, not quite believing what she was hearing right now.

She'd apologized and genuinely apologized, for lying to them and for being a bad friend, even though she hadn't realized she was even doing it.

"Right," Anita replied. "We're done with you, so you can show yourself out."

Libby felt like she'd just had the wind knocked out of her. She couldn't believe what she had just heard. She knew that this was all Charlie's doing, but at the same time, Willa and Anita hadn't exactly been held at gunpoint when they sided with Charlie and helped her kick Libby to the curb. Charlie had obviously brainwashed them. She had put ideas in their heads about things that weren't even that important because Charlie had always been jealous of Libby.

She didn't hide it very well, so Libby wasn't the only one who knew that Charlie wanted a lot of things that Libby had. Whether it was her successful career, her rising fame, or the fact that everyone saw The Brat Pack as 'Libby Evans' Brat Pack'. Whilst those things were important to Libby, and any other girl trying to make it in Hollywood, none were more important than her friends, or the people she thought were her friends. The ones who had just told her that they wanted nothing more to do with her. The ones who had just made one of the lowest points in her life that much lower.

She didn't know what she was going to do without her friends. She didn't know who she was going to talk to, or who she was going to hang out with at parties if she even got invited to exclusive Hollywood parties anymore. She didn't know who was going to join her table for Sunday brunches, and where she was even going to go for Sunday brunches. She obviously couldn't go to Silverlake anymore because it was, and would always be Brat Pack territory. It turned out that she didn't know anything anymore.

A million and one thoughts were running through Libby's mind as she silently and quickly walked out of Anita's condo. The haze that she was in meant that she didn't even hear the door to Anita's condo slam shut behind her, nor did she realize that she hadn't locked her condo on her way out. She just opened the front door and strolled right in.

All she could hear was her heart beating in her ears and all she could feel was the tears welling in her eyes. It seemed like a stupid thing to cry about, and she knew she was too old to cry about something as trivial as losing every single one of her closest friends, but she couldn't help herself. She felt the first tear roll down her cheek as she heard a knock at the front door.

Her heart jumped in her chest and the last ounce of hope she had told her that it was Willa, or maybe even Anita, coming to tell her that things were going to be OK. That she wasn't going to be totally alone and that she would have at least one friend left. In time, she would be able to earn the trust of The Pack back and things would go back to the way they were before. The way they always had been.

Libby quickly rushed to the front door and opened it without even thinking, but it wasn't Willa. It wasn't Anita either.

24

Broken

Wentworth genuinely thought that Libby was going to leave him standing in the doorway all night. The look on her face clearly said that she was not expecting him to be there, but she hadn't slammed the door in his face either, so he was taking that as a good sign. However, she hadn't said a word since they had locked eyes, so now Wentworth was starting to worry whether she was OK.

He looked at her, and even though she was the most beautiful woman he knew, she didn't look great right now. She looked like she hadn't slept since the last time he had seen her, and she obviously hadn't washed her hair since then either. He hadn't ever seen her in leisurewear, but he assumed that was what she was wearing. He could barely tell that she had a supermodel physique hiding under the shapeless top and pants she was wearing. The khaki color of the fabric wasn't helping her appearance either, making her normally radiant skin look flat and dull.

"Can I come in?" Wentworth asked tentatively.

He watched as she finally blinked. Her eyes were no longer glazed over and staring at a patch of wall behind him. She shook her head and gave him a nod to indicate that he could step over the threshold and come inside. She closed the door behind him, and, in silence, he followed her to her bedroom.

Wentworth was disappointed that it was under these circumstances that he was seeing her bedroom for the very first time. It was probably the nicest bedroom he had ever seen and reminded him of the Four Seasons they had stayed at in San Francisco. Libby's bed looked just like a fancy hotel room bed dressed in crisp white. The white sheets, probably 1200-thread-count, matched the fluffy white comforter with silver embroidery all over it, and the fur blanket tossed over one corner. That corner of the bed was also covered in what appeared to be a wooden box full of random items, including an assortment of food wrappers and empty glass bottles spilling out.

He watched as Libby straightened out a small patch of bed and sat cross-legged on top of the comforter. He looked at the white end of the bed ottoman and figured that would be the best place for him to sit right now. He felt the soft suede fabric under his fingertips as he took a seat.

"I'm sorry for just showing up," Wentworth said, watching Libby intently for her reaction. "I know it's really late."

Libby nodded, as she turned to her right and drew both their attention to the wooden analog clock sitting on her nightstand that currently read 10:05 pm. It wasn't really that late, but it was late enough that he felt bad for dropping in unannounced, especially because he didn't know if she was purposely trying to avoid him. She had, after all, not been returning his calls or texts for the last four days.

"I tried to call you," Wentworth spoke again, drawing Libby's gaze. "I tried texting too. Kind of in a bit of a stalkerish way now that I think about it..."

He watched the corners of her mouth curl into a small smile as she held his stare. Her eyes lowered, and his followed, as she silently stared at her hands in her lap. Wentworth noticed her chewed finger-nails and chipped nail polish. Things that he didn't normally see on Libby Evans.

"It's been a rough few days," Libby said, immediately coughing to rid the hoarseness from her voice.

"Yeah," Wentworth sighed. "I can imagine."

Libby looked him in the eye again. Her dark brown eyes were glossy as she did so.

"I was going to call you back," she said.

Her voice was soft. So soft that Wentworth had to strain to hear it. He was sure that she was holding back tears and speaking right now was making that harder.

"I know you were," Wentworth said. "How are you?"

Libby shrugged as she managed a small smile.

"I've been better," she replied, her eyes lowering to her hands again. "I mean, my career is pretty much over, my boyfriend dumped me, and my friends want nothing to do with me so, I've definitely been better."

Wentworth had to stop himself from jumping onto the bed and enveloping her in a hug that he was so desperate to give her.

He wanted to hug her and make it all go away. Everything she was probably feeling including the pain, the embarrassment, the frustration, and the regret of the situation she had found herself in. He wanted to hold her until he made her feel better, no matter how long it took. Regrettably, what was stopping him from doing that was the fact that she was feeling like this because of him.

"I'm so sorry," Wentworth blurted out.

He watched as Libby's eyes rose to meet his again. It was the best consolation he could offer that felt more appropriate than a hug. He waited for a second to see if she wanted to speak, but when enough time had passed, he spoke again.

"I am so sorry for putting you in this situation," he said, "for giving you an impossible choice for my own selfish reasons, and making you do something I know you didn't want to do."

"No," Libby shook her head.

Wentworth held his breath as he waited for her to continue. He knew that he was going to deserve whatever she was going to say to him next.

He came to her place tonight intending to let her lash out at him with whatever she needed to get out of her system. He came here assuming she had a massive load of built-up anger at him for being the cause of all the mess in her life. He was prepared to listen to whatever she had to say or yell. He was, however, hoping that her yelling wouldn't alert the neighbors to call security again. Getting kicked out of Sierra Towers twice in one week would probably get him put on some kind of watch list and definitely banned from the building.

"I'm a big girl," Libby finally continued. "I made the decision to go out with you and lie about it to my friends and my boyfriend."

Wentworth sat and listened, watching her as she intently fiddled with her fingers. Her gaze flicked from them in her lap to lock with his.

"I made the choice," Libby continued. "You didn't make it for me."

"But the choice I gave you wasn't really a choice," Wentworth said. "It was like a choice between Spencer Stevenson and Spencer Stevenson."

Libby laughed out loud. Wentworth could tell that she wasn't in the mood to laugh so the laugh that escaped her lips caught them both off guard.

"You did give me a choice though," Libby said.

Wentworth nodded. He wasn't sure how long she was going to let him stay here as it was already longer than he deserved. He didn't want to spend this precious time with her arguing about details that weren't important at all in the grand scheme of things.

"I wasn't ever going to leak what happened between us at the Niven," Wentworth said. "You know that, right?"

Libby paused for a minute, obviously mulling it over before she spoke again.

"I know that now," Libby replied. "I didn't know that then."

Wentworth nodded as he started to feel the tension and the awkward silence building between them, something he was trying to avoid.

Four days ago, they had woken up in his dorm room and had been making out all over Caltech campus toying with the idea of moving to New York together. Now it felt like they were back to somewhere around the time he showed up at this same condo at 1:00 am after following her home from Skybar. They were right back to where they had started, if not someplace even further back than that, and Wentworth didn't want that at all.

He didn't want to be right back at a time when he didn't know the real Libby Evans. He realized that he refused to accept that, which was the reason he moved without thinking twice about it. It was, after all, probably going to be his last chance to let her know how he really felt.

He stood up from the ottoman and moved to the side of the bed where Libby was sitting. She watched him move as he sat on the edge of the bed and reached for her hands. Wentworth sighed a breath of relief as she easily let him take her hands in his, gently squeezing them before he spoke again.

"I want to be honest with you about why all this happened," Wentworth said, just letting the words flow straight out of his mouth without allowing himself to overthink them. "About why I wanted ten dates with you in the first place."

Libby's eyes focused on their entwined hands as she took a deep breath and nodded for him to continue. She was obviously feeling very much like he was; extremely nervous and hesitant about what he was about to say.

"I've been working as a pap for longer than I've wanted to," Wentworth continued. "The money was great, and the work was easy. It was about a year into it all when I started making big money. It was enough to send home to my parents to help with my dad's hospital bills and to also contribute to my compounding college debt that they were insisting on paying because they wanted me to finish college, regardless of the circumstances."

Wentworth paused for a moment as he sorted through his thoughts and tried to figure out the best way to express exactly what he wanted to say.

"Last year, the new Hollywood Brat Pack was the biggest money earner when it came to pap photos," Wentworth continued. "Candid photos of any of you brought in big money, but you were by far the one whose photo would pay the most, especially when you started dating Ace."

Wentworth felt her hands tense in his at the mention of her ex-boyfriend and he made a mental note to avoid Ace's name again tonight. It was obviously something that was still a little too raw to talk about right now. Wentworth also knew that it was not his place to talk about the boyfriend that had dumped her, especially when he was the reason it had happened at all.

"So, it was about a year ago when I decided to put most of my energy into getting photos of you," Wentworth sighed, instantly realizing how bad it sounded as he tried to quickly steer the conversation away from Ace. "You went to Sydney late last year for the

Victoria's Secret show and I managed to see you at LAX before you took off. I couldn't understand why you were taking a commercial flight when usually the models for the show take the Victoria's Secret private charter—"

"I had a photo shoot for Longchamps in Paris a few days before, so I couldn't make the private plane," Libby said. "I had to fly commercial to Sydney and then I flew on the private plane back to LA."

Wentworth nodded.

"So, I went to LAX to get a photo of you before you took off," Wentworth continued. "I had to buy a ticket to anywhere to get into the departures terminal and when I did, I found you waiting at your gate. You were wearing black leggings and white sneakers. It was a cool day for LA, so you also had on this light blue oversized sweatshirt. I barely recognized it was you to start with because you were sitting near one of the glass windows wearing these ridiculously massive black sunglasses, and you were reading. It wasn't that I thought you were dumb because I never make that assumption about anyone, even celebrities, but seeing you reading an actual book wasn't something I expected to see. Everyone around you was either engrossed in their smartphones or reading a magazine from one of the airport newsstands, but you were sitting there reading *The Catcher in the Rye*."

"It's one of my favorite books," Libby said.

Wentworth watched a small smile tug at the corners of her mouth.

"And that's when I knew I had to get to know you," Wentworth continued, trying to capitalize on her smile that he hoped meant that she was enjoying the story.

"I wanted to get to know the girl that was not only beyond beautiful but that read *Catcher in The Rye* in her spare time for fun," Wentworth continued. "I wanted to get to know who you are. I wanted to get to know you."

He watched as Libby's gaze rose from their still entwined hands to meet his eyes.

"When I woke up that morning at the Niven and realized what had happened, I just wanted to talk to you," Wentworth said, "but then you asked what I wanted to keep me quiet about everything and I saw it as an opportunity to get to know you like I wanted. I capitalized on that opportunity to get what I wanted."

Wentworth sighed.

"I wasn't thinking about how it was going to affect you and I'm sorry for that," he said, "but I wouldn't change it. I got to know you in a way that I could have only hoped for. I got to know you, Libby, and you are even more kind, beautiful, and smart than I ever thought one person could be."

Wentworth was hoping that his words, as vulnerable but truthful as they were, would be a good place to start on the road to making things better between them. He was hoping that pouring out his soul to her would make her realize that what he felt for her was real. That this wasn't a game to him. He wanted her to know that he was serious about being with her, but as Libby's fingers and hands retracted from his he felt the opposite. Maybe his words weren't enough, or maybe they were just too little too late.

"Tell me how I can fix this," Wentworth pleaded. "Tell me what I can do to fix this. I can't just walk away from you, from this, from us. I meant what I said the other day. I'm not ready to say goodbye to you yet."

Wentworth stopped as he analyzed Libby's reaction and watched as she opened her mouth, as if ready to say something before she closed it again. He waited patiently as he watched her take a deep breath and swallow hard.

"It was the worst day of my life," Libby finally spoke, her voice soft. "The worst day, and there were paparazzi everywhere. They didn't care about how I was feeling. They didn't care about how much of a massive breach of privacy and humanity it was for them to be there. For them to be there shoving a camera in my face as I was trying to say goodbye to my mom for the last time, and you were one of them. You were there and you were one of them. Breaching my privacy. Pouring salt in the wound."

Wentworth looked at her as she spoke and when she finished, she looked him dead in the eye and that was it. It was the moment he felt his heart sink because he had been wrong.

He was worried that she didn't know exactly how deeply he felt about her. He was worried that she thought he planned all it all in San Francisco, but it turned out that the problem was that he had hurt her, and he could see that now in her eyes. He had hurt her so deeply five years ago when he was there at her mom's funeral taking photos of her to profit off. It was at that moment when she looked up at him that he also knew that it was over. There was no way to repair their relationship. There was no coming back from this. Five years ago, he had ruined any chance of being with her, and he hadn't realized that until tonight.

"I don't want this to be over," Wentworth whispered as his gaze fell to a patch of bed in front of him.

He wasn't sure if he was speaking the words to her or himself.

"But it is," Libby replied, her voice matching his in volume and in what sounded like sadness.

"Libby, I—" Wentworth started.

"Don't say it," Libby quickly interrupted him. "Please."

Wentworth nodded. She had pre-empted that he was going to say the words he had accidentally let slip the other day when Ace Thatcher had been there with them, and she was right. He had wanted to tell her on purpose this time, not by accident. He wanted to tell her that he loved her, whether it would change anything between them or not.

"OK," he nodded.

Wentworth watched her as she continued to scratch her right thumb with the fingers on her left hand, fiddling like she always did when she was nervous.

"I just need you to know that I do," Wentworth said, hoping she would know what he was talking about.

"I know," Libby nodded.

Wentworth nodded once more.

"OK," he said.

"We didn't even get to have our last date," Libby said, looking up at him with a small smile.

She was clearly trying to change the subject.

"I didn't think it was going to be our last one," Wentworth smiled back.

"No," Libby said, shaking her head. "Me neither."

"But if you change your mind?" Wentworth said.

Libby's brow furrowed in confusion. It made him smile wider. It also made him want to just take her in his arms and hold her; to kiss her and forget about this whole mess they were in.

"What do you mean?" she asked curiously.

Wentworth sighed. He wanted to draw out his next words because he knew that once he said them, that would be it. The conversation would naturally come to an end, and he didn't want that.

"Come find me if one day you see the light," he said.

Libby's eyes narrowed at him, clearly confused by his words.

"See what light?" she asked.

"The light that you've brought to my life," Wentworth answered. "The light that I've always seen in you."

He heard her breath hitch and for a split second, he thought she was going to come to him. To tell him how he could fix it. How he could fix them, but a couple of seconds passed, and then the moment was gone.

It had been less than a year, but he still didn't know how to say goodbye to her. He didn't know what words to use, and he didn't know whether he should hug her or not, so he didn't do any of it. He knew he was going to kick himself about it later when he was up all night trying to remember and memorize every single detail about her. How her hair always smelt of coconut, how her lips were always covered in pink Chapstick that tasted like strawberries and cream, and how incredibly soft her hands felt in his.

Now all he could feel was the inside pocket of his jeans. All he could smell was the overdone jasmine scent that filled the elevators at Sierra Towers, and all he could taste was the lingering regret he felt about everything. Libby Evans was so much more than he could have ever predicted when he started thinking about her more and more after that day at LAX; back when all he wanted was the chance to spend more time with her. Now all he wanted was for her to be happy and he didn't think that involved him anymore.

25

See The Light

"This is *Prosecco, Pizza & Peyton* with Peyton Song, my newest podcast where I sit down and chill in the fabulous homes of the most successful celebrities in Hollywood with a gourmet selection of pizza from Gjelina and a bottle from Marissa Michaels' new sparkling wine collection proSESSO," Peyton Song said into the giant microphone positioned perfectly in front of her face. "My guest this morning is none other than the drop-dead gorgeous supermodel, Hollywood socialite, and Privileged Pictures heiress, Libby Evans."

Libby smiled as she took in her surroundings one more time. She was currently sitting in the middle of her living room on one of the grey armchairs next to former talk show host Peyton Song, who was sitting in the matching chair about two feet away from her.

Apart from all the audio equipment surrounding them, including speakers and microphones, it looked like they were just two girlfriends having brunch together. It was 11:30 am on a Tuesday morning and they were surrounded by three different types of pizza, all absolutely covered in meat, which Libby very much appreciated, and two pink custom Peyton Song champagne flutes full of prosecco.

"How are you doing this morning, Libby?" Peyton smiled, turning away from her notepad of scribbled notes.

"Fantastic thanks, Peyton," Libby smiled. "Thanks so much for having me on your show."

"You're very welcome!" Peyton chirped as she lifted her glass in Libby's direction. "There's nothing I love more than a good glass of prosecco on a Tuesday in amongst all the chatting we are going to be doing."

Libby, in reply, raised her glass in Peyton's direction before she took a generous swig and let the bubbles dance down her throat, hopefully taking her nerves with them.

Today was the very first interview she'd done since the scandal about her and Wentworth had broken exactly nine weeks prior. She had kept a low profile since the incident as she put her life back together.

Unfortunately, as soon as the scandal broke, the Victoria's Secret Angel contract was suddenly put 'on hold', as the Victoria's Secret executives had put it. It was, however, a blessing in disguise as it allowed Libby to immerse herself in a lot of editorial shoots that she had assumed she wouldn't have time to do once the Angel contract was finally locked in. Those shoots had taken her all over the country and even to Europe over the last two months, which had been a fantastic distraction from the disaster that was her personal and social life.

"So, let's get down to business," Peyton said. "This is the first interview you've done in nine weeks!"

"Correct," Libby nodded. "I've been focusing on work a lot recently, both in the States and overseas."

"As a bit of a distraction, right?" Peyton asked.

Libby tensed up as she reminded herself to breathe.

Peyton had been honest with her when they'd met last Saturday to lock in the details for today's taping. Peyton needed ratings for her show, so Libby understood that meant discussing the scandal and Peyton had been upfront about that, something that Libby had appreciated at the time. Libby had also, at the time, agreed to Peyton's terms, but she wasn't appreciating it so much right now.

"That's right," Libby replied.

"So, in case you've been living under a rock for the last two months," Peyton explained as she looked down at her notes again, "Libby Evans was involved in quite the scandal recently that involved oil heir billionaire Ace Thatcher and a local paparazzo by the name of Wentworth Turner."

Libby simply nodded. Of course, no one could see her, except Peyton, so that was at least a plus of doing this interview as a podcast rather than a televised segment.

"So, Libby," Peyton said, "can you tell us exactly what happened?"

Libby took a deep breath.

"Look, this is obviously a very uncomfortable thing for me to discuss," she admitted, "but essentially, I made some bad decisions. I made some mistakes. I was in a relationship with Ace Thatcher—"

"Also known as Alexandre Thatcher III, a gorgeous, if you don't mind me saying, French billionaire and heir to his maternal grandfather's Mediterranean oil and gas exploration empire – Royauté Energy," Peyton added. "How long were you guys together at this stage?"

"About a year," Libby answered.

"And things weren't going well?" Peyton asked.

Libby knew she had to choose her words carefully. Her relationship with Ace was rocky and he wasn't exactly innocent in all this. He had, after all, cheated on her and not been a great boyfriend when it came to their long-distance relationship. At the same time, though, she had hurt him and had cheated on him too. No matter what he had done to her it still didn't negate the wrongdoings on her part.

"Things were rocky," Libby answered. "He had his commitments in France with the family business, and I was here in LA with my modeling and spokesmodel commitments too. Long distance is never an easy thing to do."

"Of course," Peyton said. "Long distance sucks!"

"Absolutely," Libby nodded. "So, we both struggled with the long-distance aspect, and we both made mistakes that eventually led to the end of our relationship."

"Including your relationship with Wentworth Turner, right?" Peyton asked.

"Yes," Libby simply answered as she took a generous swig of her prosecco.

"So, for those of you who don't recognize the name," Peyton said, "Wentworth Turner is a recent pre-vet Caltech graduate whose side hustle involves following the beautiful people around Hollywood as one of many paparazzi in our beautiful city."

Libby swallowed hard, trying to get as much prosecco into her before Peyton's next question finally came.

"So now, Libby, tell me about what happened between you and Wentworth," Peyton said, "because there's been a lot going around in the media and a lot of speculation and gossip about how all this went down. Some sources are saying that it was all a publicity stunt to lock in your Victoria's Secret Angel contract, whilst others are saying that you and Wentworth got married in Vegas behind Ace's back, so which was it?"

Libby laughed out loud.

"Neither of those!" Libby said. "It was definitely not a publicity stunt, and I am definitely not married!"

"Of course!" Peyton laughed. "So, set the record straight. What happened?"

Libby sighed as she prepared to give the answer that Felicity had carefully worded for her when they had prepped for the podcast yesterday afternoon.

"Look, I don't want to go into that many details about it for the sake of all parties involved," Libby said, "but the truth is that the relationships overlapped. It doesn't matter when it happened, how it happened, or why. I'm only human and having them overlap was a choice I made, even though it wasn't a great one."

"Sure," Peyton nodded. "We're all only human and we're all entitled to make some mistakes. I really think that people forget that about celebrities and the rich and famous. We're in the public eye but that doesn't mean we're going to be perfect all the time!"

"Exactly," Libby nodded.

"So, I really appreciate your candor about the situation, Libby," Peyton added, "but, listening to what you were saying before, you didn't exactly say that what happened between you and Wentworth Turner was a mistake?"

Libby paused for a moment and tried to mentally recap what she had just said.

"No, you're right," Libby replied. "I guess I didn't."

"Was it a mistake?" Peyton pressed. "Any of it? All of it? None of it?"

Libby took a deep breath to stop herself from panicking. She didn't know if Wentworth would hear the podcast when it aired, but she knew that if he did hear her say that their relationship was a mistake it was going to hurt him. As if her saying that it was all a mistake would imply that she regretted it, and she didn't want him to think that.

"I never like to think of my bad decisions as mistakes," Libby said, reaching for another piece of Pepperoni pizza to keep her cool. "I like to call them life lessons."

"Nice," Peyton nodded as she scribbled away in her notebook with a fluffy pink pen that had previously been clipped to the lapel of her trademark pink pinstripe blazer. "I'm going to use that!"

"By all means," Libby said.

A silence fell between them, if only for a couple of seconds. Libby used the time to calm her nerves by indulging in the piece of pizza in her hands. Peyton finished scribbling and then looked up from her notebook.

"So, since the scandal broke, word has it that you've been 'let go'," Peyton said, making use of an air quotes hand gesture, "from the Hollywood Brat Pack. True or false?"

"True," Libby said, crossing her legs in relaxation as she realized the worst of the interview was now behind her and she could relax a little.

"Care to elaborate?" Peyton asked.

"Well," Libby replied, "from what I've heard, The Pack is still alive and thriving, as it probably always will, but what you've heard is true – I am no longer part of it."

"So, I take it the girls were not pleased to hear about the scandal?" Peyton asked.

"They were completely in the dark about the whole thing," Libby explained, "so that didn't go down well at all."

"Oo, so they didn't know a thing?" Peyton asked, leaning further into Libby.

"I'm sure they suspected something was going on that I wasn't telling them about," Libby said, "but they didn't know anything about it until just before the scandal broke."

"Just before?" Peyton asked, using her detective journalism skills to pick out the most important part of Libby's last sentence.

"Just before," Libby nodded. "Sadly, it was one of the girls that broke the scandal to the tabloids."

The look on Peyton's face was pretty much exactly what Libby's face had looked like when she had found out that bit of news as well. It still hit a sore spot with Libby, so it was probably the one bit of gossip she was willing to give Peyton with no strings attached. Charlie Niven deserved a bit of backlash for it, and Libby was happy to admit that she was going to be that little bit petty to get that satisfaction.

"OMG!" Peyton exclaimed. "So, one of your girls actually leaked the story to the tabloids?"

"Correct," Libby nodded.

"Let me guess," Peyton said. "Charlie Niven?"

Libby laughed out loud. She had previously decided that she didn't want to publicly name and shame Charlie as her saboteur, but she knew, and Peyton had confirmed, that it was pretty damn obvious. Out of every member of The Pack that it could have been, Charlie was the most obvious guess.

"You don't need to confirm," Peyton quickly added. "That kind of thing has that blonde hotel heiress written all over it."

Libby laughed again.

"So, I take it you and Charlie are no longer speaking then?" Peyton asked.

"No," Libby said, trying to sound as polite as possible. "Charlie and I aren't speaking at the moment."

"That seems to be a common theme right now because it looks like you aren't the only one that Charlie isn't speaking with," Peyton smiled.

Libby instinctively smiled back, knowing Peyton well enough to know that she had some gossip up her sleeve that she was saving up to drop at this exact moment on her podcast.

"What do you mean?" Libby asked.

"You haven't heard about Charlie and Christie?" Peyton asked.

"Christie Ecles?" Libby clarified.

"Yep," Peyton nodded as she took a generous swig of her prosecco, her newly dyed bright red ponytail squishing behind her head as she did so. "She and Charlie had a bit of a falling out."

"Really?" Libby asked, trying not to sound as interested as she was.

"So, it turns out that Charlie and Hamish Dawson were seeing each other on the DL," Peyton said.

"Oh yeah," Libby said. "I did hear about that."

"Well, it turns out that Charlie wasn't the only Brat Packer that Hamish was seeing on the DL," Peyton said, wriggling her eyebrows at Libby suggestively.

"No way!" Libby gasped.

"Yes, way!" Peyton said, nodding enthusiastically. "This is a *Prosecco, Pizza & Peyton* exclusive that you're hearing right now listeners! Word has it on the Sunset Strip, that bad-boy singer/songwriter Hamish Dawson has been busy with his Brat Pack ladies. Turns out that Hamish and hotel heiress Charlie Niven weren't really on the same page about the exclusivity of their relationship. Poor Charlie got dumped for former backup dancer and Illuse Cosmetics heiress, Christie Ecles. My sources tell me that Christie and Hamish are getting pretty serious. Just this past week, they were spotted canoodling on Paradise Island in the Bahamas!"

"Wow," Libby nodded. "I definitely did not see that coming."

"Neither did Charlie apparently," Peyton shrugged. "What about you and the other Packers? Anita Yates? Willa Nelson?"

"Anita and I have somewhat patched things up," Libby explained. "We're on good terms now."

"And Willa Nelson?" Peyton asked.

"Maybe someday in the future," Libby replied.

"I always thought you girls were so tight," Peyton commented.

"We used to be," Libby said, "but you grow, and you change."

"And some friendships aren't supposed to last forever, right?" Peyton said.

Libby smiled and nodded.

Those were almost the exact words that Wentworth had spoken to her when they were in San Francisco and had talked about her relationships with Charlie Niven and the rest of The Pack. The words had stuck with her because they were so insightful. Now that Libby thought about it, Wentworth had been insightful about several things in her life that were in conflict, and she knew that it was because he listened to her when she spoke. He was so good at listening.

The rest of the interview went by in a blur as Libby continued to think about Wentworth as she answered all of Peyton's questions. The questions got easier as the interview went on, so Libby found that she didn't have to concentrate too hard to give Peyton the answers she wanted.

Just like Lo had said, things had eventually gone back to normal after the scandal had broken, even if it had taken a couple of weeks, and Peyton wanted all the details about what Libby was up to next in her career. Victoria's Secret had reached out again and asked her to walk for the annual show in a couple of months, which was always exciting, especially when she was sure that she had blown any opportunity to work with the brand again. Felicity had also called this morning to say that Sports Illustrated had confirmed that Libby had made the line-up for the annual swimsuit edition, which would photograph early next year. Peyton was obviously stoked to be the first to hear that news, and as petty as it was, Libby was stoked herself to hear that Willa Nelson was not one of the other twenty-four models that would be joining Libby when they shot in Tampa next March. As good as it was to be able to share her good news with Peyton, she still wished she had someone else to share it with.

Since the last time he had shown up at her condo, Wentworth hadn't reached out to her at all. She understood why he hadn't, especially when she had been honest with him about how much he had hurt her when she found out that he was one of the paps at her mother's funeral. At the same time, though, she was disappointed that he hadn't still tried to reach out. She should have been thankful that he was giving her the space she needed and the space to potentially forgive him, but all she could think about was how much she missed him.

The time away from The Pack had made her realize how much she needed real friends in her life, like Lo who had been there for her every single day since things had gone downhill. The time away from Wentworth had given her time to heal when it came to things concerning her mom and it had given her time to realize that she, too, wasn't ready for things to be over between them. Whatever it was that they had.

"Libby, thank you so much for being on the show today!" Peyton smiled as she started to wrap up the interview. "I am so very excited to see you walking the Victoria's Secret runway this November and then in the pages of *Sports Illustrated* next year. It has been such a pleasure catching up with you!"

"You too, Peyton," Libby smiled back. "Anytime you want me back on the show just let me know!"

"That's all we have time for today on *Prosecco, Pizza & Peyton*," Peyton said. "Join us next Thursday for our interview with

Hollywood director Brica Dallas as she tells us all about her new movie about the hardcore world of professional pole dancing. This is Peyton Song – peace out!"

Libby watched as Peyton hit the red stop button on the portable mixer in front of her before she took off her headphones and Libby followed suit.

"Fantastic interview, honey!" Peyton chirped, locking eyes with Libby for a second before she hopped off her chair and started packing up her equipment. "The show will air tomorrow night on Spotify and, of course, I'll email Felicity through a recording for you to keep for yourself!"

"Thanks," Libby said, also getting to her feet. "Do you need a hand packing up?"

"Aw, thanks for asking!" Peyton smiled as she folded up the two microphone stands and popped them and the microphones inside a silver briefcase. "But it's all good. Not a lot of equipment so not a lot to pack away!"

Libby sat back down silently and watched Peyton as she then packed the headphones, as well as her mixer and cables, into the briefcase. She then placed the briefcase on the floor at her feet as she sat down again to sort out things in her handbag. Libby watched as Peyton looked at the mass of Columbia brochures that were scattered across the coffee table in front of them. Lo had brought them over just the other day.

Lo started grad school at Columbia next week so she was dropping not-so-subtle hints that Libby should apply like she had been tossing up for a while now. Peyton grabbed one of the brochures on the top of the pile.

"You're thinking about going to Columbia?" Peyton asked as she started flipping through the brochure.

"Oh," Libby said, trying to brush it off casually, "kind of."

Peyton placed the brochure down and picked up her bag before throwing it over her shoulder.

"You're a smart girl, you know," Peyton said, standing up from her seat, "and I mean I don't say that about a lot of the supermodels I interview, but seriously, I reckon you could do it."

"Thanks, P," Libby smiled, as she stood up as well.

"I always wanted to go to Columbia, because I love New York City and they have an amazing journalism school, but I ended up choosing Yale because of a stupid guy I was dating in high school that I just had to follow to college," Peyton said, rolling her eyes as she did so. "My Wai Po back in China nearly had a heart attack when she found out."

"I love New York too," Libby smiled, "and the Columbia campus does look beautiful."

"I always loved that Columbia motto too," Peyton said. "'In lumine Tuo videbimus lumen'."

"Nice Latin," Libby said. "What does it mean?'

"'In your light, we see the light'," Peyton replied.

"Oh my God," Libby gasped.

She suddenly realized what Wentworth's last words to her had truly meant. Those words, after all, had been rattling around in her head for the last sixty-three days.

She figured that they'd stayed with her so clearly because she was expecting him to say something else, so she was disappointed by them in that sense. Or maybe it was because those words were the very last thing she had of him. She never in a million years thought that those words were really something much more important than that.

"Libby?" Peyton asked again. "Are you OK?"

Libby realized that she had been standing frozen in her spot, not answering Peyton, for long enough that Peyton was starting to worry about her. She was OK. Just overwhelmed by everything going through her mind right now.

"I'm sorry," Libby said, "there's something I just realized I have to do."

Peyton looked at her through narrowed eyes for a few seconds before she shrugged.

"No worries!" Peyton chirped with a wide smile. "Thanks so much again for the interview!"

"Sure," Libby replied.

"And don't forget to text me about lunch next week!" Peyton added. "Sounds super fun!"

"Sure," Libby repeated.

Libby could feel the anxiety building in her as she watched Peyton walk toward the front door. She was going at normal speed but because Libby needed her to go right this second, it seemed like Peyton was moving in slow motion. Peyton opened Libby's front door before she turned around one last time.

"Enjoy the rest of the pizza and prosecco!" Peyton again before she disappeared into the corridor.

Even before her front door closed, Libby rushed back to the coffee table as she retrieved her phone from her front jeans pocket. She felt like a madwoman as she brushed Columbia brochure after brochure all over the carpeted floor of her living room in search of the one she was after - the *Academic Planning Guide for New Students*. She flipped from the back as she knew that the page she was after was one of the very last.

Libby could feel her hands shaking as she used her index finger to trace the Directory page from top to bottom until she found the number she was after. She quickly unlocked her phone and entered the number into her keypad before she pressed it to her ear. The call rang five times before someone answered. Each ring heightened

Libby's growing anxiety. Was she right about this, or had she completely misinterpreted things? Maybe Wentworth's words didn't have any underlying meaning. Maybe they were just words.

"Good afternoon, you've reached the office of the Dean of Columbia College at Columbia University," the voice spoke on the other line. "You're speaking with Tanya. How may I help you?"

"Hi Tanya," Libby said, "this is Elizabeth Evans. This may be—"

"Oh, Miss Evans!" Tanya exclaimed excitedly. "I was hoping that I would hear from you this week."

"Yes," Libby played along, "I meant to call earlier but I've been out of town."

"Of course!" Tanya replied, "I can just imagine how busy you must be!"

"Yes," Libby nodded.

"Anyway," Tanya continued, "Dean North is very much looking forward to meeting you in a couple of weeks and discussing your future at Columbia!"

"Likewise," Libby replied. "Can you just confirm for me the time and date of my meeting with the Dean?"

"Of course!" Tanya chirped. "The Dean will see you Monday, September fourteenth at 11:00 am. Will that be a problem?"

"No, of course not," Libby replied. "I will see her then."

"Fabulous!" Tanya said. "I will confirm that in the Dean's calendar and we will see you in a couple of weeks."

"Sure," Libby said. "Thank you."

"Goodbye," Tanya said.

Libby hung up the phone call and let out a deep breath. She wasn't sure if she was more excited or nervous about the news. She had an interview with the Dean of Columbia University courtesy of Wentworth Turner. That answered her question about what

Wentworth's last words to her had meant. The only question left to answer was whether or not this was date ten.

26

Date #10

Libby had always considered herself a California sun, west coast kind of girl, but she could definitely get used to New York, especially New York in the fall. Sure, everyone always talked about how magical New York winters were with all the snow, ice-skating, and Christmas decorations at Rockefeller Centre, but Libby had decided she preferred New York fall.

After arriving in the city yesterday afternoon and taking a town car to Lo's new condo on Central Park North, Libby had found herself in the middle of New York fall and all the dreamlike colors that were swiped across the city canvas. Central Park was a mess of yellow, red, and orange all tossed in together, and Lo's condo had the most amazing view of it all. If she did end up here next year, she was going to take up Lo's offer to move in with her. There were, after all, two extra bedrooms in that new condo and that gorgeous Central Park view, which was all courtesy of the bank of Daddy Nelson.

Libby tightened her Burberry Kensington trench coat around her as she re-tied the cotton belt. She was pleased that the colder temperatures hadn't quite hit New York this week. It was, however, still chillier than her little California body was ready for, especially when she was only wearing a light viscose Stella McCartney sleeveless dress and leather pointed-toe Manolos underneath.

It was more of a New York style than her usual LA one, and more of a Columbia University college interview look than a fashion week casting call. She barely looked like herself right now, but maybe that was the point. She still felt like herself as she walked out of her interview with the Dean, but a different version. A version of herself that was maybe ready to leave The Brat Pack and Hollywood behind.

A soft breeze blew her dark straight hair out of her face as she looked out at Columbia College Walk. She had the perfect view of the walk from where she stood on the cement stairs leading down from Low Memorial Library, where she and Dean Katherine North had just finished up a quick tour of part of the grounds. After their interview, the Dean had insisted on giving Libby a quick tour before her next meeting at 1:00 pm. Libby had been admiring the Walk for only a couple of minutes, figuring out where she wanted to head next when she saw him.

A breath hitched in her throat as her eyes locked with the familiar green eyes of Wentworth Turner. Libby could feel her heart pounding in her chest as he smiled at her, and started making his way toward her along College Walk. She paused for a moment as she looked down at her feet and the steps in front of her, making sure her next step landed in the right place, so she didn't literally fall head over heels toward him. Her Manolos were beautiful, but they weren't exactly the most sensible footwear when tacking stairs, especially when Libby had to concentrate so hard on breathing properly right now.

A million thoughts were racing through her mind. She had made it here for her interview, the interview that he had locked in for her, but she hadn't even been sure that he was going to show. All throughout her interview one part of her mind was focused on answering the Dean's questions and making a good impression, and another part was terrified that she had read all the signs wrong. Maybe Wentworth wasn't going to be here today because he had moved on. It had been nearly eleven weeks after all, but he was here. He was standing less than two feet in front of her as she reached the bottom of the library stairs.

"Hey," Wentworth smiled.

Libby took a moment to look him up and down. The colder weather looked good on him. From the shaggy and rugged appearance of some newly established facial hair to the grey beanie that sat firmly on his head.

"Hi," Libby replied, a smile creeping its way across her face.

"I'm glad to see you came," Wentworth spoke again. "How was your interview?"

"You took a pretty big risk not telling me the date or time of said interview," Libby said, letting a small laugh escape her lips.

Wentworth's smile grew wider.

"I was hoping you'd figure it out," he said. "I was sure you would."

Libby's gaze fell to the pavement beneath their feet before she looked up to meet his eyes again.

Seeing him here in front of her made it feel like it had been longer than just eleven weeks since the last time she had seen him. In fact, it had also been just eleven weeks since they'd been curled up in his dorm room, in his bed, holding each other until they both fell asleep. Just eleven weeks, and yet it felt like a lifetime ago, and it made her body chill with nerves. It made her mouth feel so dry that she found herself licking her lips every few seconds so she could actually speak.

"And if I hadn't?" Libby asked, drawing herself out of her thoughts.

"Well," Wentworth replied, "I figured that if you feel even half of what I feel for you, then you would have worked on it until you figured it out."

Libby swallowed hard again as she watched as Wentworth drew his hands out of his front jeans pockets and took a step forward to further close the gap between them.

"But," he continued, "if you hadn't figured it out..."

His words trailed off as his hands reached for hers. She quickly removed her hands from her coat pockets and reached for his until their fingers met and entwined. The sight drew both their eyes. His hands were warm, even if his skin was a little dry and scratchy.

"If I hadn't figured it out?" Libby asked, urging him to finish what he had started to say.

Wentworth sighed as he looked up at her again. One of his hands detached from hers and reached for the side of her face. She felt her eyes flutter shut at the feeling of his hand as he cupped her cheek. He waited until she opened her eyes again before he finally spoke.

"If you hadn't figured it out," Wentworth said, "I was going to come and find you anyway."

Libby could feel his warm breath on her face as he inched closer to her, and it sent goosebumps down her arms. She could almost hear how loudly her heart was beating in her chest as the silence between them continued to build.

"Because eleven weeks," Wentworth continued, his voice almost a whisper, "is just too long to be away from the woman I—"

Libby had wanted him to finish his sentence but at the same time, she was desperate to kiss him. So desperate that she cut him off just like that, with a kiss she had been thinking about for longer than she probably even realized. A kiss she should have never let leave her in the first place.

After a few seconds, Libby broke the kiss and created a little distance between them. She opened her eyes and a couple of seconds later Wentworth did too.

"I'm sorry," Libby laughed. "I just couldn't wait any longer."

Wentworth smiled back at her, squeezing her hands in his.

"Well, what I was going to say before you so rudely interrupted me was—" Wentworth grinned sarcastically at her.

"I love you," Libby said, interrupting him again.

Wentworth paused for just a second as he squeezed her hands again.

"Yeah, you do," Wentworth grinned again, causing Libby to roll her eyes and start to playfully pull away from him. "Come here, you."

Wentworth laughed as he swiftly wrapped his arms around Libby's waist, drawing her right up against him. Their foreheads now completely touching.

"I love you, Libby Evans," Wentworth smiled. "I love you too."

Libby felt the pink rush to her cheeks as she smiled back at him. She wrapped her arms around his neck as she lost herself in his kiss. A tenth date kind of kiss.

ACKNOWLEDGMENTS

There are so many people to thank that helped me bring this idea from my 18-year-old imagination into nearly 400 pages of contemporary romance fiction that I hope will bring joy to people all around the world!

Mum – Thank you for putting up with me as a teenager because I know I was a difficult one. Sometimes more Charlie Niven than anyone should strive to be. Thank you for all your support as I dedicated many hours to write this. I tried to turn all that past teenage angst and drama into something productive!

Siggie – Always there on the other end of the phone for all things technical. Thank you so much for all the hours you put into creating the *10 Dates* website and for answering all my endless questions, as stupid as some of them were.

There are so many people that took a chance on *10 Dates* and read my manuscript drafts, providing reviews, feedback, and constructive criticism.
I want to pay special mention to:
Caroline (@carriea.reads) for being my very first reader and reviewer – you gave me the biggest confidence boost and I will be forever grateful!
Bec Campbell (@cleverhelpfulbitter) – the hours and hours you spent with my hardcopy manuscript and a red pen will be forever appreciated. The final manuscript would not have been the same without you!
Jerrie Tran – forever providing both positive and constructive feedback on individual chapters, secret teaser chapters, and all things social media. I realize that during your final year of high school it is difficult to find even one spare moment, so I am so grateful for all the spare moments you used to help me with this book!

My illustrators, **Maggie** and **Keeks**. Thank you for sharing your amazing talent with me and for bringing the images in my head into real life! Your illustrations are perfect and look absolutely incredible on the book cover!

ACKNOWLEDGMENTS

Joshua – Thank you for being the most supportive husband that I could have ever hoped for. Thank you for all the nights you looked after the baby and let me have my quiet time to slave over my manuscript for the 800th time. Words cannot express just how much I love you for all that you are.

Zoe – My beautiful little girl. Thank you for being a baby that loved to sleep. If I wasn't on maternity leave with you for 13 months, I wouldn't have finished this story at all. I love you so much my darling little Boots!

Bridget Van der Eyk is an up-and-coming contemporary romance author – *10 Dates* is her debut novel. She lives in country NSW, Australia, on a 5-acre property with her husband (Josh), 2 children (Zoe and Max), and 2 dogs (Kevin and Stella). By day she works as a high school Science and Agriculture teacher, and by night she is writing her next romance novel. Her hobbies include watching Korean zombie shows on Netflix, baking the best chocolate cakes you've ever tasted, and auditioning for every Australian game show she can!

www.ingramcontent.com/pod-product-compliance
Lightning Source LLC
Chambersburg PA
CBHW020259120726
47904CB00001B/262